MICHAEL FOLEY was born in Derry in 1947 and was educated at St
Columb's College, Derry, and Queen's University Belfast. He was
joint editor of the *Honest Ulsterman* from 1970 to 1971 and
contributed a regular satirical column 'The Wrassler' to *Fortnight*
magazine throughout the early 1970s. His first novel was serialised
in *Fortnight* and published in book form in 1984; his second novel,
*The D...d T... N...* was published by Blackstaff Press in 1986. He
has a... and
three... ...es in
Lon... ...the
Univ...

## ALSO BY MICHAEL FOLEY

### FICTION

*The Passion of Jamesie Coyle*
*The Road to Notown*

### POETRY

*True Life Love Stories*
*The GO Situation*
*Insomnia in the Afternoon*

### TRANSLATION

*The Irish Frog*
(versions of French poems)

# Getting used to
# not being remarkable

## Michael Foley

THE
BLACKSTAFF
PRESS

BELFAST

First published in 1998 by
The Blackstaff Press Limited
3 Galway Park, Dundonald, Belfast BT16 2AN, Northern Ireland
with the assistance of
The Arts Council of Northern Ireland

ARTS
COUNCIL
of Northern Ireland

Typeset by Techniset Typesetters, Newton-le-Willows, Merseyside

Printed in Ireland by Betaprint

A CIP catalogue record for this book
is available from the British Library.

ISBN 0–85640–626–0

They say that I am son of man and woman.

This astounds me.

COMTE DE LAUTRÉAMONT

# 1

I had a low opinion of schoolteachers. *I* was a schoolteacher. Also a scientist trained in logic. From early youth my head teemed with syllogisms – but still I was incapable of drawing an obvious conclusion. It was a long time before I developed a low opinion of myself.

Certainly I had no sense of unworthiness as I climbed the stairs to my sixth-form class. Even the fact of it being on the top floor seemed exquisitely symbolic. Was I not still a Winged Creature, a Fabulous Ascender?

The room was at the back of the new wing, looking out on the convent house and its walled garden which, even in December, had a suggestion of flowering enchantment as well as the dignity of excluding the profane. Along one of its paths a frail aged nun proceeded with careful slow steps, her eyes cast down in humble vassalage, forever a concubine of the Holy Spirit. Behind her, along the back of the house, ran a flagged area protected by a low sloping roof. Not only a walled garden but also a cloister – *perfection*. All my life I have yearned for claustral coolness and peace. Here, disgusted by venality and intrigue, the retired courtier would come to compose lapidary maxims and wise but sympathetic letters to ardent youth.

Youth arrived – all three. Such a luxury was still possible then and of course the tiny size of the class contributed to the atmosphere of exclusivity and privilege. The names of the girls I have long since forgotten but I remember their eventual grades – A, B and C. B was the ideal convent-school product – intelligent (a mathematician), talented (a cellist), articulate (leader of the debating team), exemplary (head girl). All the staff admired her and found my own lack of enthusiasm inexplicable and churlish. What I objected to was the docility that permitted itself to be so easily moulded. There should always be an element of resistance in the medium.

A and C offered resistance – but C was a garrulous scatterbrain whose escapades revealed only that youthful energy and restlessness which dissipate as swiftly and completely as morning mist on a garden suburb. A, though rarely in trouble, was a true rebel angel, arrogant, dissatisfied and resentful, possessing in abundance the terrible twin gifts of Lucifer – intelligence and pride.

'Are you coming to the sixth-form party?' C made the ritual attempt at distraction.

I shrugged, presenting my favourite posture of disengagement and indifference.

'How about the convent dinner tonight? *We're all waitresses.*' She offered the slack mouth and large vacant eyes that had already attracted male attention. A man can drown in six inches of water as well as in the deepest of oceans.

I shrugged again. 'Probably.'

Before they could pursue the matter, I enquired about the homework, two applied mathematics problems on kinetic and potential energy. When they admitted defeat on both I turned to the blackboard with the sigh of one who has found his way back to the garden. For clever grammar-school pupils, paradise lost is the elegant closed systems – logical, consistent and complete – of Euclidian geometry and Newtonian mechanics. What does it matter if these systems are wrong? Forever insulated from the squalor and perdition of the world, their beauty is pure, incorruptible, timeless. Not only was the subject matter of mechanics eternally fixed, the A-level syllabus and even the textbook were the same as those I had studied myself.

Today's questions were weighty brain-crushers from the end of an exercise – but as usual I had not prepared answers, preferring the frisson of danger in performing on the high wire without a net. Never yet had I wavered, much less fallen to earth. Nor did today provide an appointment with destiny. Beneath the squeaky chalk an elegant solution duly appeared.

$A$ objected to the reasoning in her usual vicious way – every discussion involving her seemed to turn bitter and personal. She was more intelligent and a better mathematician than I but as yet unaware of this. For the moment experience gave me the edge. I went over the reasoning again and when $B$ came in on my side $A$ ungraciously withdrew.

Leaving them to finish the second problem, I turned back to the window. The old nun had gone and in the fading light the scene was dominated by the sombre bulk of the convent house. While the senior school was a modern building, airy and bright and contemporary as befitted its ethos, the nuns inhabited a gaunt Victorian mansion which gave the impression of traditional authority exercised without concession to the age. In fact today was the only day of the year in which lay staff were permitted to cross its mysterious and slightly sinister threshold. On the last day of the Christmas term the nuns put on a dinner to 'thank' staff (and God help anyone who declined to be 'thanked'). Into the heavy dark atmosphere of the house, with its overpowering smell of tradition zealously upheld (boiled vegetables and mustiness overlaid by furniture and floor polish), came a largely female lay staff who had exchanged their decorous day uniform for evening wear that exposed arms and throats and white backs. For such colleagues to bare flesh was startling enough and for them to bare it in the inner sanctum of piety added to the shamelessness of exposure the insolence of desecration and sacrilege. Naturally the atmosphere was electric. Even the timid who stayed covered shared in the delirium of transgression. Nothing is more intoxicating than the illusion of escape from categories.

There was also the oddity of being waited on by pupils. The girls were restricted to white blouse and dark skirt but, like the son-neteers of the silver age, managed triumphs of individual expression within the strictly defined limits.

A finished the problem – but the sheet she proffered was not her solution.

'Judy Cooke's latest masterpiece,' she explained.

It was a multi-coloured copy produced on a Banda machine and showing, in different colours and shadings, the parts of the sixth-form block allocated to each tutor group for end-of-term cleaning. In fact the block was a large open-plan room whose corners could be easily indicated at the start of the cleaning period; also, each separate colour on a Banda master required a new backing sheet under the stencil, so that producing a multi-coloured master was a major pain in the hoop. Obviously considerable time and energy had been expended on a pointless exercise.

A observed me keenly, willing me to voice scorn and contempt. I had no desire to endorse idiocy – but neither could I be seen to deride a colleague. This is a familiar dilemma for the functionary. Old lags must become adepts of the equivocal response. I gave a grim little nod and grunt that were wonderfully expressive but noncommital.

There was no sense of personal shame. As yet I did not feel impli-cated in the pettiness and folly of school life. Still a master of non-attachment, I hovered above the sordid earth on powerful immacu-late angel wings. For at this time I was still fairly young and the idea that we are what we do is profoundly uncongenial to youth, which thinks of itself as a shining essence forever unsullied by its contact with the world – an essence entirely outside history, unaffected by anything that has been or will be. No capitulation or compromise can dim its inviolate radiance and the absurdities of adults, past and present, are merely a cause for amusement and derision.

Instead of throwing away the sheet, I brought it with me to the staffroom where Janet Barczyk was immersed in the gloomy depths of a Hardy novel. Only Janet had the nerve to read fiction openly like this. When I sought imaginative escape I sat at a table by the window and carefully concealed the novel behind a pile of exercise books. Of course Janet had the sanction of being an English teacher and her taste was largely confined to English writers. It would be different for a scientist to be caught reading not only literature but what one of my Irish friends described as 'that French mad dog's shite ye can never get enough of'. I was still obsessed by nine-teenth-century Frogs and in particular by the Magnificent Seven – Baudelaire, Flaubert, Rimbaud, Lautréamont, Huysmans, Barbey d'Aurevilly and Villiers de l'Isle Adam. Besides, I felt it essential to conceal this enthusiasm. The Magnificent Seven were what sus-tained me. They were the source of my lofty detachment. They were my secret angel wings.

Although I hated to have my own reading disturbed, I stood directly in front of Janet and tossed the coloured sheet onto her lap. Laying Hardy aside, she perused it with no sign of outrage or scorn. The phenomenon of the redundant chore was wearily fa-miliar to a teaching veteran.

'Silly,' she said with the utmost mildness, setting the sheet on the arm of her chair.

Justly rebuked, I felt foolish, excitable, rash, immature. Hu-miliated in fact – and thus eager to wound.

'*You* should certainly be glad to see the end of term.'

'*What?*' Startled, defensive, she gave me her undivided attention.

I threw myself into the adjoining armchair. 'After all your disci-pline problems.'

There are ways of appearing to possess authority (I could now fool a new group for up to six months) but everything about Janet suggested uncertainty and diffidence – her abrupt truncated ges-tures, her awkward hesitant gait, her averting of the head and avoidance of eye contact, her involuntary flinching as if from a blow when unexpectedly addressed. As soon as she entered a class-room the terrible haemorrhage commenced.

'I manage,' she said defiantly, flushed and hurt. 'And it's easy for those with plenty of civilised sixth-form work. We can't all be the nice-boy darling of the nuns.'

Ah! Ah! Ah! *Ah!*

Never goad a mature intelligence. You may be successful in exposing its weaknesses but fire of devastating accuracy will be swiftly returned.

I desperately wanted to refute this charge, to demonstrate instantly and conclusively that my apparent compliance was a cun-ning ruse. But self-justification, which usually comes as the leaves to the trees and best displays the human intellect's agility and power,

5

now refused to be invoked much less to dazzle. It was that most terrifying of moments when the deceiver attempts to remove the mask and finds it has fused to his face.

Unfortunately there was no time to ponder a plea. Moira Sweeney, Queen of the Staffroom, entered stage left, declaiming.

'Oh it's all right for some people. All right for the lucky ones who have no tutor group. All right for some to sit on their behinds and forget about end-of-term cleaning. Some people don't know when they're well off. Some people don't know they're living.'

Janet and I were the targets. Apparently offering the sanctuary of a study, the staffroom provides the intrusiveness of a parlour. Is there any other public space which so encourages the striking up of conversations, even with complete strangers engaged in scholarship? Earlier in the day a supply teacher I had never seen before sat down a few chairs away with the happy ostentatious sigh that invariably presages an invasion of privacy. I kept my eyes resolutely on my physics book – but of course it was hopeless. She produced and waved a sheet of signatures. 'Can you *believe* it? All these people have sponsored my daughter for . . . *a parachute jump.*' I hoped that a vague mumble about the dangers of the activity would suffice. Not a chance. As I turned back to my page a photograph of two teenage girls was firmly placed on top of it. 'Which do you think is my daughter?' Nothing for it but to choose. '*No!* Everybody picks the wrong one. *Nobody can believe I have a blond daughter.*' It is the regularity of such incidents that brings to the new recruit the shocking revelation that the principal horror of teaching is not the classroom but the staffroom. And as well as one-to-one invaders there are those like Moira Sweeney who always address the entire room.

Luckily Moira was distracted by the arrival of Terry Wills, Head of Science, and Father Kemp, a senior member of the History Department. 'And here's another two. We know why Father Kemp's so cheerful. No tutor group and no end-of-term cleaning. *Don't the men have it easy as always?*'

'No, no, Moira.' The priest laughed richly and readily. 'It's seeing *you* that makes me cheerful.'

Wills made straight for me, ignoring Janet completely. 'Could you talk to Rani Patel for me. Apparently there's some problem about her qualifications.' As always, he was trying to delegate the personnel management side of his duties.

6

'You talk to her, Terry. You're the Head of Department.'

'I think the non-tutor-group people could *at least* tidy the staff-room.' Moira addressed all of us. '*Especially since most of this rubbish is theirs.*'

Now she was looking at Terry. A wild, untrammelled, impulsive fellow, he was always in trouble for strewing the tables with books or dragging the armchairs out of position or leaving his unwashed coffee mug in dirty water in the sink. On one extreme occasion he had actually been caught attempting a calculation in chalk *on the staffroom windowsill.*

Needless to say he was entirely impervious to chastisement. Ignoring Moira, he continued to address me. 'But you're friendly with Rani.'

'All the more reason to keep out of it.'

Moira now challenged the priest. 'I thought cleanliness was next to godliness.'

'Not at all, Moira.' Kemp laughed indulgently. 'In fact it was exactly the opposite in the early Church. The saints, both male and female, used to boast about how water never touched their bodies except when they had to ford rivers in the service of the Lord. Even fairly recently nuns in some convents were forbidden to bath more than once a month. And the consequences were not shirked. Lice, for instance, were known as *the pearls of God.* If any vermin fell from the person of Benedict Labré he would immediately retrieve them and piously return them to his clothes.'

Moira was more than ready to capitulate. 'Really, Father.'

But Kemp pressed on to the *coup de grâce.* 'And Julian the Apostate used to boast about the *populousness* of his beard.'

The erudite wit of the priest drew a hearty laugh from Wills. In fact Kemp now had the attention of everyone in the room. 'I'm really here to announce that the sixth-form party is formally open. The girls are all up there waiting anxiously for guests.' He paused to chuckle knowingly. 'The presence of Mr Wills and Mr Ward is especially required.'

'Are the PE staff there yet?' Moira rhetorically cried. 'If so, there'll be no trouble attracting the gentlemen.'

Wills was known to have a weakness for the fit female body clad in PE kit – but I resented being tarred with the same vulgar brush. 'I've no interest in Amazons,' I snapped, realising immediately that to respond at all was maladroit and to reveal the intimate self utter folly. Moira had a gift for touching the quick and eliciting an involuntary response.

'*Oh!*' she cried, jubilant, mocking, malicious. 'Oh I *do* beg your pardon. I *forgot*.' She paused, turning to extend to the full audience her hideous parody of contrition. 'I forgot that our Mr Ward is a *cultured intellectual*.'

Terry grasped my arm. 'Let's get out of here.'

'Are you coming up?' I asked Janet.

'By and by.'

'But you will come?'

'All right.'

The party presented a familiar choice – to maintain reserve and be despised as a lackey by the pupils or to let go and be noted as irresponsible by the nuns. Ostensibly organising drinks and snacks with Judy Cooke, Sister Joseph, the Deputy Head, was actually keeping a close eye on things. Blissfully untroubled by dilemma, Wills seized a glass of wine and plunged into a lively bevy grouped around *C*. But of course Wills enjoyed special status. He was the school's licenced clown, a position essential in organisations which seek to impose drab conformity while appearing to admire uninhibited colour (in other words, all organisations). In return for fostering crucial illusions the clown is permitted to break many rules.

*A* approached with a glass of wine and a twisted smirk. '*Mis . . . ter . . . Ward.*' As though pulling the wings off a fly, she detached each syllable in turn and subjected it to ironic scrutiny.

I accepted the wine and took a swift grateful draught.

'I'm being *watched*.' Abruptly the irony was replaced by aggression. 'That bitch Judy Cooke. Everyone *hates* her.'

'Keep your voice down,' I had to warn. 'And no comments on staff.'

As though I had concurred in her judgement she giggled and bumped me playfully with her shoulder. Then giggled and bumped me again.

'*Mr Ward.*'

It was a summons from Sister Joseph on the other side of the room.

'Mr Ward, I think she's had . . . you know . . . ' An exonerating hand was gently laid on my sleeve. 'Not that I'm surprised.

Ooooh!' She closed her eyes and with a shudder offered the ultimate denunciation. 'She's a monkey ... a *monkey*, that one.'

We regarded Judy Cooke talking quietly to *A*. Together they moved off and left the room by the far door. Swift, efficient, discreet – the house style.

There was an awkward moment of silence. Then Joe leaned forward with an expression of intimacy and profound concern. 'And how's the little one now, Mr Ward?'

This was a reference to my baby daughter Lucy who was crying at night. But it was I who felt like an infant. 'Not too bad, Sister.'

'Ah that's great, Mr Ward.' Her pat of intended reassurance filled me instead with sudden terror. Janet was right. I was a nun's pet. 'That's great news altogether now. Thanks be to God for that now.' And, our little moment of intimacy over, she turned back to involve us once more in the public domain.

'That's right!' Moira Sweeney was crying in mock outrage as a pupil attended to Father Kemp's empty glass. 'See to the priest first. The priests are always well looked after. Don't the priests have a time of it, Sister?'

Kemp mounted his customary spirited and entertaining defence. It was not true that clerics were invariably pampered and indulged. Why, in Spain republicans would gladly *knife* a priest and even here in London there were virulent enemies. After this very party he himself would have to run the gauntlet of Kentish Town where passing Roman Catholic clergy were hounded by a renegade Irish derelict shouting the most *unrepeatable* things. On occasions *missiles* had even been thrown.

Joe scarcely knew which emotion to register – shock at the appalling behaviour or admiration for Kemp's coolness and fortitude in the face of it. Once more she turned confidingly to me. 'Isn't it awful, Mr Ward? A priest can't even walk down the street in peace.' Then she lowered her voice even further – for she would criticise her native country only to a co-religionist compatriot. 'And one of our own kind too. Sure isn't that just typical?'

She shook her head in sorrow at an Irish ingratitude and perversity she seemed to believe I could never display. Almost as soon as I entered the school she had placed in me an absolute and unswerving trust. When I was sitting in the corridor waiting to be interviewed she had rushed up to lay her hand on my arm and whisper fervently, in a tone of long and intimate acquaintance: 'The tea's just been sent in so they'll be in a good mood for you.' She had recognised me instantly as a nice boy. A pet from the very start! Suddenly my angel wings were melting. I was falling to earth.

Janet! Janet! Where was Janet?

Never one for dramatic entrances, she was standing near the door in her usual awkward diffident hunch. I had assumed she wanted time to fix herself up – but when I went across she was without makeup as always, the wild frizzy hair streaked with grey as unkempt as before. Probably she was more interested in finishing a chapter of Hardy.

'Was it wise coming up?' she enquired.

From across the room came the high musical laughter of Moira Sweeney and Father Kemp, the ringing chime of crystal goblets touched together in celebration.

'What are you doing in a convent school, Janet?' I said.

'As you so accurately pointed out, my discipline isn't the best. The Authority sent me here because I couldn't cope anywhere else. That was five years ago. I apply for college jobs all the time – but who wants a forty-three-year-old English teacher?' She paused to study me with interest. 'That's my excuse. But *what's yours?*'

This was certainly the key question. When I was working in a tough secular London comprehensive it seemed smart to make use of my Catholic background and move to the disciplined calm of a convent school. My mentor in the secular establishment, Bernard Sorensen, Head of French, argued passionately that this was craven – but I would not be dissuaded.

To the master of non-attachment all regimes are the same. None can impinge on, much less compromise, inner freedom and strength. Hence it is best to serve where the demands are least oner- ous, where protective coloration is most easily assumed and where past experience has provided the ability to deceive and charm the overlords, in this case middle-aged authoritarian Roman Catholic women. It seemed not cowardly but supremely cunning to come to Our Lady of Perpetual Succour.

And what was I doing in the lay school in the first place? Why was I teaching at all, I whose future had once seemed so dazzling, I whose parents were both schoolteachers and who had sworn never to follow in their timorous and lamentable footsteps?

According to the method of Regression Therapy, curing spiritual infirmity is a two-stage process. First there is reparenting, replacing the inadequate natural parents by a mature and perceptive new couple (Janet would obviously be mother and Bernard Sorensen the new da); then the actual regression, under the insightful guidance of the new parents painfully reliving the stunted life.

'Jack spends one and thruppence on drinks,' says Hugh Ward to the boy Pascal, reading from an 11-plus intelligence test, 'and ten pence on ice cream.' Laboriously Pascal copies down the figures with his expensive fountain pen. 'He has five pence left. How much did Jack have to start with?'

Pascal computes with painful intensity, tongue stuck out, head bent to the page.

'Five shillings!' he cries at last with a hopeful grin.

Sighing deeply, Hugh Ward turns to the doorway of the living room where Martin Ward, apparently engrossed in playing with a balloon in the hall, seems to arrive every time Pascal offers a solution.

'Half a dollar,' Martin announces now with elaborate negligence, vigorously batting the balloon towards the hallway's high ceiling.

A sharp female voice issues from the kitchen. '*Say it properly.*'

'Two and six,' he grunts through clenched teeth ('Highly intelligent, he sweats obedience all day – but certain dark traits seem to reveal bitter depths of hypocrisy' – Rimbaud).

Hugh regards his son fondly, then returns to the thankless work. 'What letter occurs twice in Digested and twice in Ended but only once in Opened?'

Again Pascal lowers his head and toils over the page, announcing finally, 'E!'

Handing the boy the test paper, Hugh goes in despair to the doorway where his wife has now arrived. 'He's very slow,' Hugh murmurs. 'Very slow. *Very slow.*'

Together they gravely and regretfully shake their heads, two concurring senior consultants by the bed of a terminally ill patient.

But of course there are alternatives to conventional medicine.

'I'm starting a Novena,' Mrs Ward whispers. 'And Greta's doing the nine Tuesdays.' Another possibility suddenly strikes her. 'We could go to Father Hegarty's Rock instead of the shore.'

'Aye,' Hugh nods, leaning close to his wife and dropping his voice even lower than hers, 'thanks be to God *we* won't . . .'

They gaze in gratitude and awe at their own youthful prodigy who, pretending not to hear but exulting inwardly at the just recognition of his genius, beams angelically and hits the balloon high into the bright vault of the stairwell. Mrs Ward turns back to the living room and addresses her nephew in tones heavy with sorrow and compassion.

'I was just getting a wee bit of a picnic ready, Pascal. Would you like to go out a run with us as far as Father Hegarty's Rock?'

Pascal nods happily but in the hall Martin's smile changes to a grimace of revulsion and hatred ('You will be amazed to see him so amenable to parental guidance – but take a look when he is unaware of being watched and you shall see him launch gobs of phlegm in Virtue's face' – Lautréamont).

At the wheel of the new family Simca, Hugh Ward negotiates traffic with frequent involuntary cries of terror ('We'll be *cut to ribbons*, cut to ribbons, look see'). In the passenger seat Mrs Ward tensely braces herself and adds her own shrieks ('Mother of God, Hugh!', 'Sacred Heart!', 'Jesus, Mary and Joseph!'), while in the back winks and giggles are exchanged by the boys. As they leave the town behind the parents gradually relax and now it is Martin who mockingly begins to issue the cry of alarm at each major junction, 'We'll be cut to ribbons. Cut to ribbons, look see.'

By the time they arrive Hugh Ward is in a grim mood not helped by the revelation that their usual picnic spot has been fouled.

'Mammy, it's *all jobs*,' Martin calls out, peering into the sheltered hollow with every sign of interest and approval.

'Well come away from it,' his mother snaps. 'Come away from it. *Come away from it.*'

Hugh, with much scowling and muttering at the vileness of modern life, sets about lighting the small spirit stove in a more exposed spot further up the high rocky headland where, according to local legend, Father Hegarty was beheaded by the English in the penal days, his severed head eluding the executioners by bouncing several times, permanently denting the rock, before plunging beyond their reach far out to sea. This miraculous martyrdom is commemorated by a shrine at the base of the headland – a coffin-shaped stone pool full of coins left by the faithful to purchase the martyr's intercession. Mrs Ward solemnly approaches and drops in several coins from her purse. Then, observing that her husband is growing angry with the stove, continually extinguished by the merciless Irish wind despite the protection of a biscuit-tin lid, she turns to Pascal and Martin. 'Go on you two now and play a wee bit there.'

Pascal, however, is profoundly reluctant to leave the shrine. 'See the much money in that there pool, hi!' Though he addresses Martin, it is the coins which hold his eyes, now agleam with an avid excitement knowledge could never inspire. 'Much de ye think's in there, hi?'

'Can't you work it out for yourself?' Martin sneers. 'Jack spends one and thruppence on drinks and ten pence on ice cream.'

Pascal looks at his cousin. 'You think you're wild smart, don't ye?' He pauses, considering how to demolish this illusion. 'But Ah bet ye can't spell *diarrhoea*.'

Martin begins – but quickly loses his way. 'All right . . . Ah can't. But you can't either.'

'Can so.'

'Go on then.'

Pascal edges away, preparing for flight, and cries in shrill triumph, '*D . . . i . . . a . . . two farts and a splash*.'

Then he takes to his heels, pursued by Martin, but in sprinting back along the path Pascal's fountain pen bounces from his pocket. Martin sees the pen fall and is preparing to avoid it when he is smitten by a new and exalted sensation – the joy of the terrible black poetry of gratuitous crime ('In evil is to be found all voluptuousness' – Baudelaire).

'*Watch me pen!*' Pascal shrieks.

Martin indeed adjusts his stride – but so that his right foot comes down on the article and shatters it into fragments on the hard earth of the path. Immediately he experiences that unique surge of ecstasy in which the artist first comprehends his vocation and talent ('I envy the Creator nothing so long as He permits me to ride the river of my destiny through a growing series of glorious crimes' – Lautréamont).

Racked by animal convulsions of pain and rage, face astream with mucous and tears, Pascal bears in cupped hands the sorry remains to Mrs Ward. '*He squashed me pen. He squashed me pen.*

*He squashed me pen.'*

Martin follows, panting wildly to indicate blind animal exuber-
ance, his eyes wide and empty but for the innocence and vitality of
youth. 'We were playin' chasin' an' it musta fell outa ees pocket.'
He pauses to simulate lack of breath. 'Never even seen it tay after.'
Mrs Ward studies him carefully. He pats his heaving breast, outwardly a clumsy but benign young dog, inwardly an exulting
career criminal ('Those who wear their hearts on their sleeves can
have no idea of the furtive joys of systematic hypocrisy, the solitary
gratifications of such as can live and breathe without difficulty
under the confinement of a mask' – d'Aurevilly).

Mrs Ward turns back to Pascal. 'Sure we can get a new pen' –
laying a compassionate hand on his head – 'as long as nothing happened to *you*. We can always get a new pen – *but we could never get a
new Pascal, eh?'* Suddenly radiant with inspiration, she looks from
one to the other. 'Why don't the two of you go in for a dip?'

Martin regards with distaste the bitter freezing North Atlantic.
He would rather go to his local swimming baths but Mrs Ward will
not permit him to mention an institution which contains, under
one roof, such potential for vice, disease, contamination, robbery,
violence and sudden death.

'Too cold,' he says, adopting the sullen, intractable look of the
grey northern waters.

Mrs Ward's radiance visibly dims. 'Well sure we'll all get a nice
warm cup of tea in a minute.' She turns to monitor her husband's
progress. 'In the meantime here's a round of tomato between you.'

Entirely unreconciled, Pascal goes off in a bitter sulk. Martin
climbs the headland to study the site of the martyrdom. Humming
a bizarre tune ('The song of nihilism, a song punctuated by bursts of
sinister gaiety and expressions of ferocious wit' – Huysmans), he
munches his sandwich and ponders the markings. Possessed by the
exhilaration of speculative thought, he abandons the path to plunge
down the near-vertical side of the headland in joyful leaps from
rock to rock.

*'Martin!'* Mrs Ward screams. *'Martin, come down outa that!'*

*'Ye'll be cut to ribbons,'* Hugh Ward roars. *'Cut to ribbons, look see.'*

Unscathed and unconcerned, Martin approaches his mother with
a frown of puzzlement. 'Did his head bounce two or three times up
there?'

'What are ye thinking of . . . jumping down rocks like that? Ye put the heart across me, Martin. Don't ye know ye could give yourself a terrible knock?' He remains unimpressed. 'A knock on the head, look see. A knock that could *come back on ye in later life?*'

Ignoring her questions, he patiently repeats his own. Despairingly Mrs Ward returns to buttering bread. 'Och Ah couldn't tell ye, Martin. Ah couldn't tell ye that.'

As a gust of wind overturns the biscuit-tin lid, Hugh Ward utters a fierce exclamation of rage.

'Easy, Hugh,' pleads his wife. 'For the love o' God will ye go easy.'

'And was he beside the first mark when he was beheaded? I mean, did his head fall off onto the ground and bounce . . . or did it shoot up into the air and bounce?'

Poised to butter a round of sliced pan, Mrs Ward regards her son in wild incomprehension and fear. Martin too is dismayed, realising the thankless nature of analysis, the tragic loneliness of the rational agent in a world of busyness and voodoo ('My metaphysical clarity fills me with terror' – Flaubert).

Studying this monster of lucidity, Mrs Ward has a sudden and terrible revelation – his luminescence is not that of the angel but of the dazzling heresiarch ('Already the child is succumbing to the rapture and intoxication of hell' – Villiers).

Martin tries a more practical line. 'Is all of him buried under the shrine . . . or just the body and no head?'

Mrs Ward looks in terror at Martin carefully studying the peak of the headland.

Over her son's head is the coveted halo – *but the halo is black.*


'You've been drinking,' Clare said at once as Paul ran against my legs with a sympathy-seeking pout that implied a major incident. Simultaneous accusation and emotional demand – the unique rewards of family life after a hard day at the office.

'I had to put in an appearance at the sixth-form party.'

'I was nearly going to phone the school. Thought you must be staying on for the other do.'

Conflicting demands have at least the advantage that one may be used to evade another. 'What happened?' I asked Paul – but it was Clare who responded.

'Attacked again at the nursery. Bitten. That Karl . . . as usual. A vicious little bastard. You should have seen Paul's arm – it was *bleeding*. And you know what Mrs Jeffreys said?' As so often, the restraint that could tolerate injury was destroyed by the insult of cover-up. 'Know what she said to me, Martin? Typical English. She said, *Karl means well, it's just his body language is wrong.* I need to get out of this country. Fucking *body language* for fuck's sake. And Paul's arm all blood.'

Paul raised his sleeve and proudly displayed the wounded arm. Why do children so adore sticking plaster? An insignia that combines the heroism of injury with the magical healing power of adults?

'Why did you let him bite you, Paul?'

'I didn't *let* him. He just did it.'

'*His body language is wrong.*' Clare's outrage had mellowed into sorrowful wonder. 'Pretend nothing nasty has happened. The English way.'

'The bourgeois way.'

She was not to be deflected. 'You know what I was thinking? I don't have a single English friend. Most of the nurses I'm friendly with are Irish. Maria's Polish. Christine's Australian.'

Increasingly Clare was subject to feelings of exile and isolation. Several other young Irish couples had come with us to London: one by one they had returned to the homeland to settle and breed. We alone of that carefree throng had become parents and property owners in the capital. A baby slept in the second bedroom and the lounge into which we were moving smelt strongly of fresh paint and newly laid carpets.

'That's the glory of London,' I said, sinking gratefully onto a sofa that released a powerful bouquet of virgin leather. 'Hardly any English in it.'

'That's rubbish, Martin. I don't think I'll ever have an English friend. And I do need friends. I know you probably don't – but I do.'

She missed the days of wine and taxis. Or, rather, the nights. It was certainly a convivial time – but, beneath their youthful insouciance, the couples were deeply conservative. The men drank and blustered but would never challenge authority. The women drank and flirted but would never go beyond a kiss.

Paul pushed against my legs. 'Can we play office, Dad?'

Was there anything to life beyond the demand to play office? 'Not tonight, Paul. I have to go out again soon.'

'That's a thing I have to tell you, Martin.' Even more than the warning, the way she sat down beside me indicated bad news. 'The agency rang.'

'*And?*'

'They want me to work tonight.'

'But you know I have this do.'

'They were desperate for someone.'

We regarded each other. 'You know it's all hands on deck tonight. The nuns expect everyone. I can kiss goodbye to the Scale Three if I don't show.'

With two children and a mortgage there was suddenly an absence of money to go with the absence of freedom. We might still be *jeunesse* but we were no longer *dorée*. Hence a hideous new principle – actions which saved or earned money took the moral high ground.

'Don't try to tell me you want to go to get promotion.' Not surprisingly, appeals to the new financial imperative tended to bring out the worst in us. Clare's mouth twisted in disgust. 'It's just to see your *lady friends*.'

Had she taken the work out of jealousy, simply to keep me from attending the dinner? Always insecure and possessive, an aversion to sex since the second birth had intensified her fear of rivals.

With the child's acute awareness of parental discord, Paul at once sensed the mood and tugged at us both with a poignant cry. 'Stop it! Stop it, you two!' Though I lusted for vengeance it was difficult to attack in front of a peace-making child.

'Besides, I have to keep in with the agency,' Clare went on. 'Otherwise I won't get the times I want.' With the air of delivering a clincher: 'They've offered me holiday rates tonight.'

In marriage, as in any form of politics, effective retaliation has to be legal. Cunning and vicious as a serpent, I attacked from an entirely new direction.

'And I suppose Lucy's been sleeping all day?' Perhaps inheriting her father's scorn for received ideas, Lucy had dedicated her brief life to disproving the cliché that second babies are easy. Fractious at best, she would certainly be impossible during the night if allowed to sleep earlier on.

'I couldn't keep her awake.' Clare was gratifyingly defensive. 'And I put her down *before* the agency rang.'

Giving her no chance to re-deploy, I opened yet another front. 'And did you tackle them about Mrs Upchurch?'

This was an elderly woman who had died during the night while Clare was nursing her. Clare had been unable to get home before her usual time but the agency paid her only to the hour of the death.

'No I didn't.' She herself was angry but unable to challenge her English bosses. A savage doormat like so many of her race.

My counter measures were obviously effective because she now retired with Paul. I crossed the open-plan living area to check the pots on the cooker. Instead of an exciting social occasion, an evening of child-minding at home; instead of the alabaster shoulders of women, a baby's shitty red ass; instead of the nuns' sumptuous banquet, a portion of curried kidney beans.

As I shovelled down the last of the food, Paul charged in, fired by the discovery that his father was after all free to play office. We went to his room where bed, chair, floor and shelves were covered with bank withdrawal forms.

'This is the office,' he explained.

I have a special affection for Huysmans because he was the sole member of the Magnificent Seven to endure not only regular employment but employment in an office – thirty-three years in the Ministry of the Interior, retiring with the terrifying title of Head Clerk.

'All right,' I said, 'you pretend to need a loan and I'll pretend to be the bank manager.'

'No no no no.' Paul frowned in irritation. 'You don't pretend. You *are* the bank manager.'

Of course he was right. Pretence cannot be sustained. We are what we do.

'OK I'm the manager and you have to fill in this form.'

Frowning in high seriousness, he accepted it and solemnly scribbled. Since chair and bed were covered with slips I had to squat on the floor.

'Now give me another.'

Thirty-three years, the largest chunk of Huysmans's life – yet the otherwise detailed and splendid biography by Baldick scarcely mentions his work. Such is the inevitable fate of our hours of paid toil – they vanish like the sweat of the anonymous slaves who hauled blocks for the pyramids.

Eventually I announced that the bank was closing, it was time to clear up.

'No no!' Paul cried in exasperation and alarm. 'We can't move any of this. We're playing office again tomorrow.'

In the kitchen Clare turned to me with a conciliatory smile that was no longer necessary. As always it broke my heart to see her in uniform – a hideous nullifying shift, plain flat black shoes and a threadbare navy gaberdine. And her face purged of makeup, long dark hair crushed into a bun – my beautiful wild gypsy girl rendered down into a skivvy for the rich.

Part of my earlier revenge package had been a refusal to ask where she was working. 'Who is it tonight?'

'Mrs Bonnington.'

'The horrible one?'

'No, she's all right. It's her daughters are horrible.'

'Will you be able to sleep?'

'Maybe a couple of hours.'

'And where did you say it was?'

'A big mansion block. Near Baker Street tube.'

Another grievous image assailed me – that of Clare mingling with the Friday night revellers but, instead of being admired and fêted as gilded youth, passing unnoticed and unremarked as one of the invisible army of drudges. Hence another grim reversal. We were not making use of the city; the city was making use of us.

Adulthood – a grim paradigm shift in which the youth joy of infinite potential is replaced by the horror of determinism.

'Take a taxi for this once,' I cried.

'What's the point of working if I waste half on taxis?'

We went out to our own foyer which opened onto the main hall. 'Would you not think of going back into a hospital after the holiday?'

'You know I can't take working in hospitals. Everything gets to me.'

She was too thin-skinned to practise professional disengagement – a reminder of vulnerability that made me remorseful and contrite as we approached the house door. 'At least it's nearly

Christmas, honey.'

A misguided attempt at reassurance. We were not looking forward to our first festive season in London. At home we could revert to our youthful selves by leaving Paul with his grandparents and going out to the bars with the old crowd. Now the bleak midwinter stretched forth with no prospect of escape.

Clare grunted wearily, as though at the feebly placatory tone of a man who has insisted on having his way. We had stayed on in London because I would not go back as a teacher. The great Martin Ward a teacher like everyone else? What was tolerable in London would be out of the question in Ireland. Being a nobody is acceptable only where nobody knows.

She descended the house steps, pulling the gaberdine about her.

'*Take a taxi for fuck's sake!*'

The face she turned was already the anonymous and fatalistic mask of servitude.

'No,' she insisted, 'it's all right.'

'John, George and Sam competed in four sports – running, jumping, riding and swimming.' Mrs Ward pauses to look at her son. He watches with eager attention, a dog awaiting the thrown stick. 'John won two and was second in jumping. Sam was first in riding and second in two others. What sport did George win and in which *two* sports was Sam second?'

Even before she has finished, he is writing swiftly and surely.

'Now that's one of the really hard ones . . . right at the end of the paper.'

'George won the jumping,' Martin casually announces, 'and Sam was second in running and swimming.'

Mrs Ward regards him in silence. 'All right,' she gets out at last, 'that's grand for now. We'll run through the rest when we get back from up the town.'

Martin's bright features cloud as rapidly as the changeable Ulster sky. 'But I can do all the hard ones already.'

'There's only *three weeks* to go to your 11-plus, Martin. And you know you're not supposed to see any Intelligence Test papers. Jean McCourt let us borrow a few till Monday *as a very special favour to me*. Now that was very decent of Jean and you ought to be grateful. There's many a one would be glad of the chance.'

'But it's *Saturday!*' ('Life calls to my youth, stronger than these notions too pure for the fiery season ruling me' – Villiers.)

'Jean needs the tests back on Monday ... they have to be done this weekend.' Going to the sink, Mrs Ward returns with an index finger inserted into a dampened face cloth. Martin backs away in revulsion. '*It's just a wee cat's lick.*' He lunges wildly in her grasp. '*Stand at peace like a Christian!*' Seizing his head in her left hand, she violently rubs the corners of his mouth with the cloth-covered finger. 'Sure it's only a wee cat's lick. Ye can't go up the town lookin' like Maggie McKay.' Martin endures in grim silence ('My mother is fantastic; one must fear and propitiate her' – Baudelaire).

The goal is a new wardrobe for the 11-plus candidate. While fully committed to the rational strategy of intensive coaching, Mrs Ward is not prepared to neglect the magical properties of appropriate dress.

They begin in Start Rite, the quality shoe store presided over by Mr Cunningham, a profoundly serious older man, darksuited, soft of voice and grave of mien, without a trace of the impertinent joviality of the newer sales staff. Indeed he is more like a senior consultant in a prestigious teaching hospital. Falling on one knee, he deftly squeezes each of Martin's feet in turn, murmuring significantly but not yet revealing his diagnosis. First he verifies it with the latest technology, solemnly ushering the boy towards the X-ray machine, an impressive piece of equipment possessed by no other shoe shop, operated by no one but Mr Cunningham and housed in an alcove like a private side chapel. Martin climbs the two rubber-covered steps and pushes his feet through an aperture covered by a small green curtain. On the other side Mr Cunningham bends his wise head to the rubber-lined viewer.

'You can see where the toe cap is too small.' He offers Martin a look. The boy stares without interest at the bones of his feet – but when he makes to step back Cunningham holds him in place. Mrs Ward must also confront the consequences of inadequate footwear. 'You can see where they're pinching.' Cunningham sighs at human folly seduced by bargains and glib sales talk. 'Not at all a good fit.'

'They're only cheap ones for school!' Mrs Ward brokenly cries. 'You couldn't keep him in good ones every day. He has the toes out of everything kickin' stones in the street. They're only a cheap pair for school and kickin' football in the street.'

21

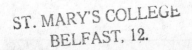

'But young feet can be easily damaged. There's a lot of shoddy workmanship on the market, Mrs Ward.'

'They weren't *all that cheap*.' She bridles at being rebuked by a tradesman. 'I mean, I didn't get them in the Black Man's or anything.'

Maintaining his air of sorrow and regret, Cunningham goes to the storeroom and returns with a stack of boxes containing monstrous leather brogues. Martin submits to fitting with an expression of violent disgust ('Bah! Let us make every imaginable grimace' – Rimbaud).

'Will ye get that old face off ye,' Mrs Ward hisses. 'Anyone would think to look at ye, ye were havin' teeth pulled.'

Cunningham fetches yet more boxes – but as always Mrs Ward is unable to choose. 'Could we take a few pairs out on appro?'

'Certainly, Mrs Ward.'

'And if we kept two pairs ye'd knock a bit off it, wouldn't ye? *What would ye make it if we kept two?*'

Martin turns away in horror ('Oh! Curses on commerce! What shame!' – Flaubert).

Next they proceed to the Diamond and a grand old Victorian department store where Martin is disposed to linger in the ground-floor haberdashery, entranced by an overhead communication system in which screw-top canisters whizz along metal tubes to a cashier magnificently enthroned in a central glass booth.

'Aunt Josie! Aunt Josie! Aunt Josie! Aunt Josie!'

'Ah, love o' God,' Mrs Ward groans.

Martin is startled to see approaching, in the uniform of a sales assistant, Mairead, the most stupid of the stupid cousins, more stupid even than her younger brother, Pascal.

'Were ye not gonnay even say hello, Aunt Josie?'

'Sure didn't I forget you were here, Mairead. Me head's addled with one thing and another these days. We're just going in to Mr Harley to get Martin some stuff.'

Mairead turns to the boy. 'God ye're as big gettin', Martin.' Then, to his mother. 'Ye'll be needin' to put him in long trousers, Josie.'

'There's no call for that,' Mrs Ward snaps.

Martin takes up the cry: 'Can I get a pair of long trousers?'

'Ye'll get *no such thing*. There's nothing worse than looking like a wee man.'

And indeed the boy acquires new short trousers, together with a Vyella shirt, Shetland wool V-necked pullover and a huge brown Crombie overcoat of stupendous thickness and weight ('O Sorceresses, Misery, Hatred, I have confided my treasure in you' – Rimbaud). So grotesque is the Crombie that Martin loses the power of his limbs and has to be helped into it by his mother who brings her face close to his for an intimate snarl: 'Do ye want to end up like that eejit, Mairead? Is that what ye want ... ah? ... *ah?*' Violently she pulls the lapels together. 'Do ye want to stand about in a *shop* all the days of your life?'

After this exhausting expedition Mrs Ward desperately needs a cup of tea before resuming. Martin seizes his chance.

'Can I go out to the street a wee minute?'

'Well make it a wee minute. Those papers have to go back to Jean McCourt first thing on Monday.'

Swift as the wind, he races to the end of the street, physically less than a hundred yards but in social terms the equivalent of the light years between galaxies. At this end live the dubious and disorderly families, many in houses *actually subdivided into flats*. Martin applies to one of these and his mentor Tony Shotter answers the knock.

'Comin' out a while?'

'Wait till Ah get me coat.' In an instant, with no need for explanations, entreaties or promises, Shotter returns, zipping an American style jacket whose casual democratic glory dazzles Martin.

'Where're we goin'?'

The overriding need for flight has prevented any thought of destination. Martin glances uneasily up and down the cold street.

'We could go down the quay,' Shotter suggests, 'and shoot a few auld commons.' From a jacket pocket he produces a home-made catapult. 'Ah've a new slingshot.'

Taking the sturdy wire frame in his right hand, Martin pulls back the strong dark elastic and exults in the murderous power that trembles in his hands ('I have closed my eyes to your illuminations. I am a savage, a wild beast' – Rimbaud).

With a heavy sigh, he returns the weapon. 'Nah. The auld doll says Ah have to be back.' Again he sighs. 'But Ah'll go down wi' ye as far as the Palace.'

Together they stroll downhill to the dubious quarter surrounding the docks. 'Where'd ye git the jacket?'

'Me da sent it.'

Ideal father – out of sight and mind but forwarding exciting American gifts. Shotter's English father rarely sees his son who, tall, authoritative and adult, has taken over as man of the house (or, rather, man of the flat). Needless to say, he has been in long trousers for as long as Martin can remember.

'And how'd ye make the slingshot?'

'The frame's off the bottom of me bed. Me ma got me the elastics. She works in the Commercial Paper Company.'

At the bottom of the hill they linger in front of the Palace, Martin scrutinising the stills with the intensity and concentration of a scholar. As always, return is proportional to investment. From a few sets of stills he can extract as much as the average cinema-goer from a lifetime of films.

Today stills for *The Vikings* teem with warriors, weaponry and ships. To be ensconced in soft plush, far from the nullity of town and age in the luxury of Technicolor mayhem and carnage ('Exceptional beings retrace their steps down the centuries and, out of disgust for the shameful promiscuities they are forced to endure, throw themselves into the abyss of the ages, the tumultuous spaces of nightmare and dream' – Huysmans).

'Wouldn't it be just great to go in?' Martin cries out in rapture.

'Seen it,' Shotter answers indifferently, glancing about him with an air of impatience.

Martin transfers his gaze of wonder to the face of his friend. '*When?*'

'Last night.'

It is difficult to know what to ask first. 'Where'd ye get the money?'

'Ah do a Pools round every Friday.' With a twisted grin Shotter withdraws from his pocket a fistful of silver. 'And afterwards Ah go to the shows.'

'On your *own*, ye mean?'

'On me own.'

Eternally seductive combination – autonomy and fabulous wealth.

'And what was it like?'

'Brilliant.' But his tone has the carelessness of surfeit. 'Ye see Kirk

Douglas gettin' ees eye put out and Tony Curtis gettin' ees hand chopped off.'

Despite Shotter's lack of genuine enthusiasm, Martin once again thrills to the savagery of the primitive ('I have always had a tender sympathy for barbarians' – Flaubert). He would like to ask more questions but Shotter is becoming increasingly restless.

'Look, are ye comin' down the quay or not?'

Already Martin is so late that there is bound to be a scene on his return. His mother shrieking, hysterical ('Where did we go wrong? *Where did we go wrong?*') and, if back from his Saturday fishing trip, his father outraged that, after a lifetime of suppressing blaggardism, he is faced with an outbreak *in his own living room* ('Doing *what*, you say? *Where? With that cornerboy* Shotter?').

'All right.'

They cross Strand Road and go down a brooding alley to the docks. Although a regular traveller on the bridge over the Foyle, Martin has never seen the river at close range. Below the rotting timbers under his feet water turbid and deep as life slaps against piles. In one direction are rusty freighters and in the other, moored at its own quay, a trim vessel in grey.

'A *warship*,' Martin mutters in awe.

'*What?*' Shotter howls in derision. 'Fuckin' HMS *Neverbudge?* Been sittin' there a lifetime. Jackie Cradden's da works on it ... clerk or somethin'.' He turns to the vessels in the other direction. 'That's a new boat. The huers'll be all down tonight.'

'*Huers?*' Martin feels the dark waters rise to engulf him. 'What are huers like?'

'If ye see a woman walkin' wi' 'er legs apart ... this kinda way' – Shotter demonstrates with uncharacteristic enthusiasm – 'that means she's rid out.'

Not from a grammar school but from Shotter the adept must acceptance be won at any cost.

Alerted by a sudden flutter of pigeons, Shotter swiftly draws his weapon and casts about for ammunition.

'Give us a shot, hi,' Martin humbly petitions.

'A shot? *You?*' Shotter regards him in wild incredulity. 'Ye couldn't hit a cow on the arse wi' a flat board.' Abruptly he lets fly himself, completely missing the target. With a fierce impatient oath he returns to searching the roadway for ammo.

'Would ye take me with ye sometime?'

'*Hah?*' Shotter looks up in dark incomprehension and annoyance.

'To the shows, Ah mean.'

Abrupt harsh brutal laugh. 'Ah'll fuckin' dance to ye, son.'

'But if Ah had money?'

'Wise up.'

Third essential quality of the aristocrat – along with autonomy and wealth, *disdain*. The hot flush of shame burns Martin's cheeks. Initiation is slow and painful – but a necessary process. 'Why not?'

Having found another stone, Shotter loads up once more. 'Because you're a *worm*.' He turns to appraise Martin with a contemptuous sneer. 'The best part of ye ran down your mother's leg.'

B ernard crossed the hall to Clare as if he had known her for years – which in fact he claimed to be the case. 'You see, this fellow' – jerking his head at me – 'believes in male friendship. Man to man. Always outside the home. He's always prevented me from meeting you. But marriage is a *symbiotic union*. You're no longer two separate people. You're *one person* now . . . *isn't that right?*'

Though she possibly agreed with the theory, Clare was disoriented by the means of expression, stammering 'Is it?' and casting me a sharp accusing look. Certainly there was little apparent enthusiasm for being one with my flesh and blood.

'Of course it is. It's the symbiotic union. Each of you alone is incomplete. I need to see the two of you together. And speaking of this other fellow, where is he?' With a hearty laugh Bernard spun round to look. 'You see, he's such a neurotic he makes me nervous. *Profoundly neurotic*. I mean, look at him standing there all hunched up and miserable. He hates the idea of us talking to each other. Don't ask me why – but he does.'

This time Clare approved of both opinion and language.

'Riddled with guilt and anxiety,' Bernard chortled. They both chortled. '*Riddled* with it.'

Reparenting was bound to involve criticism – and I even welcomed a certain amount of flagellation (the Catholic need to confess and do penance). But I had not expected an immediate full-frontal assault. Taking Bernard's coat to the bedroom, I was glad for once of an open-plan layout that permitted me to follow the conversation.

'A good white should be only *lightly chilled*.' He had produced a bottle from a bag and was displaying it to Clare. 'Twenty minutes. No more.' As they went to the fridge he lowered his voice. 'Does he permit you a decent kitchen? Or does he force you to work in squalor? He seems to find squalor romantic.'

'Tell me about it,' Clare sardonically muttered.

'I heard that,' I shouted, holding the bedroom door open with my foot (the price of liberty is eternal vigilance). 'It's a brand-new fitted kitchen. A fucking *dream kitchen*.'

I had forgotten that Paul was working at a colouring-in book on the table. Bernard was more attentive.

'I have a grandson just about your age. Timothy, his name is. When I go up there to visit, his mum and dad sometimes go out. Do you know what Timothy and I do then?' Paul considered the grey suit, grey hair and gold-rimmed chief-accountant spectacles. 'The Forbidden Dance of the Grandads!' Adopting a solemn and intense expression, Bernard performed a defiant bacchanal that combined the arm movements of Zorba's dance with the high kick of the cancan.

The family watched in stupefaction.

'Drinks!' commanded Clare, after a time.

One positive aspect of this English Christmas – the money saved on flights had been used to stock a cocktail cabinet. If we could not get to Ulster we would bring Ulster to us.

'Bushmills and water?' I suggested to Bernard.

'That would be delightful. Half and half, isn't that right? Whiskey should always be diluted. Of course no more than half and half or it tastes like liquorice water. But certainly not neat. Yet on television or the movies every time you see someone drinking whiskey they're drinking it neat.'

'Particularly westerns?' Clare suggested.

'Exactly.'

'Destroys the oesophagus?'

Bernard responded to specialist knowledge as other men to the promise of sexual favours. 'Of course, honey,' and he laid a hand on her arm in fervent solidarity and gratitude, 'I'd forgotten you were a nurse.'

Again the open-plan layout allowed me to prepare drinks

without leaving the room.

'I hope you've had *psychiatric training*,' Bernard drew close to Clare and indicated the bookshelves next to him. 'Have you seen the way he has his books *classified* and *organised?* A French shelf, an American shelf, an English shelf, an Irish shelf. The fellow's a classic anal-erotic. Obsessed with order and hoarding. I suppose he *forbids* you to move anything.'

'Don't be talking!' Clare cried, really getting into the swing of it now. 'I'd be *murdered* if I interfered with those.'

'No wonder he's fascinated by neurotics.' Bernard turned his head sideways to read the titles. 'Neurotics and bad boys. Huysmans for instance. A most peculiar fellow, Clare. In *Là-Bas* there's a Satanist called Canon Docre who has Christ tattooed on the soles of his feet so he can be *always tramping on him*.' Instead of registering disapproval, Bernard threw back his head and roared with laughter.

This was exactly the kind of remark that had attracted me to Bernard. When I first arrived in an English staffroom my thick Ulster accent made me sound like a moron. And, by the kind of vicious irony that amuses the Celestial Delinquent, while my fine mind went unappreciated my youthful body was coveted by the PE Department who actually asked if I would like to supervise the Saturday morning games session. My fastidious soul trailed through the mud of a sports field as in olden days the shield of a dishonoured knight was dragged from the tail of a horse.

Imagine my gratitude and joy when Bernard Sorensen, although outwardly as conventional as his senior colleagues, not only revealed an intimate knowledge of the Magnificent Seven but appeared to share their contempt for bourgeois values and their love of antiquity, suicide, oceans, cats and illiterate whores.

'A lady friend brings the hero, Durtal,' Bernard was saying now, 'to a Black Mass said by Canon Docre. Of course it's really just an orgy. Afterwards the lady, a respectable Catholic wife, takes Durtal to this seedy room and tries to have sex with him . . . *on a bed of soiled Communion wafers.*' Again the uproarious laughter. 'A remarkable fellow, Huysmans. And an exquisite stylist. *Exquisite.* Style is every-thing, as Flaubert said.' Accepting a Bushmills and water, he put away half in a single gulp. 'My God that's delightful. And of course reading's essentially a *sensual* thing. In fact you don't really read a book at all, do you?' He was addressing this to Clare. 'You just lie down beside it and permit it to stroke you.'

'I need to check this food.' Accepting a glass from me in passing, Clare buried half of it with an avidity and relish at least the equal of Bernard's.

'A wonderful stylist,' he repeated, 'but a nutcase of course . . . like almost all of the French. You know he ended up going back to the Church? He belongs to what I call the literature of bad temper. Always in a ferocious pique about something. Personally I think it was all due to *indigestion*. He was always eating these huge meals and washing them down with gallons of wine.'

Huysmans's sublime disgust and outrage reduced to bad temper . . . *indigestion!* Now it was my turn to down half a glass. But there was no denying the return to the Church. At the end of his life Huysmans became not just a Catholic but a dolorist, one of those who believe that suffering is both inevitable and desirable, the purpose of human life on earth. Among his last books was a biography of Blessed Lidwine, a fourteenth-century Dutch girl who enjoyed extraordinary beauty up to the age of fifteen when she was attacked by blindness, erysipelas, paralysis and a terrible plague that left her with festering wounds in which worms bred. Two monstrous boils formed, one under her arm and the other over her heart. 'Two boils, it is well,' she said to the Lord, 'but three would be better in honour of the Holy Trinity.' Immediately a third enormous pustule broke out on her face.

Huysmans's Catholicism resembled that of my mother – a mixture of dolorism and voodoo. After the publication of *Là-Bas* he believed that the Satanists were bombarding him with spells and hired a consultant sorcerer as a spiritguard. Battle was joined in occult dogfights over the rooftops of Paris and, though the defences were vigilant and strong, occasional maleficent spells got through to mount a personal assault ('fluidic fisticuffs'). On these occasions the novelist and critic, one of the most sceptical and lucid intelligences of his time, locked himself in his flat, burned in his fireplace a tablet of exorcistic paste (a mixture of myrrh, incense, camphor and cloves – the plant of John the Baptist), entered a defensive circle drawn on the floor and, brandishing in his right hand a miraculous blood-stained host and with his left pressing to his body the blessed scapular of the Elijan Carmel, recited conjurations which dissolved the astral fluids and paralysed the power of the Satanists.

The Satanists failed to get him but suffering duly arrived in the form of terminal throat cancer. He refused treatment and pain-killers and endured an atrocious protracted death. 'What a terrible slow agony in the midst of frightening lucidity,' wrote one of his friends. 'Scrap by scrap I have to pull away pieces of putrefying flesh and the stench is appalling.'

The guy may have been nuts – but he followed through.

'In fact one of his finest works is about indigestion,' Bernard said. 'I notice you don't have *À Vau l'Eau*.'

'The one about the little clerk trying to get a decent meal? One of his early naturalistic works. Dull.'

To fuel a sufficient passion and eloquence Bernard gulped down the rest of his Bushmills. '*Marvellously* dull! A little masterpiece. I *love* dull works.' Beating his empty glass into his palm, he repeated the key monosyllable. 'Dull, dull, dull, dull.'

This was no affectation. I remembered him vehemently criticising a novel for being 'too interesting'. And on another occasion: 'I thought it was going to be boring but it turned out to be' – frown of disgust – '*colourful*.'

'You've come to the right place.' Grimly I consoled myself with Bushmills. 'Crying children. Shitty nappies.'

'But the demands of children are *paramount*. And that's the other key word: *service*. What's the most important word in the language? Service. Service. Can I say it a third time? *Service*.'

Dullness and service – a delightful cocktail for the happy hour.

Nor was there affectation in his use of the second key term. After mistaking him for a believer in detachment, opposition and scorn, I was deeply shocked to discover him chairing a crowded and passionate union meeting in which staff demanded to know why canteen lunches, for which they were obliged to pay in full, were completely free of charge in a neighbouring school. Bernard calmly explained that staff who supervised pupils during lunch were indeed entitled to a free meal but, whereas in the other school teachers ate in the body of the hall, which was technically classed as supervision, here we sat at tables *on the stage* . . .

There was pandemonium. Effortlessly Bernard exerted his authority, proposing a motion (immediately seconded): 'The membership request that eating lunch on the stage be recognised as supervision in the same way as eating in the hall.'

'Not request – *demand*.'

'*Insist!*'

'Speakers on the motion. Mr Lambert.'

'I propose we simply all eat in the hall.'

'That sounds like a new motion. Do we have a seconder? *Mr Cameron*.'

'I propose an amendment.'

'To which motion, the first or the second?'

The meeting split into two camps, traditionalists who recalled the days of separate dining rooms with waitress service and progressives who wished to eat not only in the body of the hall but at the same tables as pupils (always referred to as 'kids'). A classic development – rebellion followed by civil war.

When I jeered at the absurdity of it afterwards Bernard subjected me to a lecture on civics. 'You see you're corrupted by quasi-aristocratic nonsense. You can't understand the need for institutions and participation.' A horrifying possibility assailed him. 'Have you ever even *voted?*'

'Never.' I shuddered, equally horrified. 'I'm like Flaubert – the only political act I can understand is the riot.'

Patiently he repeated the lecture, his talent for presiding over the unruly matched by his enthusiasm for enlightening the obtuse. Perhaps because he had gone to university late, he had escaped the usual consequence of education – the complete and permanent snuffing out of any further desire to learn. Not only still in thrall to exposition, Bernard was a compulsive explainer in the way that others compulsively joke, whinge, boast or flirt.

In the course of the meal he explained the relative numbers of animal species in Europe, Britain and Ireland (directly proportional to the number of land bridges connecting these three in the Ice Age); the reason for changing Fess Parker's name on the French prints of his movies (*fesse* is French for arse); the true source of Russian belligerence (lack of warm-water ports); the reason why animals never developed wheels (the problem of blood circulation in a rotating mechanism); the desirability of using American actors in Shakespeare (American accents are closer to the Elizabethan than contemporary English); the reason why birds do a number two but not a number one (no build-up of toxins to be flushed away); and, on the last course, the reason why Café Cognac should always be made with Jamaican Blue Mountain coffee (this variety shares with brandy an aroma of tom cat's urine).

As, in response to one of my sneers, he was explaining the etymology of the word 'cynic' (from the Greek for dog, since cynics copulated and shat in the street like dogs), Lucy woke up and began to cry.

'Want me to get her?' I offered.

'She'll be hungry,' Clare said. 'I'll go.'

When Bernard rose and followed her I had to go with him to avoid seeming indifferent.

'She cries all the time,' Clare said in despair. 'I don't know what to do.'

'A lot of touching and talking, honey. A lot of cuddling and stroking.'

'I *know* that. I *do* all that.' Despair so easily becomes resentment. 'But it doesn't seem to do any good. There must be something wrong with her. We must be doing something wrong.'

'No no no no no no.' Bernard laid a reassuring hand on her arm. 'You see, when people talk about *good* babies they mean *placid* babies, babies who *sleep* most of the time. Frankly I think babies like that are a bit on the slow side ... a bit lacking upstairs. But Lucy here is full of the old moxie, full of intelligence and energy, and her problem is simply *frustration*. She's full of the old moxie, raring to go, but not able to do anything yet. So you see, she's *incredibly frustrated*. And' – touching her arm again lightly, he softened his voice to mitigate a possible criticism – 'have you a bit of a temper, honey?'

At last it was my turn. 'Is a pig's arse pork?'

'Well there you are. The child is frustrated and hasn't the temperament for patience. As soon as she's able to crawl you'll have no more trouble. In fact she'll develop at an incredible rate.'

Instead of suffering from some sinister malfunction, Lucy was a frustrated genius impatient to bloom. Our weariness with explanation suddenly dispelled, we gazed in admiration and gratitude at the Wizard of Cause.

'But the other factor is this,' he went on to Clare. 'You're obviously obsessional and tense. You need a break from children. And from this fellow too. But you've this Irish horror of social and community services. Find out about crèche facilities in your local community centre. And I'll come round and babysit some evening.'

Already Clare seemed more relaxed as she settled into the rocking chair we had bought for breast feeding (one of the baby manuals claimed that motion at a certain rpm, rocks-per-minute, had a soothing effect on infants). As we returned to the living area Bernard explained the evolution of the human breast.

'You know of course that it was needed as a cushion.'

'For the weary husband? After a hard day at the office?'

Trying to deflect Bernard with wisecracks was like throwing powder puffs at a tank.

'You know how a peach will bruise on the side next to the dish? The same would happen to a baby lying on a hard bony torso. So the breast evolved to protect it.'

Among the debris of the meal was a bottle of our own cheap red still almost half full. Bernard placed a hand over his glass. 'No more for me. I hate being hungover in the morning.'

From the way he was wincing and grimacing it was obvious that the next explanations would be painful. I braced myself with a hefty snort of red.

I thought I was apolitical but in fact I was a right-wing reactionary; I thought I was irreligious but I was steeped in Roman Catholicism; I thought I was rebellious and fierce but I was inhibited and weak; I thought I was independent and free but I was a conformist mammy's boy; I thought of myself as cultured but I was ignorant of classical music as well as visually illiterate.

Remedial action – leave Our Lady of Perpetual Succour, involve myself in communal activity, regularly visit the National Gallery, use my local library's music section, henceforth address my female parent not as 'mammy' but 'mother'.

Clare called from the bedroom. The rocking chair had crossed the floor and become wedged in a corner. Lucy was still at the breast – but looking agitated and angry.

'She's not feeding?'

'Hardly any.' Clare herself was disturbed and flushed.

'And your . . . ?'

'Incredibly sore.'

Returning the rocker to the middle of the room, I placed beside it the current remedy for cracked nipples, a product whose name suggested lawnmower lubricant – Rotorsept Spray. Clare resumed frantic rocking but Lucy still thrashed. Alas, the genius theory did not explain her resistance to nourishment. Perhaps this was part of the paternal inheritance. My mother always claimed that I was an ingrate from birth.

'You have *comics?*' Paul was saying in renewed astonishment to Bernard.

'Of course. *Krazy Kat* and *Little Nemo in Slumberland.*' Hastily he turned to me. 'Not for reasons of nostalgia. I *detest* nostalgia. It's the marvellous draughtsmanship and use of colour. George Herriman and Windsor McKay were real artists . . . the *plasticity of form* . . .'

'Wouldn't know. Visually illiterate.'

Paul returned to his Lego and Bernard to his rigorous dissection of me.

I thought I was a devoted husband and father but in fact I was distracted and grudging; I thought I was a major intellect but was actually anti-intellectual; I thought I was a scientist but had little knowledge of science; I thought I was an expert on the French *fin de siècle* but, not only ignorant of its politics, painters and composers, I could not even truly appreciate the writers since I did not read them in French.

Bernard paused, aghast himself at the enormity of my illusions. 'Perhaps I'll take a little wine after all.'

In the bedroom Lucy whimpered and the rocking chair creaked and groaned (it was hastily and imperfectly put together from a self-assembly kit). Paul muttered to himself over his Lego. Bernard and I sipped the cheap wine, troubled and ruminant.

To accept his analysis would mean replacing rich Irish stew with the watery gruel of English do-gooding and culture worship, joining the washed-out living dead of committees, galleries and theatre foyers. (What horrified Huysmans about religious conversion was the prospect of mingling with the pious: 'He was afraid of being taken for a fool; the thought of being seen on his knees in church made his hair stand on end.') Impossible to contemplate – but it was equally impossible to repel Bernard's relentless onslaught. I could almost feel my deepest convictions collapsing and crumbling into dust. However I shrieked and flung powder puffs, the tank rolled on.

Suddenly there came a great need to escape and forget, to indulge in something trashy and passive, like watching a game show in bed while eating Cadbury's Creme Eggs.

This was evidence for the symbiotic union because, when she entered carrying Lucy, Clare said, with no hint of apology or shame, 'Is there anything on TV?'

There was not only a cowboy movie but an example of that late flowering of the genre known as the elegiac western. Bernard perused the *Radio Times* with a sceptical frown.

'Tepid urine, Martin.'

'But it has Jack Palance. A star with the face of a pugilist and the voice of a poet.'

Clare took the magazine and suggested, though not as boldly as before, that we could take a look at that American thing everyone was talking about.

Bernard's scepticism modulated into outrage. 'Is that one of those repulsive things about the rich?' He rose, as though to smite the television set. 'Trying to make out that the rich are having a wonderful time? Sexual fun and games day and night? The rich are all dead men. They're all dead men. Can I say it a third time? *They're all dead men.* Don't they even look like dead men – Lazaruses back from hell with the bandages just taken off? As for sex, they've never had a good bit of nookie in their lives. They're not even aware of what good nookie *is*.' Forestalling objections, he raised a calm hand. 'Take my word for it, they've never once enjoyed a decent fuck. *Never!*' Assuming a sorrowful expression, he shook his head and went close to Clare. '*Honey, they're pushing it into envelopes of loosely packed gravel.*'

'Your woman on the show's a pretty sexy bit of stuff.'

His great speech gone for nothing, Bernard's shoulders collapsed and he fell back in defeat. 'Actresses,' he sighed wearily, 'are either *lesbian* or *frigid.*'

Clare bristled. 'How do you know that?'

Bernard raised both hands in a gesture that combined compassion, wisdom, detachment and possibly even self-defence. 'Honey . . . actors and actresses . . .'

'My friend Judith's going out with an actor. And she's having a wonderful time.'

'One of these big handsome fellows? Supposedly strong but completely weak. Like Gable in my generation. You know he ended up a hopeless drunk auctioned out to women. A different woman every night.'

To a man deprived of nookie this did not seem so bad.

'Sounds all right to me. As long as he could still get it up.'

'Oh . . .' Bernard turned away in what was now terminal disgust. 'I suppose he was having *emissions.*'

Clare bounced Lucy and vehemently moved from side to side herself. Anger always made her restless and pent.

'I'd better be going,' Bernard said after a while. 'You two are obviously exhausted and need to relax. I know it's not easy. Marriage is one of the two great institutions of Western civilisation' – Clare grunted savagely – 'but of course it's actually appalling . . . the three of us know that. Both these institutions are appalling . . . but they're also *wonderful* . . . no one has devised anything better. Try to bear that in mind.'

Vigorously bouncing Lucy, Clare turned away into the kitchen area. Bernard moved towards the door, sorrowfully regarding me but, in final despair of persuasion, musing almost to himself.

'So what are the fruits of your education and upbringing? An exaggerated sense of superiority and a total inability to do anything.' He winced suddenly, as though assailed by some vicious internal pain. 'Perhaps the sensation of being intrinsically wonderful is as crippling as the sensation of being intrinsically worthless.'

As a weak man I could not prevent myself from putting the question. 'What was the second institution?'

Bernard could scarcely comprehend that there was further disappointment. He gaped at me in shock and incredulity. 'Democracy of course.'

'I know you got me this job, Mr Ward.' Anxiety clouds the vacuous features of the post office clerk, whom Martin recognises as one of the many young men – diffident, deferential, neat and dim – who present themselves at the Ward home for help in securing a white-collar position. 'But we're not supposed to hand out mail to the public. You'll get it in the morning post like everyone else.'

'Aye. All right. That's all right.' Hugh Ward speaks as one long familiar with human selfishness and ingratitude, in the tone – curt, dry, controlled – our Redeemer may well have used when only one of the healed lepers returned to express gratitude. 'That's all right,

Maurice. *Surely*. I mean, if it's *inconvenient* for you . . .'

Rarely has such confusion and anguish contorted young features. 'Well . . . Ah suppose . . .' Maurice sighs profoundly. 'Maybe . . . just this once.' The decision made, his expression clears and he turns to Martin with a chuckle. 'Couldn't wait till the morning to get your results, eh?'

As so often, horror is without warning piled upon horror. Not only is the purpose of the visit revealed as illegal interception of mail by bullying, but ignorant and innocent Martin is getting the blame.

Maurice returns with an envelope and a grin. 'The sixty-four-thousand-dollar question . . . eh, Mr Ward?'

Hugh violently rips the envelope – and his face is transfigured by that rare intensity which can radically alter our experience of time. As a man on the gallows relives in a moment a wasted past, so now, in an instant of vertiginous ecstasy, the father lives the golden future of the son.

'He got it!' he shouts in wild abandon. 'He got his 11-plus. *He got it!*'

Maurice chuckles in fond indulgence. 'Ah sure that's great, Mr Ward. That's powerful news altogether.'

Martin is also subject to an unusual sensation. As, in a near-death experience, the soul leaves the body and observes with dispassionate curiosity the frantic efforts of the surgeons, so he is now a distant spectator at his own hour of triumph ('Great minds love themselves from afar' – d'Aurevilly).

'Ye'll be goin' on to the College,' Maurice is chuckling to Martin. 'Ye'll soon be a big fella in a college blazer. Never got to the college meself. Your father taught me in St Anthony's. Did ye know that?' When Martin once more fails to respond, the clerk turns back to Hugh. 'Us crowd must've nearly broke your heart, Mr Ward. Ye could never batter anything into us. Do ye mind our class? A terrible crowd altogether.'

Hugh Ward is also unreachable. Once again he scans the letter, transcendent and rapt.

Mrs Ward appears undemonstrative but her first action is revealing. Like a general planning a triumphal march through Rome, she calls at once for a visit to the aunt house, capital and administrative centre of the empire of relatives known as 'the connection'.

Inhabited by the spinster sisters Greta and Jean, with their nephew Pascal and niece Mairead, this tiny semi-detached embodies the style of civilised living to which all the married sisters aspire. Central feature of the style: suppression of the rectilinear and hard. Every surface meant for contact yields luxuriously to the touch; there are velvet curtains and upholstery, shagpile overlaid with hirsute rugs, padded suites lined with cushions, pink marshmallow beds piled with pillows. Fireplaces, walls and furniture of course preserve the notion of firmness but straight lines have been almost completely eliminated. Fantastic whorls and curlicues pattern wallpaper and carpets and adorn mirrors, plant-holders, lamp-standards, vases, jugs, clocks, picture and photograph frames. Filigree, scallops, tassels and fringes border all material. Furniture edges are rounded and fluted; legs curve like Matisse nudes. Every trace of harshness or utility has been banished or concealed. Daylight is softened by lace curtains and scallop-edged blinds, artificial light by shades *farouche* as Ascot hats; curtain fixtures are invisible under velvet-covered pelmets; the grate is shielded by a heavily embossed brass fire screen and the coal bucket hidden in a heavily embossed brass container; even the newsprint of the *Radio Times* is concealed in a leather folder with a cover as intricately worked as the Book of Kells and the functionalism of the television set itself is subdued by a plant-holder, a lamp with a velvet shade and trim and a silver-framed photograph of Pascal in his First Communion suit.

All the tiny rooms are packed with furniture and the feeling of suffocation is greatly enhanced by overheating; high-piled fires roar in both downstairs grates. Martin pauses in the living room doorway, appalled by the clutter and fug ('Axiom: hatred of the bourgeois is the beginning of wisdom' – Flaubert). In the armchair by the fire sits Greta, eldest sister and bull aunt, comfortably wide in the beam but holding erect her armoured superstructure and fabulous cast-iron brioche of grey hair. From this source will come no overt acknowledgement of success because, in the division of labour here observed, Greta's formidable energies are reserved for enquiry, censure and recrimination.

It is Jean who advances on Martin with a familiar glad cry: '*Who's my wee man? Who's my man today?*' He submits to her embrace, for Jean is slim and golden-haired and, in contrast to Greta's mask of putty and lead, has a countenance bronzed by make-up and holidays in the Mediterranean with Molly McShane.

'Aren't you the great wee man? Aren't you great altogether?' Holding him at arm's length, she assumes a mock-solemn expression. 'But listen ... tell me this and tell me no more ... would you ever think of going on to be a doctor ... would you ever think of being a doctor and *curing my poor corns?*' Almost immediately her laugh deteriorates into a debilitating smoker's cough, in spite of which she repeats the joke for the benefit of the Ward family in the doorway.

'Ah can't see this character as a doctor.' Mrs Ward observes her son with a certain grim prescience.

Greta frowns at the boy in astonishment. 'Would you not think of going on to be a doctor, right enough?'

Martin shrugs dismissively ('For myself, who sense within me sometimes the absurdity of a prophet, I know that I shall never feel the charity of a physician' – Baudelaire).

The company take up their seats, manoeuvring to avoid bumping knees, and Mairead, who has been hovering in the hall, comes in behind with her habitual stream of sentence fragments, exclamations, chuckles and grunts. 'Well that's the boy ... sure that's ... huh huh ... oh aye ... oh that's ... it's as well ... isn't that the great ...' But as always she has to solicit individual attention, repeating the name obsessively until she is granted an audience. 'Aunt Josie? Aunt Josie? Aunt Josie? Aunt Josie? Isn't it as well there's one that's good at the books at least, Aunt Josie?'

Greta terminates the babble with a terse command. 'Bring Hugh the *Irish News*.'

Martin, man of books, goes to the books piled on the table – gigantic ledgers with rope handles and thick stiff pages of the heavily embossed and patterned wallpaper favoured by the bull aunt. For, as sensitive as any radical to the corrupting effects of stasis, Greta has exceeded Trotsky's dream of perpetual revolution with a reality of perpetual redecoration. Martin retreats to the velvet-covered piano stool at the back of the room and leans his book on the instrument he has never seen opened much less played.

'Right enough though, Josie,' Jean is saying, seriously now, 'isn't it great to get him through? I mean, after all that business ...' She pauses as Mairead enters the room with the *Irish News* and continues only when the girl has given it to Hugh and left again. 'And the same carry-on with Pascal ...'

'Pascal,' Greta grunts in sudden fierce disgust. 'Sure what

is he not?'

'Where is he by the way?'

'Out gallivantin' as usual.'

Martin bends to the wallpaper book, justified and exultant ('To know that one is a force is a consolation for the many things – cruel, bitter, lacerating, stupid – of which life is comprised' – d'Aurevilly).

'So what would you like to go on to be, Martin?'

Scarcely looking up from his book, he shrugs in profound indifference ('What is the world to me? Asking little of it, I shall let myself float on the current of my heart and imagination and if anyone shouts too loudly, perhaps, like Phocion, I shall turn and enquire: *What is that cawing of crows?'* – Flaubert).

'Would you not think of going on to be an engineer?' Greta asks. 'There's Charlie Bradley making a fortune with the County Council.'

The Ward parents turn expectantly. Perhaps the taciturn prodigy will at last reveal his master plan.

Martin merely laughs dismissively ('I fully expect to become an extremely wicked fool' – Rimbaud).

Hugh Ward returns to the *Irish News* but his wife continues to study her son in a grim renewal of ancient perplexity. 'You could get nothin' out of him, look see. He's as . . . as . . . *och* . . .'

Words proving inadequate to the mystery, she can only shake her head in bafflement. Martin contentedly turns heavy pages ('I am the maestro of silence' – Rimbaud).

'Would that be the Bradleys of Blucher Street?' Jean enquires after a while.

'*Not at all.*' Greta winces at the blunder. 'He'd be a son of Mamie McGettigan.'

'One of the *McGettigans,*' Mrs Ward explains, stressing the surname.

'Sure ye know the kind of Mamie.'

'And of all belonging to her.'

These cryptic conversations resist even Martin's immense powers of deduction.

'But sure it's no way of working.'

'There's no call for the half of it.'

Maddeningly negligible scraps of evidence! Perhaps he will become a forensic scientist, re-creating detailed histories from fibre shreds and dirt grains.

'Now!' With a cry of triumph Mairead bears into the room a tray with a china tea service and a three-level cake stand whose tiers of gradually decreasing size display delicacies of increasing sophistication; on the bottom plate are heavily buttered rounds of soda bread, in the middle slices of home-made rhubarb tart and on top a sponge flan covered with whipped cream and garnished with segments of tinned mandarin orange.

'Och Mairead . . .' Mrs Ward makes the ritual protest.

'It's just a wee cup . . . a wee bite . . .'

'It's only a wee cup in your hand,' Greta says, examining the tray and then addressing its bearer. 'Could ye not have put out the wee scones Jean made?' Wearily she sighs at the futility of explaining anything to this foolish girl. 'Those big lumps of bread.' The sight repels but also fascinates for she cannot help staring at the bottom level of the stand. '*Whatever possessed you?*'

'Sure Ah never thought. *Ah never thought.*'

'Well ye'd want to think. *Ye'd want to think.*'

Immediately Martin approaches the tray and takes the largest slice of soda bread.

'*Take another, sure!*' Vindicated and jubilant, Mairead pursues him back to his stool.

Martin is suddenly struck by the mystery of being related to this girl. If Mairead is his cousin there must be a missing aunt/uncle and a missing husband/wife. Who are they and where are they? And why does 'the connection' feel it necessary to conceal the most elementary facts?

'Give Hugh a bit of tart,' Greta commands now. Mairead promptly delivers a portion. 'And he'll take a piece of flan.'

Hugh folds his newspaper as though to defend himself with it. 'Och no.'

'You'll take a bit of flan, Hugh. Sure it won't keep.'

Mairead carries out Greta's instructions and, with a shriek of delight, adds a slice of soda bread to Hugh's plate. Martin is convinced that this apparent generosity is in fact humiliation and conquest. Will his father not rise up in wrath – or at least react in some way? ('No one has ever enjoyed rights other than those he has appropriated and knows how to retain' – Villiers).

'Boys-ah-boys,' Hugh mutters, balancing the piled plate on his lap.

When Mairead has distributed the tea things she makes to sit down herself.

Greta jerks her head at the girl. 'Get the . . .'

'*Wa . . .?*'

'The . . . the . . .' Greta grimaces at the redundancy and tedium of continually having to articulate her wishes. 'Och Mairead . . . *have ye no wit at all?*'

Jean has a word in Mairead's ear and, comprehending at last, the girl leaves the room to return with a huge heavy briefcase in light cream pigskin. Not only of monstrous bulk, the object advertises itself with a luminosity bordering on incandescence.

'Got it out of the shop on appro,' Mairead explains. 'Ye can change it if ye want.'

Mrs Ward intervenes at once. 'He'll do no such thing. Sure isn't it lovely?'

'And the best of stuff,' Greta says. 'It'll last him a lifetime.'

All look to the boy genius – but he has been struck dumb by horror.

'Have ye a mouth on ye at all?' Mrs Ward angrily cries. 'Can ye not say thanks to your Aunt Greta itself? Don't ye know that's the best of stuff? *Don't ye know that cost the earth?*'

He does know – but who covets the earth? All he wants is American comics and one-and-six for the Palace.

'He's all right, Josie.' Taking the case from Mairead, Jean places it in Martin's hand which, almost in spite of himself, grips the handle. Then she steps back to admire the effect. 'Och sure there we are now. *That's my wee man. That's my man today.*'

# 2

'Glad to be back, Mr Ward?'

Meeting Sister Joe inside the door was a brutal reminder of terrible truths – that I was a teacher in a convent school and the 'wee man' of the nuns and that ahead lay the endless frozen tundra of the dark winter term.

'Ha ha, Sister.' Wan smile and weak laugh – feeble January sun.

Seizing my arm in collusive glee, she brought her face close to mine. '*I'm certainly not glad.*' She withdrew her face to enjoy a shriek of subversive merriment, then restored it to close proximity. 'But at least there's no pupils today. The peace and quiet's wonderful. *Wonderful!* I think we should work without them all the time. What do you think, Mr Ward?'

'Great idea, Sister.'

Then, abruptly solemn: 'And how's the little one now?'

'Much improved, Sister.' To enhance the joy of the new term Lucy had wakened us twice the night before. 'Much better now, Sister.'

'I knew it!' she cried, squeezing and shaking my arm in solidarity and celebration. 'Great news, Mr Ward. Great news.' She brought her face even closer. 'And *listen*.' Another intimate squeeze. 'You might have more good news today. You might hear something interesting today.' After a final sharp enigmatic squeeze she made off, pausing a moment later to turn with a knowing wink. 'But say no more. I can't say a word now. *Say no more*.'

The official day began with a staff meeting presided over by Sister Stanislaus (Stan the Man), flanked by her genial deputy, Joe, and Sister Saviour, the school secretary, a dour ascetic young nun. First an announcement – we would all be very sorry to hear that Miss Gaston was seriously ill and unlikely to be back for the rest of the year. However, we were extremely lucky to get an excellent replacement at very short notice – Miss Phelps. A young woman stood up and smiled with suitably charming diffidence. Then Stan vehemently addressed one of the eternal great themes.

'It has come to my attention that standards of politeness and manners were dropping *noticeably* at the end of last term. Now some of you may feel that the *academic* side of teaching is what really matters.' Strategic pause, as if to encourage intervention from the supporters of this view. 'However, at Our Lady of Perpetual Succour it has always been the policy that *a certain standard of behaviour* is every bit as important as academic achievement.' Again she waited as if for a challenge – but the only response was a vigorous nod from Sister Joseph. 'Now at the end of last term, not only was there a *marked deterioration* in school but I had many more complaints from shopkeepers and residents round about. Sister Saviour, who as you know is extremely busy, has been simply *inundated* with calls.' All eyes turned to the secretary who remained formidably inscrutable. 'I would like to remind staff of certain basic rules. That at the start of every lesson a class should rise and say *Good morning* or *Good afternoon* and that at the end of the lesson they should rise again and thank the teacher *formally by name*. I think we often allow them to take *far too much for granted*. We have a superb staff here and I think it *only right and proper* to encourage the girls to be *grateful*.'

There followed a solemn recital of the rules, up to and including the ordinance forbidding consumption of solids or drinks on the journeys to and from school. 'Now of course we expect form tutors to set standards of behaviour. But we cannot simply leave it all to form tutors and year heads. *It is the duty of every member of staff to enforce the rules at all times.* We cannot ignore these things or leave them to others.' Now genuinely moved, she paused to emphasise her conclusion – a passionate call to solidarity and commitment. *'We cannot pass by on the other side.'*

Teaching itself is reasonably congenial (I was born to explain as other men are born to rule) but not the disciplinary framework that always surrounds it at lower levels. The squalid business of enforcing rules I had every intention of leaving to tutors and year heads. One advantage of a convent school was that all the lawenforcement work was carried out by women. Men generally passed by on the other side, though of course taking care not to make their detachment too obvious. Now the male staff filed out as though chastened and reformed, with lowered heads and solemn expressions, attempting not to bump the chairs.

Sister Saviour intercepted me. 'The Head would like to see you in her study for a few minutes.'

A private grilling! But how serious? Saviour's face was as pale and inexpressive as a Japanese mask.

The executive offices were on the ground floor of the new wing, dominating a dim silent corridor gravid with the latent power of authority. On one side was Sister Joseph's room and, opposite, that of Stan the Man. At the end of the corridor, directly ahead and between the two offices, a unisex toilet beckoned the unwary like bait in a trap.

All the old submissiveness and fear flooded back. It reminded me of being summoned to Tim Arthur's office after throwing pepper in the rice dessert of a free-dinners boy, an intoxicating early *acte gratuit*.

Conditioned to heavy dark opulence in the sanctums of the powerful, I was once again surprised by the austerity and brightness here – a wide window illuminating white walls, bare except for a plain black crucifix, the only furniture a filing cabinet and a functional desk of light pine.

'Mr Ward.' She waved me to a chair on the other side of the desk. 'How are the family?' The tone brisk and perfunctory. No question of intimacy much less collusion.

'Fine, Sister. All fine.'

'And you've just bought a flat, I believe? You're settling down in London?'

'For the time being at least, Sister.'

She grunted and pondered. 'And you're happy enough with us here?'

'Oh *absolutely*. Absolutely, Sister.'

This time her grunt was abrupt and pungent, the scepticism of intelligent authority inured to protestation and grovelling. 'So you see your future here . . . here in Our Lady of Perpetual Succour?'

Obviously this was setting me up – but there was only one possible answer. 'Well yes . . . I think so . . . *yes*.'

Instead of the expected offensive there came a mysterious slack silence.

'There's a few points available,' she said at last with a sudden air of weariness and boredom. 'Of course everyone's after them . . . convinced they're *entitled* to them in fact.' This revealed her mood swing's likely cause: the disgust of one who has seen too many jostling snouts at the trough. It was also clear that I had been summoned for something far worse than scolding. This was the ultimate humiliation – acceptance. The woman was actually about to *promote* me. 'Mr Wills feels it's the turn of the Science Department. And of course strength in science is incredibly important . . . especially in a girls' school. We certainly appreciate the work you all do. The results of your own exam classes are always excellent . . . *excellent*. You've really boosted us in Physics . . . we can now hold our own with boys anywhere. So Mr Wills thinks you should be responsible for Physics throughout the school.'

'Well . . . it's . . .' In moments of trauma we tend to regress to the culture and dialect of youth. What immediately sprang to mind was that most traditional of Irish queries: *would there be a pound in it at all?*

'I take it you'd have no objection to a Scale Three?'

But where did this scale start and end, how much extra initially and how soon would it arrive? Perhaps Clare could give up the night work. Certainly it was goodbye for ever to kidney bean curry.

'Well, Sister . . . *no* . . . no objection, huh huh.'

She turned to the window. The gratitude of successful snouts must be almost as unedifying as their greed.

'I suppose we'll put it down for the Physics then so?'

Why 'suppose'? Why 'put it down for'? Those exam results spoke for themselves.

'For the Physics,' I said as firmly as possible – but she was not paying attention.

'What we were thinking was that you might like to take over poor Miss Gaston's tutor group.'

Ah yes. A sweet piece of play. Even as a victim I can appreciate elegance. And, having taken the bait, all I could do now was wriggle. 'But, Sister . . . young girls . . . I'm not . . .'

'We'd like the male staff to be more involved in the life of the school. We think it's important for the girls to *see* that the men are also involved. Not to think of the men as *separate* but to see them *involved.*'

It was even sweeter than it first seemed. In return for the Scale Three she would not only fill a tutor-group vacancy but gain a crucial bridgehead among the male staff. I would not only be sucked into law enforcement but used as an example to break male resistance. Not merely a collaborator but a gender traitor as well.

'But I don't think I'm *qualified*, Sister. I mean, I've no experience . . .'

'You'll get all the help you need from an experienced Year Head – *Moira Sweeney.*'

She was effortlessly rubbing my nose in the dirt. Calling her Stan the Man did her no justice. This woman had *balls like a stallion.*

How different the outcome with Tim Arthur when, instead of confessing and 'taking my medicine', I resisted, exulting in the glory of the renegade and the rapture of the evil beyond vice.

But revolt has no career path. Only Lautréamont, the most dazzling Lucifer, understood that the rebel angel must disappear in a single flash. A citizen of late-nineteenth-century Paris, he remains as enigmatic and remote as Homer. 'My annihilation will be complete,' he wrote, 'I shall leave no memoir.' Apart from a few letters and poems all that remains is *Les Chants de Maldoror*, an institution-sized jar of industrial-strength venom, a piercing shriek of defiance at the compromised world.

Lautréamont, friend of sharks, tapeworms and lice and

implacable foe of God and Man ('My poetry shall consist of attacks, by all possible means, on that wild beast, Man, and the Creator who should never have begotten such vermin'), have pity on the humbled and compromised Lucifers, the extinguished heresiarchs whose fallen husks strew the earth!

As I was turning into the toilet to splash cold water on my burning features there came a strange, urgent whisper.

'*Wheest . . . wheest!*'

And now a low shuffling and rattling that also seemed designed to attract my attention without alerting anyone else.

Sister Joseph's door was slightly ajar. As I peered round it she beckoned in furious delight, motioning me to enter and shut the door.

'Now, Mr Ward!' Still she was whispering. 'Didn't I tell you you'd be getting good news?'

Why the secrecy, the conspiratorial tone? It seemed to be a response to the exercise of authority, a reflex so instinctive and strong that it imposed itself even when there was no disagreement with authority – *even when the whisperer was a senior executive of that authority*. As gills were developed by fish in order to breathe under water, so survival in an authoritarian environment requires the evolution of bizarre psychological features. Foremost among these is the notion that action is essentially conspiratorial. For the Irish Catholic, concealment and dissimulation are bred in the bone.

'Didn't I tell you? Didn't I tell you that now?' Her high good humour verged on the manic. 'I told Sister Stanislaus you were worth it. I told her she wouldn't regret it.'

Naked sponsorship and patronage. *Who's my wee man? Who's my man today?* This encounter promised to be as demeaning as the interview with Stan.

'And I told her it'd be great for the girls to have you as tutor. Ah it'll be great for them. *Great.*' Again the ritual laying on of hands. 'I told her you wouldn't let her down.' My mumble was wretched as well as indistinct – but she was too excited to register misery. 'You see, Sister Stanislaus is very generous really. People imagine she's hard – but that's just a front. Because she has to be tough for that job. Has to be. *Has to be.*'

'She has to be,' I glumly echoed.

'Oh she has to be. Some would walk over you if you let them.

And some of the parents even worse. *Don't talk to me about parents. Don't talk to me, Mr Ward.*' Bringing her head close to mine, she lowered her voice even further. 'And between me and you and the wall . . . *some of the staff too.*' At last something of interest – but she drew back with a knowing grunt. 'It's a very tough job . . . very tough. I couldn't do it myself at any price. Couldn't do it . . . *couldn't do it,* Mr Ward.'

'Neither could I, Sister.'

'And on top of that other job too.'

Stan the Man moonlighting? Senior Barmaid? Staff Nurse?

'She's Mother Superior of the order here . . . in charge of the convent . . . an even tougher job than Head . . . *Oh don't be talkin' now,* I could tell you some stories.'

A claustral retreat of meditation and repose – such was my notion of convent life gleaned from the sight of frail old nuns in the garden, 'their emaciated bodies secreting balm' as Huysmans claimed literally occurred in an order in Unterlinden. But of course the largely Irish nuns came from the same stock as my aunts. Spirituality was not their strong point, nor were they emaciated and frail. The convent was more likely to be a cauldron of resentment and bitterness. Especially when the bull nuns got home from a hard day at the office.

'She has to be tough, Mr Ward. But she's very generous underneath. I was telling her about your little ones and your wife staying at home to look after them.' And how similar to Greta and Jean was the hard and soft team of Stan and Joe: one the lawgiver and the other the mediator, one God the Father and the other his compassionate Son. 'You need that bit extra, Mr Ward. You need that nowadays. People think I don't know these things living in a convent.' She paused to chuckle in satisfaction, proud that a concubine of the Holy Spirit was also a shrewd today guy. '*Thirteen and three-quarters percent!*'

'I'm sorry, Sister?'

'The mortgage rate.' She laughed in unrestrained delight. 'What you have to pay on your new flat. It's absolutely scandalous. I explained it to Sister Stanislaus and she understood immediately. You see, she's very generous really. Very generous really.'

All my life I have been accused of ingratitude – but few of the gifts were without strings. Disinterested generosity is as rare as objective analysis.

'And if you make a go of form tutor, who knows, Mr Ward? There may be a new post of Senior Teacher coming up. I think myself it'll have to go to a lay member of staff.'

Next to the boss nuns at staff meetings – *a harem eunuch.*

*That's my wee man. That's my man today.*

In the staffroom an excitable queue by the tea urn exchanged ritual complaints about returning to work – but in a tone which suggested secret pleasure and even relief. No wonder Janet was not among them.

She would be in her sanctuary, the English Department store-room. Survival at work is largely a matter of finding a bolt hole. Science laboratories might appear to be a refuge-rich environment, a rabbit warren of secret passageways and priest's holes, but all the lairs are occupied by a hostile and alien species, technicians. Janet was standing on the bottom shelf, holding on to an upright with one hand while rooting on an upper shelf with the other.

'One good thing about having poor discipline – they'll never ask *me* to be form tutor.' Though she did not shriek with laughter, her tone was not without a touch of malicious satisfaction.

'*Jesus!*' I wailed, the terrible implications surging in afresh.

'Why didn't you tell her you're not qualified to counsel young girls?'

'I *did* tell her.'

Suddenly Janet went up the shelves with an agility startling in a woman her age and an indifference to modesty startling in anyone of her sex. Of course it was not as if she were wearing suspenders and open-crotch pants. Beneath her dress were heavy dark winter stockings.

'But it was bad strategy to quibble about qualifications. You should have said no straight away. *Catch!*'

Instead of commiserating she began to throw down copies of *To Kill a Mocking Bird* – dog-eared soiled defaced paperbacks patched up with Sellotape. There is something deeply melancholy about battered school copies of novels.

'How many times have you taught this book, Janet?'

'This'll be the ninth.' She descended in swift blithe jumps, apparently still unbroken by the terrible wheel of repetition.

'How could I refuse after accepting the Scale Three? She wiped the floor with me. It was beautiful. A textbook example of effective authority.'

'Authority,' Janet mused, taking the novels but looking away in sudden wonder. 'What is its secret?'

'Absence of complexity, scruple or doubt. A minimum number of beliefs held with maximum conviction.'

'No.' Janet corrected me with the gentleness of a parent. 'You're implying that Sister Stanislaus is a stupid and limited woman. In fact she's extremely clever and perceptive. I remember a few years ago ... when student protest was all the rage ... the pupils here decided to go on strike and a deputation went to Stan. Of course they expected her to make concessions and plead or else to rant and rave and threaten. Instead she just said *Off you go ... off you go then ... we'll all have a bit of peace and quiet for a change ... we've all plenty to do ... off you go now ... what's keeping you? ... off you go.*'

'And did they go?'

'Oh yes. They all went. It was very exciting.'

'But ... ?'

'They came back an hour later very sheepish and subdued.'

'Now of course,' Father Reagan begins urbanely, tilting his chair on its back legs and seizing the cord of the window blind, 'Christ was not crucified on a cross,' this apparently shocking disclosure carelessly addressed to the ceiling, uninhibited in his dispensing of dangerous knowledge because his audience is not only an intellectual elite of grammar schoolboys (the officer cadets in the army of Christ) but the elite of the elite, the top science and maths group (the officer cadets of the paratroop regiment). 'We know the Romans never used crosses as such. It was really a T-shape.'

Bringing down his chair and releasing the blind cord, he addresses them directly and solemnly – for along with the privileges of leadership go the gravest responsibilities and duties. 'But I don't want you men to be going round correcting people.' He pauses to scan the class for evidence of the sin of intellectual pride. No such evidence is found – but the very possibility makes his voice quaver a little. 'Never look down on the simple faith of ordinary people.'

As though expecting to be contradicted, he sweeps the room with a challenging gaze. The class soberly attends to recording in the manner prescribed. ('I'm not going to dictate notes to you men. You've had too much spoon-feeding already in this place. When you men go up to university you won't be spoon-fed with notes.') Satisfied, Reagan once again tips back his chair. 'And of course the nails didn't go in through the palms. You scientists know that palms could never support a man's weight. No, the nails didn't go in through the palms. They went in *here*.' Returning his chair to all four legs, he indicates points on each of his wrists. '*Something bothering you, Ward?*'

The boy is frowning in ingenuous perplexity, as though wrestling with a problem whose solution, while not immediately apparent, must be so obvious that to ask will make him appear obtuse and dim. 'I was just wondering, Father . . .' He frowns tremendously, as if, even now, the answer will surely manifest itself. About the room a few alert spirits discreetly smirk, sensing that Martin has embarked on the admirable but hazardous game of secretly ridiculing authority while appearing to display subservience and respect ('In order to escape the stake Rosicrucians used to conceal abominable formulas in ostensible prayers' – Villiers). 'I was wondering . . . you know' – he sketches a vague gesture, apologising in advance for the redundancy of the question – 'if Our Lord was crucified through the wrists . . . *why does Padre Pio always get the stigmata on his palms?*' Now he raises a brow innocently furrowed, as lovably expectant and guileless as that of a family golden retriever ('None of the sophistries of incarcerated insanity have been forgotten by me' – Rimbaud).

Rising without perturbation or haste, Reagan places his hands in the pockets of his soutane and embarks on a leisurely progress through the desks. A small slight man, his head is scarcely above those of the seated youths. Nor does he indulge in the cuffing, punching and strapping common with his colleagues. Yet every boy he passes instinctively stiffens and cringes. Finding himself face to face with dark jowls, pallid waxy flesh and sharp ascetic grey eyes, Martin is suddenly overcome by nostalgia for the homely, almost endearing, violence of the ranting brute priests. These madmen pummel the body but leave the mind unscathed. With archfiend Reagan it is the other way round. Confession, recantation and crushing of the spirit are his goals. The man is a natural inquisitor, a Torquemada of the North. ('I have seen cruel eyes where Faith burned only when reflecting the light of an executioner's torch.

To such eyes the sky is not dark enough. It is fitting that smoke from stakes blackens the clouds' – Villiers.)

'You think you're a very cool customer, Ward.' Reagan sighs in voluptuous ecstasy. 'A very cool customer . . . yessssssss . . .' Aware of having possibly misjudged his man, Ward does not respond or even move, staring impassively straight ahead. 'What mark did you get in Geometry?'

But at this reference to his genius Martin cannot suppress a flash of pride. 'Ninety-six.'

'Algebra?'

'Ninety-three.'

'History?'

'Seventy-six.'

Reagan pauses briefly. 'Religious Knowledge?'

Now Martin fails to suppress a smirk at an exquisite piece of inso-lence, a carefully calculated meeting of the minimum requirement. 'Forty-two,' he announces smugly, with a quick look round. A few subversive sniggers would help.

The class remains profoundly silent. Lucifer had his rebel angels. Martin is alone.

'Yessssss . . .' Reagan sighs with the almost unconscious rapture of a man exercising a natural talent. 'You think you'll just take what you want from this school and reject the rest. A cool customer . . . *yes*. But we'll see how cool . . . *we'll see* . . .' Now he appears to be talking to himself. And finally he abandons speech altogether.

A silence falls upon the room – the silence of space before a rumi-nant Creator.

At last Reagan permits his gaze to fall upon Ward. '*Get out of my sight.*'

'Aaagh . . . ?'

'*Get . . . out . . . of . . . my . . . sight.*'

So throwing him out of the class is the best that this arch-fiend can do. Feeling the rusty blade of Catholic chastisement shatter on his armour-plated breast, Martin gathers up his books with pro-vocative slowness, glancing about him with a smirk of triumph.

Finally the priest loses his composure. '*Get out,*' he violently hisses. 'Get out . . . *you pup.*'

Martin makes a great show of exiting with a swagger. But once outside the classroom his trembling legs almost buckle beneath him.

Vertigo creates an inner abyss on whose verge his soul trembles. Against his flushed face the cold breeze is as shocking as the waters of the Atlantic.

Nevertheless he has finally rebelled. He has become himself. ('Priests, teachers, masters, you err in delivering me up to justice. I have never been one of your people. I have never been a Christian. I belong to the race who exultantly sing under torture. I do not understand laws. I have no moral sense. I am a wild beast. You err.' – Rimbaud.)

Lower-school pupils with free periods are occasionally permitted to sit at the back of the Junior Study, a cavernous draughty hall where boarders work in the evening and, during the day, Hammy Hamilton teaches English, the public setting understood to be an attempt to enforce punctuality. However, Hammy is later than ever so that Martin can slip into a desk at the rear without having to explain himself. Now he discovers another exciting consequence of revolt: until the law-enforcement officers arrive he may carry on with his homework and possibly ensure a free evening.

Hammy enters and slams a pile of exercise books on his desk. 'We went swimming a lot. We went for a lot of walks. We played a lot of hurley on the beach. A lot. A lot. *A lot*. Does anyone know what a *lot* is?'

No answer.

'A *lot* is something offered for sale at an auction.'

How long will it take Reagan's messenger to alert the head of discipline (The Dean) or possibly even the head of the school (The President)?

Hammy distributes the exercise books by violently skimming each at its owner.

'Open your Shakespeares at Act II.' He assumes his seat with a great sigh. 'Mumble at me, Murphy.'

The period drags on and no avenger appears. Weary of vainly bracing himself, Martin begins to think of chastisement as a kind of deliverance.

Suddenly Hammy rushes down between the rows of scarred desks. Obviously he has just become aware of the brilliant transgressor at the back of the hall. Martin turns to meet his destiny but Hammy flies past with remarkable fleetness and from the hunched form of Skeets McDevitt seizes and bears aloft an incredible trophy

– an American body-building magazine. At once the expectant hall bursts into laughter.

'Stand up, sonny.'

As Skeets slowly rises Hammy's punitive zeal modulates into scorn. 'Well I suppose you'll need a strong back, McDevitt.' He turns slightly to alert the audience. 'For a life-long career of propping up gable walls.' There is a light sprinkling of chuckles. 'And pushing hefty factory girls around the floor of the Corinthian.' As laughter bursts out on all sides Skeets stares straight ahead with the terrible impassivity of a death mask ('To think that there are people who claim their schooldays were the happiest days of their lives' – Huysmans).

Hammy sighs in profound weariness at this failure in communication. 'You've the *epidermis of a pachyderm*, sonny. Don't suppose you know what that means, hah? *Hah?* Have you a tongue in your head at all? Do you know what that means?'

'No, Sir.'

'It means you have *the hide of an elephant*, McDevitt.'

The period ends without a summons for Martin. And so it is with the rest of the day's classes – an interminable agony of unrelieved suspense. On the way home he is granted a rare moment of admiration from Shotter ('Heard ye got fly wi' Reagan. Fuck me, I wouldn't take *him* on ... fuckin' *Robespierre*, that guy') but he knows that the longer the affair drags on the worse the outcome is likely to be. It appears that he has once again underestimated his man. Instead of invoking the crude disciplinary machine of the school, the arch-fiend intends to go straight to the home.

News has not yet arrived, for Mrs Ward is vacuuming the hall and in the living room Hugh Ward is asleep in an armchair, his open mouth occasionally twitching and emitting a harsh death rattle. Most of his homework already finished, Martin can treat himself to a dramatic episode of *Whirlybirds*. In a remote mountain cabin an injured boy lies panting for breath, watched over by a desperately concerned but extremely attractive mother, while, despite a raging storm and a leaking fuel tank, Chuck and P.T. ferry an iron lung in the chopper. Weather and engine noise make it difficult to hear the two men, a problem compounded by Mrs Ward entering the room to drive the vacuum cleaner across the carpet with savage purpose. Martin leans forward, wincing in irritation.

'Oh it's good to be some people,' Mrs Ward cries, giving her husband a look of extreme disgust. 'It's all right for some that can come home from their work and sleep.' With a violent thrust she drives her machine at the television. 'It's all right for them that never does a hand's turn.' Now she drives directly at Martin's legs so that he has to whip them up onto his seat with a cry of outrage ('Spurred on by revolt, we shall march with great strides against the day of our birth and the clitoris of the impure mother' – Lautréamont).

'I'm tryin' to watch this.'

'Oh it's well for the pair of yese. It's well for some.'

Martin strides angrily across the room to turn up the volume. Chuck and P.T. have delivered the lung. Safely enclosed in its iron carapace, the boy at last breathes easily and his mother turns to the heroic airmen a countenance dewy with gratitude and a pair of breasts delightfully trim. 'How can I ever thank you boys enough?'

'Why aren't you doing your homework?'

'Did it in school,' Martin snaps, experiencing the bitter emptiness and disillusion of freedom.

Suddenly the face of the injured boy contorts with fresh pain and anguish. The iron lung has ceased to function. The storm must have brought down a power line. Beseechingly the distraught mother turns to the heroes.

A terrifying possibility occurs to Martin – Reagan may take no action whatever and condemn him to a Purgatory where, instead of being expiated, his sin will suppurate and fester.

Mrs Ward stoops to lift something from the carpet. 'Everything dropped at your feet. Dropped at your feet and left for me. Not *one* of yese would pick anything up. Not *one* of yese, look see. Not *one* of yese.'

Freedom: not the fertile land of fulfilment but a desert, a void, a frightening abyss ('Freedom – the freedom to do as one likes – is a queer thing' – Huysmans).

The tempest rages with increasing fury as a repair man dangles from the chopper, desperately working against time. Ferocious winds buffet the frail craft and the fuel gauge ominously points to zero. Chuck shouts to P.T. to give up but, thinking only of that sick kid, the rock-faced ex-war-hero holds her steady over the line.

Martin knows what will happen. At the start of the next

Religious Knowledge period he will be standing outside the classroom waiting to mumble an apology to Reagan.

A machine shrieks in agony – not the death throes of the whirly-bird but Mrs Ward's vacuum cleaner ingesting something metallic. Hugh Ward gurgles loudly and seems on the verge of action or speech. Mother and son turn expectantly but he subsides into a fresh sleeping position.

Turning off the stricken appliance, Mrs Ward steps back to raise her head and deliver to the indifferent heavens a cry of Medean intensity. '*If some one of yese would even do one wee thing itself.*'

'Ah'll love ye and leave ye, Ward,' Clare would sing out as she left for her evening class, lighter in heart as well as in body (diet and exercise beginning to show results). In a typically Irish inversion she frequently used my surname as the familiar, and my forename as the formal, mode of address. Similarly, abuse was a form of endearment while politeness signified dislike. On her return to find me once again reading on the sofa: 'There you are, Ward, on your lazy fat arse.'

Much to her astonishment, Clare had discovered that the do-gooding English community centre actually promoted the acrid pleasures of rancour and rebelliousness so dear to the Gael. Although Mothers & Co had its share of baby-obsessed bores, there was also a nucleus of fiery spirits who exposed their circumstances and relationships, past and present, to a scrutiny of uninhibited candour and unbridled ferocity. (If only my mother could have lanced her boils in such a congenial forum.)

These Mothers & Co sessions usually continued in a bar, from which Clare returned at closing time, radiant and merry. 'God she's the best laugh, that Nina one. She's a case. Divorced, you know, and looking round for a new guy. She has everyone in stitches about these guys she goes out with. Anyway, she thought she'd found her Mr Right ... Ken his name is ... until he asked her ... right in the middle of things ... *can I come in your face?* Of course you'd have to see Nina telling it.'

'But what did she say?'

'You'd have to see her telling it. Really po-faced, you know, never laughs herself. *I'd really rather you didn't, Ken, if it's all the same.*'

But one evening she returned preoccupied and subdued. 'Martin, listen ... there's a crowd from the centre going to this rock pub tomorrow night. It's a benefit gig ... three really good bands that'll probably never play together again.'

'What crowd?'

'Oh ... a few from Mothers & Co.'

'Just women?'

'Nick ... the Assistant Organiser ... Nick's coming as well. In fact it was his idea. He's really into this new music ... used to play in a band himself.'

'Obviously you're keen to go.'

'We could both go if Bernard would babysit.'

Bernard had already performed this invaluable service and, sharing the traditional parent's compulsion to fetch and feed, had brought with him a Sainsbury's carrier bag bulging with art treasures – Piero Della Francesca in a *Library of the Great Masters* edition, *The Structure of Scientific Revolutions* by T.S. Kuhn, *À Vau l'Eau* in the Baldick translation (a rarity borrowed from Limehouse Library whose basement housed the French Reserve for all London libraries, a treasure house made available to the public largely on Bernard's insistence), an introductory tape of classical music made from his own records and, from two further libraries, LPs of César Franck's Violin Sonata and Fauré's Piano Quartets.

'You see, Fauré and Franck were both great favourites of Proust. In fact Proust used to summon *Fauré himself* to come and play for him. Can you imagine it? Like summoning Duke Ellington to your living room. The presumption and impertinence of the rich. And Fauré an old man at this time. Proust should have been down on his knees *kissing Fauré's boots*. The second Piano Quartet is the one. Ah ... and poor Franck. Virtually unknown till after his death. To think of him grovelling to his boor of a publisher: *I know it won't sell, I know I'm forcing you to make sacrifices, don't pay me too much.*'

After Christmas Clare had enrolled for classes in the Community Centre and on her evenings out I listened to Bernard's records and tapes. So far progress was limited but I had no desire to abandon the project in favour of pub rock.

'I think I'll pass,' I said to Clare now, 'go on your own,' injecting the merest hint of martyrdom at gross inconsistency and injustice. The issue was Clare's long history of resentment at my occasional evenings out with colleagues – but it would never do to mention this directly. Marital power play is an infinitely delicate and subtle game and the coveted moral high ground, won with such effort and pain, can so easily be forfeited by a single ill-judged remark.

'Martin, I know I haven't ... I know I've been ...' The most effective response was immensely dignified silence. 'I know I've been miserable about you going out, Martin. But things were bad for me then. And I was desperate to get back to Ireland. It'll be better for both of us in future.'

When a sinner makes an act of contrition and expresses a firm purpose of amendment, forgiveness and absolution may not be withheld. Certainly there was no doubting the sincerity of this penitent.

'The Keep Fit class will change things,' she added.

'How so?'

'If I can get completely back in shape we might have a sex life again.'

'You don't need to be fit to have sex.'

'But I have to feel attractive, Martin.'

'You *are* attractive.'

'But I need to feel it.'

'Go to your rock pub,' I said with a show of pure generosity heavily adulterated by self-interest.

Like so many bound in wedlock, she left the house with apology on her face and a song in her heart. As soon as she was gone Paul fetched the Lego and dumped it on the floor with the air of a man at last getting down to serious business.

'What are we making tonight, Paul?'

'A shopping centre.'

Reading was of course impossible but self-improvement could still be combined with play. I had just taken delivery from Bernard of his latest home-produced classical music tape.

'We made a shopping centre last time.'

'Make it again.'

Repetition, which crushes the adult, is the bastion and joy of the child.

'Now you see' – Bernard had not only recorded the music but introduced each piece himself – 'everything we've had so far, the Ravel and Debussy and so on, has been charming and seductive, music that *wants to be liked*. But I can hear Martin saying: *what is the best, what is the best?* We are now in a position to answer. Béla Bartók is the best. Unquestionably the greatest composer of this century and on a par with the greats of any other. A man of *total integrity* – but little charm. *Little charm.* With no desire to please and no need to be loved. One of these mordant iron men I prefer above all . . . men like Coleman Hawkins, Flaubert, Cézanne. And what we're going to hear is one of his greatest works, a supreme masterpiece, the second violin concerto.'

'Have we another wall piece this size, Dad?'

Slowly a shopping centre rose to the strains of the Bartók concerto punctuated by train sounds and smoker's cough – for Bernard, as primitive in his technology as sophisticated in his taste, recorded to tape by placing a mike in front of his gramophone speaker. Alas, to no avail on this occasion. To me the masterpiece sounded like forty minutes of tuning up. Obviously I was not a mordant iron man but a confection of fluff.

At midnight Clare brought in with her, like a magical force field of independence and freedom, a tonic penumbra of cold air that defied the warm fug of the flat.

'Feel!' she commanded, seizing my tepid hand and pressing it against her fiercely tingling cheek, the contrast even more extreme than she had anticipated. '*God but you're warm!*'

Though better the exalted cold of freedom than security's dull heat: now I was the cosy home bird, she the passionate adventuress.

'A good night?' I felt like some spent husk of a parent addressing a spirited teenager. Instead of replying, she straightened suddenly and swept off to the bedroom to lavish on her sleeping children a gaze of renewed devotion and love.

'No problems?' she asked, coming back.

'Only when Paul caught me trying to abbreviate his bedtime story. He knows every word of it. He was extremely cross.'

Reassured, she was free to acknowledge her own enjoyment. 'It was brilliant, Martin. *Brilliant.* I'm not sure about this new music but the atmosphere was *incredible.* This tiny room packed with people . . . you have to stand of course . . . and the band insulting the audience and everyone insulting them back.' She laughed, amazed and delighted by this reflection of her own need to display positive emotions by negative means. 'I want to go back there next week.'

Her candour and innocence and enthusiasm disarmed me. One

cold fish per household is more than enough. But my magnanimity was about to be tested to the limit. 'There's one problem though – I can't go in this thing.' Frowning in sudden distaste, she shrugged off her heavy winter coat with the imitation fur collar. 'Everyone said I looked like I was going to a Jewish wedding. I'm thinking of getting one of those black leather things.'

'*A biker jacket?*'

'Sure now you have the Scale Three, we can get a few odds and ends.'

Like most who have known real deprivation, Clare abhorred the hair shirt. (Ascetism is another luxury of the well-to-do.) As with others who embrace responsibility and adulthood too soon, she was determined to enjoy a belated good time now. For adolescence is never an optional phase; those who deny it in their teens are condemned to endure it later on.

'That money won't come through for months yet.'

'You can get them really cheap in Camden Town, Nick says.'

*Nick!* The title 'Assistant Organiser' had suggested a worthy but sexless combination of philanthropist and bureaucrat.

'This Nick character . . . what does he look like?'

Again I felt middle-aged, predictable, redundant. And what was ageing me prematurely appeared to be rejuvenating Clare. Is marriage a kind of seesaw? When one goes up must the other go down? But it was hard to be resentful with Clare in gypsy-girl mode. I have always loved her like this, exalted and radiant and mischievous.

'See for yourself,' she laughed. 'He's always saying you should come along.'

'I'd need a biker jacket too.'

She regarded me in sceptical amusement: Scale-Three convent-school teacher Martin Ward relaxing in the through lounge. 'It would take more than a new jacket.'

There was no real contempt in her laugh. Along with exaltation and radiance there was genuine compassion. But she should have been aware of the dangerous consequences of sympathy. The object immediately develops pretentions, in my own case a militant hard-on.

It seemed reasonable to expect the gypsy passion to persist into the bedroom. And indeed she came into my arms willingly – but

61

immediately succumbed to deep sleep.

The following Saturday she bought a studded jacket and, in preparation for the next gig, borrowed most of Nick's New Wave record collection, discovering that this was not just a type of music but a thriving subculture with its own style, magazines, venues, outlets and record labels. Just to read the names of the labels was sufficient: Vile, Razor, Rabid, Slash, Vengeance, Born Bad. Our musical educations could scarcely have been more divergent. While I was frowning in perplexity at Bartók, Clare was pogoing to Throbbing Gristle.

Yet we also had something in common. Ironically, New Wave was the provocation of Lautréamont finally reaching popular culture after a century as a minority taste. Even more ironically, Clare was developing an interest in the debased version just as I was beginning to question the original.

One of my tasks on the solitary evenings was defining the ethos of the Magnificent Seven.

All of them rejected the idea of progress ('It is the individual relying on his neighbour to do his work. There can be no progress [true progress, in other words, moral] except within the individual and by the individual himself' – Baudelaire), hated democracy in particular ('Universal suffrage is as stupid as divine right' – Flaubert) and politics in general ('that ignoble distraction of mediocre intellects' – Huysmans). The exception was Villiers who actually stood for election in the Ternes district of Paris – but as a Royalist candidate and on a programme which included revival of debtor's prison as a sanctuary for writers and the demolition, on aesthetic grounds, of the Panthéon, the Opéra and Saint-Sulpice.

The seven were all misogynists, though of varying degree. If relationships with women could not be avoided the advice was to stick to social and intellectual inferiors ('To love intelligent women is a pleasure of the pederast' – Baudelaire). Flaubert went even further: 'I love prostitution, the meeting point of so many things – lechery, frustration, denial of human relationship, physical frenzy, the clink of gold – that to look into its depths causes vertigo and teaches all kinds of truths. Yes, a man has missed something if he has never awakened in an anonymous bed beside a face he will never see again, never left a brothel at sunrise feeling like throwing himself into the river out of pure disgust for life.'

In fact metaphysical disgust was a permanent condition for the seven. They were disgusted not only by contemporary society but life itself which Huysmans in particular never tired of denouncing: 'this filthy hole of a carnal hostelry in which someone has decided to coop us up'. Ill fortune may have exacerbated their disgust but in no case can it be identified as the cause. 'While still very young I had a complete presentiment of life. It was like the nauseating smell that pours from the ventilator of a kitchen: you don't have to eat their food to know it will make you throw up' – Flaubert.

Contempt for action was another common theme. 'A dandy does nothing' – Baudelaire. 'Action is not life but an enervating means of corrupting our strength' – Rimbaud. 'Activity is becoming more and more distasteful to me' – Flaubert. The consequence was a peculiarly malignant form of boredom most vividly described by Baudelaire: 'Among the monsters which shriek and bellow and grunt in our squalid menagerie of vice, there is one, uglier, viler and more extreme than the rest, which, though it refrains from theatrical gestures and cries, would gladly reduce the earth to dust and swallow the world in its perpetual yawn – I refer to boredom of course.'

All seven were chronic sufferers ('Truly boredom is the God of my life' – d'Aurevilly; 'Do you understand boredom? Not the common banal version resulting from illness or sloth but that modern boredom that eats at the very entrails of a man' – Flaubert), with Rimbaud as always claiming to be the most extreme case: 'One could never imagine another life with more boredom than this. I've never known anyone as bored as I.'

Suicide was frequently mentioned and in Villiers's *chef-d'œuvre*, *Axel*, the quest for the meaning of life ends with the discovery of suicide as the ultimate good: 'The earth is swollen like a brilliant bubble with misery and deceit and, being the daughter of primeval chaos, bursts at the least breath of those who come near. Let us get away from her! Completely! Violently! With a sacred bound!' However, none of the seven made the sacred bound and Villiers himself was in the end so reluctant to attain the infinite, or even entertain the possibility, that his friends were unable to tell him that his cancer was terminal and Huysmans had to get a priest to break the news. It is true that Baudelaire did make an attempt on his own life – but the circumstances must surely call into question his resolve. Has anyone else ever tried to commit suicide *in a café?*

Instead of acting they fantasised about escape to the orient and/or the barbaric past. Baudelaire did set out for the East but gave up and came home (an awkward fact he later concealed). Flaubert travelled in Egypt – but only as a tourist, though he claims to have considered permanent residence: 'I have thought long and *very seriously* about becoming a Muslim in Smyrna.' Only Rimbaud the extremist actually tried to live the dream, with extensive stays in Java, Cyprus, Aden, Abyssynia and, perhaps most exotic of all, six months in Reading. In each of these, as in Germany, Holland, Sweden and Italy, his response was the same: 'I've not found what I expected to find, I'll not stay here long.'

Infatuated by antiquity, Flaubert produced, in *Salammbô*, fiction's greatest epic hymn to barbarism. Equally in love with the Middle Ages, Huysmans, in *Là-Bas*, gave a detailed account of Gilles de Rais and his torture of child victims. Scorning the cover of history, Lautréamont, d'Aurevilly and Villiers (who was obsessed by judicial decapitation and never missed a public guillotining) offered atrocious violence and savagery in a contemporary setting.

Again only Rimbaud moved from theory to practice.

'Put your hands on the table,' he said to Verlaine in the crowded Café du Rat Mort. 'I want to try an experiment.'

Verlaine spread out his hands – and Rimbaud slashed them with a knife.

The Occult seemed to offer a less arduous escape route. All were intrigued by Catholic mystics and the Illuminist Magi. Baudelaire, Rimbaud, Huysmans and Villiers studied the Cabbala and the works of the alchemists. Huysmans was personally involved with sorcerers (and believed they were attacking him by occult means) but Rimbaud alone tried to rend the veil: 'Wild and infinite leap to invisible splendour, immaterial delights'. Just as typically he immediately dismissed the attempt as a failure: 'I who called myself angel or magus, exempt from all morality, am thrown back on the earth with a duty to seek an uncouth reality to hold in my arms again. Peasant!'

But worship of singularity was the true religion of the seven. 'You resemble no one, the highest of all virtues,' Flaubert wrote to Baudelaire, who scarcely needed reminding ('Glory is to remain one'). Salvation was attainable only by means of personal uniqueness. All were exquisite literary stylists and at one time or another most of them also cultivated a striking personal appearance. Even Flaubert, the hermit of Croisset, was in financial difficulty over tailor's bills in the swinging sixties (nearly two thousand francs of debt, plus another five hundred for gloves).

They desperately needed to distinguish themselves from the common herd and, in the case of Lautréamont and Rimbaud, from the human race itself. For these two fanatics of distinction it was never enough to be merely sublime. Nothing short of divinity would suffice. 'The majority think an immense pride tortures him, as it once did Satan, and that he would like to be the equal of God' – Lautréamont.

Physical separation was also essential. 'I have long since come to realise that in order to live in peace one must live alone and seal one's windows lest the air of the world seep in' – Flaubert. Even Rimbaud the traveller longed for seclusion and retreat: 'What possible cloister for my beautiful disgust?' But in this respect Huysmans was the most radical ('I am convinced that the cloister is the most beautiful thing on earth') and his journey round the monasteries of France was as ludicrous and painful as that of Rimbaud round the countries of the world. It also ended in the same way: 'The cloister is all very well in imagination but in reality it is frightful.'

Next to the great mahogany table strewn with books a paraffin heater breathes and flutters, emitting heavy fumes which permeate the unventilated room. Slamming shut the lab book in which he has just entered another banal account of a tedious experiment, Martin Ward sighs with pleasure and opens *Intermediate School Geometry*. At last he is free to exchange drudgery for the joys of election. If mathematics is the language of God (and who would deny this self-evident truth?), then those who can speak it are His only legitimate representatives on earth. Ward closes his eyes for a solemn moment of gratitude and worship. Now the paraffin fumes are his incense and the flame in its window his votive lamp ('To what benevolent demon is my soul in debt for being thus surrounded by silence, mystery, fragrance and peace? – Baudelaire).

As for any sacrament or rite, devout and scrupulous preparation is necessary. Taking a ruler and a compass from his pigskin briefcase, he draws in his exercise book a neat pencil diagram of a problem in which several triangles overlap a circle. Dipping the nib of his Conway Stewart in the Stephens Blue-Black, he slowly raises the gold lever that expels air from the tube. When the pen is full he removes excess ink by drawing the nib across the top of the bottle. Finally a scribble on rough paper ensures that the ink is flowing smoothly and is not likely to blot. Then he carefully labels the diagram and underneath lists the additional given data and what has to be proved.

Now the private moment of doubt and reluctance known to even the most illustrious and committed adept. From the street come the cries of confident energetic rowdies. By his side the heater suddenly flutters as though assailed by a gust from the void. Yet once again grace is forthcoming and the solemn mystery is accomplished. As soon as his Conway Stewart touches the paper elegant syllogisms flow from its golden nib as freely as Stephens Blue-Black. Far from distracting and vexing, the raucous street cries only intensify the secret rapture of lucidity and order ('Arithmetic! Algebra! Geometry! Magnificent Trinity! Luminous triangle! While Earth reveals only illusions and moral miasmas, you, by means of your tenacious propositions and the rigorous constancy of your iron laws, you, O precise mathematics, dazzle the eyes with that supreme truth whose imprint is discernible in the order of the universe' – Lautréamont.)

The next problem has overlapping circles and irregular polygons. Ward prepares the complex diagram, exulting in its very abstruseness and difficulty.

Entering the room with the diffidence of a newly appointed housemaid, Mrs Ward advances cautiously with, in one hand, a Royal Albert teacup and saucer and, in the other, a matching plate with a buttered wheaten scone and two Jaffa cakes.

'Just a wee cup o' tea,' she whispers in a tone of profound apology for many things – the intrusion, the inadequacy of the offering, the frightful labours necessary for personal advancement – carefully setting down saucer and plate on a free corner of the table. Ward reluctantly raises his head and presents to his mother a fearsome rictus of concentration. Glancing down at the page, she sighs in awe, as though the hieroglyphs constitute a proof of the Shimura–Taniyama conjecture.

As soon as she leaves, Ward relaxes his grimace and applies

himself greedily to the snack. Then he ponders the diagram once more. But again he is interrupted, this time by the crash of a ball on a wooden surface and the passionate injunction, 'Up fir the nod, Dessie! *Up fir the nod!*' Scowling afresh, he approaches the window, going close enough to observe without being spotted himself.

Opposite the Ward home is a garage that provides the only break in the terrace and has a recessed door the right size to serve as a net for that curious form of street football in which both teams play into the same goal. Such a game is now in progress between two sides captained respectively by Tony Shotter and Dessie McAnanney.

'Git intay 'im!' Shotter screams as an indecisive team member retreats before the confident and intimidating advance of McAnanney. '*Git intay 'im fir fuck's sake!*'

Dessie brushes aside the challenge and makes the garage door shudder with a powerful drive. '*Wan noan!*'

Ward returns to the table to find his inspiration gone. He has forgotten the data and must re-read the question. The next interruption is dramatic and sudden: the delightful crash of breaking glass. Hugh Ward is quickly on the street – but already the players have vanished and all he can apprehend is the ball.

Ward composes inscrutable features for a visit from his father.

'Did you see any of those characters?' Hugh Ward can scarcely believe that a man who has devoted his life to eradicating blaggardism should not only have an outbreak on his doorstep but *may even harbour a secret sympathiser in his home.* 'Do you know any of those blaggards?'

Ward coolly returns his gaze ('His pride repeats to him this axiom: let each keep to himself' – Lautréamont).

'Never saw anything,' he says, employing his gift for investing civil discourse with the pungency of insolence. 'Doin' me geometry homework.'

Fifteen minutes later the front doorbell is rung. From his vantage point Ward is astounded to see Tony Shotter accompanied by his mother. At once he creeps downstairs and, flinging himself flat on the landing, observes through the banisters this bizarre exchange. The woman explains that her son broke the window but that the damage was accidental. Hugh Ward listens, head sceptically cocked, making no attempt to conceal his disapproval and displeasure.

'Of course I'll pay to have the glass replaced.'

'Not-at-all!' Hugh snorts incredulously at the notion of the Wards accepting money from the Shotters. '*At-at-all. At-at-all.*'

'I'd like you to send me the bill even so.'

Hugh makes an angry dismissive gesture. The Shotter woman's insistence on paying appears to be adding insult to injury.

'Now Tony wants to apologise himself.'

Shotter comes forward – calmly, with no sign of deference – and offers what is not an apology but an explanation, accompanied by much head and hand movement, of how the ball came to ricochet into Ward's window. Never has Shotter seemed so noble and Hugh Ward so base.

'Surely. *Surely.*' Entirely lacking the aplomb of the youth, Hugh Ward can barely contain himself. 'But if ye wanted to kick football why didn't ye go to the park? There's a grand park at the end of the street. Or do it *in front of your house, hah?*' He advances menacingly on Shotter. 'Smash your own windows, *hah?*'

Immediately the mother intervenes. 'I'm taking him home now to chastise him severely.'

'*Hah?* Oh surely. *Surely.*'

'You can send me the bill.'

'*I'll send you no such thing.*'

Hugh slams the door and Martin withdraws with a hiss of loathing for his father ('Scholar though I am, the blood of my ancestors, Natchez or Huron, boils in my veins' – Flaubert). Now it will be more difficult than ever to win acceptance from Shotter.

The unquiet heart may often be soothed by the purity and rigour of Euclid ('O holy mathematics, would that you might, by your perpetual commerce, console my remaining days for the evil of man and the injustice of the Most High' – Lautréamont). However, the footballers have slunk back onto the street and congregated nearby, far enough away to be outside Hugh Ward's jurisdiction but close enough to communicate their derision to his son.

'Me ma said she was gonnay chastise me,' Shotter explains loudly, pitching his voice to the upper windows. 'But when we got in home she never said nahin.' He pauses to let this sink in, then repeats with satisfaction. 'Never said a word tay me. Never said nahin.'

'Ye're lucky yer ma was wi' ye,' Dessie McAnanney says. 'He

mighta lost the rag and reached fir ye. I seen him in school – he lifted this boy off the ground *by ees hair.*'

'Fuck,' Shotter snorts. 'See if he tried tay grab me like that . . . see if he fuckin' *touched me* even . . .'

The ignominy of being trapped with a shrew and a bully in a house besieged by venomous brutes ('I have always tried to live in an ivory tower but its walls are being assaulted by a tidal wave of shit' – Flaubert).

'And he's fir fuck all as a teacher.'

'Thick as champ,' Shotter agrees.

'Thick as *pig shit*,' Dessie amends.

And now the the group proceeds to mimic the habit of the father which most revolts and mortifies his son. In what is possibly a peasant practice from the days before washing machines and disposable tissues, Hugh Ward does not use a handkerchief but, going to the edge of the pavement and seizing his nose between forefinger and thumb, violently and noisily attempts to expel its contents into the gutter, an operation which is often only partly successful and requires him to brush away lingering fronds with his free hand.

Each of those below takes it in turn to enact this procedure, striding boldly to the edge of the pavement, pinching the nose in a grotesquely exaggerated fashion and producing loud trumpetting noises followed by comically frantic attempts to dislodge clinging residue.

Suddenly calm and purposeful, Martin Ward goes to his bookshelves (the one place where his mother does not ferret and pry) and from its hiding place withdraws the terrible instrument of retribution and cleansing which he has fashioned with loving care from the finest of materials ('I love grace and elegance even in the instruments of death' – Lautréamont). A serious conduit of purification, this catapult's metal frame and heavy elastic are similar to those of Shotter's weapon but its ammunition holder is made of leather instead of cloth and the ammo box contains not stones (too misshapen for accurate ballistics) but (heavy, symmetrical and devastating, ideal for anti-personnel use) a box of the extra-large marbles known appropriately as 'shooters'. Today even these will not suffice. He selects a silver ball-bearing, magnum load for a one-shot stop.

Thus armed, he ascends to the attic workshop which is never used by the father but is the sanctuary and den of the son ('Locked in an attic from the age of twelve I illustrated the human comedy and understood the world' – Rimbaud). Here he throws himself on the floor and, working with infinite delicacy, gently raises the window a few inches. To instill a proper sense of terror it is necessary to separate an individual from the security of the herd. There are still five in the group.

Dusk, accomplice of the assassin as well as the lover, gradually falls on the street.

One by one they depart until only Shotter and McAnanney remain – but when these two go off together Ward is sure that fate has robbed him of his quarry. Displaying the infinite patience of the natural hunter, he remains at his post and is rewarded by the sight of Dessie McAnanney not only returning alone on the opposite side of the street but hurrying in the dusk with an air of·apprehension that belies the assurance of his public persona. Hands electric with latent power, Ward draws the terrible metal missile to its furthest limit but, with scarcely a tremor, awaits the perfect moment, allowing his quarry to go a little way past in order to line up not merely a head shot but a hit in the medulla oblongata (for the rigorous assassin's goal of a no-reflex kill).

Finally the moment of purification. As McAnanney reaches the end of the garage Ward fires the ball-bearing into the wooden door a few inches over his head, flinging himself flat on the floor and shrieking in hysterical exaltation at the thunderous impact and Dessie's scream.

Snow fell, causing inconvenience and discomfort but not, unfortunately, chaos. Public transport was operating. The accursed school boiler functioned. Attendance was scarcely below average.

In the staffroom Wills and Kemp strove to maintain morale. If anyone complained about the difficulty of getting out of bed in the freezing dark Terry would assume a grave frown, 'You mean the bed at home?' And when Moira Sweeney testily asked the priest if it was cold enough for him yet, Kemp responded with a vintage chuckle (vibrantly fruity, with a soft balanced finish): 'All the warmer for seeing you, Moira.' On one of the grimmest of dark snowbound mornings the staffroom was feeling so low that it actually complained about the breeziness of Terry Wills's entry: 'You shouldn't look so cheerful on a horrible Monday morning like this.'

Without a word Wills lifted his briefcase and left. Had he given up the struggle? Not a bit of it. Immediately he re-entered with a countenance of such fantastic dolefulness that even the determinedly peevish company was obliged to laugh out loud.

As well as impromptu wit Wills employed regular gags like answering the staffroom phone ('Our Lady of Perpetual Suckers, which sucker did you require?'), conversing in loud pidgin French with the young *assistantes* ('*Vous avez dormi bien? Avec* someone interesting, I hope'), and continually interfering with the staffroom noticeboard (any list requesting signatures was certain to include those of Father Kemp and Moira Sweeney so that the man of God would appear to be ordering a special-offer lady's track suit, while the sedentary Queen of the Staffroom seemed to be soliciting the sponsorship of colleagues in the Spina Bifida Fun Run). Perhaps his most famous stroke was leaving a note for a Year Head to phone a parent called C. Lyons at a number which was that of London Zoo.

Today it looked as though Wills had finally succumbed, entering the staffroom with a genuinely subdued and withdrawn air. Kemp was instantly and brilliantly perceptive.

'An evening of over-indulgence, Terry?'

'Bit of a night in the Spotted Dog.'

Releasing a light laugh of empathy (scarcely vintage but crisp and invigorating, with lots of zesty lemony fruit) the priest turned from his locker and said, apparently to Terry, but in a meaningful heralding tone that caught the attention of the room, 'Morning after the marriage feast at Cana.' Intrigued, Terry paused before his own locker. Kemp waited for silence. 'Late on the morning after the marriage feast. Joseph calls downstairs: *Mary, bring me a glass of water.*' He moved closer to Wills and, as though suddenly concerned that the story might be too blasphemous for a convent school, considerably lowered his voice. Immediately everyone leaned forward. 'But whatever you do, Mary, *don't let that fellow near it.*'

Before anyone could respond, Kemp closed his locker with a flourish and beat a brisk path towards the staffroom door. But at the corner, by the sink and tea urn, just as he was moving out of sight, he paused to look back at Terry and issue a laugh bursting with gamey flavours and rich chocolaty warmth.

Terry, convulsed, turned to me. 'He's all right, old Kemp' –

then, seeing that I too was preparing to leave – 'I want to see you about this Rani Patel business.'

Another consequence of the Scale Three was that Wills now tried to delegate even more of the tricky personnel-management tasks.

'Can't stop, Terry. Break supervision.'

'You're not on the tuck queue?'

For the secret worshipper of chaos there is nothing worse than supervision – and tuck was sold from a cupboard on the edge of the school's central crossroads and at the bottom of the stairs leading to the staffroom so that congestion and uproar were maximal and failure to control them embarrassingly public.

'The secret is to get there early, Terry.'

But he interposed his body. 'Come and quickly meet Seymour. He'll be working with Rani.'

As we crossed the room there rose to meet us a bald overweight middle-aged man with the ingenuous grin of a boarding-school swot.

'What's he doing here, Terry?'

'The usual. Discipline problems. Think he cracked up somewhere else.'

Seymour wore a dark outmoded suit and gleaming brogues and reeked of tobacco. Everything about him suggested unworldliness and bachelorhood, a spirit never touched much less tempered by the cleansing fires of relationship. To a banal question about how he had got here in such weather he described his travel plan and journey in a manner intended to demonstrate shrewdness and competence but having exactly the opposite effect. The man was obviously an *idiot savant*. Women would recoil in horror and even the meekest of convent school classes would shred him faster than a shoal of piranhas. It is only in fable and fantasy that the Holy Fool is cherished.

Already the tuck queue was a raging sea, the usual feeding frenzy exacerbated and intensified by the weather. It was dark and dismal outside, the snow at the front of the school churned to slush, windows opaque and streaming, the normally spotless floors streaked with mud. An overpowering atmosphere of confinement was driving the inmates insane. Even after a semblance of order was introduced, those at the back of the queue continued to shove, causing the front to buckle and bulge and eventually eject a pupil with the force of a champagne cork. In every case the cork protested violently that it was all the fault of the champagne. It was a disciplinarian's nightmare, universal hunger for anarchy combined with the impossibility of detection.

At least my subsequent free period was not removed by a 'Please Take' note, requesting cover for an absent colleague and the very paradigm of capricious Fate. Also free was my little table by the back window of the staffroom. Blithely I call it 'my' table. The laws governing proprietary claims on public staffroom facilities are complex and obscure. As dogs stake out a territory by pissing on walls and trees, so a colleague may attempt to claim an area by strewing it with personal rubbish – but the success of such a claim depends on the seniority, aggressiveness and social standing of the claimant. I got to the table only to find my things dumped on the floor and replaced by someone else's clutter. With a series of frightful oaths I reversed this state of affairs.

The vista was soothingly serene. The herd had not sullied this side of the school. On a row of suburban back gardens the snow was as immaculate as Mary's heart. Even in poor light it shone with a stringent purity and rigour.

And there was fiery French cognac to warm the heart – *Les Chants de Maldoror* concealed behind exercise books. 'Oh! If instead of being a hell this universe had been nothing but an immense celestial anus – note the gesture I make by my lower abdomen – yes, I would have driven my cock through its blood-stained sphincter, smashing the walls of its pelvis with my impetuous piledriving!'

Lautréamont was the Mozart of malediction – but can malediction sustain the long and difficult middle years? The author of Maldoror evaded this problem by dying at twenty-four, alone, unknown and of unknown causes, when Paris was under siege by the Prussians and its starving population was buying rats at a franc apiece and dog-flesh at one-franc-fifty a pound.

Food is the consolation of the middle years. Normally I ate sandwiches in the staffroom but, according to some contract whose source no one knew and whose terms no one studied (paternalism deters the examination of small print), staff performing supervision were entitled to one free lunch per week. My free period on Tuesday meant I could be first at the trough. Even as the pips went I was crossing the main hall, now set out with tables, and mounting the stage where food was dispensed by Mrs Morelli, a vast Mayo woman married to an Italian.

'Isn't the weather desperate altogether, Mr Ward?'

'Dreadful. Dreadful.'

'You'll need another chop so.' Her preferment was expressed in the traditional Irish way – with extra helpings of meat. 'And here's a sausage as well.'

Steaming hot food and a quiet corner – ancient bestial cave pleasures.

Someone sat down across from me: Rani Patel carrying a salad as though in reproach for my greed. 'Have you seen him?'

'Who?'

'*Seymour!*' she almost shouted, 'the character they've sent into my classes.'

Since Rani had good control but dubious qualifications and Seymour was highly qualified but incapable of controlling a class, officialdom intended to forge a single effective teacher by welding them together.

'He's going to be in *all my classes*. I've had two periods already and it's just . . . just . . .' Words were inadequate for the experience of the back end of a pantomime horse.

'He talks too much? Goes on and on?'

'I had a class of low-ability second years and he started about the Greek root of the word *electricity*. They were rolling their eyes at me, begging for something sensible. Then I had a fourth-year class and he kept interrupting and correcting me.'

'But why have they put him in with you?'

'Apparently some inspector has questioned my qualifications. Actually, with the way I was dragged round the world it's a miracle I have any qualifications at all.'

This was the first acknowledgement of the influence of background and personal history. Like the style models she expertly copied, Rani presented an image of self-sufficiency independent of roots.

'Where were you dragged?'

'Africa, India, Hong Kong . . . but what am I going to do?'

Did Frankenstein know the result of his experiment: a monster with the svelte body of an Asian girl and the bald head of a Jewish elitist?

'It's certainly a grotesque combination. Man–Woman. Age–Youth. Beauty–Beast. If you'd been Muslim the symmetry'd be perfect. Jew–Muslim as well.'

'I'm not Muslim. I'm Hindu.'

'I know that.'

She was not mollified. Always risky to mention religion or race.

'Are you aware,' I resumed, after a pause, 'that to eat on stage like this, with the pupils in the hall, technically constitutes supervision and should entitle us to *a free lunch every day?* That was the arrangement in my last school.'

'You know, he'll be in every single lesson,' she suddenly blurted. 'Day in, day out. Week in, week out. Every lesson . . . *for ever* . . . the kids always asking me what he's doing there, knowing it's some problem with me.' The prospect struck her dumb for a moment. 'I'll have to get another job.'

Certainly this humiliation was worse than anything I had to endure. It was terrible to see such a bold spirit crushed. Not only a fearless international foodie, Rani enlivened dreary staff functions by appearing in dramatic outfits from various cultures and times (on one occasion a white twenties Charleston dress whose overlapping layers of shimmying fronds were dazzling against her ochre skin, another time a flamenco dancer's dress whose tight black severity permitted itself a flounce only from mid-calf down). Yet, despite the eclecticism there remained something authentic and generous about Rani. She was that delightful contradiction: a committed post-modernist with a heart of gold. Unfortunately she was not soliciting sympathy so much as *active intervention.*

'Have you talked to Terry?'

'He says it wasn't his idea and there's nothing he can do. Referred me to you in fact. He doesn't want to know about it. Anyway, Terry *hates* me.'

Tears were close. Or perhaps I was only just noticing the results of an earlier breakdown.

'Terry's no counsellor – but hate's a bit strong.'

'No he's always hated me. He's always been irritable and rude.'

Clare once mentioned Terry behaving to her in this way. As so often there were glaring inadequacies behind the extrovert public face. But one of the problems of insecurity is an inability to recognise the same affliction in others. Clare also assumed that Terry detested her and cordially detested him in return.

'Terry has a problem with attractive girls who fail to respond to his act.'

'Whatever the reason, he's not prepared to do anything.'

Dessert was laid out on a separate self-service tray but, although I suffer from a lamentable fondness for English puddings, I was unable to rise and help myself to Bakewell tart. 'I'll see what I can do.'

'Thank you, Martin.' Her passionate gratitude washed over me in a sweet debilitating flood. Our eyes met and held. How rarely female beauty opens and offers itself! Particularly the narcissistic beauty of the age – the beauty concerned with nothing other than itself and price tags. This was surely a reward that far outweighed dessert.

As one we rose, descended from the stage and, like pastoral lovers in a sylvan glade, traversed the raucous dining hall and passed the seething queue outside. I was on the verge of speaking again when Rani suddenly turned and, with a look of indescribable fury, cried in a new deep husky voice: '*Hyacinth Onibanjo!*'

Just the name. Nor did Rani move. It was a perfect lesson in the techniques of authority. First, immense personal outrage; second, unwavering decisiveness in the choice of scapegoat; third, avoidance of confusing detail and spirit-sapping disputation; fourth, the confidence to summon the offender rather than setting off in pursuit.

Hyacinth, though a proud and refractory spirit, came to Rani at once with a hangdog air. 'Miss, it wasn't . . .'

'*Journal!*' Again the terrible voice. Again indignation, brevity, righteousness and self-belief.

Hyacinth surrendered with a sigh the little notebook which all pupils were required to carry at all times and which members of staff could demand to record disappointment and shock. Rani seized it and made a swift righteous entry.

Ward's sensors, tuned for faint encrypted signals, are overwhelmed by a perturbation so violent it all but knocks out his receiving equipment. And yet it is only the O'Sheas, a fanatically deferential southern Irish couple who were regular visitors a few years before. Ward assumed then that the husband was soliciting Hugh's help in furthering his teaching career. Either the southern qualifications were dubious or in an unacceptable subject – woodwork, he guessed, since O'Shea set about installing built-in wardrobes in the Ward master bedroom, working with an ingratiating submissiveness that Martin despised but was unable to dent ('There are some skins as hard as tortoise shell against which scorn has no power' – Baudelaire).

'*Sacred Heart of Jesus!*' Mrs Ward shrieks now in unaccountable panic and terror. 'Hugh . . . *the O'Sheas.*'

Yet she opens the door with wild cries of pleasure echoed by Nora O'Shea who advances confidently into the hall. 'Isn't that weather desperate?'

'Wouldn't it sicken you altogether?'

'At least the fishermen should like it.' Nora turns expectantly to Hugh Ward. Nothing.

'But you got a bit of sun *somewhere*,' Mrs Ward notes, with a touch of asperity.

'We got away at Easter,' cries the younger woman, one of the new ruthless hedonists without guilt or shame. 'Just for a week, you know.'

'With the children?' Again Mrs Ward attempts to insert the blade and again the O'Shea woman brushes it aside.

'Oh the kids went down to Kevin's mother in the country.' She moves into the front room, accompanied by the silent awkward men. 'The kids *love* it down there.'

Mrs Ward turns towards the living room. '*Martin!*'

He approaches, shocked to see his mother vanquished.

'Here's the *brainy one!*' Nora cries gaily from the sofa.

Mrs Ward puts her mouth to her son's ear. 'Run down to McAnanney's and ask for a good Dundee cake. A *good* cake, now, mind. And *tell him who you are.*'

Never yet has Martin told a shopkeeper who he is ('To be known is not my business' – Flaubert). And never has he felt his mother to be so vulnerable and weak.

'Can I get long trousers?'

'*What?*'

Seizing the bottoms of his trouser legs, he attempts to pull them down over his naked thighs. 'I feel a right gak in these.'

'You're no such thing. Sure those are lovely on ye. There's

nothing worse than looking like a wee man.'

'But I'm the only one left in the class. Peter McGirr got long trousers today. I'm the last one now. Wee Willie got me to stand up in Geography and made a whole laugh of me.'

'We'll see, Martin, we'll see. Don't torment me out and out. Just run down like a good boy and get me that cake.'

Swift as the wind Martin flies to the Magnet (known locally as the Maggot), his mind working as furiously as his limbs in pursuit of a hypothesis for the O'Shea affair. Surely his mother cannot have been humbled? It must be Hugh who has brought humiliation on the Wards.

Instead of McAnanney Senior, the son Dessie lolls across the counter of the Magnet, cronies disposed about the shop in attitudes of knowing indolence. As Ward enters, Dessie begins to drum on the counter, establishing a slow hypnotic Red Indian beat, to which in time he adds a solemn chant:

> On the bank . . . of the river . . .
>> stood Runnin' Bear . . . young Indian brave,
> On the other . . . side of the river
>> stood his lovely . . . Indian maid.
> Little White Dove . . . was her na – ame,
>> such a lovely . . . sight to see,
> But their tribes . . . fought with each *aw – ther*
>> so their love . . . could never *beeeeee* . . .

Abruptly Dessie stops and regards Ward. 'Do ye like "Runnin' Bear"?'

A familiar trick question to which Ward has never found a satisfactory response.

'He *loves* it,' says one of the cronies.

Dessie feigns shock and outrage. 'You're a dirty brute, Ward.' They all laugh ('Already, in many an ambush, that exalted ape, man, has pierced my breast with his porphyry spear' – Lautréamont). 'All right, young Ward, what can Ah do ye for?'

'A Dundee cake.'

This provokes another outburst. Shaking his head in amazement, Dessie turns to the shelves. 'Martin, Martin, the ducks are fartin', the geese are layin' eggs.' He tosses a cake onto the counter. 'Half a dollar to you, Ward.'

Martin pays with a shudder of disgust ('Commerce is, in its very essence, *satanic*' – Baudelaire) but as he turns to go Dessie abruptly puts a question. 'Have ye Big Hughie for Irish?' Ward cautiously nods assent, provoking a fresh shout of laughter. 'Bet he loves ye in those trousers. Does he get ye to lie on the table so he can look up yer leg?'

'*Luí ar an tábla*,' says one of the cronies, dropping his face to counter level and squinting lewdly along it.

'Fuckin' homo,' a second chuckles, 'a fuckin' arse bandit.'

The third rises from an onion bag to pout his lips at Martin. 'Give us a wee kiss, hi . . . *unless ye're a mouthwasher.*'

Ward flees the harsh laughter ('Reprisals of carnage and arson flame in his eyes – be sure that he will implement dreams of extermination during his first days of omnipotence' – Villiers).

At home he prepares a tray with a pot of tea, china tea service and a matched serving plate with slices of Dundee cake.

In the front room the animated women go on with their conversation but the slumped men turn towards the tea things with gratitude.

'The first time I met Father Harry,' Nora O'Shea is saying, 'was at the Blessing of the Throats, you know. Kevin and I were very late getting . . . Kevin was doing a wee job for Mrs Ryder . . . and the chapel was packed, queues a mile long. So then I spotted these two busmen going in to the Sacristy . . . I suppose they were on duty and in a hurry . . . and says I to Kevin, we'll go in with these two. So in we went, through the Sacristy, and right enough Father Harry came across from the altar and blessed the throats of the two busmen. But then he looked at Kevin and me . . . a *look* . . . you know . . . and says he, as dry . . . you know the way of him . . . says he to us, *you're not all busmen.*' Now the mirth, so long contained, takes possession and she bends over, helpless. '*You're not all busmen.*'

Martin waits for her to regain control ('Endless caricatures of the beautiful who take so seriously the laughable braying of your supremely contemptible souls' – Lautréamont), noting the border of pale freckled skin between her sun-reddened throat and lace cups. Eventually she straightens, lifting herself a little from the sofa in order to snap down the skirt of her tweed suit.

'Oh that would be Father Harry,' Mrs Ward has to admit.

'Now *this* is what *I* call service!' Nora looks from the tray to its bearer, effortlessly encompassing him in a monstrous effulgence. 'Not only brainy but *useful!* Where would *I* get a man like that, I wonder? And as tall getting!' Her eyes travel down his body, lingering unmistakeably on the pale blotched thighs which Ward, the tray of china in his hands, is unable to conceal ('My shame is vast as eternity' – Lautréamont).

Shortly afterwards the O'Sheas leave and Father Harry himself arrives. Again Mrs Ward summons her son.

'Bring us a wee cup of tea and a bit of that cake, Martin.'

'Can I get long trousers tomorrow?'

'Give me head ease,' she implores him, even more distraught now than with the O'Sheas. 'Give me poor head ease this night.'

'But me thighs are all scourgy. Short trousers have me all scourgy as well as everything else.'

'In the name of *God*, Martin. Give me poor head peace.'

Again tray, tea, china and Dundee cake.

The priest appears to welcome the interruption. 'Ah, Martin,' he cries jovially, 'look at the size you're getting. You must be going fishing with your father now. Do you like the fishing?'

Ward glances at his slumped father and perceives the plan. The poor vessel shattered by the priest will be made whole by filial devotion.

'No.'

'*Hah?*' The priest is taken aback. 'I think the fishing's a great thing . . . a great relaxation. Ye can be too much at the books.'

'Martin was never much of a one for the fishing,' Mrs Ward anxiously intervenes.

Father Harry continues to gaze hopefully at the youth. 'Would ye never think of comin' down to the Boys' Club? Ye needn't think we're all Holy Joes – it's just a crowd of young lads like yourself.'

Ward can scarcely credit an attempt to enlist him in the community that has annihilated his father ('Blood and hate rush to my head in boiling floods. *I* generous enough to love my fellow men! No, no. Worlds shall be seen to destroy themselves and granite glide like a cormorant over the waves before I touch the vile hand of a human being' – Lautréamont).

But of course his revulsion is lost on the priest. 'Sure it's only a crowd of young fellas hottin' it up with guitars.'

'I'm sure he'd *love* to go down,' Mrs Ward cries wildly, staring in horror at her son.

And again Ward eavesdrops on the departure, lying full length on the stairs with his ear to the banister. Hugh remains in the front room while his wife accompanies the priest to the door.

'Well I hope Hugh'll be able . . . ,' Father Harry says softly, 'you know . . . ?'

There is a considerable pause. Ward can imagine his mother's expression. 'Och sure, Father . . .'

As the door closes Martin has to nip sharply into the toilet to evade his father, laboriously mounting the stairs to the attic workshop, now converted to a single bedroom. As soon as he has passed Ward goes nonchalantly downstairs.

'*Could ye not answer Father Harry civilly about the Boys' Club?*'

'They'd only make a whole laugh of me in short trousers.'

'And why aren't ye in your bed at this hour?'

Because it is the hour of *Johnny Staccato* on television. Ward is hoping that his mother will leave him in peace in the living room. Instead she kneels on the carpet and places her elbows in the seat of an armchair. As she arranges the Rosary beads her face becomes a leaden mask. Closing her eyes, she fingers the beads and announces the Sorrowful Mysteries, in the absence of support from her family obliged to deliver both invocation and response.

> Thou, O Lord, wilt open my lips.
> *And my tongue shall announce Thy praise.*
> Incline unto my aid, O God.
> *O Lord, make haste to help me.*

# 3

Even in deep adulthood there are miracles, for instance being paid to enjoy three hours of silence with a guarantee of no interruptions. Such was the wonder of invigilation during mock exam week, the pleasure of seclusion enhanced by the memory of my own examination triumphs and the discomfiture of colleagues deprived of activity and talk. What a privilege to revel in contemplation while enjoying the withdrawal symptoms of the addicts of commotion!

And since the examinees had no classes for a week I had an afternoon off. Staff were not supposed to leave the premises till four but, after registering my tutor group at one forty-five, I went up to the old building as though to teach and, once inside, followed obscure corridors to a little side door which led to freedom of the most exhilarating kind (that surreptitiously snatched from a world which imagines you to be gainfully employed) and in the most sympathetic of environments (the heart of the tolerant capital city).

At this time no *quartier* was more louche than Camden Town, the principal meeting place for New Wave initiates with raggedy dark urchin clothes and spiky neon-coloured hair like the bristles of a worn-out lavatory brush. (Devotees of the Baudelaire legend claim that their man invented the tactic of shock locks when he dyed his hair green to outrage café society. Demystifiers, fortunately as persistent as the fabulists, point out that the green so-called dye was actually a common treatment for dandruff.) Here almost everyone had the look of an unregenerate miscreant. Among the New Wave young moved the previous generation of alienated settlers – rural Irishmen with adolescent hunched shoulders and secretive smirks, absorbed in evasions and dodges and scams, confident of putting one over on the world even as it bore down to crush them.

There is a possibility that Rimbaud visited Cork as a merchant seaman and Villiers may have come to Dublin in pursuit of an Irish heiress but, of the seven, only Baudelaire had strong links to Ireland. This is obvious from his work ('To feel no more the horrible burden of time it is necessary to make oneself ceaselessly drunk', 'There are but three beings worthy of respect – the poet, the warrior and the priest') but it is startling to discover a connection *on both sides of the family*. Not only was his mother educated by Irish nuns but General Aupick, his stepfather and crucial influence, was himself the son of a man born in Ireland and had the forename Jemis, a French version of Seamus (the surname possibly also a Gallicised version of O'Peake). To the long list of Irish glories-that-might-have-been there must now be added yet another – that, had the general appeared on the scene a few years earlier (he married Mme Baudelaire when Charles was six), he might have given the boy his forename and the legendary father of modern literature would have been Seamus Baudelaire.

Compendium Bookshop – teeming treasure house of rarities from obscure publishers, enemy of the coffee table and friend of the garret, tonically fizzing with weirdness, marginality and subversion, though the sections devoted to Surrealism and the Beats were beginning to assume a forlorn dog-eared look. Even here the triumph of the bourgeois would soon be complete. And today there was certainly nothing to bear me aloft on angel's wings.

It was necessary to return to a thoroughly bourgeois *quartier* abounding in wine bars, *pâtisseries*, coffee houses and expensive knick-knack shops with names like Lord Snooty's Gallery and La Di D'Art. Though even these streets could seem spiritual at twilight, the neon shop signs burdened with a mysterious intensity and pathos.

Clare was pacing the lounge, excited, restless, intense, and Paul, who had picked up the signals, immediately ran into my legs in obscure but fervent ardour. Clare came up behind him and I caught the sweet smell of excess.

'You've been drinking.'

'At lunchtime . . . a few drinks . . . with Nick.'

'*Nick?*'

Ferociously Paul wrestled my legs as though to make them disgorge the dark secrets of adulthood. Gently I disengaged him.

'Can we play offices, Dad?'

'Later, Paul.'

Clare leaned down to him. 'Why don't you go to your room and get everything ready? Don't come back out for your dad though. He'll come in to you in a while.'

This dismissal intensified the atmosphere of momentousness. A violent anticipatory shiver left me expectant and stirred. But Paul's departure seemed only to increase Clare's agitation. As though desperate to shake off some relentless pursuer, she paced with odd truncated gestures and constant abrupt turns. 'Martin . . .' The formal mode of address. But in a strange low tone of complicity and mischief. Then she reached for my hand. Dropping my briefcase in trepidation and wonder, I permitted her to lead me to the sofa where we sat sideways, facing, my right hand in hers. Not for an age had we been so tenderly intimate and, like a starving man given a sniff of his favourite home-cooked hot dinner, my naive and foolhardy body proceeded to prepare itself for a feast.

'*Martin* . . .' Again she tried to begin, this time halted by a half-suppressed giggle. I had a sense of joining a conspiracy against a huge and nameless authority whose spirit presided over the room. More like adolescents planning to cut school than adults on the sofa in the through lounge. 'Martin, we had a few drinks at lunchtime.' Her voice was now practically a whisper, her hold on my right palm loose and light, her thumb tenderly brushing the tops of my fingers. Nothing disturbs like gentleness. Volition drained from all parts of my body to concentrate in my cock. 'Lucy was booked into the crèche all day and Paul was at school. It was just lovely . . . you know? A few drinks like that at lunchtime can be *absolutely lovely*.' She sighed in exquisite recollection. I caught the sweet smell again. 'Anyway we came back here for coffee and . . .' Again the nervous giggle. Now I felt not so much an accomplice, more the school beauty's plain confidante. 'Well with one thing and another, Martin, *we ended up in the bedroom*.' The confession complete, she relaxed in a wondering laugh.

The first necessity was to establish the facts. 'You mean he had *sex* with you? He *screwed* you?'

'*Yes!*' she shrieked in weird hilarity.

'Here . . . *in our bedroom? Our bed?*'

She threw off the affirmative monosyllable as boldly and gladly as Molly Bloom. '*YES!*'

Far from identifying me with repressive and vengeful authority, she seemed to be once again co-opting me as a fellow conspirator, a kind of inside man supporting her bold freedom bid.

But how did she know I would not fly into a rage? And was this assumption an insult or a tribute?

'You aren't angry with me, Martin.' Less a question than a statement of fact.

'On the contrary, I'm brimming with tenderness.'

'You mean you have a hard on?'

'That's another way of putting it.'

Combining the solicitude of a mother, the affection of a spouse and the brazenness of a bought woman, she leaned across to unzip me and spring the grotesque donkey cock which, far from betraying reluctance or embarrassment, celebrated its change of fortune by flying a pennant of pre-come.

Perhaps celebration was appropriate. If Clare did not equate me with authority then *I too was free*. We could both cut school. For the first time in years a great burden was lifted. A strange exhilaration possessed me. Even a kind of *gratitude*. For this was the only way release could come. If I had had a fling it would have shattered Clare's frail confidence and plunged her into despair. She, on the other hand, could take us both along on her freedom dash.

85

Clare alone could set us free from the crushing determinism of our destinies.

For 'the connection', Colette's home in Mount Pleasant is the flagship, the show house and Colette, Mrs Ward's youngest sister, embodies the personal ideal.

'Your garden's just *gorgeous*, Colette!' Mrs Ward cries, as she and Martin advance up the curving gravelled drive.

But Colette, radiant in the porch, rolls her eyes in dismay. 'Don't be talking to me about gardens, Josephine. It's this new gardener – a real sergeant-major type. Everything in its place, you know. Everything just so. You can't say a word to him. Right enough, he's as hard-working ... but, like ... you can have too much of a good thing.' She lowers her voice and glances about in sudden mischievous apprehension. 'Eugene was just saying' – now she lays a hand on Mrs Ward's arm – 'everybody'll take us for *Protestants*.'

'Martin's going down to visit his grandfather,' Mrs Ward explains, 'so I thought I'd wait for him here.'

'As long as you don't mind *camping out*. The builders are still at the extension. We're camping out in the kitchen. Don't know whether we're coming or going. But I'm sure we can manage a drop of tea.' She turns to Martin, 'Ye'll not say no to a wee drop of tea,' leaning close in sudden conspiratorial intimacy, 'you might not get much down there.'

'Oh ... *don't be talkin'*.' It is Mrs Ward's turn to roll her eyes.

In the kitchen Eugene lays aside the *Irish News* and rises affably to greet them. Not only blessed with the ideal personality and home, Colette possesses in Eugene the optician the ideal connection husband – professional, good-humoured, docile and stupid.

'Here's Archimedes!' he cries now to Martin. 'How did the exams go?'

The youth shrugs indifferently.

'Oh I'm sure he just walked through them,' says Colette.

'I was never much good at the exams.' Eugene chuckles comfortably, not only unembarrassed by his lack of academic brilliance but possibly even regarding it as evidence of virility and common sense. ('To be stupid, selfish and in good health are the three prerequisites of happiness but if stupidity is lacking the others are useless' – Flaubert.) 'Had to repeat every exam I ever did. I think they only gave me a diploma to get rid of me.'

Mrs Ward has been peering wistfully out of the window. 'Ah Colette, that extension'll give you great extra space.'

'Sure didn't you get an extension yourself, Josie?' Obtuseness can be a problem with ideal husbands like Eugene.

But Mrs Ward is not averse to repeating the explanation. 'If you could call it that. When we were having it done the old grandfather turned up and said it couldn't go out more than a few feet.' She pauses grimly. 'And why not?' Obliged to face the terrible truth again, her expression takes a bitter set look. *Because it would put an extra shilling on the rates.* She looks at each of them in turn in perverse triumph. *An extra shilling on the rates.* That's why we never got a decent extension. And now we need a new house and it's the same old carry-on. The old man and those old country notions about money. And Hugh too bird-mouthed to speak up for himself. That old country way of working . . .' Mrs Ward is bedding down in the comfortable warmth of familiar grievance.

Eugene attempts to dislodge her. 'Where were you thinking of moving, Josie?'

'I always thought these were very good houses. I always liked Mount Pleasant.'

A bolt of terror transfixes Ward. Dangerous even to visit, to reside in Mount Pleasant would be *spiritual death* ('I am out of my element, sick, stupid, furious and utterly discomposed' – Rimbaud). He does not know what 'country notion' is blocking a move but for the first time prays that peasant obduracy may abide.

'*Mount Pleasant!*' Colette, bringing tea things, finds the idea ill-advised for opposite reasons. 'Och Josephine . . . sure the whole town's in Mount Pleasant now.' And she laughs gaily at her sister's misguided notion of exclusivity. 'Sure haven't we the Chinese even.'

'Two houses up,' Eugene explains. 'The crowd that own the Crystal Garden. Kinsella was telling me about the old fella. Doctor Kinsella, you know. The old fella's a patient and says he to Kinsella, *No breeze! No breeze!* Meant he couldn't breathe – the English is not very good, ye see . . . though the same fella's not so slow, seemingly he's opening a new restaurant in Limavady . . .'

'*Limavady!*'

'Kinsella was good value about him. Had him off to a tee. *No breeze! No breeze!*' Laughing, Eugene slaps his chest in imitation of

Kinsella imitating his patient. 'But English or no English, he was cute enough at the heel o' the hunt. Managed better than us, Josie. Because he couldn't climb stairs he got a grant for an extension with a downstairs toilet.'

'They got a *grant!*' Mrs Ward cries wildly. 'They got a grant for an *extension.*'

'Oh he's cute enough when it comes to it. And this business of the sons going to school in Glasgow – there'll be some reason for that too. They'll be claiming something for that too some way or other.'

'They'll be claiming something for that,' Mrs Ward grimly agrees.

'Though he'd be decent enough at the same time, like. He sent us over this big duck at Christmas . . . cooked some special way, with all the trimmings . . . the way they do it, you know. I'd have tried it . . . but Colette . . .'

'Oh . . . *Eugene.*' Colette finds it absurd to have to explain such a basic point. 'You only have to pick up a paper to know what they put in the food.'

'Colette wouldn't touch it so we gave it to the Vincent de Paul.'

Another limitation of the ideal husband is a heavy-handed way with an anecdote.

Colette applies her light touch. 'I rang Fonsie Burns of the Vincent de Paul and says I, *Fonsie, do you know of some family that would like a Chinese duck? Says he, Look no further, Colette.*' She pauses to look round at them. 'Fonsie has six boys.' This time her pause is to allow the laughter to subside. 'Right enough, he rang back to say it was gorgeous.'

There is a longer pause in which everyone sips tea and nibbles Battenburg cake.

'You'll have to be going round to your grandfather,' Mrs Ward says to Martin.

'Do I have to?' Frightful though Mount Pleasant may be, it is still preferable to the other. 'That house gives me the creeps.'

'Mother of God, don't say that.' Mrs Ward is genuinely alarmed – but also darts Colette a look of satisfaction and amusement. 'If your father heard you at that, Martin.'

'I think Adrian's down playing tennis with the Devlins. Maybe he'd go with you.' Colette's suggestion of his cousin's company gives Martin the necessary impetus to leave. ('Knowing nothing of the nature of friendship and love it is unlikely that I shall ever accept them and certainly not from the human race' – Lautréamont.)

In any case the grandfather requires Martin to visit alone so that he may receive the accumulated wisdom of the Wards. The old man lives in Heathfield (the park next to Mount Pleasant but neither as old nor as grand) along with two unmarried daughters whom he describes as 'the girls', although to Martin they seem as ancient as their father and with minds older still – dark, immobile and freakishly gnarled, like walnuts pickled in vinegar.

Today there is unusual vivacity. They have just had a telephone installed.

'So now,' one explains to Martin, 'when Pop wants to see you we'll phone your house *and let it ring four times*. Don't pick up the phone unless it rings more than four times. And then if you're able to come, phone *us* and *let it ring four times*.'

And at this cunning method of communicating free of charge – a practical ingenuity which Martin, for all his brains, could never hope to match – they look at the youth and cackle in glee ('In their solemn houses my ancestors – idiots and maniacs' – Baudelaire).

With a hoarse cry Pop himself shuffles towards them, employing to the full his rich repertoire of collusive signs, chuckles and winks. Now it is his turn to enjoy the delights of connivance and deception. As though wooing Martin away from the girls without their knowledge or consent, he places a hand on the youth's shoulder, winks and jerks his head towards the back of the house.

Like all careful conspirators they avoid being seen together in public places such as kitchen, parlour or front room. In winter they use the attic and in summer the garden shed, each fitted with work benches and festooned with the carefully oiled implements of carpentry and leather work. But unaffected by the seasons are Pop's many layered motley and padded bootees with zips fully open to accommodate several pairs of socks. Also changeless is the opening ploy. With a fresh outbreak of winking, nodding and chuckling, Pop draws from a special pocket sewn on the front of his trousers a small silver tin of snuff which he offers to Martin. The youth takes a pinch, inhales and, as always, turns aside for a violent sneeze. In the beginning this response was genuine. Now it is frequently necessary to dissemble so as not to deprive the old man of his glee.

This is the Ritual Wounding with which all initiation ceremonies commence. Next comes the instruction. There are only two concepts, those of 'blaggardism' and 'blaggard' (which Ward finally grasps as a corruption of the Victorian term, 'blackguard'), and wisdom consists in the knowledge that almost all human activity is the former perpetrated by the latter. Apart from close blood relatives there are only corner boys, thieves and swindlers, blaggards of every dark hue waiting to cheat and wound a young man who will survive to enjoy his inheritance only by the exercise of fanatical vigilance and profound mistrust. For while most blaggards are easily recognised, many conceal viciousness behind cunning charm. The majority of men and of course all women are fiendish, resourceful and tireless deceivers. Given Martin's limitless prospects, many women will try to *get their hooks* into him.

Today Pop appears to be fatigued at the thought of so many powerful and devious adversaries. He takes a hefty pinch of snuff and broods in silence.

'I told Hughie,' he suddenly bursts out. 'I told him. *I told him.* I told him not to be borrowing ... not to be getting himself into debt. None of the Wards ever owed anyone a penny ... *and none of the Wards ever will.* But sure she ... what's the use of talkin' ... *she* ...'

As he lapses once more into silence it comes to Martin that this is the 'old country notion': Pop has forbidden Hugh to take out the mortgage so ardently desired by his wife. Hence the antagonism between the two sides of the family. Though they also have much in common, particularly an obsession with grievances endlessly aired but never fully explained. Resentment continually bursts into speech but an even-stronger innate secrecy prevents the disclosure of facts ('It is perfectly obvious that I have always belonged to an inferior race' – Rimbaud).

'And that house Hugh was after,' Pop angrily resumes, 'I saw those houses being built. I know the cheap dirt that went into them and the blaggard of a builder that put them up. And there's poor Hughie wantin' to hand out his money ... Oh there'll be plenty to take your money, there's plenty'll be after your money. There was a fine gentleman in here' – effortlessly the tide of resentment lifts him over the barrier between anecdotes – 'a fine gentleman tappin' with a cane. Oh yes. *A fine gentleman* ... talkin' as nice as could be. But I knew what he was after. I knew his game. Says I, *you'll get nothin' from me, not a penny*. So out he went with a bee in his bonnet. Oh I chased him quick enough. I soon chased him. Says I to him, *What did you ever do for my girls?* What did my girls ever get but *emigration, starvation and the back of the country?*'

Since this is Pop's favourite anecdote Martin has long since developed a theory. The 'fine gentleman' is in fact the local bishop who is related in some way to the Ward side of the family (the cane presumably a colourful storyteller's embellishment). The visit was certainly real and in the course of it the bishop either solicited a bequest or, more likely, was imagined by Pop to be on the verge of so doing. As for the resonant punch line, 'emigration, starvation and the back of the country', this can only be a reference to the girls' former teaching careers in a village once indisputably outside the town but long since an outer suburb. Presumably Pop feels that the bishop could have arranged something more central for his own kith and kin.

'Oh yes ... a *fine* gentleman,' Pop suddenly bursts out again, so that Ward thinks he is about to repeat the anecdote immediately ('You are stifling? Have patience, O Lion of the Desert' – Flaubert).

Instead, the old man proceeds to the next stage – a guided tour of the fortifications. Blaggards are of course always attempting to break in but are foiled by a system of locks, bolts and chains substantial enough to secure a *bastide*. Pop is particularly lyrical about his hinges, also of a medieval design and weight no longer available in stores. The hinge is always your weak link. Using a plank as a battering ram, he demonstrates how the new ruthless blaggard will bypass fancy locks to smash in the pitiful hinges unloaded on a gullible public by unscrupulous hardware merchants.

But the vehemence of the demonstration exhausts him and he has to sit down on a garden wall, perhaps overcome not just by weariness but the terrible conviction that, despite all his efforts, the Goths and Vandals will breach the defences, force the maidens and strew the temple with turds. Without turning his head he waves feebly in the direction of the roof.

'But I can't do it all myself any more. I can't go up ladders. I had to get a character in to fix the roof and the blaggard botched it ... *botched it* ... never did anything I told him ... never a job done right ... never anything done right ...'

He falls silent, lapsing into vague gestures of dismissal and disgust and eventually pulling out the snuff tin with a terminal grunt. A stiff snort revives him and they return to the garden shed where, good spirits restored, he presents Martin with a purse of soft calf leather, made in this very room with the finest of materials and unstinting craftsmanship, the supple black leather stitched not with twine but bottle green leather thong.

An artefact of great beauty – but no practical use, for a purse would be laughed to scorn by the likes of Shotter. Knowing that it will join many others in a drawer, Ward accepts the gift with a smile on his lips and despair in his heart.

They move towards the front door, the girls reappearing from the parlour to see Martin out. It is at this point that Pop suddenly halts, winking and nodding at the youth. With his left hand he lifts Martin's limp right and with his own massive right hand places a florin in the centre of the youth's palm, instantly closing the youth's fingers over the coin as though to conceal it from the girls.

But if he wishes to keep the gift secret why does he wait till the girls appear? Wincing in anguish, Martin looks to them to plead his innocence. ('I have lived too many days since this dawn' – Villiers.) The telephone excitement long forgotten, they present him with masks as bleak and stony as their native mountainside in Connacht.

'Keep in with the girls,' Pop whispers loudly, holding Martin's florin hand in both of his own and shaking it up and down with many meaningful winks and nods. 'Always keep in with the girls. The girls have thousands. *Thousands!* Always keep in with them. Keep in with the girls.'

'You see? Back as soon as the music's over – I just went for the music. Back straight after closing time. *Just like I told you.*' Free from guilt, shame and fear, Clare glowed with the rectitude of the pure in heart. As always, attack was the most effective form of defence – and a pre-emptive strike the most effective form of attack.

'You had plenty of time . . . if that's what you wanted.'

'I wouldn't have missed a minute of the music.'

'Or the drink.' Again the sick-sweet fragrance was unmistakable.

'You have to take a couple to cover yourself.' Removing her jacket, she flung herself onto the sofa.

'Still desperate to get back to Ireland?'

She evaded this by lifting my book. 'The New Testament! You're not turning to *religion!*'

'What other refuge for the broken and desolate?' Solemn words gravely spoken and producing in Clare genuine alarm. What excited her was not virtue but demonic lustre (now badly faded in me but presumably burning bright in Nick). On the issue of male glamour Clare was in total agreement with Baudelaire – 'I have difficulty in not concluding that the most perfect type of manly beauty is Satan.'

'I have to stage an assembly with my tutor group. Something positive and Christian. I've been looking for ideas.'

What I sought was a Gospel theme not exhausted by mindless repetition and empty lip service. Finding one was easy – the text was full of ringing denunciations of hypocrisy. But of course there was a good reason for never having heard this mentioned in the multitude of sermons and homilies. This part of the message was no more palatable now than it had been two thousand years before.

The most successful assembly I had seen took the opposite approach. Ten girls in a row across the stage came forward one at a time to deliver ten commandments for the modern age:

1 Acknowledge the people you meet. There is nothing so pleasant as a word of greeting.

2 Smile at the people you meet. It takes seventy-two muscles to frown and only fourteen to smile.

3 Be convivial and cordial. Speak and act as if everything is a pleasure.

It continued in this vein and at the end was warmly applauded by everyone, especially the nuns. This should not have been a surprise. The Church has always been adept at finding alternatives to the difficult and disagreeable business of ethics. First it was theology. Then it was ritual. Now it was cheerfulness.

Coming back from the sink with a glass of water, Clare showed no desire to be hypocritically agreeable. 'We came home by British Rail ... on this late train ... hardly any passengers ... we were in this totally empty carriage ... it was sort of eerie.' She sat down, bright-eyed, frowning slightly in the effort of reconstruction and assessment. 'He slipped his hand under my jeans belt ... and *right down*, you know ... and then *started to finger me*.' Abruptly she threw back the tap water as though it were a bracing Tequila Slammer. 'God it was beautiful, Martin.' Once again my arousal was not aggressive but sexual. Though this was far from her purpose of pure, disinterested recall. 'And then I took out his cock and held it.' She paused – rapt, wondering, grateful. 'I offered to toss him off – but he said no, he only wanted to *ride me*.' She turned with a look of fierce pride at Nick's gallantry and selflessness. 'I even offered to *suck him off* – but he said no.'

Her startling candour was based on that unshakable confidence which inspires confidence in others. Its strong and irresistible tide would surely lift us over all the petty obstacles raised by our conventional natures. Already this new sense of empowerment had affected other areas of her life. She refused the Nursing Agency. She became a facilitator at Mothers & Co. There was even talk of her being co-opted to the Management Committee of the Community Centre.

There was a long silence. Clare swayed slightly. We too were in a lighted empty carriage, plunging wildly into the heart of the night.

'But don't worry!' she cried in sudden drunken ardour. 'I still care about you. You're really good too.'

Arm in arm, we went upstairs together. I had no objection to using Nick as a warm-up act. Who could provide better foreplay than Satan?

Give and ye shall receive: this was the great truth of the moment. It seemed that generosity would be rewarded not in heaven but on earth. I too was newly empowered and became a radiant facilitator at work. For Rani I used my authority as Head of Physics to get Seymour removed from some of her classes and redeployed elsewhere.

'I won't forget this!' Rani cried with the instant uninhibited fervour that was her most striking trait. 'I promise you I won't forget this. *I really won't.*'

For Wills I succeeded in averting a technician's revolt, negotiating with their leader, Henderson, a middle-aged Scot with a toupee so blatant and hideous it was surely worse than whatever it concealed. This contemporary Spartacus sat at the back of the storeroom, eating cheddar cheese sandwiches from a tinfoil pack and drinking milk from a small screwtop Lucozade bottle. There is something profoundly pitiful about eating home-made sandwiches at work and his flaunting of them seemed a deliberate act of aggression, an attempt to rub my nose in his dirt. He continued to eat and drink while voicing the group protest at menial tasks peremptorily ordered at short notice by arrogant staff (Rani was one of the worst offenders, he claimed). Technicians were qualified professionals, not to be treated as servants and cleaners.

Again the ancient folly and sorrow of believing yourself to be someone. Ancient source of chronic suffering, ancient wound that never heals. A little learning may or may not be dangerous, but a little qualification is usually the cause of endless trouble. Henderson's pain at the ignominy of the lab technician was no different from mine at the humiliations of secondary teaching. Despite his surliness and toupee, I felt a profound empathy and compassion. Christ would surely have been proud of me.

Wills was certainly pleased, astounded by Henderson's acceptance of a simple scheme whereby all requests were made on booking forms submitted to him at least three working days in advance.

'Terry, listening itself is often sufficient. The phoney consultation is the crucial management tool of our time.'

Wills's reward was more immediate than Rani's but much less exciting. 'Come round to the pub and I'll buy you a drink.'

'Have to get home, Terry.'

'Come on ... it was super last night.' Already he was chuckling at the memory. 'Met these girls and told them I worked as a sorter in a sewage works. Explained that I had to wear a glove. And Tommy came round later.'

Though Christ supped with Judas, I was not prepared to drink with Tommy Hogan, our Irish caretaker. I suspected that Wills bought this man pints in order to illustrate his own defiant earthiness and big-hearted love of the common people. It could scarcely be for love of the caretaker's company. Hogan was so obviously an informer, a shifty unctuous lackey entirely the creature of the nuns.

Not even Christ could be consistently Christian. It was surely enough that, while humming the exuberant opening of the Schubert Piano Trio in B flat, I would wash all the dirty cups lazily dropped in the staffroom sink − and, even more noble, abandon the congenial window corner to eat my miserable egg-and-onion sandwiches at the communal table in the centre of the room. But do not expect examples of the relentless and excruciating banality of the talk. All the terrible details were immediately suppressed. Who can stare into the Void? (Christ did not have to suffer colleagues – the guy had it easy in many ways.)

The ultimate sacrifice is for those with the temperament of the Crag to follow the Way of the Cross. According to the Way of the Crag (espoused by the Magnificent Seven), man and his world are irredeemably corrupt and the only solution is to withdraw to a pinnacle and hurl down abuse. Hence the Crag virtues are pride, detachment, solitariness, honour, rejection, contempt. But the Way of the Cross (espoused by Bernard and Janet) insists on redemption through service. It is necessary to descend to the plain and exercise the crucial virtues of humility, solidarity, commitment, generosity, compassion, forgiveness.

Is a synthesis possible? The positions appear to be mutually exclusive. All that they have in common is what they reject – hypocrisy, expediency, self-interest, self-pity, pettiness, greed.

Yet if the demands of logic could be resisted it might be possible to maintain opposing views in parallel. On one memorable evening Clare and I invested in a bottle of gin and took turns to select pieces of music, deliberately choosing them to maximise disparity and discord. I put on Debussy's *Prélude à L'Aprés-midi d'un Faune*; Clare countered with 'One Chord Wonders' by T.V. Smith and the Adverts. I played the Schubert 'Impromptu in G flat Major'; she followed with 'Xerox Music's Here at Last' by Desperate Bicycles. Since I had many of Bernard's records on loan and Clare had most of Nick's New Wave collection (another example of his selflessness and generosity), we were able to sustain this game all evening. Looking for something that would really throw her, I tried the Benjamin Britten song cycle based on Rimbaud's *Illuminations*; shrieking with laughter she turned up the volume on the Crime single 'Murder by Guitar'.

In between numbers we refilled our glasses and exchanged compliments.

'Not many husbands would be generous about Nick.'

'Not many wives would be as frank as you.'

The marvellous surrounds us like an atmosphere, said Baudelaire, but we never see it. Now it seemed to me that I was seeing Clare for the first time. By the new standard of lack of hypocrisy, her stature was suddenly and hugely enhanced. To liking and desire was added the third member of the essential trinity of love – respect.

Ironically, Baudelaire himself went seriously down in my estimation. At the same time as he was praising 'the true grandeur of the pariah', King B was busily angling for the Légion d'honneur, a seat on the Académie française (assiduously courting old duffers and viciously mocking them afterwards) and the directorship of a state theatre ('There is in Paris a theatre – *the only one in which it is impossible to go bankrupt* – where a profit of 400,000 francs can be made in four years. I want that theatre . . . I want it and I'll get it. The years go by and I want to be *rich*.') Many similar examples could be cited. Daddy Cool was not cool at all. Impossible to imagine such behaviour from Lautréamont, Flaubert, Huysmans or Rimbaud.

Is there a case for claiming hypocrisy as the sin of sins, the Mr Big who facilitates and protects all the others while never being personally prosecuted or denounced, his name not even appearing on the seven-deadly wanted list?

Certainly the rarity of candour makes it attractive and exciting. These days Clare had a natural radiance.

'Can we go upstairs?' I asked.

It was not that she was averse but that another passion still took precedence. 'Just a little more music.'

The Chopin Nocturne in B flat Minor which, by the inevitable attraction of opposites, called forth that redundant boast of Ed Banger and the Nosebleeds: 'Ain't Been to no Music School'.

Already apprehensive about his first visit to the Ward home and its grand front room, Tony Shotter shrinks back in his armchair as Martin approaches angrily waving a long brass poker ('O human creature, here you are naked as a worm faced with my diamond blade' – Lautréamont).

'What do you think *this* is?' Ward shouts, aggressively brandishing the article. Shotter shrugs at the redundancy of the question. '*What do you think this is?*'

'It's a poker for Crissake.'

'Wrong!' Ward cries in fierce satisfaction. 'It *looks* like a poker . . . *yes*. It's *long enough* to be a poker. It's *heavy enough* to be a poker.' He hefts it suggestively, as though preparing to smite the philistine. 'It *appears* to be a poker – but in fact it's *not a poker at all*. I mean, you can't actually poke the fire with it. If you want to poke the fire you have to tramp out to the yard for the *real* fucking poker. What you see here is an *ornament* . . . like everything else in this room.'

As he turns towards the china cabinet, chaos and carnage flame in his eyes and he raises the sham poker as if to shatter the delicate glass structure and all its precious contents ('My entrails burn me; the violence of venom twists my limbs' – Rimbaud).

'China tea sets that never hold tea, silver toast racks that never hold toast, Waterford glass fruit bowls that never hold fruit, crystal goblets that never hold drink, a decanter that never decants . . . *could never decant, it's sealed shut.*' With a wild swing he takes in the rest of the room. 'Brass candlesticks that never hold candles, barometer that never measures pressure, clock that never tells the time . . . and of course a shovel that never shovels to match the poker that never pokes.' Passion almost spent, he lets the weapon hang by his side, 'Find me one functional item in this fucking room.'

Shotter looks about wildly. 'The table?'

'*No!*' A fresh paroxysm seizes Ward. 'It's a dining-room table, yes . . . but one on which no one has ever dined or will dine. Even to eat at the table in the living room, you have to lay down a rubber sheet, then an old table cloth, then the *good* table cloth, then the English-hunting-scene place mats; only after all this may plates of hot food be set down. But *under no circumstances* would it be possible to eat at *this* table. Not good enough, I'm afraid. *Try again.*'

Turning, Shotter peers desperately. 'The piano?'

Ward throws back his head to release a terrible shriek ('To laugh is satanic and hence profoundly human' – Baudelaire). 'You're a clever boy, Tony. No wonder you passed the 11-plus in spite of being a slag. That is definitely a real piano that can be played.' Ward demonstrates by flinging open the lid and bringing down his spread left hand to produce a jangling discord. His right hand once again raises the poker, causing Shotter to flinch – but Ward contents himself with laying the point on his friend's chest. 'The catch is that *no one ever does play it.* Since the day I was born and probably well before, not a note has been played on that instrument.' Another great weariness, this time terminal, afflicts Ward. 'In fact there's no music of any kind in this house. Can you believe that? No playing, no singing, no record player . . . .not even a radio. You know I had to go down on my knees for a transistor. I begged them for a decent new one – but I knew what would happen . . . me da would get some poxy second-hand rubbish from one of his cronies. *I'll have a word with Tom Keegan.* And wait till you see the monstrosity he got me. I've never shown this contraption to *anyone*.'

Ward rushes from the room to return with what appears to be a medium-sized suitcase. When he lays it on the carpet and opens the lid a set of radio controls is revealed and they can hear, as though fitfully borne on the wind from some distant pleasure palace, the faintest susurrus of pop music.

'And that's it up fucking full,' Ward raves, inconsolable. 'Know how Ah hear the top twenty?' Stretching out full length on the carpet, he presses his ear tight against the machine. 'I have to lie against it like this.'

'Maybe it needs new batteries.'

'Of course it does – that's the problem. Me fuckin' heart's broke puttin' new batteries in it. They cost a fortune and it goes like this after two days. But Ah've nothin' else for music. Did you get your new record player yet?'

As Ward lapses into habitual wistfulness and envy, Shotter begins to regain his natural superiority and confidence. 'It's an Ultra,' he murmurs and adds, in an ironic tone which fails to conceal intense satisfaction and pride, 'glowing golden teak and rich black leather cloth echo the superb reproduction of this new fully transistorised record player.' There is a long moment of reverent silence. Then, as though after some climax or trauma, Shotter produces twenty Embassy Regal and delivers himself to the leisurely ritual of removing the cellophane.

'Where'd ye get the money?'

'I do the odd day with Spadge Mullen and Don Kilpy. These days they're sellin' blankets in Ardowen.'

Ardowen is a newly built council estate less than a mile from where they sit but already endowed with the legendary status of a Wild West frontier town.

'But how can you sell blankets in summer?'

'Listen, Spadge could sell dog shite for fluoride toothpaste. That guy could sell cancer. *Want one?*'

Ward has no desire to smoke but envies Shotter his Zippo lighter, a device which flaunts pure functionality.

Fluently Shotter flips the heavy lid, spins the wheel and holds the tall flame steady, casually closing it with a full-bodied metallic clunk as resonant as the door slam of a Cadillac. 'See, it's nearly all women. Spadge barges in as if he's known them a lifetime. *How're ye doin', Missus. Any danger of a cup of tea?* Know Spadge, do ye? A wee guy wi' white hair and glasses – but the women all love him. He's a one-man show. Non-stop jokes and songs.'

'*Songs?*'

'Usually begins with "Slattery's Mounted Foot" and ends with "Dear God".' Shotter sings the opening bars, '*Dear God . . . I know I'm not worthy.* You'd *love* that one. Nearly always gets him the sale. And of course if that doesn't work he takes them upstairs and screws them.' Enjoying the calm assurance of an independent man of the world, Shotter lays his head on the antimacassar (another a functionless adornment), inhales deeply and contentedly and blows a leisurely cone of smoke at the Louis Quatorze chandelier.

'But how can they pay?' Ward wants to know. 'There's no money in Ardowen.'

'No one pays outright.' Shotter laughs at this naiveté. 'It's two and six a week for a year or so.'

'And how much is a pack of blankets?'

'Three quid.'

For once Ward's mathematical skill can be applied to real life. 'But that's over a 100 per cent interest.'

'No one in Ardowen thinks that way. Half a dollar a week is half a dollar a week. That's where I come in. Spadge and Don do the selling and I collect the payments. They're well used to paying up in Ardowen. Sure if they need cash they buy something on HP and pawn it.'

While Ward ponders the comparison between this reckless embracing of credit and Pop's obsessive fear of debt, Shotter is chuckling in fond reminiscence. 'That fuckin' van though. No tax or insurance of course. A fuckin' deathtrap. And Don drives like a lunatic. *Take it easy, for Jesus' sake,* I had to say to him – and ye know what he did? *Not like me drivin?* he says to me. *Naw Ah do not,* I says. *All right you drive,* he says – and lifts the fuckin' steering wheel off and throws it in on top of me in the back.' Shotter recoils in horror at the memory. 'Fuck Ah nearly had a shit haemorrhage. Apparently the steering wheel's loose and he takes it off all the time for a laugh. He's a real spacer, Don. *All right you drive*, he says, and throws the wheel right in me lap.'

This is certainly intriguing – but Ward has an earlier investigation to conclude ('Almost all of our lives are spent in foolish enquiries' – Baudelaire). 'What if they refuse to pay?'

Shotter sighs wearily. 'Spadge sells the credit to gangsters. *They* get their money.' Confident that the questioning is finally over, he rewards his own forbearance with a deep and voluptuous inhalation.

As though visited by the Holy Spirit, Ward is suddenly radiant with exaltation and hope. Ardowen in a ramshackle van – as romantic as arriving in Dodge City by stagecoach. *Ardowen:* the name rings out with the mysterious resonance of a silver dollar tossed by a stranger onto the wood of a saloon bar top. 'Could you take me along?'

Compelled to laugh in the course of exhaling, Shotter almost chokes. '*You? In Ardowen?* They'd fuckin' eat ye wi'out salt.' Ward falls back, humiliated and crushed. 'And anyway, Don'd probably kill ye before we even got there.'

'*Don?* He doesn't even know me.'

'Naw but your da beat the head off him in St Anthony's. Took a real dislike to Don for some reason. What's this he used to always call him?'

'A blaggard?' Ward suggests miserably ('I am become like those who never glimpsed Heaven. I have forgotten how to soar above the world, how to shut my ears against the mocking laughter of mankind' – Villiers).

'That was it. Don says, if he ever sees that man again he'll boot ees fuckin' balls up to ees neck. Says he was for fuck all as a teacher as well. All he ever did was make them copy stuff from the board.'

Always supremely indifferent to his father's teaching career, Ward is now forced to see him as another time-serving bully. 'Was he passed up for some big job a while back?'

'He was Vice Principal for years . . . in charge of discipline, scared the shit out of everybody. It was assumed he'd be Principal when John Deehan retired . . . another huer's melt . . . but they put in some young guy over his head. O'Shea, I think it was.'

Hugh Ward's place not merely usurped but usurped by Kevin O'Shea, his protégé . . . *his creature.* 'How do you know this?'

'All me mates go to St Anthony's. I'm a slag . . . *remember?* Should have gone there meself. Couldn't be any worse than the College. Gettin' battered and called a slag all day every day. Fuck Ah *hate* that place.' Shotter inhales deeply and fiercely, brooding on the injustices of his own schooling. 'Especially that lunatic O'Flaherty. Used to grab me by the cheek, shake me till Ah gurgled, then shout *Are ye goin' to give us your breakfast, ye slabber* and bang me head into the partition.'

Ward considers his own absurd position – trapped in a house of appearances and denied all knowledge and experience. Can mere thought compensate for such deprivation? ('I have eaten meagrely but ruminated much' – Flaubert). 'I know less about my own relatives than most orphans,' he says at length, though more in wonder than bitterness. 'For instance there's at least one missing aunt and uncle. I've this cousin Mairead but I don't know who her parents were.'

'Her mother Sheila was a sister of your mother's. And her da was Johnny Harris.'

'Why did you never tell me this?'

'*Tell you?* I assumed you knew for fuck's sake.'

'Was Johnny Harris a big heavy man with wavy hair parted in the middle?' Suddenly Ward recalls seeing, at the kitchen table in the aunt house where only the cleaning woman ate, a huge man with laboured breathing, heavily oiled hair and an old-fashioned high-waisted suit.

'That's him. A lorry driver. Big extrovert type. Died only recently there. Everybody knew Johnny.'

Yet although this was her father, Mairead had banged down his soup and addressed him in a cold emphatic overloud tone. 'There you are now, look. Eat that there now.' Entirely undismayed, the man turned to Martin. 'Aren't you the smart one? Aren't you at the College? Well answer me this – *who's the only man the Pope ever takes off his hat to?*' At this point Jean came into the kitchen and cried out in shocking fury, 'That's enough of that old nonsense. Don't be filling his head with a lot of old nonsense.' To Martin she spoke in her usual tone. 'Go on into the living room and we'll bring you your dinner in there in a minute.' As Martin obediently turned to leave, Johnny wheezed, in immense satisfaction, 'His *barber.*'

Shotter has gone down on one knee to investigate the radio on the floor. 'Know what I think the problem is? When you shut the lid of this thing it seems to go off – but it's not *really* off. That's why the batteries run down so fast. The thing's switched on all the time. You have to turn it off at the knob as well as shutting the lid.'

Ace physicist Ward gapes at the radio. Then at Shotter the scientifically illiterate slag.

Suddenly the door bursts open and a figure enters the room backwards. It is Mrs Ward, drawing behind her a hostess trolley with tea things, buttered scone halfs, chocolate digestives and Battenburg cake. Shotter gazes upon the abundance in ineffable wonder. Already his hostess is well pleased. Savages who cannot be kept at the gates must be dazzled by the sumptuous glories of the city.

'Just a wee cup in your hand,' she explains with a smile.

Within a few hundred yards there was a dark canal, a tower block, tenements, a scrapyard, a gas works, a car breaker's, a blackened industrial chimney, a blackened brick railway bridge, a used-tyre depot, a patch of waste ground littered with mattresses and broken-down chairs (among which a character in a woollen hat rooted and roamed), a blackened derelict factory building (displaying a huge black graffito G FAWKES IS INNOCENT), a blackened functioning factory with steam issuing from rusted vents, several dingy small companies incongruously serving the luxury market (Hairdressing & Beauty Supplies, New Image Manufacturers of Exclusive Blouses & Dresses, S & S Ellis Bridal Gowns) and finally Foremost Fabrications Ltd (not an advertising agency but a steel-erecting firm).

The area was an Urban Pastoral Theme Park entirely unaware of itself. And now a sign revealed that the accompanying waterway was the Regent's Canal where, on a westerly stretch, Clare and I walked the children on Sundays. Though the Magnificent Seven adored the fury of oceans ('Why is the spectacle of the sea so infinitely and eternally agreeable?' – Baudelaire), I preferred the slumberous glory of a pewter canal.

The plenitude ended at Salmon Lane though the Hawksmoor church of St Anne's at the bottom also had a blackened and derelict air, apparently disused and shut up, daubed with the initials of the National Front. The chunky strength of the building was undeniable, especially in view of its condition and the fact that it was surrounded on three sides by council flats and on the fourth by the maelstrom of Limehouse Road. But would I have given it a second glance if I had not been warned?

In the Tower Hamlets Library I applied for membership and, with a surge of Flaubertian pride, requested access to the French collection in the basement. The system devised for Bernard's benefit moved into action. In the pages of a great ledger I added my signature to those of the discerning few, then received the Visitor's Tally (a piece of plastic with a long metal anchor that made it impossible to shove in a pocket) and followed the librarian into the open-plan offices of the Wapping Neighbourhood Planning and Economic Development Department. The term 'open-plan' may suggest an airy carpeted spaciousness sprinkled at wide intervals with the work stations of bright attractive young staffers. Instead a small stuffy room crammed with desks and cheap shelving revealed everywhere evidence of corporate and personal squalor – heaps of files, ledgers, folders, computer printout, a small plastic radio emitting weak tinny noise and a metal tray with a kettle, a pint of milk, a milk spill, several stained coffee mugs and a half empty packet of Abbey Crunch. Ageing unlovely faces looked up in displeasure as we picked our way to the basement stairs past stacked boxes, wastebaskets, bulging carrier bags of shopping and, suspended from the ceiling, a life-size inflated figure painted as a skeleton and bearing round its neck a placard: 'Applicants for planning permission may have to wait some time'.

The librarian pointed out the light switch and left me alone on the stairs. I felt like Howard Carter entering Tutankhamen's tomb; though at first sight there was no treasure. Beneath a low ceiling made even lower by massive conduits and cables was a jumble of broken furniture and heating appliances and, further back, what appeared to be several huge wooden blocks. These were the shelves which sat on metal rails and had to be rolled apart to reveal the books. It only enhanced the thrill of excavation. Soon my hands were black, my clothes covered in dust.

When I was right down behind the last shelf, checking out Villiers de L'Isle Adam, the lights suddenly went out with a resounding clunk. Still bent over, I waited for a resumption of service. Nothing happened. I straightened and looked up. Between shelves and exit was impenetrable darkness strewn with obstacles.

There came a light cough. Someone was standing on the stairs that were the only way out. Then again silence, broken only by the soughing of the wind in the ventilator grill above my head.

For the first time the lowness of the ceiling became oppressive. I also realised that I was practically against the back wall and behind the massed ranks of rolling shelves. To be crushed by tons of French literature might be an appropriate death — but this was one irony I would willingly forego. I stepped towards the centre aisle — and tripped on the metal rail tracks. From the stairs came a low mocking laugh.

It was probably the Planning Department attempting to deter French enthusiasts.

'*Oi!*' I bellowed in fear and anger, hefting the Tally that was too long to pocket but too short to be an adequate weapon.

The lights came on to reveal the true Howard Carter chuckling with satisfaction on the stairs. 'Saw your name in the book, Martin. Couldn't resist it.'

'It's all yours.' I gathered my books and made for the stairs. 'I need to see daylight.'

Laying a detaining hand on my arm, Bernard frowned in consternation. 'But have you seen the Hawksmoor?'

'On the way here.'

'And what did you think?'

Cruelty begets fear which in turn begets further cruelty. 'Just another old church.'

'Aaaaaa ...' Bernard fell back as though struck in the face. 'Wait ... you have to ... let me just. You'll have to have another look. I'll come with you. Just let me get this one book.' He rushed off down the centre aisle talking over his shoulder. 'It's this Sartre I suddenly took a notion to read. Haven't seen it in thirty years.'

'*Sartre!*'

'He was the big man in my generation.' Bernard was thoroughly apologetic now. 'Here it is ... *La Putain Respectueuse*. Always mistranslated as *The Respectable Prostitute*. You see, it should be *The Respectful Prostitute* — this is the whole point of the play. She witnesses some crime ... maybe the murder of a friend by a client ... but can't reveal the truth. This is the heart of Sartre's philosophy. If you've been a respectful prostitute all your life you can't suddenly denounce your patrons. Of course I hate reading plays — but they're good for conversational French. How's yours coming on now that you're attending a class?'

'Extremely slowly.'

'You'll have to go to France more often.' Something in my reaction made him turn to peer at me in the gloom. 'I've never thought to ask this – *you have been to France?*'

'Of course.'

Again the response only intensified his suspicion. 'When?'

'I went to Lourdes with my mother when I was fifteen.'

In the low-ceilinged confined space Bernard's wild shout of laughter was truly demonic. 'Who needed the cure?'

'Both of us.'

We went back upstairs to run the gauntlet of the Planning Department. For once it felt good to be a schoolteacher. Who else had a week off in winter when the rest of the world was chained up in darkness and servitude? Even university lecturers, the truly blessed of the earth, had to work throughout February.

'Apparently they're angry,' Bernard murmured, 'because something was stolen recently. Of course the French fans were blamed.'

Our books checked, we emerged on Limehouse Road, raucous and choking and bellicose with the start of the evening rush hour.

'God I *love* half-term holidays!' Bernard cried. 'I suppose they're all rushing home from the City to semis in Essex.'

Instinctively I hugged my books. 'Commerce is, by its very essence, *satanic.*'

'Baudelaire,' Bernard chuckled. 'But he and his followers aren't the answer either.' He patted my Magnificent Seven volumes with the qualified affection of maturity. 'They're all crazy reactionaries. All driven insane by the virulent Catholicism of nineteenth-century France.'

'But they weren't practising Catholics. Apart from Huysmans in later life.'

'I'm not talking about *conscious beliefs*. It was an attitude that grew out of their environment. The Catholicism of the time was a unique strain ... a blend of Manichaeism and Thomist theology ... but wait ...' Suddenly seizing my arm, he darted out into Limehouse Road, weaving adroitly through traffic. I assumed we were crossing to the other side but our destination was a traffic island with an ancient public lavatory.

'It's a *Women's*,' I suggested. 'And anyway it's locked up.'

'But look.'

Through the padlocked gate it was possible to read an old sign at the bottom of the steps: *One Penny for use of Urinette.*

'Now what is a *urinette?*' Bernard demanded. 'I've never seen the word anywhere else.'

'A name for a female toilet attendant? A companion term to usherette that never caught on?'

Bernard was not interested in whimsy. 'You see, it must mean they didn't want to *crap*, just to *pee*. But what kind of contraption was it? Something like a *WC à la turque?*'

'Or a name for a Parisian whore? Urinette – Specialist in Golden Showers.'

Pursuing divergent speculations, we regained our own side of the road.

'You see, according to Manichaeism the world is the realm of the Prince of Darkness and Man is a fallen creature, essentially evil. And according to Thomas Aquinas the only purpose of existence is individual salvation. These were the two powerful strands in the Catholicism of the time.' Once again Bernard interrupted himself to seize my arm. 'But *look* . . . crocuses . . . the *first* crocuses . . .'

All over the grounds of St Anne's were the confident shellbursts of purple and white. Engrossed in eulogising wrecked cars, I had missed the first flowers of spring.

'Combine the two strands and what do you get?' Bernard continued. 'A belief that any kind of human progress is impossible and that any kind of social or communal activity is a waste of time. This was the attitude at the heart of the Catholicism of the age.'

'You say this about religion and yet you're dragging me in to look at a church.'

Bernard stopped and turned to face me in bewilderment and outrage. 'I've no interest in what goes on *inside* churches. In fact I've no interest at all in *interiors*. It's only great *exteriors* that excite me. These incredible giant open-air sculptures. I mean, look at the sweep of that.' Turning to the church, he slowly drew his arm aloft. 'The magnificent *naked strength* of the thing.' Suddenly the arm froze. 'Great God, the clock is *actually working*. How *extraordinary*.'

'I suppose it has a certain brutal presence.'

'Brutal's the right word.' Abruptly dropping his voice, Bernard looked cautiously around, as though a sensitive vicar might be lingering within earshot. 'You see, I don't think Hawksmoor was a Christian at all. He was basically a pagan. There's something dark and pagan and occult about all of his churches. Just come over here.' He led me across the grass to something else I had failed to notice – a stone pyramid bearing the legend *The Wisdom of Solomon*. 'See what I mean? Obsessed by the occult . . . by ancient Egypt.'

For once I was more interested in the Catholic than the pagan. 'Go on with your theory.'

'This brand of Catholicism determined the attitudes of the age. Our psychology is derived from belief systems – even if we no longer accept the beliefs. Even if *no one* still has the beliefs. The psychology derived from them becomes independent and self-perpetuating. So all these writers were disgusted by life and contemptuous of politics and social improvement. Hence Baudelaire's famous detestation of progress.'

'But what about the chronic boredom?' I asked. 'And why are we leaving by the back gate?'

'There's another Hawksmoor church . . . St George-in-the-East . . . only ten minutes' walk. The attitude results in boredom because all the fundamental questions about existence are settled and the pursuit of knowledge is pointless. Hence no curiosity or speculation. Also pointless is communal activity. In fact *all* activity. Inevitable result – chronic boredom.'

'And hence the urge to escape? The love of antiquity and the exotic? The fascination with the occult? The flirtation with barbarism?'

'*Plutôt la barbarie que l'ennui.*'

'Flaubert?'

'Gautier.'

'But why the obsession with style?'

'Result of the insistence on individual salvation. The only duty of the individual is to ensure that he is one of the elect. And in literature, since there can be no new meaningful content, the only way to achieve distinction is by a dazzling style.'

It was proving no easier than usual to dent a theory of Bernard's.

'Misogyny?'

'Oh that was universal. Most men were misogynists at that time.'

Not so rigorous – but the elegance of the other explanations was seductive. However, the theory had atrocious corollaries. If the thinking of the seven was based on false premises then I was attracted to them not because they were right but because I was warped in the same way (virulent nineteenth-century Catholicism persisting a century longer in Ireland). So my revolt against my background was actually a manifestation of its influence. The seven were not the doctors but the symptoms of the disease.

We seemed to be working our way down to the river. As yet it remained invisible but an astringent lightness in the lower sky suggested water beneath.

'I'm taking you down by the old dock area,' Bernard explained. 'Of course it's all being redeveloped and you can't get at the river. But Rimbaud used to hang about here when he was in London. Obsessed by ships and sailors. And of course the opium dens. This was the Chinese quarter at that time.'

Nothing oriental remained. But twilight, the cunning illusionist, was beginning to render exotic and sinister the council flats and building sites. Now that we had left Limehouse Road there was no traffic or pedestrians and no sign of life in the tenements which assumed a pent, brooding look, like a character with multiple grievances drinking slowly at the back of a bar. No longer a theme park for tourists, the area was more like an open prison for the underclass. And as light departed, February reasserted itself, creating a triple melancholy of deprivation, dusk and cold.

'So basically it all comes from one source,' I said. 'The idea of original sin. Of man as fundamentally evil.'

Baudelaire: 'All the heresies are only consequences of the great modern heresy of substituting artificial for natural doctrine – I mean the suppression of the idea of original sin.'

'All reactionaries believe in original sin.' Bernard nodded regretfully. 'And what a delightfully convenient doctrine. Not only does it absolve you from any attempt at improvement or progress, it allows you to indulge yourself ... man is evil and so must fall ... while being ruthless with everyone else – man is evil and so must be kept under firm control and punished severely as an example. But *here* ... this is what I wanted to show you. A touch of the nineteenth century – there's not much of it left.' It was a wide railway bridge with a dark and dank side tunnel for pedestrians underneath. Though Bernard lowered his voice it still echoed in the cavernous gloom. 'Now don't you just feel we're Rimbaud and Verlaine on our way to an opium den?'

Despite the electric lights in the mossy tunnel roof it was possible to entertain the fantasy. And to believe that a gang of ruffians with leaded cudgels awaited us at the other end. Instead we emerged to Swift Motors Workshop for Sick and Injured Cars which, above a lengthy list of maintenance procedures, offered the following question and answer: DOES YOUR SERVICE MAN DO ALL THIS IN HE'S SERVICE? OUR'S DOES. Below the list there was poetry, traditional in the simplicity of its message but modern in the eccentricity of its punctuation and line breaks:

> Thought . . .
> Petrol is'nt cheap
> Monies not around
> But cars that do'nt
> Get serviced!
> End up breaking down

'You'll get a powerful lot of fishing done in the next week,' Jean cries to Hugh Ward in the departure lounge of Dublin airport. 'And you're getting the weather for it too. God of heaven isn't it awful?'

But it is Eugene, gravely considering the inclement sky, who responds to Jean. 'That's only good for the fishermen right enough.'

Jean turns to her fellow travellers – Greta, Colette, Mrs Ward and Martin. 'Jesus Mary and Joseph, I hope we'll not take the fishermen's weather along with us.'

'And *you* would never think of going out fishing with your father?' Greta marvels afresh at Martin's rejection of established custom.

Mrs Ward repeats the standard excuse. 'Martin wouldn't be a great one for the fishing.'

'Too busy at the books,' Eugene chuckles. 'And you'll be doing your Senior next year, ah? But sure that'll be no problem. You'll sail through that.'

'Och he'll sail through that,' agrees Jean.

They look to Martin but he fails to react ('How rare to be detached from one's knowledge. Above us, erudition is a burden and, beneath us, a pedestal' – d'Aurevilly).

'And Pascal,' Eugene murmurs to Greta,' '. . . the *call?*'

What can he mean – 'a call'? Has the most worldly of the cousins suddenly received a mystical summons to the religious life?

'*Pascal!*' Familiar derisive explosion. 'Sure, if he'd ever even sit down a minute . . .'

'Aye.' Eugene nods in solemn sympathy. 'But maybe something else . . . the Civil Service . . .?'

'Sure where would a Catholic ever get in the Civil Service?'

Rebuffed by Greta, Eugene approaches Martin. 'Are ye watchin' that new thing . . . that detective thing in the big house . . . what's it called . . . you know the one with that character in it . . . ?'

Martin nods encouragingly ('The man of intelligence, who will never agree with anyone, should cultivate a pleasure in the conversation of imbeciles' – Baudelaire).

'Can ye follow it at all at all? I can't make head or tail of it. I watch it, ye know, but' – here he peers exaggeratedly over Martin's shoulder – 'I end up sayin' to meself *that's a nice bit of stuff.*' For a moment Martin believes that Eugene is confessing to a prurient interest in actresses. 'Ye know, a nice bit of stuff on the mantelpiece behind them.'

As Eugene intensifies his pantomime of peering at background antiques, Martin is filled with an overpowering desire to be off. At last the flight is called, the men are left behind with a final flurry of warnings ('Watch yourselves in that wet on those old twisty Free State roads') and Martin can share with the women the delirium of departure. All through the flight and the transfer to the hotel, the four sisters giggle and shriek like schoolgirls.

'God forgive me and pardon me, Colette, but isn't that wee priest the image of Mickey the turf man?'

'And who would your woman be over there, Greta?'

'Sure that's a sister of Danny Hegarty's. Och ye know Danny, Jean, he was always very great with the Vaughans.'

'But did you see the way the passport man looked at you and Martin, Josie? I think he thought . . .'

'Oh God forgive ye, Colette.'

'Lord would ye feel that *heat.*'

'We'll not be worth tuppence in that.'

'We'll all be *melted.*'

'We certainly didn't bring the fisherman's weather.' Martin's drollery so convulses Jean that she has to seize the youth for support, actually leaning her head on his shoulder and seriously disarranging her new honey perm.

'Has anyone a brush on them at all at all? Glory be to God Ah'm like the Wreck o' the Hesperus.'

It is late at night when they arrive in the town which appears to consist solely of hotels. Morning reveals this as an illusion. Only half of the premises are devoted to accommodating pilgrims. The other half offer for sale every object capable of bearing the image of the sorrowful virgin in the grotto. And as if the permanent shops were not enough, the roadway in front is lined with stalls peddling yet more grotto-inscribed keyrings, pens, wallets, knives, candles, confectionery, barometers, corkscrews and plastic Holy Water bottles of every conceivable shape and size ('In Lourdes the Devil has quietly intervened to ensure that nothing decent is offered to Our Lady: that is his vengeance' – Huysmans).

Martin is appalled – but the rest of the party maintain their girlish holiday high spirits. Boldly Colette removes her cardigan to reveal a 'wee sun top' that exposes arms and shoulders already golden from an excursion to Malta.

'Lord, Colette, you got a grand bit of sun.'

'Och sure I was hardly out in it at all. Eugene can't stick sun. I could hardly get him to shift out.' Nevertheless she evaluates herself afresh. 'I suppose I did get a wee pick, right enough.'

'I never got a *blink* of sun this year.' Jean regards her own pale arms in regret and displeasure. 'Never got out much. With Greta not being well and that.'

'Och sure I was *grand*,' Greta objects. 'You could have got out *rightly*. Sure who was keeping you in but yourself?'

From one of the stalls Colette selects a jug on which the image of the grotto is more than usually discreet. Martin, brought along as interpreter, is suddenly terrified at the prospect of being required to haggle in French. How to translate, 'Is that the best you can do for us?', 'Och sure ye'll knock a wee bit more off', 'And what would ye make it if we took the two?'

Greta is outraged by the price. 'Och ... *Colette* ... have ye no wit at all?'

'Sure I *know* ... but I need some wee thing for Eugene's mother.'

Colette buys the jug and mischievously thrusts it at the youth. 'A wee birdie told me that Martin Ward *loves* ornaments.'

Like a vampire before the Christ, he retreats with a vicous snarl that makes the women shriek in delight.

'Martin loves the ornaments!' Jean echoes.

'As true as God,' cries Mrs Ward, 'it's no joke, Jean. He'd be happy as Larry on bare boards and eatin' his dinner off an orange box.'

'*Carry it for me!*' Colette pushes the article directly into Martin's chest.

'Oh stop, Colette . . . *stop.*' Mrs Ward has one leg tightly crossed over the other. 'Sacred Heart of God . . . *stop.*'

Even Greta is prepared to forgive the criminal extravagance. 'Oh Colette . . . you're the best laugh . . . Lord but you're good value, Colette.'

Martin is tempted to reveal that, of the sixty-five certified Lourdes miracles, *not one has been granted the Irish*, an incredible statistic in view of the hundreds flown in daily by Joe Walsh Tours ('God is a scandal – a scandal which pays' – Baudelaire).

Desperate for secular reward, he scans the shop fronts and eventually discovers a window displaying men's clothes and in particular an elegant pair of French trousers. He brings his mother to look – but just as she shows signs of indulging him Colette comes across. Herself a youngest child, Colette has always maintained a keen interest in youth.

'*That much?*' she cries. 'For a pair of *trousers?*' I don't think Eugene ever paid *half* that for trousers. Why would you spend that on trousers?'

*Why?* Because the dandy should aspire to be *uninterruptedly sublime.*

'Ye'd get as good cheaper at home,' Mrs Ward says weakly and, as they rejoin the others, 'we might get a few hours in Dublin on the way back.'

'Och Dublin . . . sure *Dublin* . . .' Greta shakes her head in disgust, not merely at the appalling deterioration of the fair city but at the necessity of having to explain another self-evident truth. 'Dublin now . . . sure Dublin's gone . . . sure ye wouldn't . . .'

'Can we do Dublin on the way back?' Martin urgently asks his mother.

'We'll see, Martin. We'll see later. We'll see. We'll see.'

'I don't know about the rest of you,' Jean says, 'but I need a drop o' tea.'

Martin indicates a café, another rare relief in the chain of souvenir shops, but the women recoil from the spectacle of a burly Frenchman at a window table cutting bread with a pocket knife. Instead they proceed down the hill to the Cité Religieuse, the sprawl which has accumulated around the grotto, and here refresh themselves in a pilgrim's cafeteria where they are served by a clerical student from Carrickmacross, 'a *lovely* young fellow', Colette repeats in a significant tone, implying that this modest youth would never demand outrageously priced French clothes. Martin resentfully enquires why an interpreter is needed. At least the *pâtisserie* is French. He consumes a large custard tart with aggressive relish. Much to his surprise, Greta offers to buy him another. Then a third. When it arrives she is convulsed by laughter. 'He could eat those buns to a band playin', Josie.'

Martin suddenly recognises *an attempt on his life*. The most cunning and deadly tactic of the sisters is emasculation by overfeeding, the death of a thousand prime cuts. At once he feels acutely the terrible shame of his situation, indeed of his very nature ('Men brought up by and among women are not at all like other men' – Baudelaire).

He turns to his mother. 'Can I go to Biarritz for a day? There's a coach trip advertised in the hotel. They make you up a packed lunch.'

'Ohhhhhh . . .' Colette comes forward in mischievous attention. 'I see now why he wanted the trousers. He's gettin' an eye for the girls, Josie.'

'Don't be skitin' around after girls,' Greta snaps. 'Sure aren't ye time enough for that? Get all your degrees first and let them run after *you*.'

'*I* know what *I'll* do.' Turning directly to Martin, Colette places her elbows squarely on the table and leans softly towards him. '*I* might just go along as *well*. How would you like *that*, Martin? Just the two of us. I could do with a bit more colour.' With her palms she gently caresses golden plump upper arms. 'I should have packed *my bikini*.'

Archly she watches him. Martin can neither move nor speak.

Terrible nameless things tempestuously contend within. At last she turns to his mother. 'He doesn't want to go out praying with the old ones, Josie.'

'Cary Grant's there at the moment,' Martin suddenly blurts out to Colette, regretting the remark as soon as it is uttered. To those who reveal nothing, nothing must ever be revealed.

Colette laughs in victorious delight. 'Well in that case it's a *must*.'

'He's staying in some hotel or other,' Martin adds lamely. Now the inner turbulence has abated, leaving a viscid toxic residue and a ghastly sensation of emptiness. Despairingly he attacks the third custard tart.

'You needn't worry.' Colette turns to him again. 'The old ones are doing the Stations of the Cross tomorrow. I don't suppose you'll be wanting to go up a hill on your knees with us.'

'And in this *heat*,' Greta sighs.

'We'll be *sweltered* out on that hill,' Mrs Ward grimly predicts.

'It's bad enough today,' says Jean. 'Will we even get a decent sleep this night itself? I was up to all hours with the heat last night. I had a night like a week, look see.'

'Talking of heat, Josie,' Colette suddenly cries, 'did we never tell you about being nearly baked alive out the new road? That hot hot Sunday . . . a couple of weeks ago . . . och you remember it . . . that hot Sunday. Greta and Jean and myself were out on a run . . . giving Mairead a bit of driving practice really . . .'

'Oh Mairead and the driving.' Jean rolls her eyes in comical suffering. 'Mairead and those hill starts.'

'Anyway, Josie, didn't we break down out the new road. We were stuck out there nearly an hour in hot sun . . . nearly *baked alive* . . .'

'Parboiled.' This *mot juste* from Greta.

'But eventually this man took pity on us, a civil being he was, right enough, stopped and got the jacket off and the bonnet up and started whalin' away . . . and fair play to him, he had us going again in ten minutes. So we thanked him and started off again and next thing we looked up and there he was drivin' alongside wavin' and shoutin' out of him like a *madman*. So of course we all waved back . . . *and he nearly had head staggers, look see.* He nearly had head staggers, Josie. Nearly put us all into the ditch. *What in under God is wrong with his head*, says Greta and then Jean lets a roar out of her,

*Sacred Heart of God, Greta, we're away with the man's jacket.* He put his jacket in the back seat, ye see, and *didn't we drive off with it . . .* never thinkin', Josie, ye know? And it a good suit jacket! I suppose the man was on his way to *church* or something.'

Now all the sisters laugh in delight at an anecdote confirming so many basic truths – that reckless insouciance is always leading them into situations which irrepressible high spirits soon transform into adventures, that men, while necessary for practical matters, are essentially naive and ludicrous, that formal dress is an absurdity in a random universe and that only unsophisticated dullards go to church on the sabbath.

Yet the rest of the day is spent on ritual observances in the Cité Religieuse. Only in late afternoon, when the women return to the hotel to rest, is Martin free to explore the original town on the other side of the hill. First the stalls, peter out, then the souvenir shops, and soon he is in a quarter of broken-down stone walls, winding alleys and dilapidated houses with electricity cables pinned to the walls and washing draped from windowsills. Over the entire area is an increasingly strong odour of rotting vegetables marinaded in urine. About to turn back, he comes upon a signpost for the birth-place of Bernadette Soubirous and is momentarily startled by the possibility of a rival Bernadette. It has never occurred to him that the saint had a surname, much less a home on the wrong side of town.

Returning to the hotel by a different route, he makes another discovery – a hunting shop in whose windows are handguns, shot-guns, rifles with telescopic sights, long knives like mini-scimitars with cruelly curved blades and, in a violently exciting combination of the medieval and modern technologies of death, a crossbow loaded with a traditional arrow, but attached to a rifle trigger and stock. Never a great one for the fishing, he could easily take to the hunt. With the contents of this window many unremarkable pil-grims could be elevated to the status of martyrs for the faith.

Nevertheless, evening finds him once more docile and solemn, queuing up at the Grotto with the women to deliver to Bernadette bulky packages of special requests. Seeing this unique documenta-tion about to pass from his reach, the sceptical Martin is tempted to pray for a miracle of his own – the gift of X-ray vision.

Slowly they shuffle forward with bowed heads, Martin bringing up the rear behind Colette, a black mantilla subduing the vivid blonde streaks of her perm and a crocheted shawl in loose and tasteful reverence on her olive shoulders, like tissue paper round a gold necklace.

Mrs Ward turns back. 'Martin, could you make a special request for Pascal?'

Does she think he can involve himself in this? 'Request for what?'

'That he gets a call.'

'What do you mean – *a call?*'

As so often, it takes all her patience to suffer the questions. 'A call to *training*,' she hisses fiercely.

Guessing that she means teacher training, Martin skips to the next question. 'But if his exam results weren't good enough what's the point of a special request?'

Were it not for the sanctity of the surroundings her hiss would surely be a scream. 'Because he might get a *late call*. He might get a *late call*. He might get a *late call*.'

Possibly affected by the gathering twilight, Martin has a sudden vision of a ghostly teacher-training Principal eerily calling up from the street to a bedroom window, '*Paaaas . . . caal . . . Paaaas . . . caal.*'

Straight and purposeful as a cavalry column, there approaches a line of stern uniformed nurses pushing wheelchairs with invalids whose pallid features glow with a ghastly phosphorescence in the deepening dusk. The queue of the broken-in-spirit parts to let the broken-in-body pass and Colette steps back into Martin, engulfing him in a sudden wave of fragrance. Before his eyes is the nape of her neck with a down like the fur on a ripe peach. Below that, her tawny skin glows through her shawl ('Have you noticed that a piece of sky, glimpsed through a basement window or between two chimneys, gives a more profound idea of infinity than a panorama seen from the peak of a mountain?' – Baudelaire).

As little-appreciated as the morning sun was Rani's burnished-gold beauty. We came to work on the same train but since, like all the regular travellers, she always chose the carriage nearest her eventual exit, it was possible to avoid her by keeping to the other end of the train and hanging back among the crowd. No doubt this sounds churlish but, for the weary and careworn

117

breadwinner caught between the demands of family and work, even half an hour in a herd of commuters can provide the oxygen of detachment and autonomy.

After my help with Seymour, Rani had taken to waiting by the exit with a radiant smile. Did she wonder why I was always at the wrong end of the platform? Probably not. Although by profession a teacher of Science, Rani appeared to be uncorrupted by the mania for explanations.

'I've something for you,' she said at once in typically innocent and candid delight.

'Ach ... ?' Bear in mind that it was eight-thirty on a blustery Thursday morning in March.

Seizing my arm as we descended the station steps, she put her lips next to my ear. 'I've got you some *great stuff.*'

Now my long apprenticeship to understanding was revealed as a waste and a sham. '*Hah?* Records, you mean ... music ... tapes?'

*Hypocrite lecteur,* you who would also wear the jaded mask of aristocratic omniscience and surfeit, spare a groan for the hick heart we all bear within.

'No!' she cried in sudden anger and outrage, pulling away in disgust. 'I mean *dope* for Crissake.'

If you have tears shed them now. Weep for Daddy Cool unmasked, humiliated, undone.

'Yeah yeah,' I babbled at once. 'That'd be great. *Sure.*'

Of course it was too late. The mischievous gaiety was gone, replaced by a frown of irritation. 'It's Paki Black,' she said, after a time. 'Really great stuff. The best.' Then, after another pause, in a tone of rue. 'I've been waiting for something really good.'

'I do appreciate it.' I reached out to lay a reconciling hand on her arm. 'Have you got it with you?'

No sooner was one blunder pardoned than I committed another.

'*With me?*' Again she pulled away, this time in total disbelief. 'You don't think I'd bring *stuff* to *work?* You don't think I'd bring it into a *convent school?*'

A hopeless flapping of hands was the only possible response. Words would only plunge me deeper in the mire.

'I'm going out to a club tonight. I'll drop it off at your flat on my way.'

Now it was my turn to register violent disbelief and dismay.

Imagine Clare opening the door on a beautiful, exotic and sophisticated night-clubber seeking her husband.

But the woman who opened the door was not the old possessive, insecure and frightened Clare. Instead a confident free spirit greeted Rani in the relaxed and casual manner of the emancipated and equal. It was I who was fearful and flustered, scurrying about the lounge kicking battered toys behind chairs and generally trying to minimise the squalor and shame of child-rearing. At least the nappy bucket was empty and the children themselves in bed asleep.

'Lovely flat!' Rani cried immediately on entering the lounge. But it was she who was lovely, the drab brown suit she wore to work replaced by tight black trousers of some shiny satin-like material and a short fur jacket open on a V-necked blouse of purple silk, the unruly hair that was usually pulled back in a clasp now washed and styled and cascading over her shoulders in abundant untrammelled glory. And as remarkable as her appearance was the cordiality of her manner.

'*Love* your jacket,' Clare murmured, touching it lightly in reverence.

'Picked it up in Ken market for a fiver.'

Clare received the jacket and laid it reverently across her arm. 'Can we get you something to drink?'

A bold invitation, considering what was available. Rani hesitated, assuming a wince of apology that convinced me she was about to order a cocktail for which we had none of the ingredients. In this home the happy hour was the sixty minutes after the children went to bed and before we ourselves passed out on the sofa.

'There isn't much choice,' I warned.

'Actually what I'd *love* ... is a *smoke*.' Her wince intensified. 'I have my own though.' Rummaging in a handbag like an old-fashioned school satchel, she produced two tiny packets wrapped in silver paper, one of which she handed to me before beginning to open the other.

Clare displayed an intuitive etiquette that filled me with gratitude and respect. 'No no no no. Put that away. We'll use ours. But you'll have to give us a demo.'

'We can use my cigarette papers.' On the glass coffee table Rani demonstrated how to burn a hard pellet to produce a powder to mix with the tobacco. It was a model science lesson with each step carefully and clearly explained, pupil comprehension checked by enquiring looks at each of the class.

Now I cursed my stubborn defiance in refusing to smoke with Tony Shotter. Both girls were ex-smokers and highly amused by my attempts to inhale. But my poor technique was balanced by a perfect psychological make-up ('A temperament part bilious and part neurasthenic best facilitates this kind of drunkenness' – Baudelaire, *Le Poème de Haschisch*). I got the hang of it soon enough and we had what I never thought possible on such an occasion – a mellow scene. Rani and Clare lolled side by side on the sofa, sighing with pleasure and occasionally glancing at me in amusement ('Nymphs with radiant flesh gaze at you from great eyes more limpid and deep than sky or sea' – *ibid*). In the act of coolly passing the joint to Clare, Rani suddenly sprang to her feet and rushed across the room ('There develops that mysterious and temporary mental state in which the profundity of life, teeming with manifold problems, is revealed in whatever sight, however natural and trivial, happens to come before your eyes' – *ibid*).

'You have The Diodes' LP!' She crouched to the batch of records stacked in an alcove. 'This is a great album. I love "Death in the Suburbs" and "Plastic Girls".'

'I have their single too,' Clare said complacently, neglecting to mention that the records belonged to someone else. '"Tired of Waking Up Tired".'

Rani riffled excitedly. 'And The Dead Boys ... great stuff ... "Young, Loud and Snotty".'

'Also their single – "We Have Cum for Your Children".'

Rani looked at me in grave accusation. 'You never told me you had this sort of stuff.'

Total concentration on the joint permitted me to respond with an equivocal shrug. If I did not reveal the ownership of the records presumably Clare would not mention my aversion to the music.

'Martin hates all this stuff,' she said. 'It's only me likes it.'

'They can't play,' I was forced to explain. 'They can't sing. There's no tunes.'

'Yeah,' Rani agreed, 'but apart from that it's wonderful.'

Both of them laughed so abrasively that I felt entitled to Bogart the joint – but before I could inhale again Clare repossessed it.

My need to take them down a peg was overwhelming. 'Isn't

New Wave entirely a male thing?'

'Not at all,' Rani protested. 'The Slits are an all-girl band.'

'So are The Raincoats.'

'And there's Poly Styrene of X-Ray Spex.'

'Penny Rimbaud of Crass.'

I knew of Tom Verlaine, guitarist with Television (single: 'Love Comes in Spurts') – but I had never cared for the original Verlaine. Using the Kid's name was different. 'Penny Rimbaud,' I groaned, 'of . . . Crass.'

'What about it?' Clare snapped.

'Kleenex!' Rani cried. 'Another all-female group. Swiss, they are. Really good.'

Now I had to concede. If New Wave had penetrated Switzerland it would certainly conquer the world.

Clare passed the joint to Rani and went to the records.

'Just one number!' Rani cried, getting to her feet. 'I'll have to go.'

Clare put on 'White Riot' and the girls became rapt and immobile, two wood nymphs transfixed by an evil spell.

Despite the soothing effect of the drug I had a feeling of unworthiness and shame. This New Wave revolt lacked the talent and style of the French avatars – but at least it was energetic, open, unafraid.

Rani was putting on her jacket. 'Thanks for the smoke.'

She seemed to have an English self-discipline with stimulants. But Clare and I were children of Erin where the need to forget is chronic and oblivion is the only closing time.

'Make us another of those,' I said when Clare returned from seeing Rani out.

'You know I'm going out myself in a minute?'

'Why do you think I need another?'

'Now now now.' Cannily allowing time for negative thoughts to dissipate, Clare bent diligently to the task and selflessly presented me with the result. 'Not as neat a job as Rani's.'

For once Erin's motto seemed wise: 'Sure it'll do rightly.'

'She's very attractive, isn't she?' Again I was glad of the joint as a way of evading verbal response. 'Do you fancy her?'

I exhaled as slowly as possible. 'She's too much like the old you.'

'Which is?'

'Bad-tempered, emotional, possessive, demanding. I don't think I'd have the energy or the patience again.'

'She seems to be very fond of *you*.'

'How could you tell? She hardly spoke to me.'

'These things are always obvious.' Calmly Clare received the joint and deeply inhaled. 'Why don't you go out with her some time?'

Now she too used the act of smoking to frustrate my incredulous scrutiny. '*What?*'

'Take her out some time.' She exhaled long and deliberately as though to ease the fraught silence with her mellow used smoke.

'Does this unique offer apply only to Rani? Or can I go out with the woman of my choice?'

'Whoever you like.' Clare was the very model of relaxed sixties tolerance. 'Doesn't even have to be a woman.' Sensing that this was a great exit line, she rose, gathering up papers, tobacco and Paki Black.

'Wait a minute. *Where are you taking that?*'

'Nick loves a good smoke. And you're hardly going to sit here getting stoned on your own.'

'You're taking *my dope* . . . taking *my dope to Homewrecker?*'

'I've got something for you instead.'

Another mystery gift from a beautiful woman. This was turning into quite a day. She led me across to the kitchen, opened the fridge door and indicated a gold *pâtisserie* box tied with blue ribbon. 'A French fruit tart from Maison Bertaux.'

With my pleasure taken care of, she donned the black biker jacket and followed Rani into the festival of the night.

At least it gave me the opportunity to play my own records. 'Under the influence of hashish,' said Baudelaire, 'music speaks to you of yourself and recites the poem of your life.'

This evening's poem had Rani reclining in indolent wantonness while caring supportive Nurse Clare tenderly helped me to mount.

The impulse to toss off was almost overwhelming but I saved myself for Clare's return.

Midnight came and went. Then one o'clock. By one-thirty I was dozing off on the sofa though when I went upstairs the bedroom ceiling was as cold and disconcerting as the firmament. And when I went to the window, the street too had an unfamiliar menacing look. We complain of being smothered by the blanket of habit – but remove it and the world is immediately hostile and sinister.

Some time after two there was a rattling at the door. I darted to the window – but too late to see.

'Honey, I'm sorry . . . *really sorry*.' Clare blundered into the bedroom dewy-eyed with contrition. 'We met these friends of Nick's and went back to their place. I only meant to have one drink – but I crashed out on the sofa.' She sat down heavily on the bed. 'I was *furious* with Nick when I woke up . . . insisted on coming straight home.' Consoled by this late rectitude, she pulled off her boots and dropped them on the floor. Then stood up to pull down her jeans but lost her balance and fell back on the bed.

'I was *worried*.' Entirely lacking the intended warmth, my tone was disapproving and peevish.

'Aw . . . *honey*.' She stretched out a vague hand, then resumed her struggle with the jeans.

This clumsy undressing was more provocative than a strip. Lust was a dangerous new ingredient in the cocktail of toxins.

'I was *worried sick*.' The attempt to disguise anger as concern no more successful than before.

At last she disposed of the jeans. 'You've no need to be.'

'What do you mean . . . *no need?*' Hearing the vindictiveness of my tone gave me no power to soften it. 'You're out to all hours drunk in these rough pubs . . . full of unattached violent yobs desperate for women.'

'No one would dare to make trouble with Nick.' She giggled secretly. 'If you saw him you would know that.'

'You mean he's some kind of yob himself?'

'Just incredibly protective. He has his hand on me almost all the time.' In her exalted state she seemed to think I would be reassured by this constant proprietary touching. 'But he's not in the least violent. A very gentle guy in fact. And he thinks you're great. Thinks you're amazingly tolerant. Thought it was really funny you calling him Homewrecker.'

Flattery is a ploy never neutralised by detachment and never weakened by repetition. Not even the sternest adept of Crag or Cross is immune.

Immediately my tone was less acerbic. 'But a woman . . . alone . . . drunk . . . *at this hour of the night?*'

'He always brings me home.'

'You came in alone.'

'He waits at the corner till I'm safely in. I'll tell him it's all right to come to the door in future.'

'But you have to go out on your own to meet him.'

Lifting the jeans, she rooted in a pocket and tossed onto the duvet what appeared to be a lipstick container.

A picture is worth a thousand words – and an exhibit is worth a thousand pictures. I had no choice but to pick it up. 'What's this?'

'An anti-rape device.' Now there was actual triumph in her tone. 'Nick got it for me.' And, having established the case for the defence, she threw back the duvet in a gesture which was perhaps too dramatic and revelatory. 'Aw honey . . . *at this time?*'

'I've been wide awake.' It seemed impossible to avoid sounding plaintive. 'Upset in every way.'

'But you know I'm too drunk to do anything.' She regarded the engorged organ with a look of infinite compassion and regret, like a mother consoling a beloved child for a cancelled birthday trip to the circus.

Then her tender countenance slowly began to descend, triggering a new cause for alarm.

'*It may not be too clean down there, honey.*'

Whether she did not hear or chose to ignore the warning, the gentle descent continued until comforted and comforter were one.

As with all major pleasures the physical sensation itself was only part of the experience. Equally important were the notion of being serviced and the ability to observe all the service details. (For we incorrigible *viewers*, the missionary position has become less attractive because it makes it so difficult to participate *and* watch.) No wonder cocksucking features so prominently in contemporary American fiction. For passive consumers in a service economy, fellatio is inevitably the king of pleasures as well as the pleasure of kings. (Probably a French intellectual has related the growth of the oral obsession to developments in late capitalism.)

Already the exquisite imminence was upon me. I groaned out a warning – but, instead of sparing herself, Clare made the commitment irrevocable, drawing more deeply and purposefully on the shaft while reverently hefting the scrotum like a miner's sack of gold dust.

As both service and spectacle it was exemplary. I was grateful, profoundly grateful. And yet it revealed the chimerical nature of our modern obsessions. In some crucial way it was not as fulfilling as the basic act.

We lay in silence for some time. I thought Clare must be asleep but suddenly she pulled her face up to mine.

'You're *so good*,' she murmured, imparting a kiss as sincere as the message, though what I registered was neither the touch nor the words but the shocking ammoniac tang of my own semen on her lips.

# 4

'Now,' the bishop said solemnly but with the understanding and sympathy of the experienced confessor, laying both palms flat on the table and leaning forward as though actually welcoming blows to demonstrate Christian forgiveness, 'what I'm here for is to listen to your problems, complaints, difficulties, etcetera. Whether about the school here' – he raised one palm briefly to indicate the immediate environment – 'or even the diocese in general. Of course I may not be able to offer *immediate* solutions . . . or even long-term solutions . . . but what I *can* promise to do is *listen carefully.*' He thrust his head further forward. 'So *don't be afraid to speak up.*'

With an expectant, frank and humble air he slowly scanned the assembled staff. On either side of him Sisters Stan and Joe sat in absolute immobility, their expressions austere and remote as the death masks of Caesars. The staff before them were equally still. Not a shuffle, not a cough, not a murmur, not a sigh. Only one sound broke the silence – from the convent garden, heartbreakingly innocent, the song of the first birds of spring.

Eventually the bishop turned to Stan. 'I think they've all lost their tongues, Sister.'

Not only the power of speech, the power of motion had also gone. Interpreting literally a concern to avoid rocking the boat, we were as rigid and still as if at sea in an eggshell with a top-heavy mast. It occurred to me that, like most of the staff in the room, I had no idea of this man's function or powers. What precisely was his role in the school and what could he do to me if he chose?

'Well I'm not rushing off just yet,' he consoled us. 'So if anyone wants an informal chat . . .' He turned to Joe. 'I think there'll be . . .'

'There's refreshments in the library,' Joe announced, recovering her habitual good humour.

Like children released by a bell, the audience immediately burst into animated movement and speech, noisily surging down the corridor to the library where tables were set out with snacks and drink. On these occasions it was customary for male staff to run the bar. The nuns would have liked to see me throw off my jacket, take up a position behind the bottles and glasses and, leaning towards our distinguished visitor, enquire, with that mixture of bright-eyed enthusiasm and purposeful energy so attractive in an underling: 'White or red for you, Bishop?' Instead I went to the window, a pathetically minor rebellion necessary to preserve some shreds of self-esteem. Though it was also true that the garden was superb at the moment, the glory of the blossoming trees all but obscuring the turgid bulk of the Victorian wing. Like the church it served, the school was a dark forbidding old block with a bright new front end.

A glass of wine was placed in my hand.

'Impressed by the bishop?' Janet asked.

Battered shiny black suit, bald head with a wayward comb-over, small congested face in which features crowded together as if for mutual support – the man was more like a harassed Irish subbie than a Prince of the Church. 'Bishops aren't what they were.'

Our own Bishop Farley (the one related to my father) had an opulent puce-trimmed soutane with a puce-lined cape, a chunky numinous ring with a large stone, magnificent well-coiffed silver

hair and, the most important attribute of the public figure, an oro-
tund speaking style that made the most banal of statements seem
profound. Every September he came to address the pupils of the
College: 'For some it is their first year.' Pause. 'For others it is their
last . . . and *final* . . . year.' Longer pause. 'For *all* . . . it is an . . . *important* year.' Immense authoritative pause. And every Easter I had to
visit him in the Parochial House, my scrubbed ears ringing with
maternal reminders and warnings ('Don't be pullin' down your
socks', 'Don't be eatin' sweets on the way', 'For the love of God
don't forget to kneel and kiss his ring'). Admitted by the orphans
who served the house (possibly the same age as myself but so alien
and weird that no communication ever passed between us), I would
be ushered into a dark sombre room where, lost in the mighty armchairs designed for laymen of substance, I waited for His Grace to
burst upon me, soutane aswing and face abeam, confident in the
natural affinity of holiness and innocence and as resolutely jovial as
a television chef. But when we had moved to his opulent private
chambers and chocolates had been distributed from the largest box
I had ever seen (next to it a four-legged silver cigarette case like a
model for an emperor's sarcophagus), the going was often heavy
enough and he would glance about wildly, as if to complain, *Surely
Christ's little ones were never as taciturn as this?*

'Actually I'm related to a bishop, Janet.'

'*Really?* My father was a minister . . . C of E.'

'You mean you're a *Protestant*.' I fell back in mock alarm. 'My
bishop took a dim view of mixing with those *not of the fold*. Even
more dangerous than dancing after midnight.'

'Can't do anything about being born Protestant. But I was married to a Catholic for fifteen years, if that's any consolation. A Polish
Catholic. Not that it was a happy experience.'

'Don't say anything against the Polish Catholics, Janet.'

'Why not?'

'Because where would we be without them? They make the Irish
seem liberal.'

When she laughed her awkwardness and tension momentarily
disappeared. But, as with the sexual climax, a paroxysm of laughter
is often followed by melancholy. She sipped the sweet Liebfraumilch with a mournful distracted air.

'It was a terrible marriage . . . but in many ways those early years

were the best of my life. Piotr taught astronomy at Columbia ...
Columbia University, New York. At first I was lonely and terrified. Then I discovered that Faculty wives could attend any classes
in any subject. I went to everything ... literature, history, philosophy, politics ... these world-famous teachers, you know ... some
of them just show-offs but others brilliant ... *absolutely brilliant.*'

For once the lost paradise sounded worthy of the name. To sit
without obligation at the feet of the masters! It would never be possible – but at least I had found someone who shared the dream. For
most of those who exhorted me to academic success secretly
despised learning and knowledge. Often not even secretly. The
bishop, for instance, was openly dismissive of academic achievements and told a cautionary tale of two clerical students, one a genius capable of composing Latin odes at the drop of a hat and the
other a football-crazy extrovert who had trouble with every exam.
Which one made the better priest? The footballer of course.

'And in the end I even got teaching work myself,' Janet was saying. 'I have a pretty good degree from Cambridge. So I was established as a university teacher, all I had to do was keep at it. But then
of course I got pregnant ... was out of it for a lifetime ... and you
can never get back in, especially in English. But maybe you know
the feeling?' *Know* it? It haunted me like a murdered bride. I too
once had a foot on the university ladder, teaching part-time and
researching for a doctorate. 'So now I'm stuck here ... for good
by the looks of it.'

The world is full of morose aristocrats trapped in demeaning
employment.

For instance Jean-Marie-Mathias-Philippe-Auguste, Comte de
Villiers de L'Isle Adam, the only authentic aristocrat of the seven,
with an unbroken line going back to the tenth century and including a Marshal of France who captured Paris from the Armagnacs in
1418 and the founder of the Order of the Knights of Malta who
held in check Suliman II at the head of an army of two hundred
thousand men. Unfortunately the crucial ancestor, his father, was a
lunatic who squandered the remains of the family fortune buying
up old castles in Brittany to search for buried treasure. Undeterred,
the young Villiers ('He who does not from birth carry his own
glory in his heart will never know the meaning of that word')
applied for the throne of Greece, vacant after the deposition of Otto

I and in the gift of the protecting powers, France, England and Russia. After an interview with a startled Napoleon III he was sure the Emperor had given him a definite maybe ('Monsieur le Comte, I shall think it over') – but the job went to Prince George of Denmark. Instead the penniless Villiers, Prince of Paupers (his first play was taken off after five performances and his first novel sold twenty-three copies in twenty-five years), ended up as a sparring partner in a seedy bare-knuckle gym and after that worked for a spiritualist called Doctor Latino, playing the role of 'cured madman' in the quack's waiting room.

'Marriage,' Janet was sighing, 'what a disappointment it can be. Piotr was a brilliant man – but emotionally a child. He had an affair with one of his students ... American, very imperious and sexually demanding. Poor Piotr wasn't up to it ... so many men aren't. He used to moan to me about her and I would have to reassure him. Can you imagine it – *me* reassuring *him?*' As so often, her laugh was abrupt, equivocal and incredulous. Despite her grey hair she retained the bewilderment of a child. Even in retrospect, life was a constant surprise.

Who could say she was wrong? Villiers's love life followed the same bizarre arc as his CV. His pursuit of wealthy heiresses proving as successful as his other schemes (the key to his business failure is revealed by his gleeful plans for a new magazine: 'As soon as we have a few subscriptions we must drive the readers mad'), he ended up with an illiterate cleaning woman, Marie Dantine, whom he married on his deathbed to pass the illustrious title to their son Victor, known as Totor. Noble to the last, he begged his close friend Huysmans for one final favour – to use his position as a civil servant to alter the son's birth certificate. 'Alter it in what way?' Huysmans asked. 'Change *Profession of Mother* from *Cleaning Woman* to *Woman of Property*.'

Janet was enjoying another short but complex laugh. 'In the end Piotr could hardly do it with either her *or* me. The only way was if I sat on top ...'

This diffident schoolteacher brazenly astride, her wild grey locks tossing at each vigorous downthrust ... simultaneously dominant and compassionate ...

Seymour came between us brandishing a bottle of Liebfraumilch. Though the sweetness was cloying I was glad to be topped up – and assumed Janet would be equally pleased. Instead she covered her glass and reared like a cornered wild mare. 'No no no no . . . no more for me.'

What was she frightened of? Seymour, the bizarre mixture of knowledge and ignorance, gazed in astonishment at Janet, the bizarre mixture of fearlessness and timidity. Then he turned back to me and introduced the topic which, in the conversation of teachers, is second in importance only to weather. 'Going anywhere interesting for the Easter break?'

'No. Any plans yourself?'

'Going down to Cornwall. Right to the very end. Far as you can go without falling off hah hah.'

After Seymour, but infinitely less convivial, came Moira Sweeney carrying a plate of mushroom vol-au-vents.

'You're being *rather unsocial*,' she said to me, then turned to Janet. 'But *you're* very privileged, dear. I thought Martin only talked to *pretty young Indian girls*.'

Christ changed water to wine. Many of his followers have the gift of changing wine into gall.

Moira seemed to be leaving, then swung back. 'Isn't Gina Fabrizi in your tutor group?'

'Yes.'

'I'd like you to speak to her. Yesterday on the way home I approached her about chewing gum on the street – and do you know what she said? She said, *Outside of school speak to me properly or not at all.* As bold as could be, you know . . . a real little madame.' Swivelling to include Janet, she whispered the regrettable explanation, '*Common.*' Then laid a hand lightly on my sleeve, 'You'll have a word with her, won't you?'

A brutally effective bringing-to-earth. Few things are more resented than ironic detachment.

Even if Janet and I wished to remain aloof, this was no longer possible. Like a city growing to engulf a country village, the gathering was extending to meet us.

In the vanguard was jocular Joe. 'Ah Mr Ward, aren't you great? I saw your girls first down to assembly this morning. Getting your girls into the hall before anyone else. I noticed that. Oh yes. I saw that. Don't be thinking we don't notice!' Then, turning to involve Janet. 'Isn't he a great example to the male staff, Mrs Barczyk? Isn't it great?' Janet mumbled something, surely regretting her refusal of a top-up. 'Not that I'm criticising the male staff – far from it. In fact the other day I was talking to a Sister who teaches in Holloway. *Our* men are so *scruffy* and *casual*, she said to me, but the men of Our Lady of Perpetual Succour are always *so well turned out*.' Possessed by a strange new fervour, she turned back to me. 'Always *immaculate*, she said, always in shirts and ties and nice jackets, always *such a pleasure to see*.'

Next to us, a group containing the bishop splintered in a sudden explosion of laughter. Needless to say, Joe immediately demanded an explanation.

Apparently the bishop had just come from a nearby Catholic boys' school and discovered that its past pupils included the leader of the most notorious New Wave band. Not only that, he had been shown a report which lamented the boy's lack of progress but suggested that he might 'do better in a small group'. At this there was a fresh outbreak of laughter in which Joe gladly joined. I wondered if she fully understood – but the joke itself was not important. What excited her was the bishop's success with the joke. Not a dull remote figure but a hip today guy in touch with a happening scene.

'Actually he's Irish,' the bishop said now, methodically milking the story in the efficient way of the raconteur.

'*Ah go way!*' Joe cried, her new joy immediately tempered by dismay.

'Father from Galway, mother from Cork.'

'Isn't it dreadful, Mr Ward?' The saddened nun turned to me. 'That one of our own should come to that?'

'Concentrate on the *good* Irish, Sister,' Father Kemp coolly advised. 'The best example of all. Jesus Christ was Irish.'

Joe gripped my arm. What were they going to come out with next? Who needed New Wave when our own clergy were masters of outrage and shock?

'There are three proofs that Jesus was Irish,' Kemp began, lowering his voice so that we had to draw closer. 'First, he had *twelve* drinking companions.' As though reminded of his own glass, the priest took a quick sip. 'Second, he did not leave home until he was thirty.' The bishop could not suppress a chuckle and Kemp drew back until order was restored. As we bent our heads forward again Kemp brought his own head into the circle. 'Thirdly and lastly, *his mother thought he was God.*'

This time the explosion was so violent that the splintering was terminal.

'The bishop seems to be leaving,' Janet murmured. 'Is there nothing you want to ask him?'

'Actually I did have a question.' Without any overt consultation, Janet and I were also making for the door. 'How come one of the main themes of the Gospels – the attack on Pharisaism – can never be mentioned in a Catholic school? Of course I know the answer.' In the empty corridor it was easy to be eloquent. 'All that concerns them is the surface. This obsession with manners ... *Be polite to thy neighbour,* is all it seems to come down to. They pile icing on top of icing – but *where's the cake?*' So typically Irish: craven timidity in the presence of the powerful followed by vituperation in the presence of the powerless.

'It's not always so. My father was deeply concerned with the cake ... by which I presume you mean ethics. He was always stressing how Christ put loyalty to principle first ... especially before loyalty to family. On the two occasions when he meets his mother in public Christ is extremely brusque.'

'An even better assembly theme! *Be brusque with your mother!* The Irish, Italians and Poles would love that.'

'Another thing my father loved was the way Christ was always pointing out that you can't devise rules to cover all circumstances. The teaching was made up of principles not rules – and every response should be worked out from these principles.'

'Jesus, Janet,' I said. 'No wonder your discipline's so bad.'

She moved as though to retaliate physically – but then abruptly aborted the action which ended up as an awkward lurch. Instead she got in a sharp rejoinder. 'If you disapprove of hypocrisy why is a non-believer working in a Catholic school and *posing as a Catholic?*' A key question which soured a potentially exhilarating exit from the school. Before us was a vista of dingy factories, garish filling stations, run-down bars ... the *paradiso terrestre.* 'And what of your children?'

'What about them?'

'Are they baptised?'

'Yes.'

'So you can get them into Catholic schools?'

I could have blamed Clare – but we cannot always blame others. 'Yes.'

An extra awkwardness was introduced – and walking with Janet was never easy because of her hesitant arhythmic stride.

Anxious to make amends, she sighed deeply. 'Though I sometimes wish I'd sent my son to a Catholic school.' She turned wildly towards me. 'I mean, he rings up at midnight and says, *It's all right, Mum, I'm in Hampstead police station, Mark just got bottled.*'

I reassured her with stories of my own escapades – romping through the University flowerbeds, smashing the windows of the library, proceeding exultantly home via the roofs of parked cars. In youth a hooligan and a vandal, now a lovely caring mature responsible cultured adult man. 'Even praised by Sister Joseph as an example to other male staff.'

For some reason Janet, in deepest anxiety and gloom over her son, suddenly burst out into laughter that was neither equivocal nor brief. 'She wasn't praising you, you fool. She was telling you to *smarten up* for assemblies.' She seized the open neck of my shirt. 'Not to look casual and scruffy. To smarten up and wear a tie.'

It is true that I am obtuse about coded messages. Janet's interpretation was horribly plausible. My next thought was for the only social service ever postulated by the seven – the government-funded suicide centres demanded by Villiers who envisaged a nationwide chain of houses equipped with all means of self-destruction, including crucifixion kits 'for those who, weary of being men, desire at least to die like gods'.

The consternation and anguish on my face served only to intensify Janet's mirth. Eventually she had to lean on me for support.

It would seem to be true that women are attracted to weak men.

What was startling was not so much the fact of the embrace as the experience of her body. Pallor, slightness and grey hair suggested cold but suddenly I was enveloped in a warmth that returned me immediately to the dance halls of youth and those rare generous girls who permitted the male genitals to nestle. Janet, undervalued and neglected, would be even more giving. Now her laugh was high-pitched, incredulous – and unequivocally acquiescent. We could probably have gone straight to her flat – but Clare had to go out to work soon (this an 'up' night rather than a 'sleepover') and before she left there was the madness of preparing food and getting young children to bed.

There is an incredible rumour that, finally shocked by the half-crazed brutes it is sending out into the world, the College has hired an elocution teacher to convert its older pupils into passionate debaters and eloquent after-dinner speakers. Stranger still, it is said that this stupendous task of animal training has been *entrusted to a woman.*

Not even the most credulous believe the second half of the story. Nevertheless there is a full turnout for the opening class whose membership is as novel as its subject matter, arrogant demigods of science mingling with arts riff-raff. Scarcely has Ward got used to the novelty of sitting once more beside arts-man Shotter, than he is astounded to see enter the room a middle-aged woman with a perm and tweed costume in the style of his Aunt Colette but wearing high red stilettos which Colette would find impossibly common and exuding an aura of vestigial glamour resisting surrender to the nullity of age.

He is not surprised when she reveals that she has been on the stage and intends to teach them how to enunciate and project; her own speech another revelation – rich, honeyed, precise and detached, with none of the och-sure-now familiarity and ingratiation of local women her age ('Like diamantine pearls the notes of her voice welled from her resonant larynx and resolved their personalities into a vibrant aggregate' – Lautréamont). And for those in the front rows there is the further alarming perturbation of an elusive and sophisticated scent. Her presence in the shabby classroom is like that of a sailing ship in a bottle – no one can imagine how the feat was achieved but the incredible reality may not be denied.

However, novelty and an exquisite speaking voice are not enough to subdue brutes. Already she has made the fatal error of permitting a third of the class to loll in postures of provocative indolence. Instead of snapping at them to sit up straight like Christians she distributes brochures with speaking exercises and leads the group in a chant:

> The early bird shall get the worm.
> This proverb always makes me squirm.

She looks pointedly at Shotter. 'Not squuurrrum . . . *squirm.*'

'*Squirm,*' Shotter repeats in a high piping tone with a skilful light patina of impertinent parody.

A low chuckle goes round the room – but again she takes no action.

> The early worm, for being *first*,
> Does not *deserve* to be so *cursed*.

Now there is open laughter. Ignoring it, she gets each of them to read. When it comes to Ward's turn Shotter kicks him under the desk. Suppressing a snigger, Ward begins, 'Two tired toads trotting to Tewkesbury,' then, at another kick, breaks down into laughter immediately shared by the rest of the group.

By the end of the period everyone is sprawling in near-helpless mirth.

Yet there is also much anger. The scientists, confirmed in their scorn for the arts, are furious at this waste of precious time. And the arts men are furious at being associated with absurdity and pretension.

In the storm of contempt and abuse it is difficult to acknowledge tender emotions.

'But she's not all that bad-looking,' Ward suggests diffidently to Shotter. 'For her age, like.'

'That auld *puke!*' Shotter sneers. 'Fuckin' cobwebs on it. And *no wonder*. Be like pushin' a chipolata up the fuckin' Mersey tunnel. That auld sickener'll never see fifty again.'

'Ah but . . . not bad legs . . . ye wouldn't keek her outa bed.'

Shotter composes his disgusted expression into a grimace of terminal rejection. 'She couldn't give a hard-on to the Boston Strangler.'

Next time she has abandoned the elocution books for a stack of modern poetry anthologies – but her pupils are even more derisive and insolent. Ward can see her wince and quiver as scorn is poured on her beloved poets. One of the scientists declares outright that Wallace Stevens is a load of crap. Tremulous, wounded, a doe at bay, she suggests that they take the anthologies home and choose their own poems for recital.

Ward, who has never been exposed to modern poetry, reads the book from end to end and suffers a queer ebriety at an unlikely poem with an unlikely title: *The Love Song of J. Alfred Prufrock.*

136

Again and again he is drawn back to this piece which, by some form of sorcery, persistently lures him and subtly insinuates itself into his mind. Despite its length there is no need to memorise. Trying to escape its spell is the problem, and the thought of reading it in front of the teacher makes it difficult to concentrate on his maths. Never before has he had trouble with maths. Something strange is muddying the limpid waters of the intellect.

The following week she asks Shotter to commence with his chosen poem.

'Hadn't time,' he says with that aggressive assurance that has always been his hallmark. 'Too much other work.'

The next boy takes the same line . . . and the next . . . and the next. Then Hinds, renowned for his shrewdness and cunning in evading the impositions of authority, surprises everyone by rising. She smiles in pathetic relief – but what he recites, with a knowing smirk at his resourcefulness in choosing the shortest poem in the book, is Pound's two-line image of the faces in the Metro. At once there is a great roar of laughter and approval – for nothing is more appreciated than an expression of insolence within the rules. This is more fun than a simple refusal and so the next boy rises to recite the same two-line poem. Likewise the next . . . and the next . . . By the time it is Ward's turn she is once again trembling on the verge of collapse. In the eyes that meet his there is no longer hope – only a plea for compassion and mercy. He rises, brimming with tenderness and poetry. But this is the love that dare not speak it name. Here, no love could dare speak its name. The best he can offer is a coded note of apology in his delivery of the two-line poem.

In a broken despairing voice she announces the exercise for the following week – a speech of explanation by any well-known historical character.

By this time Shotter has compiled a profile of the woman.

'She's come home to look after her auld mother . . . think the mother had a stroke or somethin'. She was probably too auld to get work as an actress anyway . . . who wants mutton dressed up as lamb? They have one of those massive old houses in West End Park . . . you know, full of shabby genteel . . . pukes that think they are somebody but haven't a bean. She probably went round the schools begging them to let her do this eejit work – *two fuckin' tired toads trottin' to fuckin' Tewkesbury.*' Shotter pauses to light a cigarette, inhales deeply and blows his smoke into the sky with fierce dismissive satisfaction. 'Thought ye were goin' to recite a poem . . . what ye call it . . . that thing . . . Alfred Poppyfuck . . . or whatever?'

Ward laughs at such a ludicrous notion. 'Nah.'

But all week he works secretly on a monologue for Judas Iscariot in which the much-maligned apostle explains that he did not betray for money ('Bah! Barely enough for wine and a clean whore') but to prevent the inevitable disillusion when Christ's human failings are revealed to his followers. And has the betrayal not been vindicated? His heroic and selfless action has been the making of Christ the Messiah although also the breaking of Christ the Man. The true sacrifice was not that of the Cross but that of the thirty pieces of silver.

Of course Ward could not possibly read this in class. Instead he waits in the school car park and approaches the passenger window of her Mini. She leans across to wind it down with a plump quivering arm, the tight skirt of her suit riding up a little. In the back are her suit jacket, handbag and a pink cardigan, on the passenger seat a box of fluffy pink tissues and on the floor below the passenger seat, temporarily replaced by flat driving shoes, the red stilettos which Ward suddenly longs to seize and bear off to the farthest corner of the school grounds, there to crouch behind the bushes crushing them against his breast forever. However, as he bends to the window he is vanquished by the scent that envelops him ('More laden with oblivion than the fragrance of cedar slivers cloven by magicians amongst the groves of the gardens of Baghdad to shame the flowers of paradise' – Villiers). It feels as though he is entering her boudoir rather than talking into her Mini.

'Why didn't you wait to show me this in class?'

He shrugs, slightly impatient. Surely that is obvious.

Instead of reprimanding him she reaches back for the handbag and withdraws a pair of reading glasses, a revelation of a secret failing that would have torn from his lips a sob of compassion had not enchantment robbed his body of all power except that required to climb into the back seat and curl up with the pink cardie over his head.

'It's very *deep*,' she says at last, peering gravely at him over the rim of her spectacles. 'But terribly *cynical*. You're very cynical for one so young.'

Deep *and* cynical! ('Genius, transported by celestial instinct, with your proud intrepid feet you will tread the summits of the empyrean and penetrate the sanctuary of the world spirit' – Villiers).

'And very French. Have you been reading French writers?' No – but he will . . . *he will*. 'You must keep writing.'

Above the tops of the spectacles her deep dark eyes hold his ('Truly it was touching to see those two beings, separated by age, bring their souls close through grandeur of being' – Lautréamont).

In class no one will admit to having prepared a monologue so she distributes a sheet of classic speeches from Lincoln to Kennedy. Shotter skilfully turns the class into a debate on the recently dead leader.

'Kennedy achieved nothing,' he announces confidently, 'and would have achieved nothing even if he'd lived.'

From her halting emotional response it is clear that she reveres the lost leader. Nevertheless she attempts to be impartial. 'Would you care to expand on that?'

'*Kennedy?* All that liberal stuff?' Shotter utters an incredulous snort. 'Bought into politics by his da . . . *a bootlegger* . . . a *crook*.'

Derisive shouts of agreement come from the class – along with other charges against the dead president. No longer even trying to respond, she trembles and turns upon Ward, dark despairing eyes shining with liquid like violets after a summer cloudburst. Never has she seemed more lovely to him ('I do not pretend that Joy cannot associate with Beauty – but Joy is one of her most vulgar adornments while Melancholy is her most Illustrious Spouse' – Baudelaire). And never has Ward himself ached with such tenderness. He would love to be her tissues and cardie – but how can a pack dog reject the pack? Regretfully he turns his face away ('You will remain a hyena' – Rimbaud).

'Fuck *me*,' Shotter mutters with incredulous disgust, 'she's going to *cry*.'

C lare looked up with a smile from stirring a pot while, in her high chair, Lucy lunged and gurgled and banged out a greeting with her spoon. It was the perfect family welcome after a hard day at the office. Except that Paul rushed at my legs with an angry shout of accusation.

'You put my pullover on inside out. I've been wearing it

like that *all day*.'

Clare's smile remained serene. 'You must be *exhausted*.'

After another a.m. return she had spent an hour clinging to the toilet bowl as though to the spar of a foundered ship while alternately retching into the bowl and begging me not to abandon her. Sadly different from her previous late homecoming. I should have been satisfied with one gift of unsolicited fellatio – it is axiomatic that ecstasy cannot be continuous or even regular – but when has the human animal been content with a single occasion of pleasure? *More!* is the quintessential and endlessly-repeated cry of the species. I was lying awake with a brute-on till Clare finally staggered in at 2 a.m.

And of course she was out of action in the morning, leaving me to organise Paul and Lucy single-handed before departing myself for a day that bristled with demanding junior classes. Only a few hours of sleep to prepare for a full day of the callous energy and egotism of the young. Pointless to reason or beg for mercy. Empathy is available only to the adult – and is exercised by few enough of those.

Today Clare was one of the few. 'Did you have a terrible day?' she asked, leaving the pot to place on my lips a warm kiss and on my flayed spirit the unguent of sympathy.

Feeling compassionate and wise myself, I knelt to try to explain to my son the difficult concept of relative importance. 'I'm sorry about the pullover, Paul. But that isn't so bad. Imagine if your *head* was inside out all day.'

'Well it's mince curry,' Clare said. 'A break from vegetarian food.'

'Mince curry!' Paul forgot the humiliation of the pullover. 'My favourite!'

We sat to steaming plates of aromatic nourishment. 'This is so good,' I had to admit.

'It's *you* that's so good.'

Normally Clare would try to make a dish stretch to two meals – but today there were liberal seconds all round. An agreeable atmosphere of amplitude and largesse obtained. Paul told us about his day at school and even Lucy seemed to want to prolong the accord, establishing a personal-best time for peaceful endurance in a high chair.

This was the joy of family life scarcely known to the seven. Villiers was the only one to marry and the only one to have a child – the boy by the cleaning woman (though, according to Villiers, the child had been sent in a basket by a princess of superhuman beauty who had passionately surrendered to him in a conservatory during a reception at the Princess Ratazzi's). The most unlikely of fathers (his endless setbacks, debts and flits make Baudelaire seem almost successful), Villiers was actually devoted to the boy, could not bear to be parted from him for more than a few hours at a time, sent money when he was out of the country ('Buy a warm suit for Totor and get his hair cut, not too short, so that it completely covers his ears – otherwise he'll catch cold') and took him along on his nocturnal wanderings round the cafés of Paris. On the way home from one such trip Totor stopped at every pharmacist's, entranced by the coloured flasks in the windows. Then, when they were crossing the Pont des Arts, a *bateau-mouche* suddenly illuminated its red and green navigation lights. 'What's that?' cried the startled child. 'The souls of the Pharmacists taking wing,' said the father.

Totor's soul took wing when he was only twenty – but Villiers is thought to have had another son, André, by an earlier liaison. André emigrated to the Belgian Congo in 1890 and returned to die in France in 1911 but had a child by a native woman in the Congo, a son who was reported alive and well as late as the nineteen fifties. It is possible that the descendants of the illustrious line of L'Isle Adam (and of the Magnificent Seven) are living on an island in the Congo Delta.

'I didn't make a dessert,' Clare said. I waved a hand in blithe absolution. 'But you've a cake in the fridge for later.'

Even free love swiftly develops its own rituals and conventions. Now a *pâtisserie* box in the fridge meant the blues in the night.

'*What?* You're going out *again?*'

Sensing that the harmony was about to dissolve, Paul departed to watch television. Lucy threw down her spoon and began to fight her way out of the chair. Possibly glad of the distraction, Clare lifted the infant.

'It's this band Nick wants me to see, Martin. Guys who used to be at his Youth Club. They were all in trouble of one kind or another until he got them to start a band. It was just to keep them occupied – but now they're doing really well.'

'But I mean . . . *two nights running.*'

'Nick only found out about this gig today. The band's stepping in for someone else. It's a big chance for them. Nick wants a good turnout.' As so often, the fun was presented as social work.

'London's full of women. Does he have to take you?'

Adjusting Lucy, she sat down across the table and laid a hand on my wrist. 'I won't go if you don't want me to.'

This too was now part of the ritual. But even the most perfervid authoritarian dislikes resorting to force. How much more agreeable to have one's wishes discreetly understood and obeyed. Use of the heavy hand is in fact an admission of failure; authority which needs to assert itself is already undermined. Also, I could see how the evening would develop if I refused. The virtuous silent concentration on chores. The brief dutiful exchanges bleached of affection and resonance. Having spent much of my life in the company of a martyred woman (my mother), I had no desire to repeat the experience.

'When have I stopped you doing anything?' Like many other long-wed couples we could spare our vocal chords by playing prerecorded tapes at each other.

'You have nothing to worry about.' She squeezed my wrist in passionate reassurance. 'And I won't be late tonight.'

Briskly she rose and, passing me the baby, returned to the sink. What variety and eloquence are possible in even the simplest of tasks! For instance, how differently she would wash up if she had been obliged to stay home. Now she went at it enthusiastically – but with shining eyes turned to the azure sky, her whole being focused on something powerfully other. Never had I noticed such fervent tropism before. But who would not blossom on such a beautiful spring evening? To meet a lover on an avenue of trees in a crescendo of bloom and to venture out together into the fragrant fecundity of the night! In one continuous burst of achievement Clare set the kitchen to rights and swept Lucy off to the bedroom.

Usually she went out in the zipped-up leather jacket – tonight she wore only a T-shirt. Briefly she perched next to me in what was probably her nurse's bedside manner – efficient, compassionate, radiant, brisk. 'Why not ring Bernard and ask him over for a drink?'

Two creeps talking books on a spring night – *ugh!*

Instead I had another crack at Bartók – the Sonata for Two

Pianos and Percussion, described encouragingly on the sleeve as a 'masterpiece with wild and energetic rhythms'. But once again the seeming arbitrariness left me unmoved and therefore dispirited; a genuine first-rate mind would surely respond to great music. (Villiers the pauper travelled to Germany to meet his musical hero, Wagner, though the visit was ruined by characteristic bad luck – war broke out between France and Germany and Villiers was bitten by Wagner's dog, Russ.)

I was asleep on the sofa when Clare returned, aglow with rectitude and pleasure. 'See? I said I'd be early. And I'm not drunk at all. Were you asleep?'

'No no,' I snapped with the shivery peevishness of Lazarus. (Why is it impossible to imagine Lazarus happy or even goodhumoured?)

'It's great to come home to you, honey.' Again the breezy nurse cheering up a miserable patient. 'You have *absolutely nothing to worry about.*'

'Just my wife going out with a guy who's younger and better-looking than me. Also more fashionably dressed ... with more interesting friends ... a higher disposable income.' Morosely I considered Homewrecker's advantages. 'Probably a bigger cock as well.'

'*Hmmmmm ...*' Clare assumed a mock frown of recall and comparison. Then she laughed gaily. 'No ... in fact his cock is *surprisingly like yours.*'

'Another shrimp dick.'

Responding to gaiety with grudging sourness was doing me no good at all. A trained nurse could possibly sympathise with Lazarus – but no woman on earth would go down on the guy.

'You seem to think it's a competition. But Nick's not competing with you. In fact he worries about you getting a lousy deal. Having to stay in with the kids all the time.' Clare reached into her bag and laid two cards on the sofa arm like a gambler playing a winning hand. 'For me and you.'

A pair of tickets for a New Wave concert. 'Homewrecker gave these to you?'

'So the two of us can get out together.'

'But it's a Wednesday night. Bernard has his evening class. Who would babysit?'

With considerable canniness she had kept her choicest news to the end. 'Nick,' she said, coolly and proudly. 'Nick's offered to do it.'

Preserving a calm demeanour was far from easy. The guy was playing me at my own game. *Homewrecker was trying to out-civilise me.*

It took strong self-control to manage a negligent wave. 'Fine.'

Had she expected an explosion of resentment and outrage? Possibly the offer was a bluff they thought would never be called. And of course my call was itself a bluff.

But the date approached and no one backed down.

On the night Clare was visibly agitated, wanting to keep the children calm but unable to prevent herself from snapping at them, possessed by a desperate impulse to tidy but aware that, for an adept of New Wave outrage, any such preparation would be absurd. It was her first experience of a common problem – how to arrange a home to impress a bohemian.

Over six feet in height and appropriately broad in the shoulders, Nick had long hair pulled back in a ponytail over a massive Mount Rushmore head. I was fortunate to know that his genitals were not on the same scale as the rest.

At once Paul rushed at him and beat at his thighs. '*You're* not my daddy.'

Manly flesh of my flesh! Loyal blood of my blood!

'Of course I'm not.' Nick displayed great self-possession. 'Your daddy's the guy with the glasses.' Going down on one knee, he extended to Paul his right lobe. 'And I'm the guy with the earring.'

Paul, a brave prince defeated by sorcery, wonderingly touched the fool's gold.

'Now bed for you, Paul.' Flushed and confused, Clare rushed off with the child, leaving cuckold and *cicisbeo* to fend for themselves.

'Beer?'

'Terrific.'

When I turned from the fridge he was sitting back at ease on the sofa, calmly taking in the floral loose covers, white walls, Bushmills-whiskey mirror and chrome-and-smoked-glass coffee table bearing a potted rubber plant. Before I could hand over the beer he rose again to his considerable height. 'I love your glasses.' Gently he removed them from my face and turned them over in wonder. Not only rendered naked and helpless, I was sure he was also deriding the spectacles.

Now he tried them on and squinted through the window. 'What's the colour of the tint?'

'Dark blue.'

'Tell me about them.'

'Only if you tell me about your tattoo first.'

With a soft laugh he returned the spectacles, sat down and took a long drink of beer. Then he absentmindedly fingered his tattooed left earlobe. 'It's the anarchist star.'

'I'm sure that goes down well at interviews.' A remark that made me sound like some ass hole careerist.

Nick swung his glass in a relaxed expansive accepting arc. 'It's a part of my past. I don't want to disown it.' Setting down the glass, he rolled up his left shirt sleeve to reveal a substantial biceps bearing two crossed guitars. 'And this is from my time in an R & B band. I broke up the band as soon as I heard the Clash.'

'And you're no longer an anarchist either?'

'Not so much.' He chuckled darkly. 'I'm a *Situationist*.'

Never having heard the term before, I had no idea whether he was serious or making fun of me again. Certainly he was beating me at my own game. It was I who should have been chuckling in dark sardonic self-sufficiency.

'What do Situationists believe in?'

'*Cultural terrorism.*' Abruptly he leaned forward, as though to illustrate precept with practice but actually to bring the explanation down to a suitably low level. 'They bang out a great fucking T-shirt, Martin.' Just as suddenly falling back, he released a harsh burst of laughter and rewarded himself with a long drink.

For want of a better reaction I took a long drink myself.

Nick continued enjoy his own joke. 'The Situationists are a weird bunch of fuckers, Martin. And they're all over the place ... there's even been a Situationist International. It's behind the whole New Wave thing of course ... and you've Alan Suicide in America, The Kim Philby Dining Club in Cambridge, Charlie Radcliffe here in London ... though Charlie was expelled from the SI for *maniacal excesses.*' Nick paused to chuckle deeply, as though this was a heresy with which he could readily sympathise. 'He got too involved with this street gang called The Motherfuckers.' Further sympathetic chuckle and sip of beer. 'But it's mostly Europeans ...

guys like Vaneigem and Debord. It's not a complete system ... more a matter of philosophical sound bites ... but it combines avant-garde art, Marxist theory and of course' – he grinned disarmingly – '*existential obnoxiousness.*'

What would any movement be without this crucial ingredient? I nodded immediately. 'Of course.'

'You'll get all their stuff in Compendium.'

I could have rubbed shoulders with Homewrecker in the radical bookshop. No – while I was upstairs with the literary mad dog's shite, Nick would have been down below in the basement among the political nutters. Even so, how encouraging that a tattooed man would seek a theoretical underpinning in books.

Clare returned with Paul ready for bed and turned to me in slight but definite irritation. 'You look as though you're settled for the night.'

If I did not get on with Homewrecker it was because I was the jealous conventional husband. And if we did establish some rapport it was immediately a threatening male conspiracy.

Clutching his story books, Paul climbed onto Homewrecker's knee.

'Bed by eight for him,' Clare said.

'Eight o' clock,' Nick repeated with a dutiful nod.

A banal but profoundly unsettling exchange. Infatuation swiftly fades – but domestic accord can last for ever.

As the summer examinations approach, Shotter continues to loll in cinemas smoking Embassy Regal whereas Ward increasingly and gratefully devotes himself to his books ('To work is less wearisome than to amuse oneself' – Baudelaire). But when Hugh Ward begins to give Mairead driving lessons his son, recently aware of his mentally dim cousin as physically radiant, displays a sudden interest in Erin's forty shades of green.

'Going out by the river?'

'Want to come along for the run?'

The son shrugs casually. 'Yeah.'

On a tranquil spring evening they drive to the aunt house which is bathed in late sunlight and surrounded by birds warbling in an ecstasy of repletion and contentment. Mairead comes to the door in a print summer dress with a white cardie draped on her shoulders but, enchanted by the balminess of the air, removes the cardie to reveal two magnificent outposts of warm flesh protected by bare arms powerful enough to repel the most brutal of ravishers (though merely clutching two bags at the moment). Her combination of strength and abundance a revelation to the scholar ('She would have intoxicated the most austere of Greek philosophers and the most profound of German metaphysicians' – Villiers).

'*God!*' she cries out at once, 'we'll all be boiled in that car.'

Martin moves to the back seat in silence, attuned to the strange vibrant chords sweetly plucked by cool manicured hands from the harp within.

'God, Hugh,' Mairead chuckles, getting into the passenger seat (for she will not take the wheel until well clear of the town), 'say a prayer there's no cows on the road the day.'

Only when the last houses are far behind does Hugh stop and walk around the front of the car. Mairead slides across to the driver's seat, removing her white stilettos and handing them back to Martin, a devoted custodian who would willingly die in their defence. Then she takes from a plastic bag a pair of flat driving shoes which, with much grunting and chuckling, she attempts to don in the front seat. As she twists and bends the youth's inner harp is joined by an orchestra and there surges up in him a concerto of almost unendurable sublimity and power, one whose inexorably building momentum could only be halted by mashing his genitals with the terrible stylus of one of the pointed heels in his hand.

'Second!' Hugh shouts. 'Down into second!' Too late – the car has already stalled.

'Sacred Heart!' Mairead wails. 'Not a hill start already.'

'It's hardly a slope at all.' Hugh repeats the instructions – but the car bucks like a wild stallion at the first touch of the rope. 'Clutch! *Get your clutch in!* Clutch! CLUTCH!'

'Jesus, Mary and Joseph!'

'*Clutch* . . . CLUTCH!'

At last the crazed machine is brought to rest. Tongue stuck out the side of her mouth, Mairead stares in consternation at the controls. 'Wait a minute now . . . kind of a way . . . wait tay Ah see . . . now . . . *aye* . . .'

When they reach the river Hugh signals her to stop and gets out to lean on the bridge, apparently oblivious to the fisherman below on the bank.

'Here,' Mairead says to Martin, fumbling in her handbag, 'ast us somethin' outa the *Highway Code*.'

He accepts the booklet, regarding her with the calm sovereign pleasure of an inquisitor before a beautiful sorceress whose pyre he will soon put to the torch. 'What's your braking distance at sixty on a wet road?'

'Any luck?' Hugh enquires at last of the silent fisherman.

'Aaaaagh . . .' The figure shrugs wearily. 'Sure the river's destroyed with poison.'

'Aye.' Hugh shakes his head at this new breed of unscrupulous poacher. 'Those blaggards'll use anything.'

'You're a bad 'un!' Mairead cries, twisting and making as though to strike the youth. 'Ast us somethin' easy for God's sake.' And she leans over the seat to threaten him with a violence for which in fact his whole body yearns, its quivering finely tuned filaments aching for the joyous hammers of the percussionist.

'What's kangaroo petrol?'

'*Sarky* . . . oooooh!' She attempts to cuff him, leaning far over the seat. Martin seizes her right wrist. She flails with her left hand. He seizes that too and they sway in a sublime dance of life that transcends earthly measure ('There are moments of existence in which Time and Duration are more profound and the Sense of Being is enormously quickened' – Baudelaire).

'Conaghan got a twelve-pounder in Wilson's Hole.' Having acknowledged the evil in the heart of man, the sombre figure on the bank can now celebrate positive achievements.

'Is that a fact now? Spinner or fly?'

'Spinner.'

'Aye.'

As Hugh makes his way back the struggle within the car abates. Mairead appears to have been exhausted. 'Ah'm not worth tuppence in this heat, Hugh. Could you drive back . . . and we'll stop at Cassoni's on the way.'

Hugh stops as requested – but when he attempts to get out of the car Mairead seizes his jacket with a terrible shriek. '*No, Hugh . . . no no . . . wait.*' Desperately she scrabbles for her handbag and turns to her own door.

'Sit where you are, Mairead.'

'NO, HUGH!' But in the act of turning she has set him free. 'Well take this itself ... take this itself, look see.' Now she attempts to press a banknote upon him.

'I'll take no such thing.'

'Sure it's only ... *here* ...'

'At-at-all. Wafer or poke?'

'Poke ... *but here* ...' In Mairead's shrieking determination Martin suddenly sees Greta and Jean.

But when Hugh returns with the ice cream she attacks the childish cone with an infantile relish entirely lacking in delicacy or self-consciousness. Martin suddenly understands that within this voluptuous body is the mind of an eight-year-old child and that this in turn is stuffed with the prejudices and platitudes of middle-aged aunts; none of which diminishes her attraction ('Stupidity is often an ornament of beauty; it gives the eyes that mournful limpidity of dusky pools and that oily calm of tropical seas' – Baudelaire).

'Aw that's *gorgeous*,' she sighs now.

Hugh also sighs in contentment, a rare condition which some-times inspires his deepest wisdom, 'Ye can't beat the Italians when it comes to ice cream.'

'But that's no way of workin', Hugh ... Ah'll ... ye'll have to ... next time ... *don't you be doin' that again, look see.*'

'Tell you what you could do, Mairead. You could come back and sit with Martin a while. Josie and I want to look at a house.'

Still the Wards will not leave Martin on his own alone in the home – though for once he is glad of the babysitter.

As soon as they are alone Mairead abandons her excruciating impersonation of an adult. 'Any comics?' she asks in an intimate conspiratorial tone.

'I'll see.'

'*American* ones.'

Martin does not reveal that it is several years since he read American comics and that, even then, what excited him most were the ads for Bowie knives and rifles with telescopic sights (one long-range shot to each of Dessie McAnanney's kneecaps, then, calmly lighting a thin cheroot and descending to the street where his prey has dragged his pitiful carcass almost to his own front door, he seizes a handful of greasy hair to raise the throat for a fluent slitting with the Bowie knife, the few seconds of dying consciousness sufficient to absorb the deadly insult: '*McAnanney-goat*'). Now all he can find is an ancient box of *Weird Tales*, American science fiction magazines that Tony Shotter once swopped for a bunch of superior Dells.

Mairead pours the comics onto the carpet and gets down beside them like a child, kicking off the stilettos and wriggling her toes in delight ('Oh! Permit me to sear my lips on your pale feet, the glory of marbles in ages to come' – Villiers). Martin sits behind her in an armchair, more than content to watch as, at each turnover, she licks her finger for a violent flip that leaves the bottom right-hand corner of the page crumpled and moist. Sighing a little in contentment, she gradually spreads her thighs for comfort and support, the tight dress riding up to reveal, near the top of one stocking, a hole that would tear a sob of compassion from a pile of breeze blocks and, at the top of the other, a fastener and an inch and a half of the flesh that is possibly the earth's supreme richness.

But now she casts aside the science fiction with a grunt of annoyance. 'Have ye nothin' only this auld space stuff?'

Martin issues a croak of apology, sure that the idyll is about to end. However, she picks up another magazine and moves back to rest her head against his chair, bathing him in the scent of springy auburn curls permed like Gina Lollobrigida's in *Never so Few* ('Long long let me drink in the fragrance of your hair – then plunge my whole face in its depths, like a man dying of thirst in the waters of a spring' – Baudelaire).

'They'll likely put in an offer for that house,' she says suddenly. 'A doctor owns it.'

She shifts her back to lean against his armchair, actually touching his knee with her bare shoulder and offering a long and leisurely draught from two filigreed cups filled to overflowing with nature at her most profligate and bounteous ('Then, from the flowering calyx of her breast, from her whole being, there arose an odour subtle, elusive and heady' – Villiers).

Possessed by a sick-sweet giddiness that paralyses the body and anaesthetises the brain, Martin is incapable of response. It is fortunate that response does not seem to be required.

'I was engaged to a doctor once ... but like ... called out at night ... wakened by calls every whipstitch ... sure who could be bothered with it ... it's no way o' workin'...'

Mairead has never before mentioned admirers (nor has anyone

else). Martin's drowsy brain is shocked awake – this comic-reader must be near thirty and must have attracted many men. However, she has obviously been programmed by the aunts to accept only suitors from the *haute bourgeoisie* – and such men need an efficient administrator rather than a Hollywood gypsy woman with the mind of an eight-year-old child. Her voluptuous and convivial beauty is doomed to wither on the branch like ungarnered wild fruit.

'Mother of God!' At the sound of a key in the front door Mairead springs erect, cramming her feet into her shoes and pulling down the tight dress. However the Wards are too absorbed in disappointment to study her. 'Did ye put an offer in, Josie?'

'Not at all' – with a weary glance at her husband – 'it'll go too high.'

'Och sure doctors,' Mairead says, with a knowing chuckle at her own shrewdness in avoiding the clutches of the medical profession.

'Ye'll take a drop of tea, Mairead?'

'No, Josie, I'd better be makin' tracks. Greta'll be bargin' a bagful.'

As Mairead departs with Hugh, Martin turns to the stairs. 'Goin' up to do a bit o' work.'

'What? You gallivant round the country and then leave it to this hour to start?' Occasionally, in moments of stress, Mrs Ward has the impertinence to question the scholar-hero.

'*Don't tell me when to study.*'

But Martin is incapable of concentration, possessed by the thought of Mairead doomed to a lifetime of squabbling and bickering with the aunts. In particular he remembers being sent to the aunt house for a meal, during which, as he was struggling through a huge plate of pork chops, cabbage and potato, Greta burst into the living room waving a completed official form. 'She left this on top of the china cabinet. Can you credit that? *Mairead!*' As Mairead arrived from the kitchen Greta turned from Jean to the culprit. 'You left this lying out. *He'll have all he wants now. He'll know all he wants now.*'

'Ah never thought,' Mairead moaned.

'Didn't ye know he was in there? *Didn't ye see him in there?*'

'Ah did! Ah did!' Mairead howled. 'But sure Ah never thought.'

'Well ye'd *want* to think,' Greta shouted. 'Ye'd *want* to think.

Ye'd *want* to think.' She paused to study the girl in renewed bewilderment and outrage. 'Mother of God, Mairead, *have ye no wit at all?*'

Cringing in shame and remorse, Mairead began to re-enact her movements in the hope that this would make them understood and be forgiven. 'See, Ah had it in me hand goin' in to the front room and then ye called for coal for in here an' Ah thought, Ah'll not get it all black Ah'll just leave it down a minute – an' then when the coal was on it just went outa me head.'

'He'll have what he wants now,' Greta shouted, waving the paper which Martin finally identified as a completed census form. Mairead must have left a classified document where Pascal could easily have picked it up.

'It went clean outa me head,' Mairead cried, rushing from the room in tears.

To break the sudden sombre silence, Jean leaned across to Martin, 'Ye'll not say no to a wee pick o' pudding?'

'Ah'm full up.'

'Och I never knew a young fellow who couldn't manage a bit of pudding.'

As Jean went out, Greta sat down, shaking her head in disgust, and laid the form on the arm of her chair. Now that the crucial document was stationary, Martin bent forward, peering. Did these dull official sheets contain a lurid revelation – or was Greta merely displaying the habitual connection reluctance to share even elementary facts? Yet another question to which he would never know the answer. The form was at a distance and upside down.

Jean returned with a typical 'wee pick o' pudding' – a large soup bowl piled with green jelly, sponge and tinned fruit.

'Mairead's makin' us all a wee cup o' tea,' she confided.

And indeed the girl soon reappeared with the classic offering of solidarity and reconciliation. Everyone was pleased to see Greta reach for a cup in apparent forgiveness and absolution.

However, the work of recrimination is endless though its agents are only human. Greta was merely taking a breather before resuming her task.

'*Whatever possessed you?*' she suddenly screamed at Mairead whose face crumpled anew.

'Sure Ah never thought! Ah never thought!'

Now Martin, seated at his bedroom table, understands that Mairead's gypsy splendour is doomed to fade slowly in an atmosphere relentlessly peevish and petty. Gazing out into the gathering darkness, he vows that her beauty will never perish entirely. Instead it will live in his heart as it was tonight, at its peak of ripeness, free from the cruelties and degradations of time, reigning for ever like a Madonna in a niche of gold, an inextinguishable lamp of worship solemnly burning at her feet.

And, having understood the desolation of love shut out, he is now obliged to recognise the terrible autonomy of encouraged love. Though he pulls away his consoling hand and fiercely clenches his body, his love insists upon complete and immediate expression. With a furious oath he pulls out the front of his trousers and rushes down to the toilet, disappearing just before a penitent Mrs Ward passes carrying a cup of tea and a plate with two rounds of buttered toast and a peppermint Yo-Yo.

'Wee cup o' tea, Martin. Where are you? *Cooooeeeee . . .*'

('For an astringent and tonic diet first tear off your mother's arms, then cut them up in small pieces and eat them in the course of a single day without your face ever betraying the slightest trace of emotion' – Lautréamont).

'*I'm in the toilet!*' he screams.

As I sat at my table by the staffroom window, gazing out at the flourishing tidy back gardens (sometimes it seemed as if the school's glad ethos had created around it an aureole of sweetness and light), Rani came to me across the room with the radiant intensity and single-mindedness of an angel charged with annunciation.

'Come on,' she said, 'I want to show you something.'

Together we went downstairs and out through the foyer to the front car park where she proudly indicated a green Volkswagen Beetle.

'Isn't that Miss Donnelly's?'

'*Not any more.*'

I remembered Mairead's first car, a second-hand Mini which she drove straight from the showroom to our house. The entire family had to come out on the street to walk round it and marvel.

'Isn't it lovely?'

'It's lovely.'

Obviously I now would be free of Rani in the mornings – but instead of the expected relief I was rent by remorse and regret. So many frigid joyless dawns of avoiding a walk from the station together! The chance would never come again. If she would only get rid of this ridiculous banger I would vow to wait upon her every morning as attentively and loyally as the page of a queen.

'Let's go out for lunch,' she cried.

In my briefcase in the staffroom were two fresh granary rolls containing slices of a ham Clare had cooked in cider and cloves at the weekend. But Clare would surely not begrudge the waste.

Usually I enjoy being driven by women (the comfort of total security spiced by a *frisson* of domination) – but Rani was not reassuring like the others. Instead of sitting back in calm mastery, she hunched forward over the wheel to direct a stream of bitter abuse at her fellow motorists. It reminded me of Villiers's story, *Akëdysséril*, in which the eponymous Hindu warrior queen plunges her chariot recklessly into the heart of the tumult, followed by exalted young heroes desiring only to perish in her shadow.

The bar at which we stopped was as dingy and dispiriting as those within walking distance of the school and offered only the weariest of sandwiches – but in all adventures and quests the journey has to be its own reward and Rani was too excited by autonomous movement to be depressed by her destination. Besides, she was probably used to worse in the New Wave venues. To gain equivalent status as a rebel angel, I hypocritically enthused about the New Wave concert for which Homewrecker had provided the tickets.

Instead of registering pleasure she frowned. 'I've sort of gone off the New Wave thing. It was my boyfriend got me into it ... and we're in the process of breaking up. That's why I bought the car ... I need my own transport now ... *you know?*' Her questioning look seemed to contain many things – certainly a determination to start anew and possibly even the offer of a place in her chariot.

Rani the Warrior Queen or Janet the Wise Grey Mother? Goddam, it was spring – why not both?

'So why are you breaking up?

'*Because he won't marry me.*' Intense feeling burst the social filters that might have withheld or softened such a personal revelation. Before I could adjust she gripped my arm fiercely and leaned into my face. 'Am I doing the right thing? *What do you think?*'

So this was not a date but a *counselling session*. I would rather have been loved as a handsome young warrior – but the new role was not without advantages. After a certain age counselling may well be the most effective method of courtship. (And did I not possess the usual qualifications of the counsellor – no experience whatever and no idea of how to live?)

'Maybe you're pressuring him too much. Clare and I almost broke up for that reason. We . . .'

Rani was in no mood to hear my story. 'It's because he's a *white boy*.' The last phrase was spat out with shocking venom. This was Kali, Goddess of Destruction, shaking her necklace of skulls. 'I should never have got involved with a *white boy*. I should have stuck to my own kind.'

'*No! No!*' Now my own passion burst through the filters. Rani had always been the embodiment of independence and escape, one who had shed the terror and suspicion of the peasant and conferred upon herself the freedom and keys of the city. Now it appeared that her sophistication was merely a façade. Though perhaps it is always so. Some façades are more imposing than others – but behind each is a quivering, shapeless thing desperate for protection and meaningful form. If the shiny new carapace is damaged the creature immediately seeks its old shell.

'Never say that, Rani. The urge to go back to our own kind comes over us in moments of weakness. We think the tribe will give us protection and strength. But it's only an illusion of strength. We end up weaker than before. I came to a Catholic school because it was easy . . . *my own kind* . . . I knew I'd be cherished and protected. But in order to regain the privileges of a child you have to submit and obey like a child. It's done me no good at all. The other school was harder – but more worthwhile. If I'd stuck it out there I'd be a better person now. I shouldn't have run to *my own kind*.' Unconsciously I had seized her hand and was squeezing it fiercely. 'And what do you mean by *your own kind?* Who exactly are they? I mean . . . where are you from?'

My own little eruption seemed to calm her. 'Oh . . . all over. Africa, India, Singapore, Hong Kong . . . London.'

'But where's *home?*'

'I was born in Kenya . . . but my people are from what eventually

155

became Pakistan. My father worked for the British in Kenya and sent money home to support his family. But after partition, when Pakistan was created, Hindus had to get out. My father had to come back disguised as a Muslim and smuggle out my mother and the children.'

'How do you mean ... *disguised?*' Were not all Asians simply Asians? Our invariable assumption of homogeneity in everything that is other.

Rani was too absorbed to take offence. 'You know ... the trousers and coat ... the hat and beard. They had to leave everything and sail from Karachi to Mombasa in a dhow. I was born much later, in Kenya. Then, after Kenyan independence, my father went back to India for a while ... but it didn't work out.'

'See what I mean? *There is no going back.*'

Now she was not only listening but looking, receptiveness tempering the intensity of her dark eyes, glistening and sumptuous and vivid as hot wet forest after rain. 'Then Singapore ... Hong Kong ... *Limehouse Road, London.*'

Even a touch of humour in the last destination. Many claim that anger enhances beauty but for me a touch of irony is the perfect embellishment – the exquisite bracing astringency, the twist of lemon in the G and T. For a moment we sipped beer in a silence at once replete and companionable, like that after sexual climax. And indeed in the great impersonal city the gift of intimate personal history could be more momentous than physical favours.

'But are you a practising Hindu?'

'I don't practise – but I believe in some of the ideas. Tolerance ... non-violence.'

'The caste system?'

'That wasn't part of the original religion. It was dreamed up as a method of social control. The Untouchables were just the darker-skinned people pushed south by invaders. They were conquered and had to be kept in their place. And the caste system was so effective that the rulers got it written into the religion.'

This explanation had the eerie resonance of a fable.

'But is it still important? *Which caste are you?*'

'It's very important in traditional places like the Gujarat. There'd be no intermarriage ... not even much mixing.'

'But which caste are you?'

'In London it doesn't count for much. I have no time for it myself.'

Twice she had evaded classification. Obviously it would have been too painful. However strongly we reject our caste systems they hold us in thrall all our lives. 'The old system is breaking up ... but a lot of the good things in Hinduism are going as well ... the tolerance ... the non-violent approach. When I was in India Hindus and Muslims went to school together and there was no trouble. Now it's different. Hinduism is more and more mixed up with nationalist politics ...'

Another familiar fable. Religion and nationalism – the one couple definitely meant for each other. If ever a union was symbiotic this was the one.

It had come about entirely by accident – but no barrister could have more adroitly lead a witness to a critical admission. 'So you wouldn't know your own kind if they crapped in your hat?'

Inducing laughter in a woman is almost as delightful as making her come. And in the mutually grateful afterglow faith returned. Again we seemed like two independent spirits combining the freedom of the city with the wisdom of tradition. Ah the tragedy of the wasted morning opportunites that would never come again! Though perhaps Akëdysséril would soon destroy her new chariot. And there was always the present moment. We arose and went out together – Kali and her consort Siva, the ascetic and madman who is also a husband and father.

'So,' I said, 'don't be pressuring your boyfriend. You'll only scare him off. Relax. Take it easy. He'll come round in time.'

'*But I want two children before I'm thirty.*'

The other aspect of Kali – the Great Mother, Giver of Life.

'You look as though you've plenty of time yet. *What age are you?*'

'Never you mind.' The playful bump she delivered was more appropriate to a lover than a counsellor. But the coy evasion was in dramatic contrast to Janet's frankness on the same subject. Janet who was almost twice her age but carelessly threw off the figure without even being asked.

Candour is infinitely more attractive than coyness – but there was also the urge to perish in the shadow of a terrible warrior queen.

Ward has taken his A-levels in one year instead of the customary two, a meaningless and even idiotic feat since he is too young to go to university and is obliged to spend the following year aimlessly hanging about, an embarrassment to parents, teachers, friends and, not least, himself. In the mornings he goes to school as usual and attends the early classes. But if the weather is fine he slips away at morning break with his books, no longer maths and science texts but the French novels, journals and poetry which execrate the vulgar herd.

Day after day Ward haunts the streets and parks, libraries and cafés – and of course the single bookshop. Downstairs are the racks of motoring magazines and gold-embossed bestsellers beloved of the herd; upstairs, banished behind the children's books in a small dingy room presided over by a stout naive old lady, is a tiny literature and classics section. Here Ward discovers the acrid pleasures of the renegade, bending behind a shelf to cram one book into an inside pocket and then straightening up with a second which he ostentatiously flips and returns, tumultuous exaltation in his soul and a smile on his face for the dim old dear ('Many characters of excessive intelligence have hurled themselves headlong into evil's arms' – Lautréamont).

Unfortunately the exaltation quickly fades and he is cast back on the tedium of a provincial town. How will he discover his destiny among ill-tempered mothers with infants and shopping? Where will Maldoror find a kindred soul?

Eventually, weary of familiar streets, he penetrates a tiny Protestant enclave – and is immediately unsettled by its brooding silence. Perhaps as a result of being cut off from its hinterland by the river, this quarter has none of the teeming street life of the Catholic terraces – Micky the turf man and Johnny the spuds man (both from across the border in the Republic), the Pools man, Betterware man, scrapman and brockman (who collects waste food for pigs in an old domestic water tank attached to a pram chassis), his hi-tech arch-rival, the 'swanky' brockman (an oil drum on a trailer behind a rusting Ford Zephyr) and of course the innumerable soliciting Church bodies, including the Silver Circle, Building Fund and Good Shepherd nuns (spectres in black who never speak – the child answering the door simply shouts, *Mammy . . . the nuns*).

Drawn by the frisson of crossing the line, Ward proceeds slowly and cautiously, alert for signs of danger and prepared for the ignominy of flight. However, no one accosts him – or even appears. There are only the neat lines of the terraces, finally broken by the rarity of a corner shop. Emboldened by hunger, he pushes open the battered door – and is brought to a halt by astonishment.

Leaning over the counter, next to a wooden tray full of hideous buns and deep in conversation with a customer, is a hugely over-weight man in upper middle age, purple-faced and with a gleaming pallid skull imperfectly covered by straggles of oiled hair drawn from a point above an ear. There is nothing unusual in this – indeed he is the very type of the Ulster small shopkeeper. But behind and to one side, erect in a doorway leading to the interior, is a tall slender dark-skinned beauty whose demure stance, neat shop coat and permed flick entirely fail to disguise a singular, imperious and regal spirit. Ward remains transfixed in the doorway ('My presence dare not approach the stunning uniqueness of that strange nobility' – Lautréamont). She is also motionless, gazing at the floor with folded arms. Slowly the dark *inconnue* raises her head and turns upon the youth a pair of eyes inconsolably disturbed, as mysterious and turbulent as the ocean. In an instant, as a condor will swoop down and bear off a child who cries out, there descends upon his helpless heart a new and terrible love, based not upon tenderness but sub-mission to mystery and occult strength ('There are women who awaken in us the instinct to vanquish and plunder; what she aroused was a wish to expire slowly under her gaze' – Baudelaire).

'Never fancied being an officer, Dougie?' the customer is enquiring.

'An *officer?*' Dougie releases a sceptical snort. 'In the *Ulster Rifles?* Have ye no sense at all? Sure their own men shot them. Boys like Ivor Turkington and Sammy Webb. If ye fell out wi' those boys it wasn't the Japs ye were worried about. Turn your back for a minute and' – without rising from the counter, Dougie raises, aims and fires an imaginary rifle – 'BANG! Ye got a bullet in it from your own men.'

Pushing herself off the doorframe, the *inconnue* approaches Ward who feels his will dissolve in her attention as flesh dissolves in a vat of acid ('My wavering wits are engulfed by such majesty' – Lautréamont).

'Could I have an apple square?'

Efficiently applying plastic tweezers, for all the world like a trim staff nurse, she lifts and bags the sugar-coated square. But the eyes she raises once more to the youth betray her impersonation of sweetness and light ('Darkness abounds in her, and all that she inspires is nocturnal and deep' – Baudelaire).

At last he has found his kindred spirit, one as noble and proud of soul and as alienated from the province in which they are trapped.

Next day he is back. And the day after that. Soon he is a regular in the shop, gaily greeted by Dougie as 'our young Fenian friend'. Ward responds easily to the raillery – but cannot speak to the woman. Though he understands that she would destroy him ('We have to imagine a youth exclusively nourished on eggs and milk and then suddenly submitted to a diet of pungent spices and condiments whose sharp burning flavour convulses, shatters and maddens him' – Villiers), nevertheless he craves intimacy ('Oh! To possess, to drink like consecrated wine the delicious and barbaric melancholy of this woman' – Villiers) and suffers agonies of shame in his ridiculous stammered words – 'Chesterbread', 'Nicky Cake', 'Cream Horn', 'Snowball'.

He is incapable of speaking to his beloved but by and by he learns a little of her story from the patrons. According to local legend she had been a princess in her native land (never accurately identified), married Dougie while he was serving there and came home with him when he left the army. Ward cannot imagine her motives. What did she think when she found Dougie's no-doubt-vaunted business was in fact a dingy corner shop in the back streets of working-class Northern Ireland? ('An inaccessible enigma was concealed within her glory of doom' – Villiers.)

As for her physical union with Dougie, even the most loyal of his cronies find it hard to contemplate. '*Jeeeesiss,*' one patron murmurs in Ward's ear, looking from the gross shopkeeper to the slim princess and back, 'Ah hope to fuck he takes the strain on his elbows at least.'

Ward is furious that anyone could even imagine such a thing and consoles himself with the fact that there is no sign of intimacy.

But one day he is appalled to see emerge from the parlour a monstrously smirking fat boy with the heavy build of mature Ulster and the golden skin of the East.

Behind the boy is the flicker of a television screen.

'Have ye done any school work?' Dougie bellows. 'Ye're only

allowed off school if ye do some work at home.'

The boy grins and lifts a chesterbread from the bun tray.

'It's not that he can't do it,' Dougie explains to Ward. 'It's just he *won't bother*. I don't think they're stretchin' him enough at that school. He doesn't want to go because the work's too boring. *Look* ...' Suddenly he stretches across the counter and grabs one of Ward's books. With a hoarse cry the youth makes an impulsive gesture of retrieval – but already Dougie is opening *Les Chants de Maldoror* and holding it out to his son. 'Read that ... go on ... read that.'

Smirking evilly and biting into his chesterbread, the boy commences in a flat mechanical voice, 'It would please me, O Creator, if you permitted me to vent my feelings. Wielding terrible ironies with a cool firm hand, I warn you that my heart holds enough of them to mount an attack on you till the end of my days.'

Anxiously Ward studies Dougie for signs of fundamentalist wrath. However the meaning of the words has been lost in a sudden rush of paternal fondness.

'See!' he cries. 'He can do it ... no bother. He's just bored with all the stuff they give him in school.' Proud, tender, triumphant, Dougie watches his son efficiently demolish the chesterbread.

Something impels Ward to look up. Tall, statuesque, terrible, she stands motionless and silent in the parlour doorway, behind her the drone and grey-white flicker of the television screen, the ceaselessly posturing and babbling face of Western man. As though aware of Ward's attention, she turns from her husband and son to bestow on the youth a look of such sulphurous intensity that he has to avert his own gaze ('Those are certainly eyes whose flame pierces the dusk, malignant and subtle orbs which I recognise by their terrifying malice' – Baudelaire).

'See?' Dougie repeats to Ward, handing back the book.

Totally granulated by the princess, the youth forgets himself for an instant. 'Maybe he's a genius,' he snaps, immediately surprised and alarmed by his own sarcastic venom.

Like so many Ulster Protestants, Dougie is impervious to irony (the weapon of the watchful and cautious minority). Instead of going on the attack he looks at Ward with new respect, as though acknowledging that there might be something after all in using taxpayer's money to educate Catholics.

161

'Dye know . . . Ah think ye might be right.'

The tourist attractions of Marylebone Road end at Baker street – but follow the road westward and you will not be disappointed. Past the Westminster Council building, guarded by two of the haughtiest lions in a lion-rich borough, is the Marylebone Public Library flanked by iron columns bearing the kinkiest cherubs in town. Ostensibly holding out laurel wreaths, an offer of a different kind is suggested by the shift riding high on one side and the podgy thigh proffered in saucy hello-sailor style. It might be assumed that the specialism of this branch is child pornography. In fact it is music.

I was here to return the Bartók record and end my unfulfilled affair with BB. One can try only so many times. Nor had I any desire to linger in a library on the first warm day of the year.

In return for the tolerance of a *mari complaisant*, Clare had granted me the equivocal gift of freedom. It was like being a wandering teenager again – the same heady mixture of rapture and discontent, energy and torpor, fascination and boredom, high purpose and aimlessness, constancy and vacillation, election and insignificance. The same half-hope of adventure combined with the certainty that none will arrive.

I rarely even spoke to anyone and, as before, the wandering usually ended in a cinema, most often a repertory art house like the Electric, the Everyman or the Scala. Mainstream cinemas reflect the mainstream ethos and make the solitary feel like a loser, hangdog and furtive and pitiful; but, at ease in an art house with filter coffee and banana cake, the solitary is an aristocrat of the spirit, a Prospero sanctioning fabulous dreams.

Tonight the destination was my French class in the City Lit, near Covent Garden, and I planned a great diagonal swathe across the centre of the city. As always I stuck to the side streets where brooding apartments gave the impression of housing spies, assassins, mistresses and fantastically specialised brothels and even the dingy ground-floor businesses were potent, mysterious and singular. Chains and franchises dominate the dismal suburban high streets – but they will never capture the heart of the city. Autonomy, obsession and oddity thrive in these quiet streets. The city's limbs are in chains – but its great heart is free.

And the little Italian place where I ate was full of unconventional types – mostly minor theatre functionaries, chorus girls, ticket sellers, lighting technicians: those who could afford only a one-plate pasta meal in a badly decorated basement where worn-out but valiant waitresses distributed plastic menu wallets containing handwritten sheets with many erasures and misspellings. In fact only their appearance and hours of work were different. The conversation was essentially the same as that of the staffroom. Like assemblies of colleagues everywhere, what they did most was complain.

Drury Lane, where Villiers attended Mozart's *Don Giovanni* with his Irish heiress, Anna Eyre Powell (one of the Eyre Powells of Clonshavoy). Marriage to an heiress was always Villiers's preferred way out of poverty and he was put in touch with the girl by a dubious matrimonial agent, one Comte de La Houssaye, whose previous business ventures included involvement in piracy and the slave trade. Villiers gave this character a promissory note for two hundred thousand francs, payable in the event of a marriage but otherwise null and void. In return La Houssaye provided the nobleman with a fur-lined overcoat, repeating watch and false teeth. However, since Anna had little French there was also a major language problem. Villiers took English lessons from his friend, Stéphane Mallarmé ('Since it's a matter of a wedding I'll learn only the future tense of the verbs').

But instead of pursuing a cynical campaign as planned, the excitable writer immediately fell head-over-heels in love and terrified the girl with passionate recitations of his work (perhaps the love scene from *Axel*: 'Do you want to trouble the stars reflected in the Bay of Naples or in the lagoons of Venice when you trail in the gondola's wake some exquisite fabric from Samarkand? Shall we let reindeer draw us across the ice or ostriches carry us over the sand?'). To whatever lyrical options were suggested, Miss Eyre Powell declared that she would prefer 'eternal celibacy and even the convent'. La Houssaye repossessed the overcoat and watch, leaving Villiers, humiliated, heartbroken and penniless, to make his own way back to Paris where, abandoning the dream of an heiress, he took up with his illiterate cleaning woman. The episode was one of his most severe disappointments – but it was not entirely without reward. He was permitted to keep the false teeth.

On the door of the classroom was a note apologising for the

absence of the teacher due to illness. As I stared stupidly at the three lines I was joined by Rachel, a fellow student, today in a sleeveless T-shirt and pants of an outmoded tightness and floral pattern now imbued with the melancholy of bygone jauntiness and daring. And not only were the trousers old-fashioned, the behind they hugged so closely was much too large for emphasis. The warm weather had obviously inspired her to rashness and vainglory – just the kind of human misjudgement to touch my heart with tenderness. And when she leaned forward to peer at the notice (she was both short-sighted and short) her feet came out of her light slippers to reveal reddish chapped heels that also moved me deeply with thoughts of the ravages of time (like Baudelaire, I can scarcely conceive a type of beauty which has nothing to do with sorrow).

There was already a little thing between us. Rachel was recently divorced, with a low opinion of the male sex in general but a keen interest in any member who appeared to transcend its faults. In discussing plans for the last class before Easter, she mischievously cried, 'Why don't the *men* bring the *food* for a change and let the *women* bring the *wine?*' The other guys responded with packets of Wotsits and Cheesy Footballs and I easily made them look like shit with my Tupperware container of *champignons au vin*. All the women were impressed – but Rachel was especially ecstatic, laying a hand on my arm to croon, 'I really *adored* your *champignons.*'

Now, as always, she was warm and cordial but, as always, I sensed a core of bitterness common in the divorced. Beneath the congenial surface was a hurt creature desperate to absolve itself and apportion blame elsewhere. Even so, if she had said, Let's go out for a drink, I would probably have been as thrilled as Axel at Sara's invitation, 'Let us venture out together, nomads clad in tattered finery, you with a blunderbuss on your shoulder and I with a harp at my waist, like bronzed gypsies singing by roadsides and in the Bohemian city squares.'

Instead she said, 'Are you going down to the office to complain?'

So I returned early – to find the flat silent and dark. Presumably Clare was putting the children to bed. The lounge was also un-usually tidy, with no toys or baby equipment on the furniture or floor. However, this was no more suggestive than the two half-full glasses of clear liquid on the coffee table. The famous three monkeys misrepresent the phenomenon of denial. It is what goes on *inside* the head that counts. When the brain refuses to think evil it makes no difference what the senses perceive.

The children's bedroom was also silent and dark. Both Lucy and Paul were asleep.

As I opened the door of the main bedroom there sprang from the bed a tall slim-waisted woman with shockingly luxuriant pubic hair and darkly tipped heavy breasts aquiver from the abruptness of her leap.

Or perhaps the normal laws of perception no longer apply in moments of trauma. Certainly it seemed to me that never before had I seen this voluptuous, limber, wanton nude. Instead of retreating or covering herself she actually took a step forward and raised her right hand to me.

I could neither move nor speak. Her beauty paralysed body and mind. Time itself was unnerved.

'*Martin . . .*'

The familiar voice brought recognition. But much remained unregistered – or was later suppressed. There must have been someone else in the room but the memory, however endlessly replayed, gives no indication of who, where or in what state of undress and arousal. All that is revealed is Clare, heartrendingly beautiful in her nakedness, forever rising from the bed and approaching the open door.

'*Martin . . .*'

# 5

'Vapid! Vapid! Vapid! Vapid!'

Familiar dramatic cry of Moira Sweeney as she dashed off a dismissive comment on the essay in front of her. No one in the staffroom answered – or even looked up. This kind of complaint was too common. Like so much disgust, it was an attempt to establish superiority by the method of contrast. What is revealed by deriding worthlessness is really the worthiness of the critic. Schoolteachers are the lower middle class of the education world, those least distant from ignorance but most concerned to point out the gap.

Not that I was any different, contemptuous of colleagues if not pupils, resentful, superior, yearning for escape. Clare's deception had changed everything. When we are hurt the laboriously forged character collapses and the old familiar temperament re-emerges in triumph. Once again I was tempted by the call of the Crag. I wanted to climb high, into pure silent air, far from women and the world.

Bernard's theory of the seven was even better than he realised for it also neatly explained their deep-seated misogyny. If the world was the empire of evil it was due to the success of evil's recruiting agents – women. D'Aurevilly made this the theme of *Les Diaboliques*, a collection of tales illustrating the depth and power of female duplicity ('The Devil teaches women what they are,' says one of the narrators, 'or they would teach it to the Devil if he did not know.').

Of course Clare hotly refuted the charge of deceit. According to her, the assignation was not planned and Homewrecker just happened to call.

'On the only evening I'm always out?'

'Yes.'

'And you would have told me?'

'Of course.'

My laugh was not entirely pleasant. 'I think he's been screwing you every week while I've been down in Covent Garden singing *Frère fucking Jacques.*'

'Well . . .' Incapable of matching such vileness, Clare threw up her hands and looked away.

Suddenly it was obvious that the moral high ground, which had seemed unassailably mine, was actually being contested in hand-to-hand combat *and could even pass from my control.*

'And why did he *happen* to call round?'

'To see *you.* He thought you were interested in Situationism and called round to lend you this.' And she tossed in my lap a thin poorly produced paperback from a small press: *The Society of the Spectacle* by Guy Debord.

A masterly surprise counter-offensive.

But behind the cannon smoke something new and horrible was taking shape. 'Wait a minute,' I said. *'Wait a minute.* This is getting *serious.* It's getting *serious,* isn't it?'

'I suppose it is,' she sighed, in sudden wonder and awe, as though some grand tragic destiny had chosen us as its instruments and we could only be grateful for the privilege.

'You said it wouldn't get serious.'

'It's Nick who's getting a bit serious.'

'Then it obviously can't go on.'

'I don't want to stop seeing him, Martin.'

And the following weekend they went to an all-day concert under the banner of ROCK AGAINST RACISM, from my point of view a carnival but from hers a solemn social duty selflessly discharged.

'Nick's really against racism. Anyone wearing a swastika T-shirt is banned from the Centre for life.'

Among the innumerable attributes supposed to be conferred or enhanced by love, a talent for sophistry has never been mentioned. Yet the most striking consequence of Clare's relationship was her ability to justify anything at all. If she could commit her secret to paper the book would be an American best-seller: *How to Secure the Moral High Ground and still Enjoy the Most Fun*.

The weekend after the concert she attended a dinner party given by Nick for a few close friends. Only after she was gone did I realise the significance of the occasion – *dining with a circle of intimates is the London equivalent of meeting the family*. She was certainly right about Homewrecker's serious intentions. In my black heart I hoped that the evening would be an embarrassing failure. Instead she returned ecstatic and jubilant, shining with the divinity of the successful performer. And this had been a difficult and discriminating audience. They were all clever, knowledgeable people, she told me, or, rather, told the room, for at that moment I scarcely existed. Elated by success, she had the star's shocking indifference to all but its own celestial radiance.

Since his sophisticated guests disapproved of meat, Nick had created an all-fish menu, with a Pernod and smoked trout mousse followed by salmon koulibiaca (not merely fish – but *fish en croûte*). Clare described each of these in admiring relish. She had always adored fish, whereas I remembered it as a penance on grim dutiful Fridays and based my own primitive cooking almost entirely on red meat. There could be little doubt that Homewrecker was making me look like a hick. I was being comprehensively out-refined by a tattooed man.

Now I had more freedom than ever. I could go where I wanted, spend what I liked, enjoy the favours of anyone who would have me. But the Celestial Ironist displayed his usual wicked dexterity. While with one hand he bestowed on me the freedom I craved, with the other he quietly withdrew the self-esteem necessary to enjoy it. Now attractive *inconnues* had a self-sufficiency and indifference that were terrifying to behold. A horrible new fear took shape – that of being cast out for ever from the paradise of the flesh. Not that Clare had ceased to let me. She performed with the frequency of old – but in the traditional joyless manner of the dutiful wife.

'Vapid! Vapid! Vapid! Vapid!' With Moira's dismissive cry ringing in my ears, I left the school and took the Tube to Charing Cross.

Bernard was waiting at the appointed place in the National Gallery foyer.

'Just one thing before we start.' He led the way into the twentieth-century gallery and paused before a Picasso still life. 'This used to be called *Fruit Dish, Bottle and Guitar*. A superb example of Rococo Cubism. But look at the instrument. Note the four strings over a bridge, the two S apertures, the curved neck. A guitar has six strings, no bridge, one circular aperture and a rectangular neck. This was obviously a violin, not a guitar. I had to write to the Director to point this out.'

'You wrote to the *Director?*'

'I suggested that he would not wish the *Young Woman Seated at a Virginal* to be described as *Young Woman at a Harpsichord* . . . and that Picasso deserved as much as Vermeer.'

'What did he say?'

'I had a nice letter from the Keeper of French Paintings. He thanked me for pointing out the error, promised to correct the title and enclosed the current edition of *National Gallery News*.'

How did Bernard retain his crusading fervour and self-belief? Another consequence of Clare's escapade was a deepening of my natural reluctance to enter, much less attempt to reform, the world. Heavy upon me lay the fatalism, inertia and indifference of the years.

'But why bother? What's the point?'

'I want the bastards to know that someone is keeping an eye on them. *J'ai l'oeil*, as we say in France.'

Exactly the kind of ardour, vigilance and steadfastness advocated by d'Aurevilly ('Let us never take early retirement from ourselves').

'And who will keep watch when you're gone?'

'On Clare's advice I've given up smoking, butter and puddings. So I may be the first man to live for ever.'

It would have been pleasant to tarry among the giants of the current century – but the purpose of this trip was to go back to the beginning. As we entered the early Renaissance galleries I failed to suppress a reluctant groan. 'All this religious stuff.'

'It has nothing to do with religion,' Bernard snapped. 'It's all about coloured shapes and forms. Once Giotto broke with the icon, art as we know it was born. The kind of period I always prefer. I love beginnings, origins ... people trying to invent something. Of course Giotto was back in the twelve hundreds – and naturally things took time to develop.' He paused, transfigured, rapt, wondering, like the multitude before a paralytic who has taken up his bed. 'Then, at the start of the fifteenth century ... *the child gets up on its feet and walks.*'

'A child of the Church.'

'But not the Catholic Church we know. A Church essentially classical and pagan. They went in for Annunciations, Epiphanies, Adoration of the Kings ... Madonna and Child of course ... but not so much crucifixions. They loved life, you see ... no interest whatever in the glorification of suffering. Take our first man ... Fra Filippo Lippi ...'

'A monk.'

'A monk convicted of violating fourteen nuns.'

'Already the guy is growing on me.'

'Look at this Annunciation. You see, I *love* Annunciations. You have the two halves – Mary on one side saying, *No not me ...*' Bernard turned sideways and, assuming a look of consternation, crouched in a semi-kneeling position. Then he straightened up and repeated the pose, facing in the opposite direction. 'And the angel on the other side saying, *Get used to it, honey, you're the one.* Renaissance painters loved the Annunciation because it coincided with the vernal equinox, an ancient pagan festival. And of course the binary structure of the scene itself.'

'What's so great about two halves?'

'It's something they can take and develop. Like a riff in jazz. Like "Perdido".' Nodding on the beat, he moved off to another Annunciation. '*Ba dee dum ... ba dee dum ... ba dee dum ...*'

Where Lippi was bold and stark, Crivelli was ornate and teeming – a child hiding from her mother, rugs hanging out to dry, kitchen utensils and bowls on a shelf. Though not all the details were homely.

170

'What's the laser beam?'

'The Holy Spirit entering the Virgin.'

'And this?' In the foreground loomed an apparently redundant apple and a large sinister gherkin.

'Crivelli's trademark was fruit and veg. To symbolise the fertility of the Lord.' Apparently feeling that I was suitably warmed up, Bernard eagerly pressed on. 'Now ... Piero Della Francesca.' He paused for a quick genuflection. 'At his name every knee shall bow.'

In a long and solemn silence we gazed at *The Baptism of Christ*.

When Bernard finally spoke it was in a hushed and reverent whisper. 'You see, he's touching the same chords as Vermeer and Chardin. That mysterious timelessness. The cool still landscape ... frozen into immobility. The inscrutable expressions. Look at the strange face of that angel behind the tree. *Staring right at us.*'

'The one who looks like a rent boy?'

'I don't care for Berenson but he has a wonderful phrase: *the art of ineloquence*. No bravura. No rhetoric. No heroism.' He gave an intensely human sigh in which wonder and disillusionment were strangely combined. 'But you don't like it, do you?'

It was true that nothing was happening. One man's immobility is another man's rigor mortis.

'You like it enough for both.'

The speaker was a pale Renaissance virgin, Bellini's Madonna of the Meadow.

'I do beg your pardon,' Bernard said. 'I'm afraid I have rather a loud voice. An occupational hazard of teaching.'

'Not at all. I was enjoying your enthusiasm.' The authentic Marian sweetness and empathy. 'You really like that picture.'

'*Like it?*' Bernard spun back to Piero with a fiercely appetitive abruptness that woke a nearby attendant from his doze. '*I could eat the paint off it.*'

Laughter softened the Madonna's demure countenance. 'Would you mind if I went round with you? You seem to know a lot about art.'

Who would have believed that it was possible to pull by lecturing on the Early Renaissance? The Virgin was older than she had seemed at first – long hair and a slim figure created the illusion of youth – but intriguingly combined a girlish manner with the schoolmarmish severity of a tartan suit and a high-necked blouse with a black bow.

'Of course!' Bernard cried. 'Though we're looking only at a few of my favourites.'

The Madonna introduced herself to Bernard as Jocelyn Moorehead. I trailed along behind the two of them feeling insignificant and worthless.

Even in the fifteenth century the Flemish painters were astoundingly naturalistic. Without the titles it would have been impossible to identify as Madonnas or Magdalens these real women at ease in real rooms with windows open on real towns – van der Weyden's Magdalen cosily reading, Campin's Madonna with curls and a strikingly long nose instead of the conventionally anonymous straight hair and regular features, the halo behind her head actually a fire screen. Also this Virgin was topless, one breast exposed prior to a feed.

'The child is too old,' I suggested. 'Should have been on solids long ago. It's a bit kinky in fact. Like a lot of these Virgins with Child.'

'The Church had strict rules,' Bernard explained. 'The humanity of Christ would have to be obvious. There's a well-known monograph on the subject: *The Penis of the Christ Child in Renaissance Art.*'

In Campin's *Virgin and Child in an Interior*, the left hand of the dreamy child stroked Mary's chin in the knowing gesture of an adult lover, while his right hand . . .

'*He's pulling his wire!*' I had to cry out in astonishment.

Bernard sighed and turned to his companion. 'I'm afraid he's a coarse fellow. Excitable. I'll have to take him home.'

Jocelyn was desolate. 'But Leonardo . . . Titian . . . Tintoretto . . .'

Bernard betrayed the shadow of a wince. 'I prefer the early period. It has the freshness of the spring flower . . . the vernal moment. The High Renaissance is the blown rose . . . *the blown rose*. Too much fanciness and perfection. And of course the rich have got in on the act.'

'Van Gogh?' In a small pitiful voice Jocelyn pleaded for Saint Vincent.

The wince blossomed. 'I find him an embarrassing fellow.' As though the sensitive artist himself might be eavesdropping in the gallery, Bernard dropped his voice to a whisper. '*He breathes in your face.*'

Jocelyn gaped, mesmerised, like a woodland creature trapped in the gaze of some monstrous predator. 'How about a cup of coffee instead?'

Bernard issued a sceptical but tolerant chuckle. 'That would be very nice indeed.'

We proceeded in two-and-one formation to the restaurant but, as Jocelyn went for a tray, Bernard suddenly pushed me in front of him. 'You go first and I'll do what you do.'

It took me a moment to comprehend the discovery of Bernard's Achilles heel: *the man who knew everything was frightened of restaurants.* The revelation was welcome but not sufficient compensation. Still in need of comfort, I chose a large slice of passion cake (for me, unhappiness in love will always be associated with a craving for *pâtisserie*). Behind me, Bernard chose the same. Suddenly Jocelyn swept past to the till and paid for all three of us. As the man at the front it was I and not Bernard who looked stingy and feeble. To make matters worse, Jocelyn herself had only a cup of black coffee. With our gaucheness and huge slabs of cake, Bernard and I had the appearance of schoolboys taken for a treat by a kindly aunt.

As soon as we sat down Bernard launched into a lecture on Piero's geometric genius and masterly use of the golden section. 'You see, this fellow's supposed to understand these things.' He made a denigrating wave in my direction. Familiar recourse of the publicly awkward – lay into your friends. 'This fellow's supposed to be some sort of mathematician and scientist.'

'Didn't Piero work for the Princes ... the *rich?*' I had to fight back – but it was foolhardy to challenge Bernard on his home ground.

'For the Pope and Duke Montefeltro of Urbino. But he was no court parasite. He always came back to his home town. One of his greatest works, *The Resurrection*, is in the tiny local church.' Bernard paused to savour first his passion cake and then a calm *coup de grâce*. 'He had a post on the civic council. And he served as a watchman, patrolling the walls at night.'

'You've been there?' Jocelyn asked.

'Borgo San Sepolcro.' Suddenly falling back in his seat, Bernard sighed with the melancholy tenderness of a roué recalling his first love. 'No ... I've never seen it.'

'Wouldn't you like to go?'

As though Jocelyn were offering to sweep him straight off to Italy, Bernard assumed a furtive hunted look and began to speak of large, mysterious scholarly projects which occupied all his free time and would prevent him travelling for the foreseeable future. He was now facing her directly, talking in a low serious tone and unaware that his mouth was encircled by crumbs of passion cake. I gave my own face a quick wipe – for messy eating was a failing we shared. (Further evidence for the Watchmaker Theory of God – in his infinite wisdom the Great Designer has balanced a talent for rigorous thought with a humbling inability to keep the gob clean.)

Far from being repelled, Jocelyn finished the conversation by requesting an exchange of phone numbers with Bernard. He laughed indulgently, as though this were some sort of ludicrous adolescent game. Still she persisted, producing a diary from which she tore a page with her number inscribed. A guy twenty years my senior with gold executive-officer glasses, grey hair and grey suit – *and this attractive stylish woman was forcing her phone number on him.*

The message was brutally clear – I was sexually null. And the reason for nullity was also clear. Damaged self-esteem creates a precipitous downward spiral in which lack of confidence brings about rejection or indifference which in turn inflict further damage which in turn … etcetera. Watching Jocelyn's elegant figure depart, I experienced the melancholy certainty of never receiving an annunciation from such an exquisite angel.

Apparently divining my inmost thoughts, Bernard held out the phone number.

'Would you like this? You're fond of mature ladies.'

'It's you she's hot for, Bernard.'

'*Hot?* She's a classic daddy's girl.'

'Y ou're Martin Ward? *The* Martin Ward? The Martin Ward with great exam results?' At last he is the chosen one, the honoured guest. 'I'm Angela Neville. My daddy Frank taught with your daddy … *God rest him.* You must know Frank. He's teaching your mother to drive at the moment.'

Finally his caste is providing an appropriate reward – an enchanting creature in whom, to the petite and slight frame of the convent school girl, have been added the heavy breasts currently prized by the material world. As they move out to dance, Ward casts a fierce glance of triumph to where Tony Shotter presides over the record player at the far corner of the party. However, Shotter, eyes screwed up against his own cigarette smoke, concentrates frowningly on record sleeves in the search for music that transcends the vulgar taste of the herd. Having for some time rejected the triteness of song lyrics, indeed the very idea of song itself, he now restricts himself to the purity of instrumental pop music. Even within this limited subdivision he is fantastically selective. The record he plays is not a hit but an American obscurity: 'Pipeline' by the Chantays ('It is good to teach the contented of this world that there are happinesses superior to theirs ... more sophisticated, more grand' – Baudelaire).

But since the music is impossible to dance to, the throng on the floor cry out in protest. Angela glares at Shotter in vexation. '*Who is that character?* Why doesn't he play something *decent?* Why doesn't he play the Swinging Blue Jeans' records I brought? I had to search the whole house for them tonight. And it was just crazy in our house.' Distracted by the memory of commotion, she turns animatedly to Ward. 'We were all *up to high doh* in our house tonight. I was running round trying to get ready and looking for "The Hippy Hippy Shake" and my sister Anne was going to her college dinner dance. Malachy Armstrong was taking her ... you know Malachy, the solicitor's son? Och ... the Armstrongs from Mount Pleasant ... ever so ever so ... very awfully awfully. Anyway it's the custom for the boy to bring the girl a box of chocolates ... and didn't Malachy turn up at the door with a thruppenny packet of fruit gums. *A thruppenny packet of fruit gums!* Of course he had a big expensive box in his car the whole time. But he didn't let on for *ages.* We were all having *kittens.* We were having *canaries.*'

Ward listens, enchanted ('Her pretty chatter would bring to life even the most saturnine prince of the blood' – Villiers). It seems that he has scarcely to respond, much less direct. Everything happens with the inevitability of a fairy tale and, as in a fairy tale, she must disappear at midnight before the end of the ball ('Daddy's picking me up').

When they go to retrieve Angela's records Shotter swiftly appraises the discs and snorts in vicious disdain. 'Peter and Gordon ... fuckin' nancy boy wankers.'

Hot points of fury blaze in Angela's eyes – but her voice is cold and assured. '*I* happen to think they're *very good.*'

When Ward returns from seeing her to the door, Shotter dramatically clasps his own throat, extends his tongue to the limit and makes a violent retching noise. 'Jesus, what a *fuckin' puke!* What a *sickener!* That wee girl'd give ye the *fuckin' dry gawks.*' To restore his equanimity he takes a long draw on his cigarette and riffles once more through the records. 'All this stuff is *poxy.*'

'Why didn't you bring your own?'

'Bring me own records? To be ruined at a party? Get your head looked, son.'

Ward gazes wistfully at the door. 'She has good cans,' he suggests with a hopefulness that makes Shotter look up in sharpest suspicion.

'Ye haven't made a date wi' Fuckface?'

'Actually Ah have.' Ward is almost as surprised as Shotter. Like the rest of the convivial encounter, the assignation seemed to have arranged itself.

Even so, when Ward meets the girl he is careful to keep himself on the outside of the pavement, as etiquette demands, and in the Golden Grill he gallantly proposes the expensive sirloin garni.

'My *spare tyre!*' Angela cries, leaning back to let her sweater ride up and seizing a handful of warm golden flesh.

Instead she orders a chicken salad and, pecking delicately, enquires into Ward's brilliant future. Everyone knows that it is certain to dazzle – but in precisely what way?

He shrugs casually, a weary aristocrat much too fastidious to covet the baubles prized by the world. 'I'd like to get right away ... you know? Not just work with a team in an ordinary lab.' ('I have such a hatred of the commonplace that even discoveries bore and disgust me when they become widely shared' – d'Aurevilly). 'A scientific expedition somewhere ... Antarctica maybe.'

Angela has a mild attack of vertigo. '*Antarctica!*' she manages to shudder at last, hugging her own ample bosom, epitome of comfort and warmth. 'I just couldn't *bear* anywhere cold. I *love* sun. I lay out our back all weekend in my bikini.' For once at a loss for words, she watches him spear several French fries with calm ruthlessness and precision. '*God Ah nearly forgot!*' Burrowing suddenly in her handbag, Angela produces a piece of paper bearing a mathematics problem which she says has defeated her brother, himself no slouch at sums. 'He's tried *everything* and he says it just *can't be done.* If you do it, Martin Ward, I'll just *die*. I will ... *die* if you do this ... I *promise*.'

A mechanics question about colliding spheres, it presents a formidable amount of given data but, as with so much that appears intimidating, this is mostly noise, bluster, interference, camouflage:

> One end of a light inextensible string is attached to a mass of 5 gm which rests on a rough horizontal table, the coefficient of friction between the mass and the table being one third. The string at right angles to the edge of the table passes over a smooth fixed pulley at the edge, under a smooth movable pulley of mass 4 gm and over a smooth fixed pulley, and has a mass of 3 gm attached to its other end. Assuming the portions of the string to be vertical between the pulleys, find the accelerations of the masses and the tension in the string.

The core problem is simple, unworthy of his talent, merely a matter of writing down the three equations of motion and solving for the three unknowns. Ward dallies with it as a master swordsman might toy with an oaf before ending his doltish existence with a contemptuous thrust.

'You know Daddy's always going on about you,' Angela says. 'He's always telling our boys to study and get on like Martin Ward.'

'Just the boys?'

'*Puh!* I was never smart. Daddy's in raptures if I pass *anything*. He never thought I'd get *hedumecated* at all ... couldn't believe it when I got through O-level. He bought me this *beautiful* bikini ... as skimpy, you know ... but *really expensive*.'

Ward pushes the solution across the table. Angela snatches it up and stares at the hieroglyphics in wild-eyed speechless admiration. 'Oh!' she cries at last. 'I just don't *believe* it. Is that *really* the answer?' Ward nods casually ('After the pleasure of being astonished, none is greater than that of causing astonishment' – Baudelaire). 'Oh my God!' Angela claps the paper face down on her sweater and shuts her eyes in disbelief. Then she has another peep. 'I just don't *believe* this. I ... simply ... *do* ... *not* ... *believe* ... *this*.'

So inordinate is her gratitude that it seems only natural to suggest a stroll on the scenic hillside locally notorious as a haunt of the lower class of courting couple. Far from being shocked or insulted, Angela appears to welcome the proposal.

'So this is where you take all your girlfriends,' she laughs, apparently happy to be brought to an infamous location by an experienced seducer. In sumptuous sunlight and high spirits, they gladly ascend the hill of love, Ward gallantly helping her over the steeper parts and carrying the jacket she is soon obliged to remove. This affords her considerable relief, for the sweater, although heavy, tight-fitting and roll-necked, is now revealed to be without sleeves. Her spirit is simultaneously released. With another sudden shriek of recollection, she opens her bag and produces a tiny transistor radio. Swiftly tuning it to a music station, she immediately sings along with the song, apparently in a transport at the feeble tinny emanations.

'Oh I love this one ... "Sorrow" ... the Merseybeats. I *love* the Merseybeats.'

Ward smiles tolerantly. 'Not the Merseybeats. *They* split up and two of them then formed the *Merseys*. "Sorrow" is by the *Merseys* ... not the Merseybeats.'

'What difference does it make?' Irritated by this pedantry, Angela turns up the volume. 'With your long blond hair,' she sings gaily, more for herself now, 'And your eyes of *bloo ... oooh*', the upper half of her body swaying from side to side in time. 'Talking of long blond hair, do you know Dolores Page at all?'

'Is she at school with you?'

'Not at all. She lives up near us. Really sexy, I think. She has a lovely figure, you know, and she wears these tight tight sweaters.' In Angela's voice is a tone of wistfulness and envy, as though she is unaware that her own sweater is neither loose-fitting nor inadequately filled. 'All the men are always after her ... and she always has loads of boyfriends, you know. She goes through boyfriends like no man's business ... but then didn't she get married all of a sudden last month.' Sudden high musical laughter enchants the slumbering hillside. 'A real rush job, you know. No engagement or anything.' Another high peal of mischievous understanding, even complicity. '*We're all counting the weeks.*'

Nor does it seem unnatural to leave the main path for a secluded sun-dappled glade. Irrepressibly buoyant and limber, Angela puts down the radio to dance around the clearing in an ecstasy which, apart from the heavy breasts bouncing in harness, resembles that of an enraptured wood nymph released from a thousand-year spell. Eventually exhausted, she falls to the grass and lies supine with arms outstretched, as though pinioned by a Hairy Wild Man of the Woods. Surely these are unambiguous signals. The lengthy symphony of love is at last approaching resolution. Ward lies next to her in silent communion. After a time he turns and, though yearning to crush her to him, settles for raising her shoulder, moving his body gently against hers and seeking her lips with his own. Angela's lips suffer his for a moment – and then turn aside to release, into the warm afternoon, the cold terrible tones of an alien creature who lives in her depths. 'You're *hurting me.*'

At once the enchantment is broken. The very sun seems to dim. Frightened wood spirits flee in dismay.

Apparently unaware of any change, Angela resumes her former gaiety on the return journey. Although they are going downhill, Ward is now obliged to move slowly and carefully, hampered by the chafing of his sensitive penis head, exposed by a subsiding erection which has trapped the prepuce behind the head. Unable to pause for adjustment, every step is a trial. And by and by there is added to this a dull persistent ache in the testicles, which Shotter will later diagnose as the common affliction of lover's knackers ('The energy of voluptuous feeling ends in discomfort and positive suffering' – Baudelaire).

Thus is established the pattern of their meetings, a pattern made even more bewildering by a claim of Shotter's. 'Know Barney Gillan . . . the guitarist with the Florida Showband? He used to live beside her. Claims he rid her when she was fifteen. Broke her in, he says.'

'That's impossible.'

'You mean, she's giving *you* nothing.' Shotter laughs and offers advice typically terse. 'Fire her down and ride her.'

Ward is devastated by this new mystery. 'She couldn't have given it to Barney.'

'Well now.' With obvious relish Shotter removes the cellophane from twenty Embassy Regal, withdraws a cigarette, lights it with the Zippo and inhales deeply. 'This is the question, isn't it?' He releases smoke with a sensual sigh. '*Did he or did he not tie her diddy in a knot?*'

Compared to human conundrums, those of mathematics are

absurdly simple. The world is still at Ward's feet but now he can see that it is not a treasure house but an evil vortex of ambiguity and deception. Far from corresponding exactly, reality and appearance have nothing in common. When he ceases to see Angela the action seems only to strengthen the linkage. Mrs Ward, his friends, café society, everyone believes that the two of them are a couple; Angela Neville is Martin Ward's girl.

But whereas it was fun for the relationship to start by itself, its continuance against his will is not so amusing. Alarmed and disillusioned, Ward returns to his books and on the sofa in the front room he eventually attains a kind of peace ('Happiness is not possible; but tranquillity is' – Flaubert).

Familiar high melodious laughter in the street. Ward leaps from the sofa in terror. For a moment he remains rigid and petrified, his face contorting in wild disbelief. Then, with a terrible oath, he rushes out of the room and upstairs, disappearing just as his mother opens the door to Frank Neville and his daughter.

'There's Angela, Martin!' Mrs Ward calls out. 'I'm away for a bit of driving with Frank.'

Angela goes into the living room to wait. Cautiously emerging from his bedroom, Martin peers through the stair rods. Not a sound.

But after a time Angela comprehends and begins to frisk around, rustling newspapers and flipping through magazines while all the time humming a breezy tune.

Still gaily humming, she goes out to the kitchen to make tea.

Snarling, Ward grips the stair rods with the impotent fury of an imprisoned murderer. As many another before him has discovered, mere rejection of one's destiny is never sufficient. You have to seize the brute by the throat and squeeze the breath from its body.

*Sweet Jesus, now she is making for the stairs!* His Destiny is about to climb the stairs and beard him in his den.

In blind panic he rushes back into his room, throws himself on the bed and pretends to be lost in the oceanic depths of Nelkon and Parker's *Advanced Level Physics*.

She is only going to the bathroom.

Eventually Frank and Mrs Ward return.

'Where's Martin?'

Angela glances up from *Women's Own* as though the question has only just occurred to her. 'Still upstairs, I suppose.'

'You mean he *never came down.*' It takes Mrs Ward a moment to grasp the enormity of the snub. 'You mean you were *left on your own the whole time?*'

'Oh I was fine,' Angela cries airily. 'I made a cup of tea ... and I found these magazines.' Dropping *Women's Own*, she springs to her feet with a radiant smile.

Frantic, Mrs Ward rushes at the magazines. 'Take them with you, sure.' And lifting the entire bunch, she attempts to force them on the girl. 'I never look at magazines. They're only auld things Bibi Drummond brought me in hospital.'

Politely Angela refuses, reducing the older woman to desperate pleading. 'Sure stay a wee minute for a drop of tea itself.'

'I'm only after one, thanks.'

Father and daughter depart with the quiet dignity of the morally superior. As they drive off, Mrs Ward, broken, humiliated and vengeful, turns her darkening features towards the stairwell.

'*MARTIN!*'

'I see they have blue roses in Japan,' someone murmured contentedly, without looking up from the paper.

'*Blue roses!*'

'They cost *fifty pounds each.*'

'*Fifty pounds each!*'

'Apparently they stand them in blue ink.'

I was trying not to listen. The human mind shies in terror from a nothingness infinite in time and space. Banality is as frightening to contemplate as Pascal's Abyss.

Beyond the window, above the convent house, hung a dolorist sky heavy with the burden of present suffering and the promise of more in the years to come.

'And there's Martin by his window. In solitary splendour as usual.'

'Oh he wouldn't lower himself to talk to the likes of us. We're not up to his intellectual standard, dear.'

'He looks as though he's miles away.'

'Don't you believe it. He's taking in every word.'

At least there was the start of a breeze which could shift the oppressive looming clouds. Into the field of vision rose a torn and tattered carrier bag. Ecstatically it soared, hovered, looped the loop and suddenly swooped back down with rapturous authority and control. The message of this performance was clear. Only the disencumbered are free. Shed your burden and fly.

'Rubbish everywhere,' someone behind me complained. 'Is there anything in the paper about the dustmen's strike?'

'They've just turned down the latest offer.'

'Soon they'll be earning as much as us.'

'Soon *everyone*'ll be earning as much as teachers. You wouldn't mind if they did something for it. Have you seen that crowd supposed to be mending the road outside? All they ever do is sit in a hut and drink tea.' Ensconced in an armchair, the speaker fell into a brooding silence consoled by a sip from the mug at her side.

'Dustmen earning as much as teachers. Teachers who've spent *years* being trained for the job.'

'Oh I'm sure some are already earning more than us, dear.'

'And they have the perks as well. I believe they're always finding the most *marvellous* things.'

At precisely the instant I turned from the window Janet looked up from her novel.

A secret look would have sufficed – but she crossed the staffroom to sit at my table and whisper, 'I'm having a few people over on Sunday afternoon. *Would you like to come?*'

'Sunday?' Instinctively I recoil from invitations.

'No one else from here of course.'

Familiar joy of being the chosen one, the preferred, the elect. Obviously Janet was about to propel the relationship into the inevitable new phase. ('The friendship of women,' said d'Aurevilly, 'is virgin love or widowed love. It is *before* or *after*.')

'And of course you must bring Clare too.' Janet assumed her habitual expression of wistfulness and yearning. 'I saw the two of you on Finchley Road on Saturday.'

'Why didn't you say hello?'

'You were laughing about something ... you looked so happy together.'

I considered telling her the truth – but it was too flattering to be seen as the dream marriage, the show couple, the laughing young lovers.

'I don't know about a babysitter.'

'Bring your kids along. Other couples will have kids. And my daughter's mad about children.'

Would any young woman be capable of such consideration? Janet's dark eyes revealed deep compassion and tenderness. ('A soul which has lived its life is surely a more formidable mystery than one which has only just begun' – d'Aurevilly).

However, Janet's concern for the entire family was not enough to enthuse Clare.

'I can't stand that bastard Wills.'

'No one else from the school is invited,' I snapped.

Though not reassured, she could scarcely deny me this triumph of preferment.

How long was it since I had been invited to a party? The tight jeans, abandoned for years, just about fitted still. When the zip finally went up I felt like d'Aurevilly strapped into his corset ('If I even took Holy Communion I would burst'). A theorist of dandyism before Baudelaire, Barbey was the only one of the seven to retain a fanatical concern for appearance. Up to his death in 1889, at the age of eighty-one, he continued to dress in the style of the twenties – a severely waisted frockcoat over a waistcoat of lurid red ('the colour of power, war and love'), glove-tight checked trousers and a shirt with lace ruffs and sleeves, his accessories a pair of musketeer's gauntlets and a wide-brimmed hat. No doubt as preposterous a sight as myself, propelling a double pushchair in skintight Levis, cowboy boots and a heavy studded lumberjack shirt.

Janet's flat was in one of those magnificent Bayswater town houses whose Palladian splendour has been humanised by subdivision and neglect. Wide imposing steps led up to strong Doric columns supporting a pediment – but the steps were worn hollow, paint was flaking from the columns and the pediment was riven by structural cracks. We hauled the pushchair up the steps only to find the hallway obstructed by a bicycle on one side and, on the other, a rickety table littered with mail. Beyond the table was a payphone surrounded by the notes and messages of supportive community-conscious tenants. The contrast with our own sombre foyer was dramatic and revealed the extent of our apostasy. Although our home was still in flatland, we were already developing the sclerosis of the suburbs.

Janet appeared on the stairs with a cry of welcome that was full of sincerity and warmth but somehow got lost in the upward toiling with pushchair and children. Laughing awkwardly, she led us into a second-floor flat in the style of the hallway – poorly lit, cluttered, run-down, functional – but with a reassuring ambience I recognised as fifties intellectual. Along the walls were old wooden bookshelves full of faded hardbacks with tattered dust covers and, above the shelves, paintings that were theoretically original but in fact poor imitations of various modernist movements and styles. And every-where, on the shelves, on the floor, suspended from the ceiling, were pots which varied in size from trinkets to giant plant-holders and waist-high Aladdin jars.

As we came to rest in the living room I waited in fatherly antici-pation for Janet to make much of the children. She looked at the pushchair, gave an incredulous laugh and turned to offer us white wine.

As Janet went for the drinks Clare appraised her with a frown of distaste. 'She doesn't do much with herself.'

I had a glimpse of Janet through Clare's eyes – the pale unmade-up face, crazy anyhow hair and cheap nondescript clothes. In Clare's culture dignity was expressed by unremitting attention to personal appearance.

Suddenly I was conscious of my own absurd get-up. A provin-cial trying desperately and getting it hopelessly wrong.

Janet returned immediately with wine – but I could feel her drawn by the magnetic field of the other guests.

'Lovely pots,' Clare said weakly.

'I make a lot of pots. I have the use of a kiln. It keeps me sane.' Janet lurched and gave a high-pitched nervous laugh that ques-tioned the success of the therapy.

There was an awkward silence. I praised a derivative exercise in Cubism on the wall nearest us.

'The artist's over there!' With a wild cry of hostess triumph Janet indicated a man with a black roll-necked sweater and an impressive intellectual baldness. Before I could stop her, she took my arm and drew me across the room.

'Martin's a fan of your painting, Ivan,' her heavy stress of the second syllable of his forename (Eee-*van*) adding a cachet of East-European seriousness to an already formidable presence.

The artist turned from his group, taking in my leisurewear and, behind that, the wife with the pushchair and children. Then both of us looked to Janet – but she used her momentum to sail on. Eee-*van* waited with patience and courtesy but no initiative or interest. Clare was bent over the pushchair. Lucy had wakened and was angrily struggling against her straps.

When Lucy let out a roar of frustration I went back to the loved ones. Clare released the infant and took her up in her arms. Paul, who had been cautiously assessing the room, now made for the only fun item – a basket chair suspended from a chain fixed to the ceiling.

'He'll pull down that whole fucking thing,' I warned grimly.

'Maybe you'd like to take him away from it.' Clare bounced Lucy on her shoulder in a vigorous manner perhaps intended to calm herself as much as the child. 'Where's this daughter that's supposed to be mad about children?' Everyone in the room was middle-aged and almost all of them were men. We were the only youngish couple, the only couple in leisurewear, the only couple with children, no doubt the only Irish couple as well. 'I feel like a *fucking gyppo*,' Clare went on. 'Get me a cardboard box and I'll go round with Lucy begging for coppers.'

'We'll have to speak to someone.'

'*You* speak to them.'

The company turned out to have another chilling advantage. They were nearly all university lecturers, colleagues of Janet's ex-husband (who was also present, keeping his distance but subjecting me to a searching scrutiny when he got the chance). I had to keep admitting that I taught in a comprehensive school. In one group Janet attempted to improve my status by mentioning that I had done postgraduate research.

'Where was that?' someone dutifully enquired.

'Queen's.'

'Queen's College Oxford ... or Queens' College Cambridge?' The question came so quickly that it was possibly ingenuous.

'Queen's University Belfast.'

There was a moment of silence. Then someone else said that he had actually been to Belfast. 'And I thought this was significant. The boat turned right round' – the speaker himself turned his back on us, thrusting out a large behind and peering over his shoulder in comical apprehension – 'and went in *very carefully ... backways ...*

*like this.*' With exaggerated caution and fearfulness he manoeuvred his great behind into our midst. There was a certain amount of guarded laughter. 'But in fact I had a great time,' he added, straightening up and turning to present me with a reassuring grin. 'The Irish have such a great sense of humour.'

'English egotism,' noted d'Aurevilly, 'the most terrible since that of the Romans.'

When I went to take Lucy, there was little in Clare's expression to suggest the uproarious fun-loving Gael. 'Let's get out of here,' she muttered.

'We can't leave this early.'

One reason for staying was that the company included a philosopher, not merely a teacher but the author of several highly regarded works on ethics. I had never seen a philosopher, much less had a chance to talk to one. Though the prospect was as daunting as arguing with Socrates, it was not an opportunity that would soon present itself again.

This man had the ugliness of Socrates but not his asceticism. As I approached, he seized the woman on either side and pulled them against himself with a great roar of laughter. I experienced a surge of puritanical distaste. With a girl on each arm, he was more like a Mafia boss in a nightclub than a thinker preoccupied by existence and essence.

But it was too late to turn back. 'You're an authority on ethics?' And I began to explain about the crag and the cross.

'*What?*' he interrupted almost at once, with a humorous look at each companion in turn. 'Define your terms.'

The fact that the 'girls' were both middle-aged women made the situation even more repellent. They sniggered in the insolent knowing way of camp followers everywhere faced with an unwelcome intruder. Of course I could see the absurdity of it – a half-drunk Paddy in leisurewear attempting to discover the meaning of life. Yet, though all men in leisurewear are idiots and I was indisputably in leisurewear, I was definitely not an idiot. But as I tried to explain the terms they grew more and more vague and Socrates more and more impatient. At last he burst out in irritation.

'It's just the old Pagan–Christian divide.'

To the professional it was merely a question of terminology. And to most nonprofessionals this kind of speculation would be futile and ludicrous. 'Philosophy,' sneered d'Aurevilly, 'a hole made with a corkscrew in a cloud.' For the warm-blooded, life is its own justification. But the rest of us are not so fortunate. Cold hearts need faith. And the fact that it has to be arbitrary is not a deterrent. Villiers put it with a typical flourish: 'Since you cannot escape your own illusion of the world, choose the most divine.' Flaubert said something remarkably similar: 'Since all alternatives are absurd let us choose the most noble.'

Eventually Janet's natural solicitude prevailed and she took Lucy from us so that we could go to the buffet. It was instantly obvious that she had no way with children. Her problems with discipline went back to the cradle. Immediately Lucy began to struggle and roar. Pale but determined, Janet took her from the room.

The intellectual indifference to appearances extended also to the food which consisted of shop-bought cold meats and a salad as unimaginative and limited as those thrown together by my mother on our return from Sunday devotions in the summer. Clare frowned with contempt – but filled her plate in disciplined silence.

As soon as we sat down to eat, Paul fell off the swinging chair and landed on his head.

There was quite a little commotion, in which the intellectuals displayed their customary ineptitude and horror of blood. Clare alone was magnificently calm and controlled. The cut was superficial and there appeared to be no damage done.

'He could have one of the bedrooms,' Janet offered. 'If you wanted to put him down for a bit.'

'That's the *last* thing you should do after a knock on the head.'

Clare's tone had a hard cold edge. It was definitely time to go.

In the street she immediately flung back her tortured head. 'Jeeeeeeeesus.'

'All right,' I snapped. '*All right.*'

'Jesus, Martin.'

'*All right.*'

'Jesus ... I've never felt more like a gyppo in my life.'

'All right, we shouldn't have gone. *All right?*'

'I'll tell you something now, Martin. If that's the sort of people you want to mix with ... *fine*. I mean, if that's the sort of friends you want ... *fine.*'

'They are *not* my friends.'

'I mean, go and see them . . . *fine* . . . but just don't ask me along . . . *OK?*'

'They . . . are . . . not . . . my . . . friends,' I pronounced each word slowly, with great care and calm. 'I knew no one but Janet. *They are not my friends.*'

'You spent enough time with them. *Leaving me to look after the kids.*'

'*Looking after?*' An incredulous embittered cry directed not at Clare but at the objective neutral heavens.

'What *exactly* is that supposed to mean?'

'Paul's split, isn't he?'

'*My* fault of course.' Now it was her turn to address the sky. 'All my fault . . . *oh yes.*'

It was a long time since both of us had appealed to the firmament like this. In the early stages of marriage both parties, overwhelmed by outrage and despair at injustice, look around for an impartial judge to absolve the innocent and convict the guilty. When none is discovered an imaginary arbiter has to be invented and impassioned pleas are addressed to skies, ceilings, roofs – whatever lies overhead.

'*All right!*' I screamed suddenly, trembling. 'It was a terrible mistake. We shouldn't have gone . . . OK?' Clare was momentarily silenced by the force of this outburst. I should have left it there but, like a man out of the trenches and over the top, a kind of suicidal fury drove me on. 'It's just that *beggars* can't be choosers . . . *can they?* I don't get invited out all the time. Nobody buys *me* tickets. Nobody takes *me* out to restaurants. Do they? I mean, *do they?* Hn . . . *Hn?* I suppose if I was going out *three nights a week* I might start getting particular. I'd probably be a bit more *choosy*. You *know?* Hn? But in fact I don't go out *any* nights. I don't go out *anywhere*. So I'm afraid I'm not choosy. I'm not choosy at all.'

'Stop it! Stop it! Stop it!' Paul covered his ears against the rant.

Clare began to talk in a calm conversational tone, addressing a wise and just but unfortunately imaginary person at her side. 'Here it all comes now,' she was saying, with a hideous fatalism that almost seemed to welcome violence. 'It's all coming out now. I knew this was bound to happen. Here it all comes now.'

To Paul this was even more distressing than rage. 'Stop it! Stop it!'

So we went home in sullen silence in the creeping desolation of Sunday twilight, through streets that were now shabby, hostile and alien. This is the other side of the city experience – all that is exhilaratingly exotic when you are up will seem correspondingly squalid and threatening when you are down. Above all, it seemed absurd to be in charge of young children in such a place. We had to haul the pushchair up a long broken escalator, then change a nappy on the platform and coax Paul into holding his water until we got home. I wanted to let him pee on the track but Clare had some horror about electric shocks passing up the urine jet and frying the insouciant pisser to a crisp. As a physicist, I should have been able to dismiss this – but I could not think how.

Most depressing was the memory of the scene with the philosopher. Not only personally humiliating, it seemed to dispel any hope of illumination or guidance. There was no ideal, no way, no guru, no code. Nothing but gathering Sunday dusk and our petty, aggrieved, squabbling selves.

At home I fought an impulse to sit down with a gin and tonic and grimly threw myself into getting the children to bed. Routine domestic chores are invaluable in the course of a violent quarrel. Not only do they permit a silence free from the accusation of sulking, they also strengthen the two essential convictions of martyrdom and rectitude. Best of all, they provide distraction for hands that itch to encircle a throat.

But soon there were no chores left. I poured a stiff one and drank it standing up at the kitchen sink.

Clare came into the room with a purposeful expression.

'Drink?'

'No thanks.' Failing to offer her one sooner was another thoughtless surrender of rectitude. 'Listen, Martin. I've been thinking about this whole business. It's just not worth it if you're going to throw fits in front of the children. I mean, I just can't take that sort of thing.' She was calm, composed, grave. 'I think it's better if I don't see Nick again.'

Of course this was what I wanted – but not in a scenario which granted her all the nobility and selflessness. My long months of dignity and forbearance were not to be so easily set aside.

'I'm not ordering you to give him up.'

'You're obviously extremely angry. Possibly violent.'

189

'On one occasion I've lost my temper slightly. *Once!*'

'But it shows you've been furious all along. I always thought you were generous. It's better if I don't see Nick any more.'

'You mean you want to go on seeing him but have to submit to your brute of a husband.'

'It's better to break it off if you feel like this.' Her expression took on an even more sombre hue. 'And I won't go back to the Centre. I'll give up my courses.'

'*Oh . . . beautiful!* That's a lovely touch. All knowledge and culture abandoned in a sacrifice to the brute.'

'I couldn't go back to that Centre.'

'So everyone will know you've been chained to the wall by a jealous husband. Martin the fucking barbarian.' I thrust my face into hers. 'But I spent the first half of my life with a martyred woman . . . *and I've no intention of spending the second half the same way.*'

'I'm not going back to the Centre.'

'Of course not. But why stop there?' Now my face was practically against hers. 'Why not take the *fucking veil?*'

In the movies, when women hit men it is always sideways, across the cheek, with a comically ineffectual wrist slap and no follow through. Clare swung from the hip and caught me on the jaw with a heavy clout that bent me back over the sink and knocked my glasses across the work surface. Instantly I clouted back. Improving on the concept of turning the other cheek, she thrust her whole head forward in an angry defiant invitation. I would have been only too glad to oblige – but it was her turn to strike. When she continued to offer herself I threw the contents of my glass in her face. With a hideous shriek of satisfaction she shook her dripping head at me.

What I longed to do was seize her throat and choke off her breath. Instead I turned and hurled the empty glass at the far wall, the open-plan area permitting a long full trajectory before a deep rich detonation in which the sound of breaking glass was only the topmost musical component. As with any explosion, there was an eerie moment of silence before the realisation of damage and injury. Then Clare crumpled, sobbing bitterly, supporting herself on the work top.

According to Shotter, the Florida Showband is full of sophisti-cated musicians condemned to perform the frightful trash demanded by the Irish dancing public.

'What they really want to play is jazz. You know they backed Louis Armstrong when he toured Ireland?'

'I never knew that.'

'And he said he wanted them again when he came back. He really rated them – but that was the last time they got to play decent music.'

In response to this rejection of their true talent, the band now deliberately seek out the most tasteless and vulgar material, a posture of aristocratic nihilism which Ward finds invigorating and noble ('To the public one should never offer the delicate fragrances which infuriate them but only meticulously selected and graded Class I *merde*' – Baudelaire).

For the solemn occasion of the Florida Showband playing the Mecca, Shotter, ever in thrall to the USA, wears a light tan mohair two-piece (whose official colour of 'biscuit' does not do justice to its rainbow iridescence), a white shirt with a tiny collar made even more compact by a gold pin underneath a slimline tie just wide enough to avoid being classified as 'string'. Ward, enamoured of tradition, wears a heavy dark three-piece with his grandfather's silver watch-chain across the waistcoat and, at his throat, an old silk tie of his father's in a loose Windsor knot ('Dandyism is the last flicker of the heroic in a bourgeois age' – Baudelaire).

There is no question of dancing with, or even looking at, girls. Shotter leads Ward to the chairs beside the stage where they face the band and resolutely ignore the rest of the hall. At first there is Dixieland jazz but when the hall fills up singer Gregory joins his colleagues to perform a jaunty quickstep set whose highlight is 'Don't Lose Your Hucklebuck Shoes'. This is followed by a slow set ending with 'Five Little Fingers', a heartrending ballad narrated by a father coming home to baby after news of Mammy's death in a crash with her lover, the eponymous fingers of the infant reaching for those of its daddy. 'And then those five little fingers touched my ha-aand' – too moved to sing the conclusion, Gregory shuts his eyes and, stretching out his own hand in unconscious empathy, recites in a broken tearful whisper – 'five little fingers ... *too young to understand*.'

Shotter chuckles in knowing delight. 'They fight each other to get doing numbers like that.' But though Ward is alert for contempt beneath the sentimental words, he is unable to distinguish the renditions of the Florida from those of the genuinely vulgar bands.

Now guitarist Barney Gillan steps to the mike for 'Sea of Heartbreak', undermining its sombre message not by irony or contempt but by winking and grinning at a group of girls who have approached the stage to watch him sing.

'Barney's a wild man for his hole,' Shotter explains with a laugh. 'He'd get up on anything that moves. And the women are all dyin' about him. He was tellin' me Gregory's wife tried to get off with him – but he only dry rid her ... too much trouble already in the band.'

Eventually Ward takes to turning sideways and casting surreptitious looks down the hall. At the top, in the snack bar, sit the bourgeois girls whose disdainful poses and expressions make it clear that the only applicants considered will be those exceptionally endowed with money, transport, breeding and looks. At the bottom end, around the ladies' toilet, is a large closely packed and excitable throng, many in lime green or shocking pink, encumbered with lighters and twenties of Embassy Regal. In between the two groups, and apparently belonging to neither, is a tall girl with pale features framed in long hair black as jet that falls to her shoulders in a shining straightness untormented by the curlicues and confections typical of the seething mass behind. Standing apart, impassive, silent and still, without the solace of social superiority, companions or even cigarettes, her severe and solitary distinction is almost allegorical in its power ('The greatest praise one can bestow on a diamond is to call it a solitaire' – d'Aurevilly).

Ward has a technique for asking a girl out to dance. Approaching with a countenance entirely devoid of interest or warmth, he stops a few feet away, touches the point of her elbow with the tip of his middle finger and, when she looks at him, briefly raises his eyebrows the merest fraction of an inch ('That ease of bearing, that sureness of manner, that simplicity in the habit of command, that calmness revealing strength in every circumstance – one of those privileged beings in whom the formidable and the attractive so mysteriously combine' – Baudelaire).

Equally expressionless, she follows him onto the dance floor and, tossing back her long hair, moves into his arms.

It is some time before he speaks. 'Like the band?'

She shrugs briefly. 'They're all right.'

Assuming an expression of profound disgust, Ward lays his left index finger along the left side of his nose and with his right hand makes the motion of pulling down a toilet chain ('If what is divine in man is three-quarters madness, then his wisdom is three-quarters contempt' – d'Aurevilly).

'A sarky type.' She studies him for a moment. 'You have a sarky face.'

Despite himself he smiles, pleased that she can see shining on his brow that mysterious sign which reveals those who despise the ritual fatuities of the herd. 'Actually they're not as bad as they sound. They have to play crap for dances – but they're really jazz musicians.' He pauses respectfully. 'Like jazz?'

'No.'

They dance.

'What music *do* you like?'

Frowning a little, she offers her favourite response – the shrug.

After they have danced for a time. 'Are you from the town?'

She shrugs and grunts, then adds in a pungent dismissive tone, '*That famous city.*'

Now Gregory raises his mike with a meaningful grin. 'Thank you. Thank you. We continue dancing with ... "The Bold O'Donoghue!" '

As the crowd cheer a bucklep, Ward frowns in distaste. 'I hate this Irish crap. Like it?'

'No.'

> *Oh I'm the boy to squayze her and I'm the boy to tayse her and*
> *I'm the boy to playze her and I'll tell you what I'll do*

The dancers shriek with delight and kick out. Already some enthusiastic men begin to 'swizz' their girls. Grimacing, Ward looks about for a refuge.

> *I'll court her like an Irishman with the Irish blarney too if I can,*
> *It's the hulligan-mulligan hulligan-mulligan Bold O'Donoghue!*

'How about getting outside for a while?'

She shrugs. 'All right.'

After the noise and heat they are struck dumb by the cool and silent immensity of the night. Beneath a sky teeming with stars the dance hall is revealed as an ugly excrescence, a crude concrete cuboid hastily flung up in a field on the outskirts of the town. Clad only in a short sleeveless minidress, the girl suddenly clasps herself, as though in involuntary self-defence against the mercenary expediency of man and the pitiless indifference of the universe.

'Cold?'

'I'm all right.'

Still holding herself, she walks by his side around the corner of the building, placing her flimsy shoes carefully on the uneven ground and as carefully averting her eyes from the couples at intervals against the wall. Entranced by the grandeur of the night and thirsting insatiably for the infinite, Ward throws back his head to the heavens where he would like to soar aloft with the powerful wingbeat of the Andean condor, exulting in freedom and space and a blackness as hideous as man's heart, emitting wild piercing cries which make the dogs of the farflung farms of Ulster snap their chains and rush in circles, foaming with frenzy.

'I suppose you're at the College,' she says suddenly, with a hint of resentment and bitterness.

'What have you got against college boys?'

'Oh' – she glances quickly at him, attempting to plumb the mysterious plenitude of the brow and the gleaming eyes beautiful as suicide – 'they fancy themselves.'

There are no spaces along the side wall. Still apparently strolling at random they turn the corner at the back.

'And what do you do yourself?'

'I work in a sweet shop. Canning's.'

'Like it?'

She laughs bitterly. 'Canning's a bad animal. A hateful pig. Cares about nothin' but money. And he hates me like poison. Maybe because I'm bigger than him. I must be a foot bigger. Or else because I don't suck up to him or the customers. He's always telling me not to have such a *face* on me.' Another one incapable of learning the banalities which appease the herd! Ward glances at her in sudden approval – but she is too absorbed in her story to notice. 'And he's always giving the other girls rises and telling them not to let on to me. Of course it always comes out. There's this one . . . Gloria . . . she gets the most because she's always lickin' up to him.' Pause for a harsh bleak laugh. 'And the best of it is this, Gloria's robbin' him blind the whole time. Hands out free fags to everybody belongin' to her.'

This unexpected bitter eloquence rouses Ward from his detachment. He studies her perceptively. 'And Gloria isn't tall either?'

'A *midget*,' she spits out in violent contempt, turning suddenly and, in a single lithe movement, bringing her body against him, placing her arms about his neck and lifting her parted lips to his, which receive them in gratitude and pleasure ('Stranger, permit me to touch you and let my hands, which seldom consent to touch the living, venture forth upon the nobility of your flesh' – Lautréamont).

When he draws her closer to him she shifts, not to evade the lower grossness but to arrange its comfortable accommodation, moving her legs to permit him to grip one of her thighs between his. After a time he moves his hand to the top of the zip at the back of her dress – but squanders the coolness of the experienced libertine by fumbling hopelessly with the catch.

'Havin' some trouble there?' She draws back her head to regard him, mischief glinting in veiled eyes like a sliver of moonlight on a somnolent canal. Then, to his astonishment, she reaches back herself and swiftly undoes the catch. As he draws down the zip, two things simultaneously slip out of place – the front of her dress and his indifferent mask of surfeit.

'Like what you're lookin' at?' she tartly enquires.

'Very much.'

But when he feels for her bra catch she firmly removes his hand. 'No.'

And when, shortly after, he attempts to raise his hand along her inner thigh, she brusquely seizes it and flings it away.

Although he would never admit it, Ward is secretly pleased by this allowance precisely calculated and strictly policed, well above the miserly norm but with a clearly defined upper bound. As unsatisfactory as total denial would be total surrender now. For the small are as incapable of receiving as of giving. The gift of her arcanum would be too overwhelming.

By the time they return the dance is over and Shotter is signalling impatiently from the stage door. Something in Ward's careful gait makes Shotter grunt knowingly.

'Did ye *fire*?' He casts a swift glance at the girl who waits a few paces behind. 'She gave ye a dry ride, uh?'

'So called. It's actually one of the wettest experiences I know.' Gingerly Ward slips a hand in his pocket and detaches his trousers from the soaked underpants.

'But dark trousers don't show.' Shotter grunts disparagingly at his own biscuit mohair. 'These fuckin' light suits are *desperate*.'

In the back room Gregory and Barney Gillan are drinking from half bottles of Bushmills.

'We're shagged out,' Gregory complains. 'Met these two Yanks in Dublin. Says Barney, *we've no mission here* – and right enough ye wouldn't have thought to look at them . . . ye know? But Jesus they bucked like *rabbits*.'

Producing twenty International Dunhill, Shotter, without bothering to ask anyone, proceeds to throw a cigarette at every man in the room except Ward. Nor do the recipients respond, other than by catching the cigarettes against their chests and, almost absentmindedly, placing them in their mouths. Shotter takes one himself and goes round with the Zippo.

'They have us destroyed,' Barney agrees, inhaling hungrily. 'And Jesus we were broke dead when they went home. Took them out to the airport and they had all these presents for us – fancy lighters and monogrammed handkerchiefs and what not. The two of us were *broke dead*. Broke dead, look see.' Shaking his head, he takes a sharp belt of Bush to ease the pain. 'Didn't seem to bother *them* though. Wild characters altogether. Gregory says his wanked him off with her toes.'

Anxious to avoid any suspicion of drunken exaggeration or fantasy, Gregory looks around for somewhere to set aside his bottle of Bush. Finding nowhere suitable, he has to rely on naked sincerity. 'I swear to Jesus,' he says, 'that's the God's honest truth.' After staring into the faces of Shotter and Ward in turn, he assumes an expression of the utmost solemnity. 'It was the Gresham Hotel in O'Connell Street. Just lie back, she says, and *wanks me off wi' her toes*.'

Chuckling deeply, Shotter casts a triumphant look at Ward who is indeed impressed by a rejection of the natural worthy of Baudelaire. After drinking deeply, Gregory draws on his cigarette and passes his bottle to Shotter. Barney passes his to Ward with a nod at the waiting girl in the doorway.

'Is she a big ride? Looks like a *big ride*.'

'What's she called anyway?' Shotter asks.

'Clare.'

'*Claa .. aare*,' Gregory sings a snatch of song, 'was ever a woman so rare?'

Barney exhales decisively. 'A big ride.'

Suppressing a shudder, Ward raises the bottle to his lips but refrains from drinking the fiery liquid.

'We're goin' on to Thran John's,' Shotter explains to Ward. 'Comin'?'

Clare leans against the door frame, impassive, silent and statuesque, registering neither impatience to leave nor a desire to approach for attention.

'Fuck *me*, she *is* a rare duck,' Gregory chuckles, gratefully accepting the return of his bottle from Shotter. 'That's a dour-lookin' one all right.'

'Comin'?' Shotter asks Ward again.

'Nah,' Ward grunts, returning his bottle to Barney. 'Said Ah'd leave her home, didn't Ah?'

'D'Aurevilly has several stories about unfaithful wives.' At once Clare displayed gratifying attention. 'In one, the husband covers his wife's genitals with hot sealing wax and stamps it with the pommel of his sabre. In another, the husband has the young lover brought before the wife, then cuts out the lover's heart and throws it to his dogs.'

'Charming,' Clare said. 'Which will you do?'

'Why not both?'

'Why not indeed? From your recent behaviour I'd say you were well capable.'

The problem was that, in the second story, the wife instantly plunged to the floor and attempted to eat the heart herself (though of course an aristocratic lady could not compete with hunting dogs). The husband's vengeance was counter-productive and the death of the lover intensified her love.

'Possibly those fates ennobled the lovers too much. Villiers has a story where the husband, instead of killing the lover outright, merely wounds him fatally. Then, as the distressed wife bends over the dying man, the husband seizes her and tickles the soles of her feet, compelling her to burst out laughing in the face of her expiring beloved.'

'That's more your true style,' Clare readily agreed.

Is there any point in struggling against our basic temperaments? Better to accept the fact of my nature and retire to a crag, there to live at last the congenial Crag ethic – proud, free, strong, solitary and honourable, justifying giving nothing by asking for nothing.

But of course the problems were legion. First and foremost the children. Then the colossal energy and commitment required to find even a single room in London. And the economics of separation: how could we maintain two establishments? I suggested to Clare that we live separately in the flat, designating areas of privacy and drawing up a contract on the use of joint facilities and care of the children. Such contractual cohabiting was common, I suggested, even among married couples. Clare told me to fuck off and wise up.

Something would have to be done, I insisted, both to Clare and myself. Those who lie down get sat upon and walked over. (Blessed are the meek for they shall upholster the earth.) But the action, when finally it came, was both characteristic and absurd. I refrained from intercourse with Clare. By now it was entirely dutiful on her part (with nothing of the whore in her make-up, she was incapable of feigning enthusiasm) and one way of maintaining dignity was to stop the charade. There was also the desire to punish by self-martyrdom, a strategy that comes to the Gael as naturally as leaves to the trees.

Recrimination persisted through all this. 'The only reason I put up with it was because you said it wasn't serious. You said it would never get serious. You said you would never leave me.'

'I haven't left you yet.'

'Yet!'

Another genuine symbiotic union – that of alcohol and grievance. I rose to fix a stiff one.

'You realise that's the last spirit glass?'

On the back wall of the living room there were now three dents left by flying gin glasses, three perfect crescent-shaped craters like hoof marks in clay. This was yet another reason for restricting my sex life to the bathroom, where I leaned over the bowl and jerked off into a wad of toilet paper. Endless squabbling and screaming had produced a great weariness with relationships and I could not

believe in the romantic dream of a redemptive simplicity and succour elsewhere. As Huysmans tartly put it to one of his importunate
female admirers: 'Remember, Madame, that nothing happens as
one would wish.'

'So I can't afford to smash the last glass. Want one yourself?'

'No.'

'*I'll* use a wine glass.'

'No.'

All the dignity and strength were with Clare. 'You don't understand, Martin. I've never got on as well with *anyone* ... male or
female. And Nick says it's the same for him. I've never been able
to talk to people – all my life I've been tongue-tied and awkward.
Now there's no silences or embarrassment. I can talk endlessly ...
and it's not just chatter as *you* probably think ... *serious* conversation
... he treats me as an *equal*, Martin.' I made a gesture – but she
brushed it aside. 'I know you cook a bit and help with the children
... that's not what I mean. Nick *listens* to what I say. He's actually
*influenced* by my opinions. When we go to the pictures he asks what
*I* want to see. And not just out of politeness. He's *interested*, Martin.
With us it's always you who chooses the film. Things like that are
important. It's not just the sex. Company's what I enjoy most. He's
great company, Martin. He ...' For a moment she paused and pondered. Only something truly frightful could have interrupted such
eloquence. 'He makes me laugh too. He makes me laugh all the
time ... something you never did.' Again a brief hesitation – but
she trusted in the healing power of truth. '*You have no sense of humour
really, Martin.*'

No one can wound like a spouse. And what made it worse was
the absence of any intention to wound. If only it had been spiteful
retaliation, a reflex return slash with the Stanley knife. But there
was no malice in the remark. It was simply the truth as she saw it.
No doubt a necessary revision. Those who desire to alter history in
the future usually begin by altering it in the past.

I was certainly glad of the gin – and of restful shadows in which
to slump. For years I craved overhead irradiance of operating-
theatre intensity – but recently I had yielded to Clare's taste for
soft indirect light. Now two lamps, low and shaded, discreetly
guided into corners their subdued yellow beams.

Strong drink and weak light: the home helps of the frail.

Any lingering desire for vengeance was removed by Clare's passionate sincerity. *Les Diaboliques* depicts women as treacherous and resourceful temptresses and deceivers. The stories are lurid and thrilling – but false. D'Aurevilly was a posturing fool. Like so many who advocate pride and honour, he failed to display either himself. When *Les Diaboliques* was threatened with prosecution he immediately withdrew it from circulation. Baudelaire and Flaubert went through with their immorality trials; the fanatic of honour backed down.

Clare was neither treacherous nor deliberately seductive – but she was unconsciously tempting as she sat on the sofa with her bare feet tucked up beneath her, bare upper right arm extended across the sofa back, her right hand gesturing, supporting her face or toying with her long black hair. This familiar favourite pose was now invested with something subtly extra which made her heartbreakingly beautiful. It was certainly not her clothes: old jeans and a well-worn short-sleeved cotton blouse. Perhaps a new aura of self-belief. Before, there had always been something hunched and apologetic in her posture, something hunted and evasive in her eyes. Now there was a new voluptuous ease in the way she spread herself out, a thrilling new boldness in the way she tossed her head and thrust back her hair. Even the hair itself seemed more luxuriant and lustrous and her pale skin had an opalescent glow like the mystical light that emanates from a vapour at the critical point. She had become like the other demoralising women of the capital – mysterious, confident, articulate and remote, unattainable except in pitiful masturbation fantasies. She may even have superseded her rivals. I was certainly tossing off regularly to feverish images of my own wife.

'You know, I dream of Canning's shop almost every night, Martin. Nightmares, more like. I'm always back working there . . . and I hate it more than ever. I'm in the shop and Canning comes in . . . back from his golf . . . and runs his finger along one of the shelves to show me the dust. He used to always do that. And I remember as clearly as anything the day I got that job. I remember coming down the stairs and seeing Mrs Canning at our door and knowing straight away why she was there. Canning always sent his wife to the house when he needed a new girl. And I remember thinking, *I don't want to work in your lousy sweet shop.*'

'So why did you?'

'He was a well-known Catholic business man. He had a big car. He always wore suits and had his tie in a tie pin. He handed round the money baskets at the end of Mass in the Cathedral. My parents didn't refuse people like that. Maybe they even thought it was some kind of *honour*. Anyway, my mother agreed ... *without even asking me if I wanted it*. Without even enquiring about the *wages* ... buttons of course ... or the *hours*. In fact the shop was open to all hours at night, even at weekends. So that's how I went to work for Canning ... and we hated each other from the start. You know, often we'd have to do extra work ... in the Christmas rush ... or at Easter to make up baskets. At the end of it he slipped you something ... if you were lucky.'

'There was no agreed overtime rate?'

'*Overtime?* Don't talk nonsense. We never heard of that word. He'd sort of come up to you sideways and slip you an envelope without catching your eye. Always less than I expected. Always less than the other girls got. They weren't supposed to tell – but Gloria could never keep her mouth shut.' Clare paused, momentarily overwhelmed by the memory. 'The man's ten years in his grave – and still I dream about him almost every night. Can you understand that, Martin? *Almost every night.*'

'So what are you saying? Because he's not around you want to take it out on me instead? The husband as universal scapegoat and punchbag?'

'What I'm saying is that people have been telling me what to do all my life. Making all my decisions for me. Never consulting me.'

'You were the one desperate for marriage. It was you who pushed us both into that.' The old trick of answering one grievance with another.

Clare ignored the ploy. 'And can I tell you something else? You know I failed the 11-plus?'

'I've never asked you about that.'

'You didn't have to. And I knew you knew. All my life I've been ashamed about it. Feeling like a moron. An ignorant person. But now can I tell you *why* I failed? Because I was never taught for it – that's why. The nuns didn't even want to enter me ... only my sister Kathleen went down and made a fuss. Kathleen never got doing it herself and she was always angry about that. So in the end the nuns entered me all right – but they never asked me to the special class. They had this class on Saturday morning for 11-plus girls. Doctor O'Donnell's daughter. The daughter of Mrs McCabe the teacher. People like that. I was never asked and of course there was no one to help me at home. I knew nothing about the exam. Didn't even know it was in two parts ... didn't know an intelligence test came first ... didn't even know what an intelligence test *was*. Everyone else had been doing them *until they were blue in the face* ... and comprehension tests as well. I never saw one of either. *Never even saw one.*'

'Jesus,' I groaned. 'Am I to be punished for the sins of the Ulster Catholic bourgeoisie?'

But perhaps she was justified. The seven's misogyny, based on fear of women, led to a preference for lower-class partners who were less of a threat. I had always been proud of marrying below my caste – but maybe the choice of Clare had been cowardly rather than heroic, dictated not by rejection of the bourgeois but fear of dealing with an equal. Maybe the relationship was wrong from the start and Clare somehow sensed that the wrong could never be put right. No choice based on fear is likely to work out well.

'No one's blaming you, Martin. I'm just explaining that I never had a chance. I never had a chance to do anything better.'

'So you've been trying to get into the bourgeoisie as desperately as I've been trying to get out of it.' I uttered a short mirthless laugh. 'We're like two people wedged in a doorway – all we've done is block each other.'

'I have never wanted to be bourgeois.'

'No?' I stamped my foot on the Vancouver Shagpile from Allied Carpets. 'Then what's this?'

'Look around,' she said. 'We bought hardly anything except the carpets. Most of this is from your relatives.'

It was true. Tables, chairs, curtains, bookcases, three-piece suites – all from the houses of my aunts or mother. The connection began gathering furniture as soon as it was discovered that we were potential home owners (since the concept of purchasing a flat was too weird for Ulster, my mother told everyone we were moving into a house). As pointless as ever to decline their generosity. My mother even paid the movers. So that now, by a truly grim irony, I sat in the very armchair once favoured by Greta. If you attempt to flee your destiny they send it after you in a van.

Only the need for another gin got me out of the armchair's terrible embrace.

Clare now found her own history as strange and perplexing as I did mine. 'I was totally innocent, Martin ... so innocent. You know I never understood why you suddenly went limp. And I used to think the stain on your trousers was because you'd peed yourself a bit.'

For once we pondered the same memory – beneath a dark Sacred Heart picture a youth in a three-piece suit falling asleep on a sofa on top of a half-dressed girl, a pocket watch and silver chain hanging out of his waistcoat, a dark stain slowly spreading on the front of his pants.

'You know I was crazy about you, Martin. You have no idea.'

Blind youth, that never knows the value of what it gives or receives. Or that the time of the gifts is soon over and that henceforth everything must be earned.

'I would have done anything for you, Martin ... absolutely *anything*.'

The first wild extravagant love of a young girl – so absurd and wearisome at the time – was now revealed to me as the greatest gift life has to offer, the one human glory surely envied by the gods.

'It could be like that again,' I suggested, not even believing it myself.

'No no no no ... it could never be like that again, Martin.'

We sat for a long time in silence. I finished most of the new glass of gin.

'But surely I made you laugh *sometimes?*'

She looked up quickly – and saw that the question was anything but flippant. 'Well ... *sometimes*, I suppose.' Compassion beckoned for a moment. Then Truth drew her back to its cold steely breast. 'Sometimes ... *but not very often.*'

A plush alcove in the Squealin' Pig Lounge and a table for two by the fish tank in the China Garden – such is the evening of sovereign opulence planned by Ward to demonstrate further his mysterious combination of the attractive and the formidable, a schedule requiring such a sum that his mother cries out in terror: 'Jesus, Mary and Joseph, Martin, you'll have us in Stubbs.' Wearing a Burton's ready-made two-piece ennobled by a scarlet brocade waistcoat, a collarless red-striped shirt and a scarlet bandanna, Ward climbs on a balmy summer evening to the vast council estate of Ardowen, which covers a hilltop above the town, and there, with the cool élan of a crown prince taking a turn in the Tuileries, traverses its paths of hard earth beaten through scraggy waste ground.

The entire estate seems to be out of doors to savour the last of the sun. Hunched men go by with hard masks of inscrutable rumination and purpose, groups of women linger in doorways, girls play ball against gable ends ('Catchy . . . catchy-bouncey . . . ricketawally . . . under-the-leggy') or spin round lampposts on rope swings ('Hi mister push it up a bit higher for us would ye mister?'), boys play tip's-your-kick on the footpaths ('My keek . . . ye touched it . . . ye touched it . . . my keek'), furtive cowering dogs root in gardens (Ward particularly struck by the shocking pink of a huge raw wound on the back of a limping mongrel – 'The charms of horror intoxicate only the strong' – Baudelaire) and on the iron-hard earth of the Big Field rages a tempestuous soccer match in which even now a man of at least forty thunders goalward with a single-minded fury and conviction that scatter younger men before him ('Somebody git *intay 'im* fir fuck's sake!'), his tremendous shot immediately the subject of an altercation ('A fuckin' mile over', 'Nah it was a good goal hi').

Although there are hard men everywhere, Ward betrays apprehension only at the sight of a figure in a wheelchair. For this is the legendary Ironside who uses the immunity of his chair to issue vicious personal insults exceptional even in a city renowned for the imaginative vigour of its abuse. As Ward hesitates, regretting the sublimity of his outfit, Ironside observes, across the street, a passing youth afflicted by acne of shocking extent and virulence. 'Hi, Kirby!' Foolishly the youth turns, recoiling a little when he sees who has hailed him. 'Ye've a face like a busted sausage, Kirby!'

And while the disabled relishes the shame of the disfigured, the dandy smartly nips by on the inside of the pavement.

Although Ward is early, Clare is waiting in the street and, seizing his arm, pushes him back the way he has come.

'What's wrong?'

'I don't want my mother to see.'

'I know – I'm not good enough.'

'Very funny.'

'What then? You're eighteen after all.'

'My mother's a bit strange that way.'

Ward can feel his exaltation subside. Why exhaust oneself in passions doomed to fail and be forgotten? ('Young girl, you will become as other women. Appear no more to my scowling suspicious gaze. In a moment of aberration I might seize your arms and twist them as one wrings water from washing, or snap them with a crack like dry branches, forcing you afterwards to eat them' – Lautréamont.)

Clare darts him quick sidelong looks. 'I didn't think you'd come.'

'That's why you were out on the street.'

'I was going to my friend's after ten minutes.'

A most inauspicious start – and ahead lies the terrible Ironside, though luckily once more distracted, this time by a youth with straight shoulder-length black hair parted in the middle.

Ironside hails him. 'Hi, Jesus!'

Instead of cringing, this youth crosses the street in smiling serenity.

'Really think Ah'm Jesus?'

Ironside is uneasy – but has little choice. 'Aye.'

Still disturbingly genial, the youth lays a hand on the seated one's head. 'Then get outa that wheelchair an' walk ... *spastichole*.'

Clare glances at Martin's scarlet waistcoat and bandanna. 'We can cut off here and go round by Lisnarea Drive.'

Secure at last in a booth of the Squealin' Pig, Ward ignores Jack and the Jackpots (a beefy singer accompanied by a doleful organist and an indolent drummer swirling brushes) to question the girl. 'Why did you think I wouldn't come?'

'Because it happens all the time. Everyone says I'm too dour, they can't talk to me. All I ever get is *Cheer up it might never happen*.'

Again Ward is encouraged by her lack of those consecrated expressions which placate the vulgar herd. But soon he experiences the problem himself. For a long time scarcely a word is spoken.

'Canning's any better than it was?'

'No.'

'Then why don't you leave it?'

She shrugs grimly. 'To do what?'

A fatalism terrifying in one so young. 'There must be *something* you'd like to do.'

She ponders this. 'I thought of nursing once . . . got the forms and all . . . but never applied.'

'Apply now. I'll help you. I'm good at embroidering application forms. By the time I'm finished you won't recognise yourself.'

Who could resist such an enthusiastic offer? Yet Clare sits in silence, her mouth a grim line.

A beautiful teenage girl with a heart that is empty of ambition and desire?

Ward is glad to go to the bar for drinks – and undismayed when a friendly hand is laid on his shoulder.

'How's about ye, young Ward. Still ridin' away?'

It is none other than Quelchy Quigley, a legendary stick man and slag who left the College at the earliest opportunity. With appropriate expressionless laconic calm, Ward issues the greeting he has heard Shotter use.

'Fuckin' Quicksilver Quigley – three strokes and he's home.'

'Least Ah'm gettin' intay *weemen*.' Standing back for a better view, Quelchy considers the waistcoat and bandanna in relaxed humorous wonder. 'But what about *you?* Have ye turned fruit or somethin'?'

Ward indicates Clare with a complacent nod. To his great surprise and consternation, Quelchy grimaces in sudden distaste.

'That real stuck-up one. That *snob.*' An inarticulate Ardowen shop girl *a snob?* Before Ward can put a question, Quelchy takes him by the elbow and turns him back to the bar. 'If you're comin' up to Ardowen try big Delia McMenamin. *Delia Delia come ere tay Ah feel ya.*'

'Takes a length, does she?'

'*Takes a length!*' Quelchy is forced to exclaim in outrage at such an extreme understatement. '*It's bitin' the fuckin' leg off her.*' ('Life teems with innocent monsters' – Baudelaire.)

To establish his own heterosexual worldliness, Ward mentions another famous Ardowen beauty.

'*That auld bag?* Don't believe all ye see in this world. She stuffs her bra wi' the *Belfast Telegraph*. An Ah was that fuckin' bored, Martin, *Ah took it out an' read it.*' Shaking his head, Quelchy withdraws into a sombre rumination on the deceptions and disappointments of life.

'So what are ye doin' with yourself these days, Quelchy?'

'Ah'm out in Henderson's, Martin, ye know?' His expression assumes an even darker hue. 'It's wild altogether. There's this auld English boy in charge. Wild sarcastic, he is. Every time he sends ye for somethin' he says, *Did ye stop off for a bottle of Guinness on the way back or what?* Wantin' to know where ye are the whole time ... ye know? Edgar Fuckin' Lustgarten investigates.' Quelchy shakes his head in disgust. 'Ye couldn't stick him. Ah'm on me way up to the Rockin' Chair to get *arseholed*, Martin.'

For a moment Ward imagines that the youth is proposing to sell his body to men. Then he realises that Quelchy is referring to the conventional escape of drinking to coma. Ward would willingly tarry with such a congenial companion but Quelchy suddenly seizes Ward's wrist: 'What time is it, hi?' A thoroughly existential hero, he carries no time piece on his person – nor does knowledge of the late hour dismay him. He executes a merry jig. 'Ah'm gonnay get *arseholed* the night.'

Ward assumes that Clare will be impressed by his easy mingling in this tough milieu. Instead she is just as disapproving of Quelchy as he was of her. 'I know the Quigleys,' she mutters grimly. 'They're from *Ardowen Heights*.'

Whereas Clare's home is on the town side of the estate, Ardowen Heights is a raw new settlement on the edge of the wilderness. It must be the familiar story of early aristocratic settlers despising newly arrived trash.

'My friend Moira lives next door to the Quigleys,' Clare goes on. 'The house is full of dirty weans ... the smell of it would turn your stomach. Seemingly Mrs Quigley has no smell in her nose – that's the only way she could stick it, I suppose. Moira says they're always runnin' into her house asking for pliers.'

'*Pliers?*'

'The weans have pulled all the knobs off the cooker. The only way you can work it is with pliers. And because she's no smell Mrs Quigley never knows if the gas is off or on. You ought to see the state of her – she's had all her hair and eyebrows burned off twice.'

Careless, ignorant, lazy and blind, Ward has always regarded the social world beneath him as a rigid homogeneous mass. Now, in a moment of sudden insight ('A lightning flash of perception with the invincible brute force of those ideas which not only violate but impregnate' – d'Aurevilly) he has a vision of tumultuous plurality and a social scale that, far from stopping at his own level, is minutely calibrated (district by district, street by street, even *house by house*) all the way down to zero.

But Clare's comments on the Quigleys prove to be her last major contribution. It is certainly fortunate that the China Garden provides a fish tank for entertainment. And when her chicken and pineapple arrives, Clare can only pick at her plate.

'I thought you said you liked Chinese food?'

'I *do*,' she hotly protests. 'I *love* it.'

'And you said you hadn't eaten since lunchtime'

'*Neither Ah have.*'

Frowning in concentration, Ward moves to investigate the remaining area of the problem space. 'Is there something wrong with it then?'

'*No! No!*' Now her voice has the desperation of a cornered animal. '*No . . . it's fine. The food's fine.*'

Weary of a mind so impenetrable, Ward is glad to desist ('Taking your head between my hands in soft fond manner, I might sink my greedy fingers into the lobes of your innocent brain, thence to extract with a smile an unguent suitable for bathing eyes sore from the eternal insomnia of life' – Lautréamont).

When they return in silence to Ardowen, she asks him to wait in the street while she goes on to investigate the house.

Soon she comes back with a look of renewed desperation. 'Me big brother's still up. He's tryin' to teach the dog tricks.'

Ward casts over the dark estate a look in which wonder succeeds in predominating over frustration ('O world! And the limpid song of dolours new!' – Rimbaud).

She suggests a walk around the block.

'So how many are there in the family?'

Every attempt at soothing small talk seems to intensify her discomfiture. 'Eleven. Eight boys and three girls.'

Even to contemplate such fecundity exhausts Ward. 'Jesus wept!'

'There's fifteen of the Quigleys,' she snaps.

When they arrive at her house for the second time, Clare foregoes reconnaissance to plunge straight in with Ward. On a sofa in the parlour, beneath a Sacred Heart picture, is a youth whose left hand holds a cigarette while his right attempts to calm a tiny over-stimulated mongrel. 'Sit, Jip. *Sit* now.'

Ward recognises a rough diamond who was a year behind him in the Wee Nuns but whose face will be remembered forever due to one of Sister Perpetua's more imaginative punishments – parading the boy around all the classes dressed as a girl. Neither of them acknowledges the previous encounter.

'How're ye doin'.'

'How're ye doin'.'

After this mature and virile exchange Clare plants herself squarely in front of her brother. 'Get lost, Bob.'

Unhurriedly he rises. 'I'll put the dog out.'

As they wait for his return Ward has a chance to survey the room. On the back wall is a portrait of Pope John, a framed work perhaps technically a sculpture since the pontiff rises up out of the background in a three-dimensional simulation of reality. The side wall has a plate bearing the Kennedy brothers' profiles, Bobby's a little lower than Jack's, their parallel visionary gazes directed at some utopia in the skies. And next to the window is another plate delivering its inspiration in words: 'Some people make you feel at home. Others make you wish you were.'

Ward nods at this maxim. 'Which are you?'

'*Wouldn't you just love to know?*'

Bob returns, passing through with a manly nod and grunt for the guest who suddenly remembers the offence which brought such terrible retribution. At the end of the year in the Wee Nuns the main landing was given over to a display of prizes, a cunning mix of sweets and religious goods from which the winners were free to choose and thus reveal their true souls. Ward, a major prizewinner, incurred the contempt of Sister Perpetua by selecting a tin of toffees instead of a statuette of the Virgin – but young Bob, not one of the chosen, called down the wrath of the nuns by helping himself to a similar tin.

Ward gently takes Clare by the elbows. 'Is Bob older than me? He was a year behind me in school ... but if he's your big brother ...'

Yet again harmless small talk seems to have a violently negative effect. The girl pulls out of Ward's arms and abruptly turns her back on him.

'*Clare?*' He touches her shoulder – but she shrugs him off. He has

209

to walk round in front of her to study her expression. Still it is concealed by the long black hair that completely veils her lowered face. '*Clare?*'

Holding back her hair, she lifts to him a countenance alarmingly distorted and stricken. '*I'm not eighteen. I'm only fifteen.*'

'What?' he gasps, incredulous. 'I'm a *baby-snatcher?*'

With a howl of anguish she breaks away to plunge through the kitchen and out the back door.

Ward hesitates, apprehensively listening to the silent house. How many tough vengeful males await arousal upstairs? When there is no sound from above he follows Clare out the back door and gropes carefully forward. His legs encounter knee-high growth. A crop of some kind. Then his hand is torn by a currant bush.

'*Clare?*'

From the darkness ahead comes a deep racking sob. Homing in on this signal, Ward is soon by her side.

'*Go on,*' she sobs at him. '*Go home.* You don't want to go with me now. *Go on.*' And she abandons herself to huge involuntary convulsions, an unstaunchable haemorrhage of sorrow and grief.

'It's all right,' he says, glancing anxiously back at the house. 'It's OK.'

'That's all right. You don't want to go with me. You don't want to be a baby-snatcher.' Suddenly she stamps the ground in wild distraction. 'Anyway I can't talk to you. I can't talk to *anyone.* Go home, Martin. *Go on home.*' Now the sobs are tinged with anger and despair as she turns violently this way and that, a trapped raging thing, stamping the ground.

From an outhouse somewhere near them a dog begins to scrabble and bark.

'*Shut up, Jip,*' she hisses fiercely through her tears.

Ward regards her in amazement. 'I don't mind if you're only fifteen. It's all right.' Tentatively he reaches out a hand – and this time she does not shrug him away. Gradually the twisting and turning stop and the spasms subside. 'Come into the house.'

Snuffling, shivery and hunched, she permits herself to be led back.

'You didn't want me to help with the application form because I would see your real age?' She nods vigorously. 'And the Chinese meal?'

'I couldn't eat with you watching.'

In the parlour Ward once again pauses to listen for stirrings upstairs. While he is still preoccupied and tense, Clare flings her arms about his neck, crushes her body against his and kisses him wildly on the lips. Ward has held girls in his arms – even encountered desire – but there has never been anything like this, the arms fiercely binding him, the body attempting to fuse with his, the fragrant hair and tear-wet face pressing themselves to his lips as though desperate to be consumed. He understands that he can have his way completely, enjoy all the pleasures he thought he came here to find. And she would not merely permit but *give* – bestow, lavish, shower, heap on his head with reckless abandon the petals of the unplucked first flower jewelled with the tears of the storm.

Momentarily exhausted, Clare buries her face in his shoulder but signals no loss of intensity by holding him even more fiercely. Ward rocks her gently, observing in wonder the dark room.

The Pope leans out of his frame. The Kennedys gaze up at the sky.

# 6

Clare returned earlier than usual and, without pouring her usual glass of iced water, made straight for the sofa. Immediately I killed Debussy (having failed with Bartók I was moving back in time and making some progress) and got up to make the drink myself. For as soon as Clare said that it could never be as good again I doggedly set about trying to make it as good (nothing is more violently coveted than what we are told we cannot have). Hence renewed zeal in child care (rising early on weekend mornings), home improvements (installation of self-assembly kitchen units), housework (unremitting attention to nappy bucket and dirty dishes) and cooking (an exciting new range of vegetarian and fish recipes, and a dinner for Clare's friends from Mothers & Co). Now no service was too demeaning or demanding. The Cross was in, the Crag was out.

'Not great music tonight?' I suggested, handing over the glass.

'I'm starting to go off New Wave a bit. There was a guy in a Cambridge Rapist mask. And a character selling this magazine showing sex with amputees.'

Was her disaffection merely with existential obnoxiousness – or had there been a rift with Homewrecker?

Perhaps my dedication, humility and sacrifice had finally touched her occluded heart. It was certainly worth persevering with the Way of the Cross.

In any case the impossibility of the Crag had been demonstrated by its advocates. Rimbaud's *Illuminations* chronicle his failure to achieve divinity in a garret. In Villiers's *Axel* the aristocratic hero withdraws to a castle in the forest but ends by committing suicide. Huysmans's *À Rebours* is a parable of the Crag; the aristocratic Des Esseintes devotes his limitless imagination and wealth to the creation of a perfect lay cloister full of esoteric art and rare books (above the chimney piece Baudelaire's *Anywhere out of the World* inscribed in missal lettering on vellum) – but he too ends in defeat and despair ('The waves of human mediocrity are rising to the heavens and will engulf this refuge for I am opening the floodgates myself, against my will. Ah! My courage fails me and my heart within is sick'). In Flaubert's version the heroes are not aristocrats but the copy clerks, Bouvard and Pecuchet (an example of the preference for the ordinary over the exalted that infuriated d'Aurevilly – 'Flaubert has soiled the gutter by rolling in it'). Yet the humble suffer the same fate as the noble. Exhausted by the freedom a legacy offers, the clerks end by returning gratefully to their copying desks.

Clare was sitting back on the sofa with a furrowed ruminant expression. Now she leaned forward and sideways and her frown modulated into a grimace as she grunted and released a long, sputtering, disgraceful, luxurious fart. 'Ah God,' she sighed in profound relief and gratitude, 'that's one good thing about a husband – ye can let off whenever ye like.' And immediately she availed herself once more of the privilege, this emission brief and succint but apparently more potent. 'Oops!' she cried, desperately fanning the air. '*Sorry!*'

The advantage she had conferred on me was scarcely ideal – but I was not about to reject any form of preferment.

'Zephyrs from heaven, my angel.'

Things could be going my way. All I had to do was maintain the service policy and avoid stupid blunders. Clare sat back again and resumed her puzzled, concentrating look. 'Before the music,' she said at last, 'Nick took me to this fancy fish restaurant. He ordered salmon . . . and then hardly touched it. Can you believe that? Left most of his salmon . . . and it cost *an absolute bomb.* I had to finish it for him. Couldn't bear to waste salmon.'

I should merely have nodded in silence – but the urge to point up a comparison was overwhelming. 'You've come a long way since your chicken and pineapple night. Remember? You couldn't even eat your own portion. Now you can put away both.'

Too absorbed to follow this up, she pondered frowningly, drinking deeply on her iced water as though to stimulate the sluggish brain.

'So what was wrong with him?' I had to ask in the end.

'Oh . . . lots of things.' She made a gesture of impatience that consoled me like a blessing. 'He thought one of the waiters fancied me. And he says I'm too bourgeois. In love with my cosy little nest. Too cowardly to leave.'

The most terrifying statements are often those made in an offhand way. The lack of any desire to impress can make a revelation frighteningly impressive.

'You mean he's *asked you to leave?* He wants you to *move in with him?*'

'Not move in with him where he is. He would get a bigger place . . . and in a better area.'

So the tattooed anti-bourgeois wanted to establish his own cosy nest. Like so many apparent rebels, what angered him was not so much privilege as the fact of his own exclusion from it.

'You mean you're *considering it?* You're *thinking about it?*' So vast were the implications that it was hard to know where to begin. '*And what about the children?*'

'He's quite prepared to take them. He's very good with them in fact.'

Again the casual assumptions were breathtaking.

'Oh he is, is he? That's very nice of him.'

'Listen, Martin.' She came forward decisively on the sofa. 'You don't seem to understand. This guy is deadly serious. He'd do *anything* . . . absolutely *anything* . . . if I agreed to go with him. I mean, he'd give me every penny he had . . . go anywhere I wanted . . . do anything I wanted. This is an incredible thing for me, Martin. Not like you with your fifty-page contract.'

She drank down the last of the water, as though now to cool a racing over-heated brain. It was fortunate that I did not have a glass or I might have been tempted to add another hoof mark to the wall.

'Why don't you go with him if he's so marvellous and I'm such a shit?'

'I don't think you're a shit, Martin.'

We fell silent again. As though it had just awakened to the pain of some great wound, the fridge in the kitchen began to shudder and groan.

'So when can we expect a decision?'

Clare sprang to her feet with the cry of a creature intolerably beset. 'Make a decision . . . make a decision . . . that's all I ever seem to hear these days . . . morning, noon and night, that's all I seem to hear now.'

The next day was Saturday but lack of communication between the adults was easy to conceal in the servicing of children. After lunch Clare said that she needed a few things in the local shops.

Lucy went down for her nap and I sat on the sofa with the homework for my French class. As always the sword was mightier than the pen. Paul slashed the notepad from my hands with his plastic sabre and waited, fully dressed for war in his plastic helmet, cloak and shield. It would never do to have Clare come home to an unhappy child. I took the other sword, fenced, received a fatal wound and died with melodramatic cries. Then we brought out the Lego garage.

Neither would it do to let an infant over-sleep during the day. Without a thought for myself I wakened Lucy at the appointed time. She was not obviously leaking and did not absolutely have to be changed. Rejecting not only inertia and laziness but also the easy option of a disposable nappy, I went for tricky and stressful terry cloth, hoping that Clare would come in just as my left hand lifted Lucy's ankles while my right briskly removed clinging excrement and my face radiated loving approval and pleasure: 'Who's a great girl today? Who's as good as gold today?'

But Clare did not come in at this point. Nor, later, when I was skilfully feeding Lucy mashed soft-boiled egg (strictly no convenient tins or jars), opening my own mouth wide in smiling encouragement and gaily zig-zagging the spoon to turn the meal into a game.

It was eight in the evening before a phone call produced a surge of relief not reflected in my tone.

'For Christ's sake,' I shouted, 'where the fuck are you?'

'Don't swear at me, Martin. *How are the children?*'

'You're with that bastard, aren't you?'

'I'm not with anyone. *How are the children?*'

'Where are you? When are you coming back?'

'I need time on my own . . . time to think. I won't be back for a while.'

'You're with that bastard.'

'*How are the children?*'

'The children are fine. *Where are you?*'

'I'll be in touch, Martin.'

Instead of changing Lucy into her sleep suit I dressed her in a warm jacket and strapped her into one side of the double pushchair. As always nowadays, Paul wanted to walk – but this was not the time for a dawdle. With both of them firmly strapped in I could maintain an urgent pace that had startled pedestrians skipping aside. It took about fifteen minutes. The house had a steep flight of stone steps – but the bells were clearly labelled and there was no entry phone.

Nick opened the door with a flourish – only to fall back in confusion and alarm.

'Is Clare here?'

'No.'

Innocence did not allay his fear. Yet his troubled gaze fixed on the children rather than on me. Lucy was asleep in the pushchair but Paul had got out to negotiate the steps and was looking up with the ready grin of a child expecting a warm welcome. Possibly Nick envisaged some kind of insane dumping scene. *You want my children as well? Here they are. Take them.*

He and Paul turned to me for the next move – but now that I knew Clare was not here there was no next move.

Situationist and Dandy with double pushchair – a bizarre tableau in the gathering dusk.

'Come in and check if you don't believe me,' Nick said at last.

'I believe you.' All volition and fervour gone, I glanced in confusion down the darkening street. 'It's just . . . she went out before lunchtime to shop . . . hasn't been back . . . I got a bit worried . . . *sorry.*'

Immediately Nick's apprehension changed to solidarity and concern. 'She'll be with Nina.'

'Probably. But I don't have Nina's number. And it's too far to drag the kids at this time of night.'

'I'll drive you.'

'You don't have a car.'

'I have the keys to the Community Centre minibus. I'm taking the Young at Heart Club to Southend tomorrow.'

I experienced a pang of solidarity myself. A Situationist taking pensioners to the seaside was surely every bit as grotesque as a Dandy at the helm of a double pushchair. We are one people, immured in absurdity, sacrifice and toil.

When we got to the Centre I was horrified by the ramshackle minibus – but Paul was thrilled and rushed to fling himself across the back seat. The pushchair we managed to wedge in the aisle without waking Lucy. Then, just as we got under way, Nick suddenly slammed the steering wheel and shouted at the top of his voice: 'Fuck it. Fuck it. Fuck it. *Fuck it.*' An approaching junction obliged him to concentrate on steering but, as soon as we had turned the corner, he repeated, with increased vehemence and venom: 'Fuck it anyway. Fuck it. Fuck it.'

Anger and violence – the last things we needed. This bizarre caravan was surely ill-advised and rash.

At length he calmed down enough to explain. 'We share this bus with two other centres. They're supposed to fill it with petrol when they're finished – *but the fuckers always leave it empty.*'

At Nina's flat he seized the initiative, leaping out of the bus to take front position at the door. As the senior man in every sense I was not at all happy about being pushed into the background – but I was hampered by the need to keep an eye on the children in the double-parked minibus on the road.

'Is Clare here?' He also assumed the role of spokesperson, looming over the tiny bare-footed Nina with a righteous assertiveness bordering on aggression. It came to me with a shock that he disapproved of this girl. I had classified all of Clare's new friends as mellow fun people who adored each other. Again the lazy and

217

thoughtless assumption of homogeneity.

'No.' Obviously frightened of Nick, Nina looked to the man she knew as a mild and self-effacing chef. Then her gaze travelled further and became a look of stupefaction. She had just caught sight of Paul waving enthusiastically from the minibus.

When we returned to the minibus ourselves there was a long moment of silence. Nick, the natural leader, had also become deflated and aimless. His great granite head brooded in darkness.

'In a way I'm glad she's not with that little bitch,' he said at last, rooting suddenly and furiously in the glove compartment.

'I suppose we'll just have to sweat it out,' I said.

'Let's go to the police.'

'But she's been on the phone. I mean, she's obviously all right. They'd laugh us out of the station.'

Nick found the tape he was searching for and savagely jammed it into the machine. It was a New Wave band who were friends of his. We listened in impotent melancholy silence.

'They've just split up,' Nick said suddenly, as though some universal disintegration linked the break-up of the band to the disappearance of Clare. 'Or rather the band's finally ditched the singer. I mean, the guy was doing *Tuinal* for fuck's sake.'

'Ah.' I had no idea what he was talking about but nodded wisely several times.

'Fucking *barbiturates* for Crissake.'

This time I shook my head.

'They were in Japan ... going from Osaka to Tokyo or something ... apparently the roads are so crowded you have to take trains ... they had this train hired and the guy was dosed to the eyeballs ... steps out of the carriage and flat on his face on the platform ... start of the tour and his mouth smashed up ... hotel full of lawyers and agents and orthodontists and Christ knows what ... the rest of the band meet in a bedroom and decide enough is enough ... the hardest decision they ever made ... I mean, they've known this guy *from time* ... at school together and everything ...' Nick paused to brood on the sadness of human folly and waste. 'And the guy has such talent. I mean, he never knows where he is but his pockets are always full of these incredible songs scribbled down on scraps of paper.' To demonstrate the careless profusion of outpouring genius, Nick slapped each of his own pockets in turn, shaking

218

his massive hewn head at the pity of it all.

I too was deeply affected by this image of pockets overflowing with scrap-paper masterpieces. My own pockets were also permanently stuffed – but with stilted, childishly written notes from parents explaining that their daughters had not been at school because of 'bad stomach cramps'.

For a time we listened to the doomed singer.

'You really admire this guy,' I softly suggested, impressed by a passion so intense and sincere.

Nick glanced at me in sudden surprise, as though his rapt concentration on the music had made him forget the presence of another. 'Fucking Amadeus, Martin.'

Yet this moment of intimacy made the end of the encounter more difficult. I had the feeling that Nick wanted to come home with me to help man a Missing Person Crisis Centre. And just as wearisome as the prospect of violence was the thought of the two of us wallowing drunkenly in some emotional bubble bath. All I wanted was solitude and my usual nightcap – an angry and anguished toss-off. Of course an invitation had to be issued but I did it so reluctantly that he had to decline. (The ability to register lack of enthusiasm is a natural gift.)

Clare phoned as I was putting the children to bed.

'Where were you?' she snapped. A bold pre-emptive strike.

'Where was *I*? That's a good one. That's rich. Where the fuck are *you*?'

'Stop swearing, Martin. *How are the children?*'

'What are you playing at? *Who are you with?*'

'I'm not with anyone. How are the children?'

'But where are you? When are you coming home?'

'Certainly not tonight. How are the children?'

'The children are fine. *Where are you spending the night?*'

'I'll ring later, Martin.'

Normally our telephone conversations were protracted and relaxed, a leisurely murmuring of banalities which both of us were reluctant to terminate. Brief, ferocious and clinical, these recent exchanges were more like fire fights between rival crack units.

It was disturbing enough to warrant breaking a rule against drinking alone. For me alcohol has always been exclusively social. And in fact a series of gins did encourage me to socialise. Like a punchy old wino on a park bench, I sat in an armchair and talked to myself. Or, rather, disputed with myself. There was little agreement between the parties – but at least no glasses were smashed.

At seven a.m. on Sunday there was a visitation from a terrible warrior, brutal, determined and merciless as Attila – Paul in full battle dress. And his rush to war had wakened Lucy who was gurgling in happy anticipation of another day of attention and service. In an instant the reality of single parenting was brought home to me.

A possible strategy for difficulties is to attack them before they attack you. The answer was not to evade or minimise but to embrace the responsibility with fanatical zeal. ('Is it not by martyrdom that virtue is brought to perfection? By outrage that grandeur is rendered more grand?' – Flaubert.) Thus I did not distract Paul with television or feed Lucy from jars (though I did take the disposable nappy option for, despite intensive coaching in the triangle-and-three-corner technique, I had never made a go of cloth which invariably sagged, pinched or leaked – and sometimes all three).

After lunch there was the perfect family outing – a trip to feed the animals in Golders Hill Park. Often men propel pushchairs in a deliberately detached and desultory fashion, standing aside and at an angle with only one hand on the grips, in a powerful body language statement that, far from constituting a destiny, this involvement is temporary and casual. Not for me such fastidiousness and reluctance. Vigorously seizing both handles and hunching forward in unequivocal head-on commitment, I drove the double pushchair through the crowds like one of those who outraged and disgusted Des Esseintes ('the appalling boors . . . who, without expressing or even indicating regret, drove the wheels of a baby carriage into your legs').

Now I could see that there was something ludicrous about the disgust of the seven. Withdrawal to a Crag, supposedly the cure for disgust, in fact appears to have made it worse, producing a discontent almost comical in its universality and vehemence. Flaubert the hermit could tolerate nothing at the end of his life ('Everything annoys me and hurts me; and since I control myself in the presence of others I am occasionally seized by fits of weeping during which I feel my end has come.). Even the simplest of actions became unendurable ('It bores me to eat, dress, stand on my own feet etcetera') and of course communication was increasingly impossible ('The

220

simplest conversation exasperates me, for I find everyone idiotic').

The later years of the seven are a salutary lesson in the consequences of cosmic disgust. Although often presented as a sophisticated, mature and even noble response, disgust is in fact only the
acceptable face of self-pity; instead of whingeing about being too
good for the world, we whinge that the world is too base for us.
Essentially a form of self-indulgence, disgust is incapable of providing fulfilment.

Mothering, on the other hand, is the true Way of the Cross.
Whereas the ordeal of the Redeemer was public, finite and grand,
that of the mother is invisible, endless and petty. Christ may have
suffered the little children to come to him – but he did not have to
clean shitty bums or rise in the middle of the night to change a
vomit-soaked bed. Men are certainly capable of sacrifice – but only
if it happens under a spotlight, only if it is melodramatic and brief.

And the difficulty of mothering is related *exponentially* to family
size. A second child does not double but *quadruples* the problems.
Lucy howled with frustration if she was put in the playpen – but
as soon as she was taken out rushed to destroy whatever Paul and I
had made. And if I concentrated on appeasing Lucy, Paul was
immediately pressing for attention. Needless to say they could
never be left alone together. From time to time the stupendous size
of Clare's family came to me. But it was not a prospect on which I
could dwell. My mind, which could easily contemplate the black
infinities of outer space and the human heart, shrank in terror from
the enormity of eleven children in rapid succession.

Nevertheless I was coping, discovering techniques and strata-
gems as old as motherhood itself. The trick was to turn everything
into a game for three. Instead of dumping Lucy in her pen and
ordering Paul to behave while I cooked, bring them both into the
kitchen and give them something to mess with (as management
theorists have recently discovered, the illusion of involvement is a
panacea). Instead of the tight-necked-vest-and-sweater dressing
ordeal, making Paul howl at a renewal of the birthing trauma, turn
it into a game by dropping the garment over his head and crying to
Lucy in mock consternation – '*Where's Paul?*' Paul's gone. *Where's
Paul?*' – so that Paul himself eagerly shoves his head through and the
whole family laughs aloud in delighted relief.

I am not claiming to have discovered a technique for every

circumstance (the logistics of going for a crap still defeated me) but by and large I think I was pretty good in there. Goddam it, *better* than good. I was *Mr Hospital Corners* (another aspect of male sacrifice – it insists on recognition and gratitude).

When Clare phoned on Sunday night I adopted an entirely different tone, no longer angry and resentful but independent and proud, that of a happily-coping single parent unconcerned about her return. I even suggested she stay away longer since the Monday was a bank holiday. Indifference is smarter than indignation and the quickest way to renew bondage is often an offer of freedom.

I was also preparing for the return. Lucy had started pulling herself upright and edging along the seat of the sofa. It looked as though she might by-pass crawling and go straight for upright locomotion. What a coup if she could be coaxed into taking her first steps now! What a magnificent reproach if the absent mother missed this! (I seem to have a talent for personalised punishment – in a more congenial age I would have made a superb inquisitor.) Every few hours Paul and I lined up the sofa and armchair only one short step apart, stood Lucy against the sofa and, getting down on the carpet by the armchair, yelled out encouragement as the dockers in *On the Waterfront* exhorted the badly beaten Brando to stagger in and register for work: *Walk in, Terry! Walk in! Walk in!* However, Lucy, though enjoying the game, declined to reward her attentive father by taking the one crucial step.

Paul was easier to manipulate. When Lucy went down for a nap, with a shamelessness worthy of an American politician I put him to work on a giant home-made card that bore the message in huge print, surrounded by heart-wrenching child drawings and batteries of Xs: WELCOME HOME MUM.

What I envisaged between the adults was a tearful and infinitely tender reunion, accompanied by renunciation of Homewrecker and a passionate renewal of the marriage vows, this in turn leading to a dramatic resumption of physical relations. For in this respect the reconciliation experience is unique. Gourmet sex can be enormous fun (and I would never disparage it) but for pleasure of the most exquisite intensity and sweetness, simple reconciliation intercourse is the ineffable sublime.

Those of the seven who did not live with women came to regret it in later life. When Huysmans, misogynist and would-be monk, discovered that a young married couple had moved into an apartment across the street, he could not refrain from observing them and astonished his admirers by sobbing bitterly over the emptiness of bachelor life. Even Rimbaud the extremist ended by yearning for conjugal bliss: 'Solitude is a bad thing and I'm beginning to regret never having married.' He also longed for a child, 'a son, at least, whom I shall spend the rest of my life training according to my own ideas, providing him with the best and most complete education obtainable today, and whom I shall see grow up to be a famous engineer, a man rich and powerful through science'. And Flaubert, who declared that 'marriage would be an apostasy which it appalls me to contemplate' and that 'the idea of causing the birth of someone fills me with horror', was later to write: 'I adore children and was born to be an excellent papa. It is one of the sad facts of my old age that I have no little creature to love and caress.' When the poet Heredia met Flaubert he was astounded by the great man's request – to be taken along to a children's party. And even more astounded to observe Flaubert deeply moved by this experience.

After teatime on Monday Clare returned and rushed straight to the children, lifting them in turn and hugging them ardently. As soon as he had an opportunity, Paul presented the Welcome-Home card. Clare marvelled over every detail of the construction – but gave the architect scarcely a glance.

At last I could no longer refrain. 'Where have you been?'

'With a cousin who lives in Purley.'

'First I've heard of a cousin.' Querulous, grudging and petty – absolutely the wrong tone.

'I have over thirty cousins, Martin. Many of them living in England. I never discuss them with you because you've never had any time for my family.'

Again the emphasis on my failings instead of my generosity over the weekend. And when we got round to discussing the three days it was not my heroism that captured her attention but the weird events of Saturday night. 'You took the *children* out in the *pushchair!* You took them round to *Nick's flat!* You all got into the *Centre's minibus!* You all went round to *Nina!* My God, you had to drag *Nina* into this too! Did you announce it *over the whole city?* Is there *anyone* in London *who doesn't know?*'

As for a final decision, surely the purpose of her weekend retreat, there was in fact no decision and no date for a decision – nor would any further mention of the word 'decision' be entertained.

As though to repel the orderly and fastidious, stacks of paper coal bags full of rubbish line the landing, leaving barely enough room to pass. Alerting Clare with a wink, Ward throws open a door to reveal Shotter squatting cross-legged in an armchair, eating Ambrosia Creamed Rice from a tin and regarding a tiny television set placed in the centre of the floor and attached by a gently swaying cable to a light socket in the ceiling. As they watch, the picture detaches itself from the bottom of the screen, shudders slightly as if in memory of bondage and gently proceeds to roll over.

Shotter turns in irritation. 'Shut that door to fuck.'

Ward chuckles delightedly and, with the pride of a young wife conducting a tour of a showhouse, ushers Clare into his own sanctuary and cloister, his antechamber to the sacred threshold. She pauses at the door, taking in the threadbare sofa and rug, cracked linoleum, rickety formica-topped table, bookcase made of planks and bricks, broken-down bed sagging like a hammock and, in the corner, the huge discoloured jawbox fed by a single tap drizzling to the accompaniment of a deep groaning lament.

'Doesn't that drive you mental?' She nods in wonder at the droning tap.

'Can't be turned off,' he explains.

'Why don't you just change the washer?'

'*What?*' ('To be a useful person has always seemed to me particularly horrible' – Baudelaire.) 'That's for the landlord. Take your coat off and make yourself at home.'

Clare clutches the garment to her. 'It's freezing in here.'

'I'll light a wee fire. It looks fine with the fire on.'

Tearing open a new bag of coal and piling fuel on top of an extravagant scatter of firelighters, Ward soon has leaping flames if not yet much heat.

Clare opens her coat to reveal a sumptuous uniform. Over a dress of heavy mustard-coloured material, with metal buttons on the front and studs on its starched collar and cuffs, is a white apron bearing a watch and a starched belt secured by a further four studs.

'I have split shifts,' she apologises, consulting the pinned watch.

'No time to change.'

'But it's ... it's ... *magnificent*.' Intoxicated, he seizes her.

'*Get lost!*' she shrieks, laughing. 'You'll ruin it.'

They wrestle strenuously, blundering into the bookcase and table.

'You're strong,' Ward has to admit.

'Ah could always beat up me brothers.' Seizing his head in a violent armlock, she deftly positions her leg behind his, trips him and throws him towards the floor. Ward is unable to stay upright – but succeeds in pulling her down with him.

'Strong,' he cries, '*but not strong enough*.' Freeing his head, he rolls over and forces back both her arms, pinioning them to the floor with his knees and then sitting back to enjoy her heaving subjugation in the calm insouciance of pride surfeited with power ('Our young lord is so vigorous that he strangles wolves with a single grasp, not even deigning to draw his hunting knife' – Villiers).

'Give in?' he suggests.

With a sudden fierce lunge of her lower half, she throws him completely clear and leaps wildly on top.

'*Watch me glasses!*' he has to yell.

There is a violent banging on the wall. 'You're wreckin' this TV,' Shotter cries. 'Ah'm tryin' to fuckin' watch *Bonanza*.'

Clare rises, examining her uniform for damage and dust.

'That jammy bastard Shotter,' Ward growls, remaining on the ground as though laid low by fate. 'Fuck all to do ... like the rest of the arts people. A couple of tutorials a week and that's it. And of course, to go with English he picks Ancient History and Psychology. They're well known to be the easiest to pass. Nobody ever fails those. Practically no work involved.'

'So what does he do with himself?'

'Plays cards in the Union mostly. Whereas I have practicals every day ... Jesus, I hate those labs. Some creeps love it of course ... never out of the labs ... *those cunts in white coats*.' He rises defiantly to his feet. 'That's one thing I won't do at least. I refuse to buy a white coat. I won't be forced into uniform.'

'It's well for some,' Clare observes drily, adjusting her collar in the spotty mirror and perching cautiously on the edge of the bed. 'I suppose this is full of fleas.'

'When Flaubert went up the Nile to visit the famous whore –

Kuchuk Hanem – what excited him about her was the mingled aroma of bedbugs and sandalwood.' Ward assumes the cold mask of the sated voluptuary. 'I like a touch of bitterness in all my pleasures.'

'Speak for yourself.'

'Flaubert ...' sighs Ward, with a yearning glance at the bookshelves. 'You know what Shotter once told me – he never read a book for pleasure in his life. He hates having to read ... and I'd give my right arm to do it. The work he complains so much about would be relaxation to me.'

'Then why are you studying science?'

'Why did you work for Canning? It was what was expected of me. At the College if you could do science you did it.' He sighs deeply. 'But at least you got out of Canning's.'

Though only to be tyrannised by another dictator. Sombrely she tells him about Sister Patterson, the terrible pint-sized potentate of the children's ward.

'Know what she did today? We were really busy and she wanted this admission done in a hurry. It was a child with gastroenteritis and you're supposed to always wear a gown. But she said, never mind the gown for once, just get on with the admission. So of course the bed was screened off and I didn't see the Matron coming. I got absolutely torn to shreds for not wearing a gown. Patterson never said a word about making me do it.'

'But why didn't *you* say?'

'A wee junior nurse? Are ye *mental?* Patterson'd have *murdered* me afterwards. It's bad enough as it is. She always arranges my time off so I never get my day and half-day together ... and of course *never* at the weekend.' A note of deep despair enters her voice. 'I don't know when I'll see you at the weekend, Martin.'

Ward can scarcely admit that he is partly grateful to Sister Patterson. He needs time alone, firstly to heal the wounds inflicted by the herd and secondly to journey with lamp and staff to the sacred portals where his spirit will finally be emancipated into its own incommensurable being ('Recognise yourself! Proffer yourself to the Essence! Child of the incarcerated, save yourself from the prison of the world!' – Villiers).

'I've a half-day Tuesday. Could I stay here Tuesday night?'

'*Stay?*' Ward looks about him in amazement, as though at a loss to know how to make the room sufficiently unattractive. 'What would you tell the Nurses' Home?'

'That I'm going for the night to my mother's.'

'And what will your mother think you're doing with your time off?'

'Staying at the Nurses' Home.'

Ward ponders. 'You realise we've no money to go out?'

'Yes.'

'And that I have no radio or television . . . there's nothing to do here but read?'

Clare looks pointedly about her. 'There seems to be no shortage of books.' The matter settled, she takes from her bag a square of starched white cloth which, in an instant of astonishing legerdemain, she fashions into an elaborate coif and pins on top of her piled hair. 'What do you make of that, eh?' Essentially pill-box in shape, two dramatic side projections make it a kind of Winged Victory. 'And there's a cape as well. A big bright-red cape. But you're not allowed to take that out of the grounds.' She lifts her coat and draws herself erect – a fabulous Winged Victory of Order over Chaos and Filth. 'Anyway Ah'll love ye and leave ye, Martin.'

'The cape,' he begs. 'You'll have to bring the cape.'

'Get lost. I'd be *murdered* if Patterson caught me.'

So it is, that, on Tuesday evening, entirely stripped of splendour and mystery, she squats on the broken-down sofa in her everyday clothes, legs cosily tucked up beneath her, frowning intently over the black Penguin Classic edition of *Madame Bovary*. At the table Ward is composing a lab book by means of the twin tools of genius – invention and theft. Maladroit with equipment and bored to extinction by lab work, he steals what results he can from the white coats and, as a job applicant will attempt to make haphazard experience seem a long preparation for a post, arranges the available data to appear the fruit of purposeful speculation supported by experiment.

Late in the evening Clare lays aside the book for a study of her own hair, drawing out each of the long strands and examining it carefully for split ends.

'Bored?' Ward grunts impatiently.

'No. No. No, I'm fine.' Finishing a minute examination of the current hair, she carefully selects another. 'But I wouldn't mind going to bed soon.'

A god interrupted in the cosmic fury of creation, Ward lifts his head to cast her a fierce look ('Wolves and lambs look not on each other with gentle eyes' – Lautréamont). But it is Clare who attacks, rising to circle behind the creator, seize him in a half-nelson and throw him to the floor where she pinions his arms and gazes down with fire and mayhem in her eyes.

'I always beat up our Kevin,' she cries happily. 'Used to drive him mad. I'd always fight with him and lock him out of the house. Once he got so angry he put his fist through the window.' Hoping the memory will cause a lapse in her concentration, Ward lunges for freedom – and is instantly thrust back. '*Give in!*' A pitiless female Attila, she straddles his puny breast in triumph, flushed and panting, dark eyes flashing furious fire. Ward shudders in thralldom.

'Ah said *give in!*'

'All right.'

As soon as he yields she rises calmly, adopting the casual chattiness of a wife. 'You know, I was the most bad-tempered one in our house, I was *terrible*, everyone was scared stiff of me.' In fact her manner is that of a wife after decades of marriage; as she talks she steps casually out of her clothes. 'I was terrible altogether. Don't know how anyone stuck me.'

Not only is the bed a tiny single but irremediably spavined so that they both roll into a central trough as deep and desperate as an oubliette. Clare shrieks with laughter – but Ward is discomposed and vexed ('The grotesque aspects of love have always prevented me from giving myself completely to it' – Flaubert).

'I'll never sleep like this,' he snaps.

'*I'm* the one who has to get up at six. And isn't it lovely to snuggle in?'

Although Clare has presented no obstacle to intercourse, Ward has refrained from this final step. Beholden only to his own severe and lucid angels, Ward has entered into a pact with them to the effect that avoidance of avowal and consummation will absolve him from the responsibility of commitment ('I am he who wills not to love. My dreams know another light, eluding the terrible blow with a svelte bound' – Villiers). Instead he restricts himself to fingering which, since books and films have indicated that sexual pleasure is associated with frenzy, he pursues with frantic enthusiasm. Clare is obliged to educate him in the ways of gentleness. 'Easy, Martin. You're hurting me a wee bit there. *Easy*.'

Not only does Clare now come to the flat every half-day and day off, she even suggests that, on the nights when Rapunzel is imprisoned in the Nurses' Home, her prince should scale the back wall of the hospital grounds, approach the home under cover of the rhododendron bushes, wait in these bushes for the prearranged signal and finally effect a tryst in her bedchamber via the opened corridor window.

'*Wha* . . . ?' Ward cries, aghast. 'What dye think Ah am – *fuckin' James Bond?*' ('Beware of the moon and the stars, beware of the Venus de Milo, of lakes, guitars, rope ladders and love stories' – Baudelaire.)

'The other boyfriends do it all the time.' Clare is deeply disappointed by this lack of gallantry. 'They say it's dead easy.'

'Aren't the days off enough? Doesn't anyone think about anything but *courting?*' He pauses, dumbfounded by a vision of a barracks teeming with love-lorn maidens and surrounded by lustful swains lurking in bushes. 'Don't these girls ever enjoy their own . . . or each other's . . . company? Don't *you* ever want to be with *them?*'

'Those eejits?' Clare has turned sullen. 'Runnin' about screamin' and throwin' buckets of water over each other.'

'But don't you have *any friends?* Anyone else you want to see?'

'I just want to see you.' Hurt, brooding, ashamed, she lowers her head and allows her long black hair to veil her troubled countenance. 'Though there's a young doctor always pestering me to go out with him.' She looks up in hopeful expectation of outrage. 'Good-looking too. All the other nurses are mad about him. They think I'm *mental* to turn him down.' Still there is no response from Ward. Desperately she tries her last shot. '*And he has his own car.*'

Since her off-duty is frequently arranged at the last minute, Clare is likely to turn up at the flat without warning. Ward's annoyance on these occasions she attributes to thwarted assignations with a rival. If out when she calls, he is far from apologetic or concerned on his return. On one occasion she spends two hours with Shotter who, in contrast to his flatmate, is entirely too hospitable. But when Clare protests to Ward he merely laughs, as though such betrayal and infamy are only to be expected from a friend.

One Friday afternoon Ward returns from a frustrating session at the lab (possibly suspecting him, the white coats are taciturn and vigilant) to find Clare on the doorstep with her only female friend – Emma Bovary. At once she springs up to explain that she has realised every nurse's dream – that of concatenating the day and a half from successive weeks to create a *stupendous three-day weekend break*.

'I thought Patterson would never allow that.'

'I'm on a different ward now – geriatric.'

But something in her demeanour suggests that the tyranny is not at an end.

'Isn't it good to get away from Patterson?'

'Aw wait till I tell ye, Martin.' Laying a hand on his arm, she lowers her head and leans brokenly into him. 'The first night I was on the new ward Sister told me to collect all the false teeth and wash them.' Her grip on his arm tightens and her tone becomes tremulous. '*And didn't I collect the whole bunch and throw them into a sink in the sluice.*'

'Isn't that what you were supposed to do?'

She shakes his arm in despair at trauma compounded by obtuseness. 'Didn't I mix them all up? They couldn't tell whose were whose. Sister was ready to *kill* me. She was fit to be *tied*.' Worn out, Clare falls against Ward and lays her head on his shoulder.

Dutifully patting her hair, he frowns impatiently down the street. 'OK – but I have plans for the weekend.'

At once her face darkens. 'You have another girl.'

'The last thing I need is *another girl*.'

'You're seeing someone else. I know it. That's why you don't want me around.'

They mount the stairs and go along the landing, now more easily negotiated since Clare has been reducing the rubbish mountain by several bags a week. In Ward's room she throws her case onto the bed.

'You don't know what I had to do to get this weekend. Swop my offs with everyone. Agree to do their bowel days.'

'Their *what*?'

'Every Monday. On Sunday night all the patients get Dorbanex – a laxative.'

'Why a laxative?'

'*Why do you think?* They never get exercise. Some are totally bedridden. And on Monday morning they get a suppository.'

'Which *you* . . .'

'Not for all of them,' she says. 'Not all of them make it that far.'

'So for one half of the patients you administer . . . and for the others you have to . . .'

'It makes Mondays even more popular than usual.'

To reach him she will swim across an ocean of geriatric shit.

'And even worse than that, Martin, I have to do a night duty next week. No one wants to do nights because this is the ward with the *black dog*. Apparently it started about a year ago. It was after three in the morning and there was just a wee junior nurse on with the Sister. The junior nurse heard it first . . . this padding and panting noise . . . a dog walking about somewhere. Then the Sister heard it too . . . and this was a sensible middle-aged woman . . . a saved Protestant from Belvoir Park . . . doesn't drink or wear make-up or anything. Says she, *there's a dog somewhere on this ward*. So the two of them looked everywhere . . . no sign of a dog . . . but all night they could hear it walking around the place and panting . . .' Here Clare pauses to grip Ward's arm. 'And next morning one of the patients was found dead in his bed.' She moves closer to him, holding his eyes in hers. 'That dog's been heard five different nights since . . . and every time there's a patient found dead in the morning. So now nobody'll go on that ward at night.' She moves against him for protection. 'I'm on that ward on Wednesday night and I'm going to be in the nerves the whole time. I know I'd just go *mental* if I heard that, Martin. I'd just run straight out of the ward so I would.'

Suddenly she clasps him so fiercely that he almost loses his balance.

'If this dog has never been seen,' he enquires, 'how do you know that it's black?'

Instead of replying, she rises on her toes and presses her mouth against his in a passionate affirmation of life over death. Her short A-line mini rises over Ward's hands which now hold the bare backs of her upper thighs. He strokes them in tender reassurance and presently moves a hand round to the front to offer equivalent consolation to the soft inner thigh. Before he can complete even one stroke Clare clamps her legs shut on his hand and doubles up as though violently punched in the stomach.

'Martin,' she groans desperately, '*Martin.*'

Clenching her face shut, she writhes on his hand which, at last schooled in gradualism, gently draws aside her gusset to part the intimate lips. In the silence tremendous gouts of lubricant rattle shockingly on the lino. Yet her expression suggests not pleasure but the terrible hermetic solipsism of pain. Falling back on the bed she undoes him in swift, almost unconscious urgency, and guides him into her with a simple directness that may not be refused. Wonderingly he observes her pleasure take its course ('Even when two lovers are passionate and full of mutual desire one of the two will always be cooler and less self-abandoned – one the surgeon or executioner, the other the patient or victim' – Baudelaire) – until, with a sudden wild cry, she thrusts him away and, turning her back, bursts into violent rending tears.

After a while he timidly touches her heaving shoulder. 'Did you ...?'

'I don't know. I don't know.'

She cannot explain. No more can he, except that he has not reached climax, so that their love is still technically unconsummated. ('You will think I am selfish, that I fear you. I admit it. I am terrified of your love' – Flaubert).

When her sobs show no sign of abating Ward touches her softly once more. 'What's the matter?'

'I don't know. I don't know. Don't ask me. *I don't know.*'

'Life,' said Baudelaire, 'is a hospital crowded with patients obsessed with the need to change beds.' As the deadline for giving notice approached, the staffroom was more excited by career moves than the gorgeous renewals of nature. Not only were the English and History Department Heads leaving, an entirely new Deputy Head post offered further hope of advancement.

'I'd enjoy the challenge,' Kemp said seriously to Moira Sweeney when asked if he was applying for the History job. 'Although it's come at a difficult time for me. My mother and I were hoping to sell the house and get something smaller in town and maybe a little bungalow at Eastbourne. And you're going for the Deputy Headship?'

'I think it has to be a lay person,' Moira said, as though her candidacy were in disinterested and reluctant pursuit of this goal. 'The nuns mean well enough in their way – but they don't understand the concerns of lay staff.' Leaning close to Kemp, she whispered, '*Living over the shop, you know.*'

Terry Wills also saw himself as the new Deputy Head. 'They're all saying it'll have to be a lay person.'

'*Lay*, Terry,' I said, 'not *heathen*. It's between Moira Sweeney and Judy Cooke.' Moira Sweeney was assumed to be the favourite but her naked righteousness and authoritarianism belonged to an era that was past. Judy Cooke, on the other hand, was the perfect bland executive of the future, a priceless unit of corporate ectoplasm that would assume any shape required. 'And I think it's Judy Cooke's job.'

'I've been here as long as her,' Terry snapped. 'And I've seen how she operates. Nobody's impressed by her telling off kids in the corridors.'

'On the contrary, that's *exactly* what impresses. What have *you* got to offer?'

'I've done my share for the school.'

Three astonishing truths about promotion: first, that so many should crave it; second, that all of these should believe it possible; and third, more astounding still, that all should somehow succeed in convincing themselves they *deserve* it. Obviously Terry felt that his work as licensed clown should be recognised – that, in the way famous old hams are rewarded by knighthoods, he too should now be elevated for his services to entertainment and drama.

When I failed to acknowledge this likelihood his irritation deepened into bitterness. 'I would have thought it was in your interest for me to get it.'

'Why's that, Terry?'

'So you could go for Head of Science.'

Cue for Flaubert: 'Honours dishonour, titles degrade, status annihilates the soul.' And, on the subject of careers: 'As for a job or post, my dear friend, never! never! never!' Yet even The Incredible F Man was almost embroiled. When his rapacious niece and her husband left him destitute at the end of his life (a fittingly ironic reward for his advising her to marry a bourgeois), Flaubert's friends arranged a post, never actually taken up, as special curator of the Bibliothèque Mazarine. Flaubert negotiated what may well be the most exciting job spec in the history of employment: 'I accept the position: three thousand francs a year and the *guarantee* of no duties whatever.'

Janet and Rani were also applying for jobs, Janet in her customary fatalistic despair and Rani in mounting anger at the injustice of life.

'No one's even offered me an interview,' Rani raged.

'Seymour's probably as unhappy as you. If he leaves, you'll be left in peace.'

To the restless patients of the hospital of life, advice to accept the current bed is profoundly unwelcome. 'You think I could stay here after the way I've been treated? Being publicly humiliated every day. Kalpesh won't even speak to me.'

'*Who?*'

'Kalpesh Raichura – the new Indian supply teacher.'

Now I remembered the youthful mathematics graduate whose air of haughty and remote disdain had afforded me a certain grim amusement. If he remained in the teaching profession his fastidious nose would soon be rubbed in the dirt.

'But he's only just arrived. And he's temporary. He hasn't spoken to *anyone* much.'

'But why hasn't he spoken to *me?*'

'Why should he? He's in the Maths Department.' She flashed me a fierce look of contempt and I understood, too late, that she expected Kalpesh to approach her as an attractive and eligible Hindu girl. All her sophistication and independence seemed to have been jettisoned in favour of tradition. 'He might not be interested in *sticking to his own kind.* You weren't so keen on that yourself at one time.' My heavily ironic tone was wasted. The capricious and wilful hate to be reminded of yesterday's overriding urge.

'But he hasn't even *noticed* me.'

*Noticed?* I felt a sudden stab of anger. Who has the right to insist on being *noticed?*

'Could you . . . you know' – her anger suddenly became coyness – '*have a word with him some time?*'

To approach a proud spirit like Kalpesh as some kind of *peasant matchmaker* . . . or, even worse, as *Rani's pimp!*

What upset me most was probably the implication of my own sexual nullity, her blithe relegation of me to the sexless role of go-between. It chimed too well with the low self-estimate caused by

234

Clare's continuing refusal to decide in my favour or acknowledge my strenuous attempts to please. Accustomed to glory and praise, I believed that success was the inevitable consequence of commitment and determined application. It was simply a matter of making an effort. But, far from being won over, Clare was increasingly irritated by my constant attempts at ingratiation. The realisation that I could actually lose her triggered a terrible new phenomenon – *turbulence*.

Rational analysis has never found it easy to explain why orderly behaviour should suddenly become chaotic and unpredictable. For centuries physics evaded the issue and even the legendary Heisenberg is reputed to have said on his deathbed that he had only one question for God: *why turbulence?* Why indeed? And the emotional version is every bit as mysterious as the physical. Behaviour is suddenly deviant. Laws no longer apply.

Not only is turbulent emotional behaviour hard to explain, it is also excruciatingly embarrassing to reveal. What follows is the most difficult and painful part of this narrative. Yet it is also the most necessary. Baudelaire put it with typical cogency: 'Although ashamed to remember, I desire to forget nothing.'

First, my professional confidence went. Blankness descended in the middle of an A-level mechanics problem, although I was able to bluster through and conceal the failure from *A*, *B* and *C* (this is the guilty secret of experience – what is lost in ability is made up in cunning). The public deterioration of my tutor group could not be concealed. I should have ranted about falling standards but I looked away and let them fall. Moira Sweeney had to give me a severe telling off.

Then there was the violent compulsion to purchase. Book and record shops were especially irresistible, though not from love of literature or music. Frequently I would not even open the book or play the record but, although awareness of this possibility brought me out in a cold sweat, I could hardly ever leave a shop without buying something. The constant compulsion to eat was a variation on this theme. Comfort eating is a subset of comfort consumption.

Deteriorating appearance was another obsession. After the minibus excursion Christine remarked to Clare that I seemed to have 'aged terribly'. Clare passed on the remark in her usual offhand way, entirely unaware of the terror that invaded my rational soul (which should have known that cuckoldry and sacrifice were scarcely ingredients of the elixir of youth). I began to ransack our bathroom cabinet for cleansers, moisturisers, emulsions, anti-wrinkle oils and rejuvenating creams. (Most impressive was Clarins *Double Sérum Multi-régénérant Jeunesse du Visage*: 'A youthful facial appearance depends on the five vital functions of the skin – revitalisation, nutrition, hydration, oxygenation and protection. The "Hydro Serum" and "Lipo Serum" act in synergy to stimulate these functions and prevent, postpone and minimise the effects of the ageing process.') Panic about thinning on top made me write to a hair transplant clinic (and I was pestered for months afterwards by phonecalls exhorting me to come in for a 'free consultation'). I also embarked on a regime of rigorous dieting, power walking, press-ups and work-outs with a bizarre and dangerous device Clare had bought (as a joke) for ten pence in a jumble sale in the Community Centre (you were supposed to bend it to develop the biceps but its spring was so powerful that it always threatened to break free and knock my teeth out).

However, the effects of this fitness regime could not be displayed because of the demands of another new concern – fashion. 'That whole tight thing is out,' Clare informed me, as though it had been some brief whim of fashion – whereas, for men like myself who came of age in the sixties, tightness was a deep-seated philosophy, an entire way of life. Now I would have to wear loose-fitting trousers (preferably from the Covent Garden men's shop favoured by Nick) instead of the tight jeans I dearly loved (even though they made my balls scoot every time I sat down) and credited with any residual allure (once Rani glanced thrillingly at my fork and murmured, *You'll drive the nuns mad*). Even worse, baggy boxer shorts would have to replace the snug briefs which I had always believed showed the beasthood to advantage ('Nick wouldn't be seen dead in anything but boxer shorts now.') I could not deny an edict of Clare's. Shamelessly I copied not only the outer apparel but also the foundation garments of the rival (though I drew the line at soliciting the name and address of his tattooist).

None of this helped with what mattered most – sex. In the way that a full bladder gets increasingly importunate with the proximity of a toilet, sexual desire for Clare had grown imperious in the belief of an imminent decision. When it became clear that no decision was forthcoming some crucial restraint broke and desire raged out of control. Now I wanted only to be in her company and as close as possible to her body, marvelling at a beauty and radiance to which I could pay homage only by grunting over the toilet bowl with a wad of tissue in my hand. Why had I never appreciated her unblemished beauty? Even the simple urge to touch her made me tremble like an ague – though it was cancelled out by an equally powerful dread of rejection and permanent displeasure.

In the end there was nothing for it but to beg. Clare suffered me in silence, making no attempt to co-operate or conceal her disgust. Most humiliating of all was the fact that she was totally dry. Never before had this happened. Penetration, always so swift and inevitable, was now lengthy and difficult. I was haunted by Bernard's terrible phrase – *pushing it into an envelope of loosely packed gravel*.

Regret, remorse, shame, fear, obsession, self-abasement and weak will – just a few of the more obvious novelties. The symptoms were manifold and florid. Love is a Many-Splendoured Thing.

The only consolation was that Homewrecker was undergoing a parallel disintegration – and his was even more public. My youth of constant dissimulation gave me the ability to conceal many shameful things from Clare (at last the Catholic upbringing was coming into its own) – but Homewrecker had no training in, or talent for, concealment. Clare was immediately made aware that he had lost the ability to play guitar, then the ability to do his job. Everything was going from bad to worse. In the Youth Club heroin was replacing amphetamines as the principal drug threat. Racism was rearing its ugly head. There were fights in the Youth Club disco; white gangs ambushed black youths outside. Nick was accused of discriminating against whites, who left the club in droves to swell the gangs lying in wait. A message was daubed on the hall in giant letters: NICK'S JUNGLE DISCO – COONS ONLY WELCOME.

Convinced that Clare's retreat had really been a weekend of secret passion, Nick reversed his assessment of her. Before, she had been a cosy home-loving *bourgeoise*; now she was a ravening and fickle adventuress, a wilful Brett Ashley figure who loved to destroy talented young racing drivers and matadors. Having successfully accomplished the ruin of a talented young musician (himself), she would be looking round for her next victim.

'He thinks I have an endless stream of lovers,' Clare said in weary amazement, after coming in to throw herself on the sofa. 'He thinks I go through them like a dose of salts.'

'Gin?' I asked, indicating my half-full glass. Regular drinking alone was another degenerate new habit.

'Just some water. I don't want more drink. I get no effect from it these days. When we go to a pub Nick thinks every man in the place is lusting after me.' She shook her head in dismay. 'And that *I'm* lusting after *them* too. He's jealous of absolutely everyone, Martin.'

I took a quick snort of gin and got up to pour her a glass of water. 'Everyone except me.'

'He's scared to even go for a piss in case I run off with someone. I mean, can you imagine that? And all the time threatening to hit guys he thinks are leering at me. My God, he even thinks I'm having *a lesbian affair with Nina*. He's always disapproved of her ... for being too flighty or something ... and now he's jealous of her too. Isn't that just incredible?'

Handing her the water, I shook my head gravely, sombre commiseration on my features and exultation in my heart.

'And when he's not angry he's maudlin. Crying into his beer about how I'm tired of him and he's losing me.' Before, Clare had drunk her water as though it were alcohol to prolong the gaiety. Now she drank it as though it were alcohol to dull the pain.

Clare was attracted to confident disdainful bad boys (or, more precisely, boys who liked to pretend to be bad) and had replaced me in her affections with a newer and brighter antichrist. Yet both Nick and I were now tearful and craven, utterly without pride or dignity, disintegrating before her eyes. Incredulous and disgusted, she was compelled to face the terrible truth which comes in time to all women – that there is no such thing as a strong man, there are only degrees of weakness.

She drank from her glass slowly and deliberately, hunched around it as though for comfort. 'He really thinks it's all over. Tonight he was even asking for a memento.'

'Photos?'

'A pair of my pants.'

It was important not to seem too eager. A sip of gin was a useful distraction. 'Why bother to ask? Can't he have those anytime?'

Once again Clare displayed her extraordinary talent for making the most momentous statements in a matter-of-fact and even throwaway tone. 'We haven't had sex for a while now. The way he goes on puts me off.'

I concentrated on finishing the gin, holding the lemon slice down with a finger as though intent only on extracting the last drops of alcohol. The hand that held the glass was steady – but something flapped inside me like the wings of an agitated bird.

Needless to say, I assumed that Homewrecker's loss would be my gain. England's trouble has always been Ireland's opportunity.

I stood up, shaking the empty glass. 'Should I have another or not?'

'Suit yourself.'

'I won't bother,' I said, with an air of great sacrifice, and turned to the sofa as though on a impulse.

What made it worse was that Clare waited until a few moments after I had sat down beside her and then spoke in a calm measured tone that enhanced the venomous contempt. 'Fuck off, Martin. I really mean it. Just fuck off and leave me alone tonight.'

It was obvious that she would do anything to escape the attentions of her importunate suitors and when Pascal chose this time to come to London on a course Clare went off with the children to the cousin in Purley. Despite the prayers of his aunts, Pascal had never been accepted for teacher training but, after several attempts and many more fervent Novenas, he had finally been taken to the respectable bosom of the Northern Ireland Civil Service. His precise function in the Ministry of Agriculture was, needless to say, never explained by the connection but must have involved carrying out checks on farms, for there were many anecdotes about the ingenuity of the farmer's in planting produce in Pascal's car so that, try as he might to avoid it, he would invariably return from a visit to discover, hidden in the boot or under a seat, a ham, a turkey or a side of beef. 'The farmers are as cute,' Mairead would chortle. 'Ye couldn't watch them, look see.'

Now Pascal had worked his way up from the clerical level and was in London to learn management skills. He emerged from the tunnel at Heathrow beaming happily and, when I offered to carry something for him, he handed me a carrier bag full of discarded plastic meal trays, dirty containers and implements. 'Says I to this lassie of a hostess, do ye mind if I keep me stuff for the kids? Says she, how many do ye have? Says I, *four*. Says she, hold on a wee minute.' Then he dropped the other bag with a grunt, 'God isn't this heat desperate?' – recovering to jerk his head in the direction of two nearby black cleaners, 'No wonder some o' these fellas have a great tan, eh?' These last two remarks announced the twin themes of the visit – humorous comments about blacks and Asians (both referred to as 'Ballymena men') and complaints about the warm spring weather ('How do ye stick it? – it has me feet destroyed.'). Other traumas included London prices ('Guess what Ah paid for a sausage roll?'), rush-hour congestion ('Do people have to put up with that carry-on *every day?*') and the frigid solipsism of his fellow travellers ('Nobody would say a word to ye at all.'). On the other hand he was excited by street markets, hugely amused by the condom machines in public toilets and deeply impressed by the people running his course – not for their knowledge or presentation skills but for their astuteness in setting up such a nice earner. 'God that's a good number they're on to there, eh – thirty or so of us at two hundred a skull? It's a wonder ye wouldn't think of gettin' into that racket. Teaching the McKenzie Grid and all that sort of stuff, eh? Says I to this Welsh fella, do ye understand this? Haven't a clue, says he. Says I, *join the club.*'

Yet despite the heat and long gruelling days of management games, Pascal had the phenomenal energy that seems to come to all London visitors. When I tried to persuade him to watch television in the evenings he would rise to his feet with a happy grin. 'Ah sure we'll go out for a bit of a dander. Sure aren't we *bachelor gay?*'

It was not just the ordeal of being seen with a short squat overweight man in a grey suit and bri-nylon shirt, relentlessly facetious and embarrassingly familiar with strangers. There was also a nightmarish feeling that this visit was fated, that Pascal had been sent to teach me something or to show me my destiny. If I were God and wanted a laugh at the expense of a smart aleck, Pascal would be the ideal unwitting tool.

Towards the end of the month Sister Joseph drew me aside in the corridor. I was sure that she meant to criticise my handling of the tutor group (and continuing failure to stage an assembly). Instead it was to inform me of a teaching vacancy in St Margaret's Training College in Northern Ireland. Had I heard of the college? she asked.

Had I heard of the province's provider of Catholic female lay teachers? Almost every woman I knew had been there – my mother, several cousins, Jean, both paternal aunts and Angela Neville.

'Well it so happens I'm very great with Sister Rita . . . the Vice Principal of St Margaret's . . .' In her excitement and eagerness Joe came close to me. 'Now don't say I told you this . . . we certainly appreciate you very much here . . . but I happen to know that *they need a Physics lecturer there.*' Her expression a blend of mischievousness and triumph; she stepped back a little to observe the effect.

My first reaction was of horror. To be once again the nice boy working for nuns (not merely Irish nuns but *Irish nuns on their home ground*), in an establishment turning out the female type I most disliked (Angela Neville a typical latterday student) and promoting Catholic separatism, opposing the integrated education that would surely help to heal the grievous divisions in the North.

Against all this there was the prospect of shaking off Homewrecker and attaining the most hallowed of titles – *lecturer*. Now that the Luciferian flame was extinguished I understood the universal hunger for status, the need for something external to confer substance and form, a raiment sufficiently imposing to disguise the pitiful husk and with sufficient weight to prevent it from blowing away in the wind.

'Now I know you're far too well-qualified for us, Mr Ward.'

'I don't know about that, Sister.'

'Ah go way now. Go way. Of course you are, Mr Ward. *Go way.*'

Obviously the seven had been right all along and the intelligence controlling the world was malign. Only the Prince of Darkness could have offered me what I wanted, at exactly the time when I was most in need, and used as his agent a kindly rosy-cheeked white-haired nun.

'And *listen*,' Joe said in ever-heightening collusive excitement. 'Didn't you tell me you were related to Bishop Farley?'

Not only favouritism, nepotism as well. But even Flaubert, man of iron integrity ('May the United States perish rather than a principle') was not above making use of his connections. In the prosecution of *Madame Bovary* the defence case rested largely on the solid bourgeois reputation of the Flaubert family. ('So you presume to attack the younger son of Monsieur Flaubert. No one, sir, not even you, could give *him* lessons in morality.') Is there anyone who can honestly claim *never* to have invoked an available privilege? Even Christ occasionally made use of the fact that his father was God.

'I am,' I heard myself saying, 'but he's not a very close relative.'

'*Och!*' She waved aside the irrelevant issue of degree. 'I just told her you were related to the man. *Never mind how.* And listen, Mr Ward, she was saying they want to build up the Science Department ... everyone's crying out for female science teachers these days ... so she was *very interested* to hear you were well qualified and had lots of experience teaching girls science ... *anyone getting in now could really go far in that college.*' (Flaubert: 'What a shower of honours descends on those who are without honour!') Again the familiar grip on my arm as she leaned close for what was meant to be the ultimate reassurance. '*And sure ye'd be back among your own kind, Mr Ward.*'

Commanding a rise over-looking the Foyle, the private park of Mount Pleasant has large detached houses on three sides of a rectangle whose interior is a communal garden scrupulously maintained but never used. Ward has always been puzzled by the garden's perpetual emptiness but eventually concludes that this immaculate central area is a kind of open-air front room.

Pausing between the mighty pillars that frame the entrance to the park, Ward and Clare cannot help but be cowed by its inviolable hush.

'My Aunt Colette's house,' Ward whispers, with a wave at the substantial dwelling on their left.

'Better rush me past before someone sees me,' Clare sarcastically mutters.

It is a relative of Clare's they are coming to visit. Annihilated by the effort of rearing eleven children, Clare's mother has largely abdicated in favour of her eldest daughter, Kathleen, in whom the authority of early responsibility has been reinforced by affluence. Her husband, Jack Barrett, has his own business fitting burglar alarms, a booming trade in an age of rampant blaggardism and one which has enabled him to afford the dignity of a distinguished old park. So the girl Ward has found in Ardowen brings him back to Mount Pleasant.

Apparently unintimidated by the surrounding reserve, the

Barrett home is lit by garden spotlights and has in its drive a van marked PMH Security, a bulky station wagon and, next to the house, an enormous new caravan. Ward pauses on the driveway in sudden repugnance. Clare rushes on to ring the bell, only to be nonplussed when Jack Barrett comes to the door.

'Is Kathleen around?'

'*Around?* Sure Ah can't get rid of her. Put her out every night with the milk bottles and she's still there in the mornin'.' Jack looks past Clare to Ward. 'Thinks she's guardin' them.'

Behind Jack, Kathleen appears at the top of the stairs and Clare cries out in bitter reproach, 'You didn't sell the old caravan, Kathleen!'

'Och that old thing.'

'But those holidays! I have really happy memories of those holidays.'

'Sure there was nothin' in it, Clare.'

Behind Kathleen are three children, two boys and a younger girl, obviously keen to descend. As one of the boys places a tentative foot on a lower stair, Jack goes back down the hall to speak with the immediacy, conviction and terseness of true authority. '*Up.*'

'Let me just say goodnight to Daniella,' Clare begs, already mounting the stairs in brazen dereliction of her duty as sponsor and protectress of Ward.

'How're ye doin', Martin?' With this deep mature greeting Barrett ushers the youth into a lounge combining elements of the hotel lobby (a huge leather sofa extending around both sides of the far corner) with a taste for the luridly hirsute (dyed sheepskin rugs everywhere on the shagpile and even one, or at least something hairy, on the wall).

Jack goes straight to a cocktail cabinet and produces a bottle of Paddy.

'I can't really drink whiskey,' Ward protests.

'But have you tried Paddy? Irish is smoother than Scotch and Paddy's the smoothest of all.'

'Just a small one then.'

'God never made halves.' Jack pours copiously and presents the youth with a chunky tumbler. 'That'll put hair on your chest.'

Ward carries his drink to the extended sofa which is not only lower than it looks but also more yielding at the back so that his behind seems to come to rest practically at floor level. As he lifts the glass to his lips a large boxer dog rises from a rug and, padding swiftly across the room, places its front paws on his genitals and attempts to lick his face. ('I attract madmen and animals; is it because they sense that I understand them, because they feel that I enter their world?' – Flaubert).

'*Rebel!*' Jack calls sharply, adding, in a softer tone, to Ward. 'He won't hurt you – he's just being friendly. Boxers are the friendliest dogs around. *Isn't that right, Rebel?*'

At this invitation the dog abandons Ward to bound at its master who leaves aside his drink and falls on one knee to engage in a mock sparring bout, delivering a series of strong manly cuffs which produce in the drooling brute a frenzy of love and respect.

Eventually Jack rises to resume seat and drink and turns with enthusiasm to Ward. 'So what are you thinking of doing when you graduate?'

Disinclined to submit to interrogation, Ward merely shrugs ('Pride imposes silence on pride' – d'Aurevilly).

Barrett is undeterred. 'Now if I had a degree in Physics I could really go places. See, I just install alarms and respond to call-outs – but if I could make up my own systems the business would really take off.' Jack puts down his drink and leans confidentially forward. 'What I need is an electronics expert I could really depend on. If I could find the right man I'd set him up, ye know … *properly*, I mean … with a workshop and a few young fellas under him to train up. I'd look after all the installation and business side of things.'

Ward is shocked to realise that he is being offered a position. An offer to *go into business!* In this *remote and godforsaken province!* As a *protector of the bourgeoisie!* As a *protégé of the loathsome Jack Barrett!* ('A man so little spiritual he would disgust even a solicitor' – Baudelaire). At last Ward is grateful for the support and consolation of the Paddy. 'I'd think I'd like to go away for a while.'

Surprisingly, Jack accepts this. 'I can understand that in a young fella. Had to get away meself. Where did you have in mind?'

Ward shrugs, relaxed and careless now that he feels out of danger. 'Oh I don't know … London maybe …'

'*London!*' Jack angrily approaches him over the sofa ('It is a wonderful thing how no one will allow anyone to live as he likes' – Flaubert). 'Sure London's finished. England's finished. Wait till

244

Ah tell ye, Martin.' Adopting the gravitas and concern of a mentor, he advances closer still. 'The last time I was in London, Martin, I went up to the top floor of the hotel and took a good look round.' Now he grips the youth's arm, intimate, confidential, shrewd. 'How many tower cranes do ye think Ah saw . . . *ah?*' Ward makes a show of frowning in deep consideration. 'Ah'll tell ye how many Ah saw . . . *five*. Five tower cranes in a capital city the size of London.' Jack sits back, satisfied that his point has been proved. 'That shows ye how much is goin' on. I was supposed to go in with an English crowd – but I pulled out. Wouldn't touch it, Martin. *Wouldn't touch it*. London's finished. A young fella should go where the action is. Ever thought of Saudi?'

'*Saudi Arabia?*'

As though determined to take the youth straight to the airport and put him on the first plane to the Middle East, Jack grips Ward's elbow and draws him up from the sofa. 'Come on.' ('Royal soul surrendered in one forgetful instant to the crab of debauch, the octopus of weakness of character, the shark of individual abasement, the snake of absent morals and the monstrous snail of idiocy' – Lautréamont).

And indeed they go back along the hall and out the front door towards the van – but here Jack stops, content to greet the vehicle with the same hearty affectionate slap he used on his dog.

'Know what PMH stands for?'

'No.'

'See, I was working for this crowd in Saudi and says I to meself, it's wide open out here, why should the firm get all the profit when Muggins does all the work . . . *eh?* So I decided to go out on me own. But this Arab character says to me, says he, what's your company called? you can't work out here unless you're a company. *Pogue Maw Hone*, says I to him. *What?* says he, a bit suspicious . . . ye have to be careful out there. That's the name of the company, says I. And that's where PMH comes from, Martin. *But don't be tellin' anyone that*. Four years I was out in Saudi. Never looked back since.' Still leaning casually on the van, Jack turns to look back contentedly on his other possessions.

'You've done very well.' Ward's touch of sarcasm is lost on his mentor ('There are some tortoise-like carapaces against which contempt ceases to be a pleasure' – Baudelaire).

'Sixteen men workin' for me now,' Jack explains. 'Not all permanent of course. I take people on when I need them. Though some characters round here don't seem to understand that. They think ye should get a pension book the first mornin' ye start. Only ten of those'd be permanent ... workin' shifts to go out on alarm calls with the dogs.'

'Your own men go out? Aren't there some rough customers round here?'

Chuckling happily, Barrett places a reassuring arm about the youth's shoulders. 'Those fellas know how to handle themselves.' He chuckles again in a significant way. 'Used to go out meself actually ... when Ah was just startin' up.'

Now he disengages decisively from the van and guides Ward back to the house. Clare's voice issues invitingly from the lounge – but Jack propels the youth down the hall and into an under-stairs cupboard where he clears away a layer of sports gear to reveal a full wine rack. 'All good stuff ... *Ah?*'

Already feeling the alcohol, Ward fears that Barrett will make him drink wine on top of whiskey ('The spirit of every business man is completely depraved' – Baudelaire). However, it seems to be purely a demonstration of the quality and extent of his cellar.

'That's good stuff,' Ward agrees, turning impatiently back towards the hall.

Jack bars his way with a gentle hand. 'Listen,' he says, bringing his face close to Ward's in the under-stairs gloom and adopting a new tone, low but intimate and urgent. 'You know I'm very close to Clare ... sort of a father to her really ...'

'*Uhn?*' Again Ward makes to move and is gently restrained.

'It's just Ah wouldn't like anything to happen to her. Wouldn't be very happy about it' – Jack drops his voice again but compensates by bringing his face even closer – '*know what Ah mean?*'

Finally it comes to Ward that he is being threatened ('Tumultuous torrents of undying hatred mount like heavy fumes to his head' – Lautréamont) but before he can react Jack adroitly turns away and goes back up the hall.

In the lounge it is impossible to retaliate.

'Fancy a few years in Saudi?' Jack is asking Clare, adding mysteriously, 'Chop-Chop Square.'

'Jack!' Kathleen remonstrates mildly.

'Chop-Chop Square – that's the place. Every morning. Seven or eight guys.' Jack delivers a nifty kick with his left foot and follows it up with a vicious slicing motion of the hand. 'A wee kick in the arse and then *voooom . . .* off with the head.'

Clare cries out in revulsion. '*They chop people's heads off?*'

'Oh yeah.' Elaborately casual, Jack apparently concentrates on his drink while watching Clare over the rim of the glass. 'Every morning in life. Chop-Chop Square. You can go and watch while Martin's at work.'

'Oh *Jack!*' This time Kathleen's objection has a note of genuine dismay. But, powerless to control the outrageous fellow, all she can do is advise her sister, 'Don't pay any attention to him, Clare.'

'No messin' with those guys,' Jack says in deep satisfaction, glancing at Ward as though to suggest that a spell under such a regime would do the youth a power of good.

Now Clare and Kathleen express a desire to see the caravan holiday movies.

Jack is glad to oblige and soon they are diverted by images of Clare howling, pursued by Jack with a crab, Clare howling, dumped in the sea by Jack, Clare howling, captured changing into a bikini, Clare, in the bikini, playing beach tennis, Clare at a table in front of a caravan, rising to flee with a howl as Jack approaches with some hideous insect.

Kathleen, seated on Ward's right, brings her face to his ear in an intimate and confidential manner that seems to promise criticism of her husband. Ward presents her with his undivided attention.

'That was the old caravan,' she explains – and then suddenly shrieks at her own first appearance on screen. 'Would ye look at the size of me! That must have been after I had Daniella. But you're as skinny as a rake, Clare.'

'Sure didn't Jack used to call me Chicken Legs.'

Observing Jack grinning as the screen Clare, clad in a towel, flees along the beach in terror, Ward now feels that it is Barrett who would benefit from the traditional justice of the Orient ('You know the incident of the forty pounds of human eyes which were brought on two gold plates to Shah Nasser-Edin on the day of his ceremonial entry into a rebel city?' – Villiers). As their screen counterparts wrestle, Jack and Clare exchange laughs on the sofa. ('The execution of the rebel leaders was more formal. Their teeth were first extracted with pincers and then hammered back into their skulls, specially shaved for the occasion, in such a way as to form the initials of the glorious name of the Shah' – Villiers).

At last it is over and they are released. Ward wastes no time in violating the solemn hush of Mount Pleasant. 'How can you stand that fucker Barrett? How could you think of going on holiday with a dirty bastard like that?'

'Jack and Kathleen were very good to me,' Clare shouts. 'They always took me on holiday in that wee caravan.'

'We know why of course.'

'Those were the only holidays I ever had in my life. My parents never took us anywhere. It's easy for you to talk ... you don't know what it's like to have nothing ... but I had the time of my life on those holidays. Jack Barrett might be a bit of a blow – but he was always generous to me. Always paid for everything. And generous to the rest of the family too. The only good thing that ever happened to us was Kathleen marrying a man who did well.'

'Kathleen's certainly grateful. Practically *pimping* for him for Chrissake. *Filming* him chasing you. That's right – *run away*.'

Clare plunges through the pillars of Mount Pleasant. Ward waits for a moment but, when there is no sign of her returning, follows, crossing to the other side of the road and keeping twenty yards behind. In this way they proceed to the centre of town and the hospital bus stop.

Even while she waits for the bus Clare does not acknowledge the figure on the opposite side of the street. And when the bus arrives she enters morosely, without looking up. However, she takes a seat on Ward's side and, as he turns to go, sullenly opens the window. 'I've a half day on Wednesday.'

Jocelyn had exchanged her National Gallery elegance for jeans and a cheese-cloth blouse tied in a jaunty bow at the waist. Both items looked as though the price tags had only just been removed. Beneath the jeans, rather forlorn and loose on her slim figure, a pair of new sneakers shone with the virgin purity of first snow. It was obvious that she had bought a special outfit for an evening with 'the young ones', a depressing sign of ingratiation, of playing to the supposed strengths of others instead of relying on her own. All her mystery and sophistication disappeared in an instant. The Wise Virgin was revealed to be as naive and insecure as the rest.

Bernard, in the act of handing Clare a bottle of wine, cocked an ear to the New Wave music.

'They're over-excited,' he suggested eventually. 'They're over-excited fellows, aren't they?'

'*What?*' she cried, flushed and angry.

'Well *I* like it.' Jocelyn cast Bernard a look of playful defiance. 'Just you play what you like in your own home, Clare.'

The familiar sour taste of futility: my chronic spiritual heartburn. This dinner party, intended to demonstrate to Clare my independent social life, was suddenly revealed as an act of folly, a waste of time, energy and cash.

Now Bernard was being negative about aperitifs. 'You see, it's the hangovers I can't stand. I hate it when the computer isn't functioning properly ... when it's not receiving *sensory data*. We need to take in sensory impressions *all the time*.' He touched in turn his eyes, ears and nose. 'These are our data terminals. Our data terminals. We ought to be registering all the time. The sensual ecstasy, my God.'

Jocelyn ignored this advice to order a large gin and tonic. Clare made and distributed three drinks, affecting to notice Bernard's consternation only when we raised our glasses for a toast. 'I thought you didn't want any.'

'I'll have to have one, won't I, if everyone else is?'

When I crossed to the kitchen to get on with the cooking, Jocelyn followed to offer assistance. 'Someone's been going to *a lot of trouble*.'

'It's only a fish casserole.'

'It smells *absolutely delicious*.' Her voice descended to the chalumeau register. 'I'm sure you're a *wonderful cook*.'

Was this not what I wanted – attention and praise from an attractive woman? The perfect cure for ailing self-esteem? An incentive to return to the sexual marketplace?

In fact the episode depressed me. It was not the flattery (never believe anyone who claims to dislike it) but that this attempt was so superficial and lazy. Effective flattering needs ability and effort like any other skill. Goddam it, you have to locate the clit.

If the Jocelyn experience was typical, the allure of the strange was likely to evaporate and leave behind a familiar residue of complication. But having to leave London for a new job would provide the perfect escape. A window of opportunity suddenly appeared and exuberant sunlight streamed in. My lamentable existence could still be redeemed by valedictory intercourse with Janet or Rani.

It might seem presumptuous to take them for granted but both women had reacted emotionally to my possible departure. Rani had been especially stricken, holding me in a long sorrowful gaze and actually seizing my arm as though to detain me by force. Clare, on the other hand, had scarcely shown any response to the news, possibly dismissing it as another empty threat from a weak-willed fool – or possibly not considering it at all. Beset by emotional demands and ploys, she was increasingly inclined to ignore anything Homewrecker or I said or did.

As always the cooking took longer than I expected and we had finished a third aperitif before the food was ready. Bernard ate with gusto but held back on the wine. Jocelyn picked at her food but accepted every refill of her glass.

'What would you think,' she cried suddenly to Clare, 'of a man who refused tickets for Mozart?'

Immediately Bernard put a cupped hand to his mouth and produced an exaggerated cough. 'I couldn't sit in a concert hall with a chronic condition like this.' He turned in mock solemnity to Clare. 'Perhaps honey here can recommend a cough medicine.'

'A cough should never be suppressed,' Clare firmly declared. 'It's an essential mechanism of the body.'

Always entranced by ex-cathedra pronouncements from the Big Nurse, Bernard forgot that he was merely play-acting. 'But a cough can go down into the chest.'

'Only an infection can do that.' Confident expertise always commanded Bernard's attention and respect. And if the expertise was medical he became as submissive as a child. 'You've probably gone back to smoking.'

'Only one or two in the evening,' he pleaded.

'A cough takes *three times as long* to clear up in a smoker.'

'It isn't the cough,' Jocelyn suddenly cried. 'That's not why he won't go to Mozart.'

Bernard turned to face her. 'It's true that I don't care for the fellow.' He grimaced. 'All that ethereal tinkling beauty. You see, I don't care at all for your Michelangelos and Mozarts. It's all too

250

sanitised and perfect. Art should be a by-product of living ... *like sweat.*' Forgetting himself in his passion, he seized his glass and took a great slug. 'It's the grit that makes the pearl.'

'Now he's attacking Michelangelo!' Jocelyn cried in despair, looking round for support. Surely someone would spring to the defence of the gods of Culture – Mike 'n' Mo?

Bernard was only getting into his stride. 'You see, they worked for patrons ... and patrons always want cissy stuff. Something to glorify themselves and confer respectability. Because who were they really, these so-called enlightened patrons? Chieftains, bandits, robber barons.' Suddenly he turned on his hosts. 'You two probably believe you're descended from Celtic chieftains. But you carry a chieftain's name not because you were related to him but *because you were his property.* You were his *slave.* And if the Goths and Vandals hadn't come down from the north to smash the Roman aristocracy you'd still be slaves.'

Despairing of reasoning with such a maniac, Jocelyn concentrated on the rest of her audience. 'Now he's praising the Vandals and Goths.'

'*Yes!*' Bernard shouted defiantly. 'Fuck aristocratic culture!' Viciously he slashed the air with a sudden horizontal stroke that caused the table to shake and the wine in our glasses to slop. 'Let the Goths and Vandals ride in and fuck the whole lot.'

There was a long pause, heavy with the awkwardness of transgression. Flaubert's fondness for barbarians now came to mind.

In silence Clare served the dessert which was her contribution to the meal (nothing would ever convince me to become an adept of sweetness).

Jocelyn reaffirmed her belief in civilised values by emphatically complimenting the chefs. 'I thoroughly enjoyed all of that. Thank you both very much.' Then she returned to the argument. 'And after he turned down Mozart, claiming he really preferred jazz, I asked him to come along and meet some friends of mine who love jazz. *What do you think he said to that?*' Clare and I waited attentively. 'He said, *if there's one thing I hate more than philistines it's people who share my tastes.*'

The desire to laugh was overwhelming. Bernard, the self-styled enemy of aristocrats, was in fact displaying aristocratic fastidiousness and perversity. Was this passionate advocate of the Cross a man of the Crag in his heart?

'It's true,' he agreed, though with a suspect readiness. 'I hate people. I hate life.'

Again the echo of Flaubert was uncanny: 'I have a hatred of life. There: I have said it. I will not take it back.' Yet Flaubert, for all his whingeing, had two of the greatest gifts life has to offer – a private income and an easy death. Integrity ('I am more than ever intransigently idealistic and resolved to die rather than make the slightest concession') is easier to proclaim when there is no need to scratch around for a living. And his courage in remaining outside the Church (the only one of the seven known to have done so) was never put to the ultimate test of a lingering painful demise. Could he have withstood the bullying of his mother? Chroniclers tend to pass over the fact that The Incredible F Man was a mammy's boy. Not only did he live with his mother until her death, when he himself was over fifty, the legendary realist and destroyer of fantasy made his servant Julie wear the deceased mother's clothes to create the illusion of maternal presence. And when the success of *Salammbô* briefly permitted him to maintain a base in Paris as well as the family home at Croisset, instead of relishing the freedom, he rented a second apartment *in the same house* for his mother.

It could be argued that Flaubert never had to face life or death. But all that matters is what we make of the givens. Morally, intellectually and aesthetically The Incredible F Man was a giant. And he alone of the seven offered practical advice ('One should live like a bourgeois and think like a demigod').

Apparently satisfied by Bernard's admission of misanthropy, Jocelyn rose and went to the bathroom.

'You're far too hard on her,' Clare accused.

'Indeed I often think I'm doing her a disservice by talking seriously. The poor angel can't cope with unpleasant truths. It's like putting stones into a wet paper bag.'

'Then why do it?'

'Because I have to show her that there's more to life than she imagines. She thinks it's all tinkling with the right hand.' Bernard demonstrated by touching imaginary keys with delicate fingers. 'She has to see that there's also the rolling bass underneath.' With an outspread left hand he struck deep heavy chords.

'*Why?* Why does she have to see that?' Clare's vehemence made

252

it clear that she was arguing not just for Jocelyn but on behalf of Novelty, Adventure and Fun, those wayward gods whose recent withdrawal had left her resentful and baffled (her most recent night out on the town had ended with Homewrecker attempting to strangle her for looking the wrong way at a man in a bar). Another unwelcome truth was imposing itself – that Fun is not an automatic reward for casting off shackles. Instead it is every bit as demanding as duty and possibly more work than work.

'It's my way of letting her down easy. I could never reject her outright. Instead I let her see what I'm really like ... and that the whole thing's impossible.'

With his customary skill Bernard had guided the interrogation towards a revelation of his motives as selflessness, compassion and charity. Clare's angry persistence was admirable – but in order to defeat Bernard in argument you would have to be Descartes to fault his logic and Torquemada to make him admit it.

'But why is it impossible? She's a lovely person, highly attractive ... and obviously mad about you.' Now Clare, still undecided between husband and lover, was arguing desperately in favour of romance.

'I would crush her, honey. I would crush her, wouldn't I?' As always the softness of Bernard's tone was proportional to the hardness of the current truth. 'You see, she's not a sophisticated girl.' He grimaced and sighed in deep reluctance. 'For instance, in spite of her marriages and lovers she's still coy about sex. About nakedness for example. And she says she likes sucking men but doesn't want them to tongue her because of the smell of her cunt. Now that's a *very unsophisticated* thing to say ... isn't it? That's a very unsophisticated thing for any woman to say.'

'I still think she's a very nice person,' Clare insisted. 'I'm sure you could make a go of a relationship if only you put your mind to it.'

'No, no. It happens only once, Clare. Once if you're lucky, that is.'

'But the world's full of people happy in second and third relationships.' Clare was desperate to preserve her dream. But she was fighting that most implacable of foes – determinism.

'I can only tell you what happened. My wife's been dead over twenty years – and yet I still dream about her every night. I don't mean that approximately or figuratively. I mean that I've had a substantial dream about her every night of my life for twenty years. The terrible thing is that we're always quarrelling in the dream. Always quarrelling bitterly. Of course we did frequently quarrel in real life. That's inevitable in any deep relationship where sex is involved. These couples who never fight have some kind of tepid asexual brother-and-sister thing. Anyway, in the dreams Pat is always reproaching me for something. But about once every six months we're happy in the dream. My God, the mornings after those dreams are incredible. Such bliss, Clare, such absolute bliss. It would be wonderful if I could have something as good again ... even half as good ... a quarter as good ... but I think it happens only once ... I think you're only capable of it once ... when you're both young. It happens once only ... and then it's over for good.'

Instead of Hillcrest or Glen Avon burned into a varnished tree-trunk slice, this apparently ordinary Ulster house has its name around the arch of the doorway in dark Gothic script: Le Grand Chateau Mysterieux. To the door comes Scott Copeland himself, Ward's exciting new artistic friend, gifted, exuberant and convivial, certainly 'no spring chicken' but somehow still untainted by the fearful conformity of his native province, apparently content to live in rented accommodation and survive on a precarious income from writing.

'And this must be Clare.' Scott advances to seize the girl boldly and kiss her full on the lips. Then he looks questioningly at the third member of the party.

'Tony Shotter,' Ward explains, almost groaning with encumbrance. First Clare sulked until asked along to the party. Then it seemed that Shotter could not be left behind alone. Now Ward feels that he is climbing the steps of the Temple of Art with a Catholic ghetto strapped to his back ('One does not forge one's destiny, one can only submit to it' – Flaubert).

'Let me show you round!' Scott leads them upstairs, flinging open rooms and wittily describing their absent tenants, an impressively diverse group with apparently nothing in common beyond a lack of concern for privacy and rejection of conventional furnishings and decor.

Turning from Ward, Copeland addresses polite enquiries to Shotter. Shotter replies – but, instead of looking at Copeland, *keeps his gaze firmly fixed on Ward.* The mighty Shotter, always so superior and scornful, is revealed as another timid peasant. For the long years of fraudulence and the revelation at this most inopportune moment, Ward could willingly strangle his inadequate friend ('I would like to suppress you without anger, as I would kick a piece of dirt from my path, without your death interrupting even one of those lofty thoughts which remain forever beyond your grasp' – Villiers).

Clare meanwhile is considering a huge ornate gilt frame which so exceeds its present purpose that the area it encloses is largely taken up by a mount, leaving only a small central square for the artwork itself – a crumpled pair of red Y-fronts.

Scott gathers the wandering attention of his audience. 'Let's see if Henry J. Tonk's in.'

'Won't he be downstairs at the party with everyone else?'

'I don't think so.' Scott drops his voice to a dramatic whisper. '*I'm sure he's still in his room.*' Tiptoeing across the landing, he knocks softly and apologetically on a door with a brass name plate: HENRY J. TONK. When there is no reply he knocks again and at last tentatively opens the door.

Lolling in an armchair facing them is a life-size rag doll with a huge papier-mâché head on which has been painted a lopsided grin.

Intruders and tenant consider each other in silence.

'Henry J. Tonk,' Scott explains. 'He's agreed to look after the coats tonight.'

Divested of outer garments, they proceed to the top landing, where most of the space has been fenced off for an aviary with rock pools and branches imaginatively arranged to resemble trees, a miniature sylvan paradise where colourful tiny birds flit in an understandable ecstasy of song.

The guests gape like beasts enchanted by a fairy princess. Nothing in their brutish existence has prepared them for such melodious delicacy and grace.

Shotter speaks for all three. 'The only thing *I* ever saw in a house was a budgie cage.'

'But it's not even your house,' is all Ward can say to Copeland. 'I mean, you just rent the place.'

'Yip,' Scott agrees cheerfully. 'And we're going to be thrown out soon.' In some fantastically perverse way he seems almost to

255

relish the prospect. 'We'll have to find somewhere else when I get back from the States.' He lays an avuncular hand on the youth's shoulder. 'Are you coming out with me? There's plenty of work, as I said.'

In the idyllic safety of a protected world the innocent birds flutter and chirp.

Called away by the front doorbell, Scott indicates another stair-case. 'Party's that-a-way. Follow the noise.'

'The States,' Clare says at last, acidly. 'Just you of course.'

Ward suppresses a surge of anger ('What do you mean by self-ishness? I should like very much to know whether you too are not selfish and quite impressively so' – Flaubert). 'Jill isn't going either.' Another of Copeland's astounding achievements is a childless mar-riage in which the couple lead separate lives with separate friends and even, it seems, separate lovers.

'I'm not Jill.'

'*Look* . . . it's only for six weeks . . . and you know I've no interest in American girls. Physical separation might be difficult – but there's an answer to that.' Eagerly Ward expounds a solution of typical ingenuity and elegance. 'All we have to do is agree a time and masturbate *simultaneously* thinking of each other.' Clare presents him with a terrible countenance of lead. 'Taking care to allow for the time difference of course.' He grins encouragingly to show that he has grasped the parameters of the problem. 'On the east coast I'll be about five hours later than you.'

The leaden mask is not lifted. 'Fucking *drop dead*, Martin.'

As though in gladness at having been spared the human condi-tion, the birds suddenly combine in an outburst of carolling. With a sharp bark of disgust Shotter makes for the stairs.

'I want to live a little,' Ward cries. 'I've never been anywhere. I've experienced nothing. I have to be able to go *somewhere* without *you*.'

'But you *never* want me with you. You don't want me here now. I'm just a nuisance. I'm showing you up. I'm holding you back.'

'That's not true. I never said that.'

'You don't want me with you. I'm going.'

'Where you're going is the party.'

Grimly they descend to what is surely the most cosmopolitan gathering in the province, a sophisticated company which effortlessly transcends the barriers of age, religion, nationality, colour, sexual orientation and class.

'How about ye, Ward?' In the kitchen they are enthusiastically hailed by John Bell. 'After the drink as usual, I suppose.' Bell turns to Clare with an earnest expression. 'A terrible man altogether. He'd drink it out of a dead bear's bum.' Shaking his head in mock dismay, he addresses Ward once more. 'You missed a ferocious session in Lavery's the other night. *Desperate.* Wild altogether.' Now he turns back to Clare and, laying a hand on her arm, gazes into her eyes with an expression of solemn resolve. 'Ah'm puttin' it all on tape for the blind.'

'I need a pee,' Ward says.

'Faulty washers.' With a laugh Bell moves closer to the girl.

'I need to go too.' When Clare seizes Ward by the elbow he throws back his head in a bitter ironic laugh.

Walking a few steps ahead of her in the hallway, he stops and, without looking back, snaps his fingers and points at the ground by his side. 'Here, girl. *Heel.*' When nothing happens he repeats the gesture. 'Come on, girl ... *heel.*'

Clare approaches and digs her nails into the pointing hand. 'That's not fucking funny.'

Ward regards the marks with a show of surprise. 'Bad doggie.' Moving on a few yards, he repeats the performance. This time Clare viciously gouges the hand. Ward inspects the damage. 'Blood.' He laughs horribly. 'Excellent.'

Pushing past him she runs up the stairs. Ward catches her as she enters the cloakroom and glares at the dummy.

'I'd like to kick that fucking thing to pieces.'

Always alert to injustice, he moves to defend the helpless lodger. 'Just remember I never asked you to come here. I told you you wouldn't like it.'

'Well I'm going now ... *all right?*'

'I mean, who could meet your demands?' Ward suddenly shrieks. 'You want me with you night and day, you expect to be entertained night and day. Yet we have nothing in common. You don't like anything or anyone I like. We have nothing to say to each other.'

'Nothing in common,' she repeats dully. 'So that's the way of it. Nothing to say to each other.'

In the oppressive silence which follows the dummy appears to be watching them with an ironic smile. Ward himself suppresses a sudden urge to tear off its head.

'Maybe we should finish altogether,' he softly suggests.

'If you say so.' Calmly she dons her overcoat.

'It'll be better for both of us in the long run.' ('Later you will thank me for having had the courage not to be more tender' – Flaubert).

Clare departs without fuss. Convinced that she will soon be back, Ward waits in the company of grinning Henry J. Tonk. When the silence persists his heart begins to pound and a terrible vertigo engulfs him. Is it exaltation or despair? Or can these can these two opposites co-exist?

Downstairs Shotter is nowhere to be seen. Instead there are elegant, mature women, most of them gathered round the writers. Ward joins the group round a middle-aged bearded critic in a safari suit. The man is holding the right hand of a woman in his left hand and frowningly scrutinising her palm as if it were a multi-layered post-modern text. Eventually it comes to Ward that appearance is reality; this is an exercise in palm reading. Now the critic seems to have arrived at an interpretation, though he looks for corroborative evidence before making it public, glancing up sharply into the subject's eyes and then down again to her palm which he strokes caressingly several times.

'I'll tell you this much,' he finally breathes. '*You're all woman.*'

Ward prepares to join in the laughter – but no one laughs. Instead those awaiting interpretation press forward a little, attempting to hasten a subject obviously disposed to linger, gazing with admiration and gratitude into the eyes of the exegete stroking her hand.

The insularity of life in the province is being lamented by the group around Copeland who reveals that one of their leading poets has never been across the Channel.

Ward seizes a chance to reveal his knowledge of cultural events. 'But didn't he just do a reading in Oxford?'

The silence is sudden and calamitous. Everyone gazes down into a glass.

'The English Channel,' Copeland explains. 'Not the Irish Sea.'

Ward can scarcely comprehend his error. He whose multi-coloured maps of the tropics astounded a generation of Geography teachers and who could barely repress a shout of derision when some buffoon at the wall map mistook Formosa for Hong Kong, has now himself committed the most hideous elementary gaffe.

The group has moved on to criticise the pusillanimity of local broadcasting.

'Derryck Hunter's the only revolutionary in the BBC.'

'And Derryck's leaving.' Scott's light tone belies the extent of this tragedy for, as all present know, it is Hunter who has championed Copeland's work.

'No, Scott!'

'*Never!*'

'Oh yes.' Copeland shrugs casually. Can *nothing* upset this guy? 'He can't take the crap any more. No support at all, you see. We need to get more good people in there.' He goes on to exhort the men of talent to abandon their ivory towers and seize control from the creeps. There is nothing dishonourable in using a popular medium. If Shakespeare were alive today he would be writing for television.

Ward has often heard this argument. Tonight it occurs to him that if Flaubert were alive he would most certainly not be writing for television. ('To practice art to earn money, to flatter the public, spin facetious or dismal yarns for reputation and cash – that is the most ignoble of professions.')

What has happened is that Clare and Copeland have succeeded in cancelling each other out. Earlier, Copeland's relaxed independence discredited Clare's desperate possessiveness. Now Clare's innocence and authenticity make Copeland seem a phoney pretending insouciance. Each has annihilated the other. Nothing remains but ashes and gall.

Ward returns to home to hear voices issuing from Shotter's room. Shotter himself cautiously opens the door to reveal a wine bottle, glasses and Clare, tearful but silent.

'She came back for her stuff,' Shotter explains.

Ward turns to go – but Clare leaps to her feet and pursues him. 'We didn't do anything, Martin.'

'It's none of my business if you did.'

At this confirmation of the end Clare cries out in anguish and throws herself into his arms. 'I don't want to finish with you, Martin. I don't want to finish with you. I don't want to finish with you.'

Ward, an empty thing without volition, is pushed back against the sofa and falls down in a sitting position. Clare straddles him and attempts to kiss his lips.

He starts back in sudden terror. 'Your teeth are black.'

'It's the wine. His old cheap red wine.' Desperately she licks her teeth with her tongue – and then actually begins to scrub them with a finger.

'It's all right,' he murmurs, touching her arms in reassurance and in this action registering her physical presence on his lap.

Immensely grateful, she presses against his lips an avid mouth sick-sweet from wine. 'I don't want to finish with you,' she repeats, though in a calmer tone now, regarding him with rapt worshipful eyes. And her next kiss is infinitely tender and light, a mere brush of the lips. Delicately her lips withdraw ... and return – withdraw and return. Whimpering in contentment, she reaches down to take his genitals in a firm proprietary grasp. And, pressing with lips and hand, she leans her body into his. 'I don't want to finish with you, Martin.' They sway gently together. With a sudden imperious movement, she unzips him and urgently seeks his member. Again they sway, whimpering a little. But to hold is not to unite, much less to fuse. With an anguished grunt she pulls down her pants and guides him unerringly into her. Then, tranferring both hands to the back of the sofa for purchase, she bears down with decisive unequivocal strokes.

Ward tries to speak – but she seals his lips with the sick-sweet mouth. He has to pull his head free. 'Honey, I can't ... it's too ...'

'Stay in me, Martin,' she whispers, without breaking the rhythm, 'stay in me. *Stay in me now.*'

Taking a firmer hold of the sofa back, she presses her upper body against him so that he has her considerable strength to contend with as well as the force of gravity and the natural inclination to tarry in the honey pot.

Fear is stronger than all these. With a terrible hoarse cry, he breaks free and shoots his load over the seat.

# 7

Like many an old lady my mother had a large house at her disposal but lived in a tiny cluttered parlour on an armchair equidistant from the fireplace and the television. So over-furnished was this room that the other armchair was awkwardly jammed into a corner and the sofa tightly wedged between a dining table and a sideboard. Also, the deep shagpile did not provide a stable base so that sitting down on the sofa, however gently, made the lamp on top of the television totter and the sideboard tremble on its spindly legs, rattling the twin brass door handles and the Waterford glass collection within. But when I suggested that we use the front room she was shocked and reluctant though able to offer no reason other than the habit of years.

To put her at ease I served tea in the proper manner, on a doily lined tray with china cups and saucers and milk in a matching china jug. And began with the congenial topic of my forthcoming job interview, the reason for this visit home.

'You should have finished your research,' she said. 'You should have got all your degrees.'

'Sure I'm getting a word put in for me. Better than a lorry-load of degrees.'

But it was pointless to reason with a classic grievance. Not only disappointed in my personal failure, she felt that she had been cruelly cheated and mocked by the Great God Education who, far from rewarding her idolatry with an appropriate position for her son, had filled his naive youthful head with appalling mad dog's shite.

In this respect she resembled the terrible Madame Rimbaud. Fanatically righteous and proud, this woman rejected her easy-going husband and slow-witted eldest son (when he became the local postman the family were herded into a back room to avoid communication during deliveries), investing all her ambitions and hopes in the academically brilliant Arthur. At fifteen the Kid swept the board in examinations – but immediately threw it all over for poetry. The mother rejected him in turn, bitterly resenting having to send books to Africa, declining to visit him during the two and a half months of his slow death in Marseilles but doing her duty in the end by bringing the body back to Charleville for a funeral of the *première classe*. In fact so much did she loathe literature that when a monument to Arthur was unveiled in Charleville she refused to attend the ceremony or even look at the statue. Madame had her own way of fostering her son's reputation. Dissatisfied with the family grave, she had Arthur and his sister Isabelle dug up and moved to a more imposing tomb. Arthur's *première classe* accommodation was still intact – but Isabelle's cheaper coffin had disintegrated. The workmen were horrified – but not the Iron Matron. The resourceful Mme Rimbaud herself transferred her daughter's bones.

'Weren't you trained in St Margaret's?' I asked. 'What was it like in those days?'

'Well of course there were no grants,' she said, with the undisguisable satisfaction of the natural martyr. 'We had to make do with a lot less. You know what *my* treat was? Going to this wee shop that sold broken biscuits. We were only allowed out on Saturday afternoons and all I could afford was this shop. *Tuppence worth of broken biscuits on Saturday* – that was my treat.' As though in compensation she helped herself to another slice of Dundee cake. 'People were a lot easier pleased in those days. I remember one Saturday meeting these two young fellas I knew from down the country. I asked them where they were going and they said they were on their way to Lipton's to see the new bacon slicer.' She gave me a slightly reproachful look, implying that my fanciful 'notions' were no advance on the simple pleasure of watching meat being sliced.

What struck me was the phrase 'down the country'. Like my father and Mme Rimbaud, my mother had begun life as a peasant, though up to now her secrecy and the absence of maternal grand-parents had concealed this crucial fact. Is there anything more crippling than the fearfulness and caution of peasants who have just entered the lower middle class and are determined to climb higher?

'You'll need a house,' she said suddenly, triggering another familiar grievance. 'If you'd bought when I wanted you to, you'd be well away now.'

'The flat in London is a good investment.'

'But if ye'd bought in London sooner ye'd be even better off.'

'We didn't want property sooner. We didn't want to be burdened with a mortgage.'

'Och sure you're just like your father. Some old country notion about debt. Everyone in the world had a mortgage – but not Hugh. Nothing would do Hugh but buy for cash. And in the end he waited and waited until the cash was worth nothing.'

'But you bought a perfectly good house. What's wrong with this house?'

'It was too small and dark – but your father bought it without consulting me. That was always his way of working. He just went out and put down the cash. I never liked the house. There was only a poky garden for you – and no storage space at all. For years, every time I opened a cupboard a heap of fishing gear fell out. For years – even after he died – I had to look at fishing gear every time I opened a door.'

'What happened to it in the end?'

'Pascal said he would take it for me.'

Sudden whiff of a familiar scent: Essence of Pascal. Only Pascal could make it seem that, in accepting expensive equipment, *he* was the one doing a favour.

At every break in the conversation 'the room' swiftly re-established its sempiternal decorum. Waterford glass glinted discreetly in the china cabinet, patterned rugs lay at peace on the patterned carpet, velvet curtains hung in solemn plush folds. Everything obeyed the fundamental principle: superiority is most effectively communicated by reserve.

Only once had this hegemony of silence been challenged – when I acquired a record player and tried to establish it on a coffee table. Every time I wanted to listen to music I set it up – but as soon as I left the house my mother removed the equipment and put it back under the stairs.

Throughout the silence my mother had been brooding. 'If ye'd bought a place when ye first got married. But no, no – I had to listen to the same old nonsense about mortgages. The same as I had to listen to for a lifetime from your father.'

I was stung by this persistent attempt to equate my bohemian irresponsibility with Hugh's peasant caution. And also by her attempt to blame all the fearfulness on Hugh. Framed in filigree silver on top of the china cabinet, Hugh appeared to be begging me to intercede on his behalf.

'You know that in all the time since he died you've never said one good thing about him.'

Such brutal directness was ill-advised but the thought had passed into speech before I could suppress it. She was certainly taken aback. Among the women of the connection complaint was such a way of life that they probably never noticed the total absence of approbation.

She did attempt to answer the charge. 'Och no no … I didn't mean to give that impression, no.' There was a short perplexed pause. 'Your father was good enough, I suppose.' Further pause. 'He was always very good to me. And he was always very good to you.' In the even longer pause which followed it seemed that she was seeking to define the positive qualities of her partner. 'It was just that old way of working. You see, I was expected to pay for everything out of my salary … food, clothes, bills, *everything* … so I could never save much. Your father kept his money … I think there were shares … and maybe other things in the Free State … but I was never told anything about it and of course it was all lost when he died.' She had slipped back into the familiar groove. Once again she could warm to her task. 'It was all that country cuteness about hiding money and not trusting women . . . the money was all in the Free State and in other people's names. But none of his crowd ever came up with a penny of it after he died. It was all lost . . . *lost*. Not that I wanted any of it myself . . . but it would have set you up nicely.'

'I *am* set up.'

'He had this big metal box that was always locked. I was never allowed to see into it . . . not that I ever asked . . . and after he died I threw it out.'

'*You mean, you never even opened it?*'

'You know that your father died before *his* father. After Hugh's funeral I went down to see the old man . . . to console him . . . it must be a terrible thing to have your children die before you. But you know what he said to me?' A sudden surge of outrage brought her forward and fiercely erect. 'He said to me, *you know, we don't give money to strangers.*' Her eyes blazed and she brought her fist violently down on her arm rest, luckily deep-pile velvet. Even so the impact made the Waterford glass in the china cabinet tremble. 'The old man thought I was looking for something from him. He thought I was down after his money. And to describe me as a *stranger* – me that had known him thirty years. I came straight back here, look see, and threw that old box to the back of the coalhouse. For all I know it's still there . . .'

I had an over-powering urge to rush out and check. But now she had drifted off into general complaints about Pop. 'Sloostering about the house in all those heaps of old rags. There was no call for that. When my father . . . God rest him . . . was an elderly man he always wore a three-piece suit and a watch chain. Even just to sit in the parlour. Though of course he went out for his walk every day. But that character footered about the house in rags for fifty years. *Fifty years*, look see. Fifty years since he went out to a day's work. Sittin' about the house making purses since he was a man in his forties.'

This very early example of very early retirement was intriguing enough to distract me from the subject of the box. 'How did he manage it?'

'He was in the old RIC . . . and it was disbanded after the Free

State got independence. They all got pensions for life. And he was a sergeant so he did really well.'

A chilling revelation: my grandfather was a native member of the colonial police. And a trusty – a *sergeant*.

'I suppose he couldn't go back to his own place,' she was saying now. 'For fear someone would settle an old score. So he came up here to the North.'

I had never longed to be descended from the hallowed heroes of the independence struggle – but a quisling for an ancestor was not an exciting alternative.

After this 'the room' got the better of us and re-established its solemn hush. My mother went to visit Colette. I rushed out to the coalhouse.

There it was, an ancient black metal strongbox of the type carried by stagecoaches in B-feature westerns. Unfortunately the padlock was missing and the lid hung awry. If the box had contained anything of value it had been stolen long since. Exquisite irony: the strategy designed to foil blaggards had handed them the valuables on a plate.

All that remained was yellowed paper. I carried the box to the garden seat (bringing it back into the house would have been a gross violation).

The Hugh Ward Archive was a lifelong chronicle of petty cash transactions – cancelled bank books and savings certificates, bills, statements, receipts and pages of financial calculations in the scrupulous archaic penmanship of the Dickensian clerk. However, he must have had some extravagance and fantasy in his soul. Halfway down was a wad of tickets for the Malta government lottery of June 1966, boldly inscribed 'Sixty-Eighth National Lottery – to be held in public in Malta on Sunday 26th June 1966' and bearing on the reverse the solemn message: 'WARNING – do not purchase this ticket unless the seller is known to you as a trustworthy person'. Below the tickets was a copy of *Hibernia* from 1943, rusted staples spreading an orange stain into the yellowing paper.

This issue had an article by Madam Marie MacEgan on 'Our Waterford Glass' ('the acquisition of a piece of our incomparable native glass, known immediately by its touch of warmth and softness, ought to be the ambition of every Irish person who sets store upon our cultivated past'), a report of the speech of the Supreme

Knight of the Knights of Saint Columbanus at the Supreme Council Meeting ('Our social reconstruction can only succeed if it is based on the Divine Order, that is to say, on Catholic teaching. This will necessitate a fundamental modification of the many social institutions which arose out of the mind of the Protestant heresy.'), and, beside an intriguing ad for Tom Cullen (Rubber Services) Limited (Belting, Hose, Insertion, I.R.-Sheet etc), an article on 'Educational Reconstruction' by H.J. Ward. Instantly I closed the pages of the journal. I could not bear to look on my father's reactionary Catholic rantings. The dark age of crusades was over and the theories of Knights and Supreme Knights better forgotten. But eventually curiosity overcame better judgement. I could not resist a peek and, far from rabid extremism, the article turned out to be a banal and stilted appeal for lower class sizes, better facilities, free milk and school meals: 'The remarkable increase not only in weight but in mental alertness shown by children who have been supplied with milk and regular meals proves the desirablity of an extension of the innovation.' Only towards the end was there something to make me snort. 'We are migrating towards a new epoch: better still, a change of heart. Hitherto Irish education has been centred round the examination. But education means more than an examination. In the years to come it must lean towards the emotional, teaching children to feel rightly. They must be drawn towards the Pure and the Beautiful and things of the spirit or good report. Theirs should be a devotion to Truth, Justice, Culture and the Tradition of Ireland.'

Suddenly it struck me that, although I had spent my entire life, man and boy, in the company of Irish schoolteachers, I had never heard from any of them a word of belief in, or commitment to, teaching – and in this respect too I had failed to break with tradition.

Below the journal was another layer of financial detritus, among it a letter to the effect that two thousand shares in the Donegal Bottling Company, the property of H.J. Ward, were being held in the name of F.X. Ward. Further exquisite irony: after a lifetime fearing 'strangers', Hugh had been robbed by his own brother Frank.

Below the final layer, right on the bottom of the box, was something small, a mere torn scrap of card that nevertheless produced the alarming and nauseous sensation of a sudden precipitate descent in a possibly-out-of-control lift. Skeletal fingers played an icy arpeggio on my spine; a bone hand squeezed my heart. What I was staring at was a photograph of myself – *but one that had never been taken.* I knew that I had never worn these clothes or seen the river I was standing beside.

Gradually the vertigo subsided. This was a photograph of Hugh at exactly the age I was now.

Normally invigorated by a visit to Colette, my mother returned with a troubled look.

'So how's Colette?'

'Oh she's grand.' The tone also grim. 'Grand.'

Obviously it was not a good time – but the secrets of the box demanded acknowledgement. I persuaded her to sit down in 'the room' and gave her the accountant's letter to read.

Instead of expressing outrage, she merely shook her head and sighed. 'Och sure Frank ...' With another definitive shake she demonstrated the peculiar talent of her family for compressing a lifetime of disgust into a single monosyllable. '*Frank.*'

'We could do something,' I cried.

She handed back the letter. 'This is legally worthless. That crowd aren't even properly qualified accountants. *More friends of your father's.*'

'I could phone Frank.'

'You'll never get a penny out of that character. Frank is far too cute.'

'I don't want money. Just the pleasure of telling him he's a crook.'

Even this limited project failed to excite her enthusiasm. 'Och Martin ... I've had that much about wills and money ...' There was a pause in which, for once, I had the sense to shut up and wait. 'You know, just before Jean died she told me that Pascal and Mairead were putting terrible pressure on her. Everything was supposed to come to me but they were forcing her to leave it all to Mairead. Jean was very soft, you know ... she wasn't able for that pair. At the heel of the hunt they marched her down to the solicitor and a few days after that she had the first stroke. I'm sure the stress of the whole business was what brought it on. Then straight after her funeral Pascal drove away in her car ... that was his reward ... it was practically new, hardly driven at all. I'm sure he had his share of the money too. I said nothing – but a few days after the funeral

Mairead turned up here and tried to throw money at me. I mean, she *literally* threw it at me. Of course I wouldn't touch a penny. She ended up bawling . . . pleading and crawling about on the carpet . . . there were bank notes all over the floor.'

Terminal estrangement over wills – classic nemesis of the peasant and the subject of innumerable bad Irish plays. Grotesque to think of it happening here. Life not only imitates art, it imitates tenth-rate art.

To introduce a more positive note, I handed her Hugh's article. Without the least sign of interest she riffled the pages and handed it back. A shocking lesson in the way obsession shuts out the world. In her mind a single tape loop of grievances played endlessly – and she wanted to listen to nothing else. Is this what age has in store?

Urgent lesson: *Stop hoarding grievances.*

'Your father was a very committed teacher at one time,' she said now, corroborating the gauche idealism of the article. But the phrase 'at one time' seemed to confirm that the mature Hugh had become a clockwatcher. 'And later he took that promotion business very hard. He was never really the same after that. I often think that heart attack . . . you know?'

Further chilling revelation: *My father died from lack of status.*

An appropriate moment to produce the photograph. This she did study carefully, though also with a renewal of her earlier perplexity. I waited for involuntary memory to do its work – but after a few minutes she handed it back.

Nothing. Not a word. *Nada.*

As always, ore had to be gouged from the rock with bare hands.

'Don't you think he's the image of me?'

'I always said that, Martin.'

I was tempted to give up – but when would there be a better opportunity?

'Was he this age when you met?'

Her face contorted with familiar annoyance at merciless harassment.

A chilling possbility to accompany the chilling revelations: *Perhaps my taste for the Crag was merely my mother's chronic fear of intimacy rationalised and given an intellectual gloss.*

Even as we flee our parents we are inexorably becoming them.

Yet I had a feeling that a desire to talk was struggling against her ingrained reluctance.

'Nooooo . . . he'd have been a bit older.'

'So when did you meet?' I adopted the familiar tactic of softening and dropping my voice.

'Och Martin.' Her grimace intensified. Cosmetic measures were not enough to lay the ancient taboos. 'It was so long ago.' This in a helpless beseeching tone, as if to plead that, although she desperately wanted to testify, it was impossible to surmount the habits of a lifetime – the compulsive secrecy, hatred of examination and horror of the intimate.

In the beginning our pet habits are given a nice cage and fondly indulged. Later we discover that we are the pets and they are the cage.

Further urgent lesson: *Talk to people for Chrissàke.*

'All right. *How* did you meet?'

'I told you I can't remember now.'

What I sought was evidence against my own atrocious theory. According to this, each of two peasant families had pushed a child up the social scale by means of education, then looked around for a mate at an equivalent level. Having been found 'good enough', the man and woman would lie down together, not for pleasure but to form the next layer in the Pyramid of the Living Dead, a tyrannical long-term project whose ultimate goal was to lift fortunate descendants into the bliss of professional fees and an ivied mansion in Mount Pleasant. Everything I remembered seemed to support this theory. But memory is essentially caricatural – it selects, exaggerates and condemns. I wanted her to tell me that there was something more human, that they had also been sweethearts, at least for a time. And suddenly I thought of Clare and experienced a wild surge of longing. Goddam it, we all need a sweetheart.

'It doesn't sound terribly romantic,' I suggested now, with the utmost mildness.

This succeeded in stinging her into a response. 'Well you have to remember that this was during the war. Times were hard . . . people had very little . . . and parents were stricter in those days.'

Blame the parents, blame the age – the tactics of every generation. My own excuses were no different.

Third urgent lesson of the day: *Stop attempting to transfer the blame.*

This saga of pleasureless duty cast a chill over my soul. If I was coming home to this place I would have to get my experience in first. Valedictory intercourse was not only desirable but *essential*. The London experience had to be crowned with an incandescence bright enough to illuminate even the farthest reaches of the dark and dismal time ahead. The only question was whether it would be with Rani or Janet. Once again the choice was between image and content. Rani was pleasanter to look at but Janet was more likely to be a circus in bed.

My mother was brooding with a harried violated look. And then, with the desperate ingenuity of the hunted, she suddenly gave her pursuer the slip and headed back to familiar terrain. 'What I do remember is that your father and I had very little at the start. We certainly didn't have it easy. That's why I want to see you set up.'

'I *am* set up,' I said again. Now it was I who felt like screaming. 'I could buy a house anywhere. I could buy a house in Mount Pleasant.'

But our filthy age had sullied even the paradise of the private park. 'Och Mount Pleasant. Sure I'm only back from there and Colette was saying she wanted to move. She was saying the whole town's in Mount Pleasant now.'

In other words the likes of Jack Barrett and Tony Shotter.

When Shotter and his wife returned from teaching in Africa they did not invest their savings in a bungalow but rented a house in Heathfield owned by an old friend of my mother's, an elderly teacher whose poor health had forced him to live with his daughter in England. My mother was certain that the Shotters, 'a cute pair if ever there was', took the house only in order to get it for a song as sitting tenants when the old man died. And they did indeed purchase it cheaply, reselling at once for a huge profit and buying a mansion in the private park.

In the silence we slumped on our seats like exhausted boxers between rounds. Her dodging and weaving and counter-punching were wearing me down.

I had the energy for one last attack. 'Daddy has a full head of hair in this photo. Did he lose it all at once ... you know, *quickly* ... or was it a more gradual thing?'

Surely the physical inheritance at least could be explored? No, the familiar defensive grimace immediately formed. 'Your father had a wonderful head of hair, Martin.' She consented to take the photo again. 'He always said it was using someone else's comb.'

I allowed her a few moments to relish his hirsute glory. 'But did it happen quickly?' I was terrified of my own hair suddenly falling out. 'Like over a year or two?'

The grimace became a look of persecution. 'Nooooo ... like, it wouldn't have been ...'

'*But at what age did he go bald?*' Losing patience with gradualism, I put a straight question – and immediately regretted its double harshness.

She too was weary of indirection. 'But your father wasn't bald,' she suddenly screeched. 'Your father *wasn't bald*, Martin.'

I tried not to look – but it was impossible to desist. Inexorably my gaze was drawn to the photograph on the china cabinet, the top of Hugh's skull agleam like a dining room table after a polish.

But though the skull shone like polished mahogany, the features no longer seemed wooden. In the eyes there was a hint of amusement I had never noticed before. Amusement and other common human emotions – sadness, yearning, disappointment, disillusion and reproach.

J ust as Flaubert, after slowly and painfully climbing the Great Pyramid of Cheops, attains its summit with torn hands, bleeding knees and scorched lungs, only to find inscribed in black letters on the ancient stone, *M. Buffard Wallpaper Manufacturer 79 rue Saint-Martin*, so Ward has arrived on the pinnacle of science to find it claimed by a buffoon. For although Ward's research is in theoretical physics ('Enthusiasm applied to anything other than abstractions is a sign of weakness and disease' – Baudelaire), he is obliged to work in a laboratory full of the apparatus he has abandoned and to share it with one whose research involves repeating the same experiment endlessly with infinitesmal differences in temperature. Despite the repetitive nature of his investigations, Wesley Blair happily toils late into the evening yet is invariably first at his post the next day.

'Good afternoon,' is his cheerful morning greeting to his heavy-hearted colleague.

'How come you're never late?' Ward sullenly enquires.

'Because I have four alarm clocks.'

'*Hah?*'

'The kids, I mean. I have four of them.'

'*Four kids?*' A spasm of terror seizes Ward. Even in this exclusive sanctum banality and convention have sought him out.

'Eleven, nine, six and three.' After rattling off the ages Blair waits for Ward's full attention before adding, with the happiest of chuckles, 'Then Ah shot the milkman.'

In the morning they go for coffee to the Great Hall (referred to by Blair as the 'Great Hole'), renowned for its fresh wheaten scones, and in the afternoon to the Students' Union ('the Onion') which at this time of day offers another Ulster delicacy – a strawberry jam sandwich of scallop-edged shortcake rings with the top of the upper ring heavily iced.

'Time for the Onion!' Wesley cries now, shocking Ward with the lateness of the hour. Can there have passed another day in which he has once again failed to wrest shining theorems from the bowels of chaos? Slowly but surely his magnificent brain is silting up ('O sad relic of an immortal intellect, created by God with such love' – Lautréamont).

Outside, a monstrously burdened sky broods over the city.

'Going to be great weather for golf,' Wesley suggests. If it was sunny he would have said it was time they brought out their bikinis. Filled with melancholy and foreboding, Ward is unable to reply. Habit and ritual, those ruthless imperialists, are colonising his proud soul.

An unexpected innovation – Blair forgoes his shortcake ring.

'Roberta has me on a diet,' he explains gloomily, turning to scrutinise the troubled sky for portents. 'If it rains it's going to be desperate out the dual carriageway. It's bad enough on Friday at the best of times.'

'Where do you live exactly?'

'Out past Supermac.'

They fall silent, oppressed by the empty cafeteria and the leaden sky beyond.

'Back to porridge,' Blair dramatically sighs when the allotted twenty minutes have elapsed.

In the lab Ward is yet again unable to work. The mathematical symbols, once so obedient, now assume a frightening autonomy and mockingly cavort before his eyes.

The phone rings. Blair answers. 'Hello – Buckingham Palace.' Then his face clouds. 'For you.'

It is the secretary of the Prof, Ward's research supervisor, an English physicist of great brilliance and growing international reputation. He too is completely unpractical – but, as so often with the unworldly great, is served by a brutal and ruthless minion.

'The Professor would like to see you at ten o'clock on Monday morning.'

'But I can't . . . it's not . . .'

'Ten o' clock sharp on Monday.' Ward is sure that she has just flashed one of her hideous momentary smiles – like a klieg light briefly switched on inside an iceberg.

'But does he know . . . ?'

'Ten o'clock.'

Ward has no work to bring to this progress meeting – and now the urgency of buckling down makes it finally impossible. With a fierce oath he flings papers into his briefcase and springs to his feet.

'Poets day!' Blair cries, employing an expression new to Ward. 'Piss Off Early Tomorrow's Saturday.' Unable to maintain this astonishing level of novelty, Blair now reverts to the familiar. 'Don't do anything I wouldn't do.' Then, just as Ward opens the door, 'And if you can't be good be careful.'

Desperate, a driven man, Ward leaps on a bus to the city centre and scours bookshops for something to alleviate his despair. But in the end all he acquires is a tin of tuna, two tomatoes, a loaf and a cream horn for dessert.

Today the dreary old student house rings with light girlish laughter. On the living room sofa, feet out of shoes and legs cosily tucked beneath her, is none other than Ward's ineluctable destiny – Angela Neville. Still the girl has retained the priceless gift of inevitability. All her plans and arrangements seem pre-ordained, sanctioned by natural law and thus impossible to oppose without appearing perverse. Now she leans on Tony Shotter's shoulder a calm proprietorial elbow – as though the two of them are children of noble families pledged to each other from birth.

'Angela's up for the weekend,' Shotter explains. 'She's on teaching practice.'

Once so scornful and proud, Shotter is not only allied to an archetypal *bourgeoise* he despised, but is himself also training to be a teacher.

'In *Omagh!*' At the absurdity of a jewel such as she condemned to languish in a rural backwater, Angela utters a laugh of the most delightful musicality, like a Waterford crystal goblet gently struck by a silver spoon.

Another of her natural gifts is the power of instant colonisation. Although only just arrived, she seems to inhabit and possess the flat more fully than either of the paying tenants.

Ward retires to the kitchen and, after a frugal tuna salad, takes his briefcase to his room ('One must work if not from inclination at least from despair' – Baudelaire). But in a dingy back bedroom the equations of theoretical physics look as bewildering and indecipherable as the hieroglyphics on the Rosetta stone. A terrible drowsiness assails him. Yet when he yields and goes to bed he becomes immediately wide awake, his first experience of that delight of mature years – rampant narcolepsy in the armchair followed by insomnia between the sheets.

Late in the night he falls into an uneasy sleep, waking briefly to musical laughter in the morning and, later, to heavy drumming rain that disposes him to remain in his winter teepee of heavy blankets and overcoats. He rises finally, in the crepuscular light of late afternoon, to a world rinsed but unredeemed, doused in water but not born anew. After finishing the tin of tuna and second tomato, he returns to his equations. ('At every moment we are weighed down by the conception and sensation of Time. And from this nightmare there are only two means of escape – pleasure and work. Pleasure consumes us. Work strengthens. Let us choose' – Baudelaire).

Still unable to concentrate, Ward is driven out onto the streets to roam in blind despair until it is time for his assignation.

With a smile of enchanting gladness, Clare descends from the hospital bus and displays to him a carrier bag containing the latest of many gifts from grateful patients. 'Look – a new handbag. Isn't is lovely? Better than this old thing I'm using. Just been given it by an old man in the geriatric ward.'

Ward is strangely moved by this evidence of a caring, blithe and hopeful world.

'What's the matter, Martin?'

'Let's go for a drink.'

In one of the anonymous bars favoured by Ward he reveals the problems with his research.

'I feel like a wind-up toy with its spring broken. It used to be simple – turn the key and the tin man runs. But something's snapped. I think I've realised I've always been working to please other people – never myself. And now I can't do it any more. I'll have to give it up.'

'And do what?'

'Any job. I don't care what it is or what people think. Preferably something repetitive and mindless. Digging a hole every morning and filling it in every afternoon.'

'What will your mother say?'

He grimaces and sighs. 'She'll have a shit haemorrhage.'

'And what will you tell your supervisor?'

'The Prof?' He sighs again. 'Some story or other.' Suddenly it occurs to him that he can use native voodoo to hoodwink the great rationalist. Already the Prof is acutely aware of unrest in the province which he seems to feel has cunningly tricked him by remaining peaceful only long enough to lure him onto the Chair of Physics. Ward can claim that he is engaged to a Protestant girl and that the star-crossed lovers will have to flee for their lives.

Clare is thoughtful. 'Things are changing, aren't they, Martin?'

He shudders. 'Definitely.'

'But they're changing for me too.' She turns to face him frankly. 'I don't want to go on the way we're going.'

Startled, he studies her and seizes her hand in dread. 'What's wrong with the way we're going?'

'It's leading nowhere, Martin.' Gently she disengages her hand. 'My sister Kathleen was telling me about an uncle of yours. He always went out with girls who worked in this factory he managed ... Kathleen used to work there. He went with them for years – but never married any of them ... they weren't good enough, I suppose. Kathleen says he'd walk the feet off them for years and then leave them.'

Ward does not know which aspect of this speech is more disturbing – the fact that everyone seems to know more about his relatives than he himself or the fact of being presented with an ultimatum in his time of deepest travail.

'So what are you saying?' he enquires coldly, after a time.

'I'm saying I don't want anyone to walk the feet off me for years.'

276

'In other words marriage or nothing. Sign on the dotted line. Shape up or ship out.'

The rest of the evening passes in cool, polite estrangement, Ward reflecting that perhaps it is this very relationship that has broken his spirit, that his sordid sexual needs are dragging him down into the mire. Already he has broken his contract with the gods by failing to deny the girl his essence. ('Upon a sensual body the Mantle frays and wears thin. In the left hand of the lewd man the Lamp flickers and dims' – Villiers). He resolves to refrain from touching her and to rise at dawn, pure and strong, to re-apply himself to research with renewed concentration and zeal.

But he does not rise at six. Nor is he capable of refraining from contact ('Eternally my privates present the lugubrious spectacle of tumescence' – Lautréamont). Enfeebled by indulgence, the lovers fall back into a deep sleep and fail to awaken until early afternoon.

And so it is that the four of them sit together in the living room at that hour of the sabbath when a zealous God's grip on the province is most unremitting and close. Now nothing stirs in the silent streets and sodden parks. It seems that the entire city, including even its rabid and tireless assassins, has succumbed to fatalism and failure of will. Shuttered houses withdraw into themselves. Above, the sky is a sullen immobile grey wash. Even the rain appears to be paralysed, suspended over the empty pavements in a saturated emulsion.

Can it be that potential and imminence have passed for ever from the earth? Without interest or enthusiasm they turn the pages of newspapers. Curiosity, born with the universe, is dying of inanition in the Ulster gloom. ('Those provinces which are the analogues of death – there the sun only obliquely kisses the earth and the slow alternations of light and dark suppress all variety, increasing instead that monotony which is the twin of Nothingness' – Baudelaire).

Shotter flings down his paper. 'Why don't we go a run some-where? Now that we have a car for once.'

Even Angela's vibrancy is muted today. 'Tony, I have to drive back to Omagh tonight. And with all the trouble recently I don't want to be on the roads late.'

'You have *your own car?*' Clare is deeply impressed.

'Daddy bought me a Mini when I started the teaching practice.'

For Ward, only the business and sports sections remain. ('How many the signs from God that it is *high time* to act, to consider the present moment as the most important of all moments and to take for my *everlasting delight* my accustomed torment i.e. work' – Baudelaire). He is haunted by a familiar but terrible scene. At his desk the Prof hunches over papers, scribbling rapidly, a few lines to each page, revealing to Ward only the top of his head, bald except for a single quiff which he continually plaits and unplaits with long fingers carefully manicured and scrupulously clean. In fact all of the Professor is scrupulously clean. His body, like his mind, is unsullied by life. Awkwardly Ward hesitates in the centre of the room, incapacitated by a severe attack of spud-in-the-gob, that syndrome which afflicts the Gael in the presence of superior Brits and whose symptoms are cold sweat, paralysis, faintness and the feeling of a large dirty misshapen potato crammed into the mouth. Eventually he sits down without being asked. There is another long wait – until suddenly the Prof glances up as though surprised to see someone there: '*Oh!*' With profound diffidence Ward lays on the desk the folder of inadequate work to be savaged ('Oh to behold one's intellect in a stranger's sacrilegious hands' – Lautréamont). For the Prof does not entertain the possibility of insoluble problems. When violence broke out in the province he demanded of Ward how long it was likely to last. Ward murmured that, since there appeared to be no solution, ten years seemed the regrettable but likely time span. White with sudden fury, the Prof abandoned his quiff to slam a pale hand flat on the desk. 'No solution? Of course there's a solution. *Send in the tanks.*'

With a heavy sigh Clare throws down the colour supplement and begins transferring the contents of her old handbag to the new one, desultorily examining receipts and scraps of paper, trying old make-up tubes on the back of her hand.

It comes to Ward that what is required is a wild, redemptive sovereign gesture. Instead of cowering in submission he should rise and drive his titanium cock through the blood-stained sphincter of the universe, smashing the very walls of its pelvis with powerful and impetuous thrusts. His soul can still be redeemed by an act of defiance so exalted it transcends all the categories ('Are not good and evil one thing by which we furiously acknowledge our impotent passion to attain the infinite by even the maddest of means? – Lautréamont).

'Do you need your old bag, honey?'

'I'm dumping it out in a minute.'

With a single bound Ward has reached her side and seized the bag. 'Now *listen*.'

Arrested by his brilliant transgressor's voice, all three look up and are transfixed by a countenance, cold as the marble slab on a sarcophagus, in which eyes blaze like stars in a firmament they illuminate but leave cold. 'All four of us shite in this bag' – his eyes seek each in turn – 'then we close it up and leave it out on the pavement across the street.' When he jerks his head towards the window they follow his gaze but are immediately drawn back to a visage irradiated by Divine Lumen. 'Then we pull our chairs to the window and wait.' He himself illustrates this by pausing. The Lumen blossoms in a terrible effulgence. '*We wait for some greedy fucker to come along and pick it up.*'

In a foretaste of the enchantment which a sentence of death can cast over the world, the decision to leave a place invests its most humdrum details with the plangency of transience and valediction. Everything is stricken and heart-rendingly beautiful. Everything holds out a promise of fulfilment and wonder. Everything implores us to relent and stay.

Now a mere routine trip on the Tube was as fraught as the descent of Orpheus into the underworld. As though to torment and madden, moving stairways offered a succession of exquisite *inconnues* in summer ensembles. In the corridors posters for European movies were a chorus of soul-wrenching sirens, while currents of warm air caressed my features like fragrant zephyrs from paradise.

When I broke the news of my job success to Clare, I expected a dramatic scene of outrage and defiance. Instead, not only was there no resistance, she even accepted the move with something close to relief (albeit at its most uneuphoric and muted). This may have been because it spared her the agony of having to make a decision (nearly impossible for those formed by authoritarian cultures) and offered an escape from Homewrecker's importunings, apparently now even more of a trial than those of her husband. The revelation of my interview had plunged him even deeper in self-pity. 'You're just going to let yourself be whisked off,' he had wailed to Clare. 'You'll probably sneak away without even telling me.' And as Homewrecker had disintegrated so had Clare's new personality based on belief in his nobility and lustre. Like rocks in a subsiding sea, the old familiars re-emerged – hatred of England and the condescending English, fear of bringing up children in the evil capital city, yearning for the conviviality and reassurance of home. So our emotions were bizarrely inverted. Clare, with reason to stay, was content to depart. I, with reason to go, was heartbroken at leaving.

Now I wandered in the city at every opportunity and, on my last day at Our Lady of Perpetual Succour, abandoned my tutor group and the end-of-term cleaning for a solemn affecting pilgrimage. A sombre grey sky would have been the appropriate background but, as though in pointed contrast to Ulster where the sunshine is always temporary and every evening brings a chill, Camden Town was bathed in a warmth of Mediterranean durability and plenitude. Another treasure insufficiently cherished: the magnificent iron railway bridges of London! Passing beneath an imposing metal arch, I turned right into Royal College Street where shabby businesses coexisted with terraced houses in peaceful senescence. According to the cliché, it is spires which dream – but a spire is too self-important for this kind of abandon. Obscurity, neglect and insignificance – these are the preconditions of dream. The top of Royal College Street was richly endowed with all three and its spell was already strong when, after fifty or so yards, what appeared to be a gap in the buildings was revealed as a quiet curving stretch of that old friend – the Regent's Canal. Like a languid voluptuous woman mischievously poking a warm thigh from under the bedclothes, London was coyly tempting me with what it knew I loved most. The message was potent and unmistakable. The city was offering itself. *It would let me.*

Nor was Number 8 a disappointment, residual flakes of paint clinging to a cracked dingy façade whose windows were veiled by tattered lace. At ground level twisted iron railings protected a deep and sinister area and on top of the front was a crown of tall weeds. It looked as though nothing had been touched since the event commemorated by a plaque on the wall: 'The French poets Paul Verlaine and Arthur Rimbaud lived here, May–July 1873.' Central London teems with oval blue plaques (mostly for successful and forgotten mediocrities like architects, surgeons and portrait painters) but this was a rectangular white stone presumably erected by a private enthusiast. Even after more than a century the poets were too disreputable for officialdom.

Once again the city appeared to be wooing me, carefully preserving the key house when all about had been razed and rebuilt. Across the street was a new council estate divided into blocks bearing those synthetic English-village names (Camelford, Dulverton, Lydford, Hartland, Calstock) planners no doubt hoped would confer a sense of community and tradition. But if you turned your back on this everything was much as it must have been on the earlier July day that ended the poets' sojourn.

Down the sunny street comes Verlaine, the foolish virgin, carrying salted fish for the evening meal. Rimbaud, the infernal bridegroom, leans from a window and offers a fatefully sardonic comment: 'If only you knew how fucking stupid you look with that herring in your hand.' Immediately Verlaine turns on his heel and walks all the way to the docks where he boards the first boat for the Continent. Eventually realising the seriousness of the situation, Rimbaud follows – and arrives just as the gangway of the Antwerp boat is being raised. On deck is the offended poet. Rimbaud signals wildly. Verlaine shakes his head and looks away.

Such was the end of their London experience, one of the calmer episodes in the five-act tragedy of Rimbaud's life.

### ACT I — THE BRILLIANT BEGINNING

Reared under the thumb of the ambitious and tyrannical Mme Rimbaud, the Kid reveals exceptional intelligence and achieves outstanding success in examinations at fifteen.

### ACT 2 — REBELLION AND POETRY

Instead of pursuing his studies he runs away to Paris where he shouts *merde* at the literati and shocks Verlaine's bourgeois wife by leaving strange insects crawling on his pillow. Verlaine explains that these are lice which Rimbaud cultivates in his hair to throw at priests in the street.

Alone in a garret, the Kid imagines himself a seer, a magus, the equal of God. More like Satan, concludes Verlaine, who spends two years in a Belgian prison after shooting his partner in Brussels. Back home in Charleville the Kid finishes *Les Illuminations*, has it printed at his own expense and sends copies to everyone in the Paris literary set.

He himself returns to Paris to be fêted. It is a public holiday and the Café Tabourey is crowded with artists and critics. Many know the Kid but no one will speak to him much less mention the book. Rimbaud sits on his own and slowly suffers the revelation of the mocker – that those who reject the established order will be rejected by it in turn. Of all the violations of convention, contempt is the most severely punished. The invulnerable phalanx of mediocrity will now be firmly closed against him.

When the café shuts he walks home, not across Paris but thirty miles to Charleville where he arrives at dawn to provide an *illumination* of a different kind – a bonfire of all his manuscripts.

## ACT 3 – THE WANDERING YEARS

He goes north as far as Scandanavia, east to the jungles of Java (abandoning a trip to Russia at Vienna), west to the jungles of suburban Reading and finally south into Africa, building up along the way a CV of unsurpassed splendour which includes service in the Dutch army and the British merchant navy, a tour of northern European capitals as manager of a circus, a spell at Suez as a wrecker and looter of ships, work as the foreman of a desert quarry and as ganger of the fifty men building the summer residence of the governor of Cyprus, lengthy periods as an exporter of coffee, gum and hides from Aden and Abyssinia, two years as a gun-runner and, possibly most bizarre of all, six months as a teacher in Reading.

None of this brings him satisfaction. Isolated in Harar, the only Frenchman in a settlement of mud huts, he begins to think of Mme Rimbaud with affection and tenderness: 'Dearest mother, try to rest and take care. You have exhausted yourself enough. Spare your health at least and rest.'

## ACT 4 – GUN-RUNNING

Desperate to make money and escape Africa, he invests all his savings in a scheme to run guns to Menelik, King of Shoa. From the start everything goes wrong. The political situation changes and he cannot get a licence to import arms. Of his three successive partners, two drop dead and the third is murdered. When the arms finally arrive there are no camels for transport. Eventually he sets off, without partners, only to find that his route traverses some of the worst terrain on the continent and the territory of its most feared tribe, the Danakil, whose males are considered suitable for marriage only after they have killed and worn as personal adornment the genitalia of the victim (thus putting into practice that most extravagant of threats – 'I'll tear your bollocks off and wear them for earrings'). For four months the party journeys in a lunar landscape, under constant harassment and attack, with nothing to drink but what has been transported in goat hides smeared with old tallow and bark tar, a hot yellow cocktail of brackish well water, rancid mutton fat, goat's hair and bark.

When they arrive Menelik cannot be found and, when found, no longer needs the guns. Moreover, he holds Rimbaud responsible for the alleged debts of his late partners. As soon as the Kid pays, other creditors spring up. He honours the claims of the poorest and ends up with virtually nothing himself.

For although the colonial trading and gun-running are often taken as evidence of cynicism, the record shows exactly the opposite. To his mother he writes: 'I would like to do something useful, something good.' In another letter home: 'On the route I enjoy quite a bit of consideration due to my being human with the people.' One of his employers, Bardey, put it like this: 'His charity was lavish, unobtrusive and discreet. It is probably one of the few things he did without disgust and a sneer of contempt.'

Despite applying the keenest intelligence, most single-minded self-discipline and most inexhaustible stamina, the Kid makes no money whatever. For none of these qualities can compensate for corruption by the Crag and the Cross. He is too proud to haggle with merchants and too compassionate to cheat the natives. 'Those unfortunate people were always honest and in good faith and I permitted my heart to be touched.'

ACT 5 – THE BITTER END

Taken ill in Africa, he believes that he can recover only in France in the bosom of his family. At Marseilles he is hospitalised and his right leg amputated. The prodigious walker, who covered twenty miles a day, can now barely hobble a few yards. And when he gets home it is to find his mother as taciturn and remote as ever.

Now he believes that he can recover only in the warmth of Africa. Once again he goes south, nursed by his pious and simple-minded sister Isabelle. In constant pain, semi-delirious, penned into a corner of a railway carriage by boisterous holiday makers, he passes through Paris totally ignorant of the fact that he is now a famous poet, the toast of the capital and already a legend. (Baudelaire claimed that establishing a cliché was the proof of genius and he himself laboured mightily to achieve this goal. Rimbaud established half a dozen clichés without even trying – the artist as starving loner in a garret, as shocker and scourge of the bourgeoisie, as systematic deranger of the senses, as visionary seer besieging the infinite, as bohemian wanderer endlessly searching and as action-man shunning white-collar work for virile employment.)

Again he is hospitalised at Marseilles. Gradually paralysis spreads through his body (and no sooner is it complete than his new artificial leg arrives). Constantly harassed by his sister and the nuns, the proud rebel who scribbled *Merde à Dieu* on park benches and believed he had stolen the celestial fire, at last submits and is received back into the Church, thus fulfilling the terrible prophecy of Baudelaire: 'He who would aspire to be the equal of God ends by falling below his own nature.'

Mme Rimbaud does not visit her son in hospital – but has the body sent home for the *première classe* funeral, in which five principal singers and a choir of eight with pealing bells precede plumed horses drawing a hearse draped in the richest of black hangings, and containing the most expensive coffin available, behind it choirboys, several priests and a score of orphans with lighted candles. No expense is spared – but the ceremony takes place unannounced. None of his schoolfriends are present, not to mention friends from Paris, Verlaine, or his own older brother. There are over forty paid attendants but only two mourners – Mme Rimbaud and Isabelle.

*He permitted his heart to be touched.* Worldly success never came to the seven but those who survived into maturity had a measure of recognition, physical comfort, the company of like-minded friends. Rimbaud enjoyed none of these. Instead his proud soul was broken and he was forced to eat shit. (Beware of crying *merde* or you may be required to eat your word.) It is possible that his only satisfaction was in leaving places behind (his mother may well have appeased his unquiet spirit by moving the body to another grave). The last written statement is a letter dictated to a steamship company on the day before his death: 'I am entirely paralysed and so wish to embark early. Please let me know at what time I should be carried aboard.'

What absorbed his final years in Africa was the quest for something to take home. A similar motive kept me lingering in Royal College Street, uneasily aware that the council estate behind me was beginning to stir into lunch-hour life. There was also activity across the street. The door to Number 10 suddenly opened on a couple with a child in a pushchair and a large alert Alsatian dog. The humans cast me a brief suspicious look and the animal loped across the street to give my genitals a cursory sniff.

Was there anything to be gained by lingering? Yes – the detail that a casual inspection would have missed. At the bottom of the door, on the right, was an ancient Victorian bootscraper that could easily have been there in Rimbaud's time. I was not worthy to touch the Kid's boots – but perhaps I was entitled to touch his bootscraper. Praying that no one would notice and demand an explanation, I swiftly darted across the street and bent to touch the black metal, warm from the sun.

It was a gesture of renunciation – goodbye to the seven, goodbye to London, goodbye to the Crag and the Cross. Another of Rimbaud's unique qualities – he alone understood that the choice was between Crag and Cross. 'Charity and scorn, each is right,' he declared. And in another poem he wondered if he had made the right choice: 'Would Charity have been the sister of death for me?' In Africa it is possible that he did change – or at the very least was torn between the two.

Like the Kid, I was seeking an honourable reward for the years of servitude and waste. The touch of warm metal was not enough; it would take the touch of warm flesh.

I had arranged to meet Janet and Rani at the function for leavers but neither was in the staffroom an hour or so later when Judy Cooke presented me with the official reward – a ballpoint pen and a card covered with humorous good-luck messages. In fact this was a muted, dismal occasion, for also absent were the great theatrical lions, Moira Sweeney, Terry Wills and Father Kemp, all of them boycotting in protest at being passed over for jobs. Kemp himself was leaving in a pique for a surely unsuitable post as Head of

Discipline in a Catholic Boys' School. No more of a natural disciplinarian than I, Kemp had always been protected by vigilant NCOs for whom disrespect to a priest was among the most heinous of crimes. He was incapable of providing authority for himself much less others.

Judy Cooke, still ecstatic at securing the top job, was doing her best with the presentations but her excruciating impersonation of gaiety was the equivalent of a tone-deaf non-musician attempting to fiddle an Irish jig. How different from the Christmas Convent House dinners when, on behalf of the assembled staff, master presenter Terry Wills gave Joe a box of spirit bottles which were known to be for entertaining Convent guests but which the outrageous Terry pretended were soon to be consumed by Joe herself; as fond laughter continued and a blushing Joe reached out to collect, Wills would make as though to drop the packed box so that the poor nun was almost at her wit's end with the fellow. Today even Have-a-Go Joe was finding it difficult to raise a smile. There was universal gratitude when, after receiving his propelling pencil, Seymour hoisted onto the table a suitcase packed with Jewish delicacies prepared by his mother to reward the school for sheltering her sensitive son. Joe shrieked and enthusiastically fell upon the food, demanding from Seymour a detailed explanation of the provenance and ingredients of each dish.

The snacks certainly looked appetising but Rani would not be pleased to find me enjoying Seymour's largesse. Moodily sipping wine on my own by the window, I turned to find the absent beauty actually a few yards away, waiting to maximise the drama of her arrival by allowing me to discover her myself. Such a stratagem was hardly necessary. She was wearing a gold-trimmed purple sari, her midriff bare between the fitted top and long skirt, her right shoulder bare and her left shoulder covered by a swathe from the skirt. It is not always true that our most successful performances are impersonations of ourselves – but Rani had never been more effective. Her European outfits, though stunning, had always the suggestion of dressing up and, while play-acting can often be fun, it is rarely capable of authentic splendour.

'The sari . . .' was all I could mumble, helplessly waving my glass, and understanding for the first time the insight that beauty is the beginning of a terror we are still just able to endure.

'You like it?' She laughed and stood back to let me take it in, points of amusement dancing in her dark eyes like fireflies above a forest pool. Still chuckling, she raised her right hand with a clash of bracelets and drove it boldly into the heart of her thick wavy hair, lifting and holding it up for a moment, her bare right arm an ingot of unpolished gold and her smooth ochre diaphragm tranquilly stirring like a tropical sea in the evening sun.

In a twist entirely typical of the Celestial Prankster, Janet now appeared behind the Asian princess, hovering painfully for a moment, then going towards the noisy group at the table and finally, as though in sudden pique, abruptly leaving the room.

'Is it . . . ?' I vaguely waved my glass at the sari. 'Is it all one piece?'

She laughed in delight and adopted the patient tone of an adult instructing a slow-witted child. 'Two pieces. A blouse' – golden hand briefly alighting on a snugly encased breast – 'and a skirt' – a lithe graceful gesture indicating the purple material that fell in sumptuous folds to her feet.

'Are you wearing this for Kalpesh?' A cunning question designed to flush out her true allegiance. 'He isn't here today.'

She made a brusque gesture of dismissal at a notion too absurd to be dignified with speech. But the irritation did not last. Her manner, too, seemed to have altered. She was patient and reconciled, sweetly submissive. As though in the charmingly coded avowal of a chaste and diffident well-born maiden, she took from my left hand the ballpoint pen case. Reverently, tenderly, she withdrew the pen and gently clicked it several times, observing with wonder and interest the appearance and disappearance of the point. It was as if she had taken out my cock and eased the foreskin back and forth. Surely pledged beyond all impediment, we were transported to the east coast of Africa where a smiling child placed a garland of flowers about my neck and native drummers in long white woollen robes established a steady hypnotic beat.

'Kalpesh!' she snorted in sudden disgust. 'No, I've met a nice Indian boy . . . another teacher . . . I'm on my way to his staff do now . . . they're a really lively staff there' – she glanced in contempt at the guzzling gourmets – 'not like this bunch here.'

Suddenly my mouth was like a long-dry river bed – petrified, gaping, cracked and parched. 'But . . . a glass of wine at least . . .' I was begging desperately again. It was now my destiny to beg.

287

'One at least . . .'

'No I must go . . . I just came in to wish you good luck.' She placed the pen case in my hand and patted it – the case, not the hand. 'Thanks for everything.'

In her eyes there was no regret or yearning or loss, no acknowledgement that we could have been lovers or that it might be sweet to steal an hour of pleasure from our jealous and possessive destinies. There was no longevity, ambivalence or overlap in her emotions. She was happy for her destiny of the moment to be a tyrant who could neither be evaded or made to wait. All her beauty and adornment were for the nice Indian boy. He would be wise to accept them today.

What would *I* receive today? Was I to leave London in tears carrying a ballpoint pen?

Janet was in the storeroom. Without discussion or even greeting we made our way out of the school and slowly walked to a nearby park that was lovingly tended but mostly empty. Again I had the feeling of secret sequestered dreaming peace, of idyllic desert islands available all over the city.

'God I love London.' A spontaneous cry of regret.

Janet believed in the examined life. 'Then why are you leaving it?'

'Many reasons. Most of them bad. But I'd go to Greenland to get out of teaching.' Denied honour, the guilty seek instead the comfort of company and attempt to impart to everyone else their own venality and weakness. 'Wouldn't you?'

Janet sighed. 'I'll never get out of teaching.'

Despite strong sunshine, the day had an air of circumscription and indigence, of the grey afterlife of maturity when enchantment and potential have died. Of all the adults I have known, only Bernard has succeeded in escaping the sense of diminishment that comes with the years. Perhaps his going to university late made adult life seem rich and his youth the thin shrunken time. Could it be that lack of expectation is the key to later fulfilment? Perhaps promise itself is the worst enemy of promise. Rimbaud's cosmic discontent could be the consequence of his early academic success. Nothing could ever match the expectations this raised.

Janet was still pondering entrapment and the ethics of escape. 'And you could be asked to do something even worse in Greenland.'

Another accusation that cut me to the quick.

We climbed slowly to the top of a hill by a path between trees where squirrels scurried back and forth. Here the shy woodland creatures could venture out unafraid. In the ravaged parks of Northern Ireland they would have long ago been bricked to death.

Janet's disapproval persisted. As always I tried to cover up with a joke.

'Look on the bright side, Janet. Father Kemp's leaving.'

'I have mixed feelings about that.'

'Why?'

'He owes me money.'

'For what?'

'He commissioned a chalice and cruet set from me. For saying Mass, you know. It's not so much the materials as the labour. I spent ages designing the things . . . researching previous styles . . . discussing it with him . . . trying out possibilities . . .'

An interesting problem in theology: can the sacrament of the Mass be valid if celebrated with stolen vessels?

'Didn't you ask him for the money?'

'I gave him a price early on and he agreed it.'

Although moving very slowly we could not postpone descending the hill and going back towards the gate.

'Anyway,' Janet said abruptly, looking away, 'you'll be missed.'

My twisted temperament reacts to accusation with facetiousness and to praise and fondness with acerbity. 'Anyone could do that lousy job.'

'I didn't mean the job.'

This was the cue for a fervent embrace to initiate the valedictory sublime. But neither of us seemed to be capable of action. Janet was *English*, I suddenly remembered. It would surely be a frightful thing for a Paddy to violate an English Rose. Rani's rejection and erasure of history had destroyed my frail confidence. Perhaps my gaping admiration for Rani had had a similar debilitating effect on Janet. It was possible that we shared desire and certain that we shared a lack of belief in desire.

'We'll keep in touch, Janet,' was my pitiful response.

Not only inadequate but untrue. All my life I had carelessly shed people. It would be no different this time. I would lose touch with both Bernard and Janet and their influence would die with the link. The dream of reparenting was over.

But if we were unable to come together we were equally unable to part. Arriving back at the front gate, we lingered on the pavement outside the park. The afternoon provided a fatal illusion of dreaminess. It seemed as though we were in the legendary land in which it is always afternoon. If we could tarry long enough Fate would push us together.

Fate did indeed intervene – in the shape of a tiny red sports car which screeched to a halt next to us. An angry Terry Wills leapt from the driver's seat.

'Where have you been?' he shouted at me. 'I've been looking for you everywhere.'

He had no idea of what was between Janet and me. Because the concept was beyond his imagination, his senses were incapable of registering the reality. I had a sudden violent perception of the essential vulgarity and coarseness of the man.

'You weren't going off without saying goodbye?' Brusquely, angrily, he seized my arm. 'Come on. I'll give you a lift home.'

'But it's completely out of your way. You live in the other direction.' Fatal, fatal, fatal, fatal. Never begin by questioning details – reject the principle at once.

'Doesn't matter. I'll give you a lift.'

He had the blind seething impatience that is so difficult to resist. Though scarcely able to believe it, I allowed myself to be bundled into the passenger seat of the sports car which was so low-slung that I felt as though I were sitting on the road. As Wills went round to take the wheel I looked back at Janet. She had not spoken or moved and did not respond to my feeble wave.

Violently we roared off into the traffic and, to the unpleasant sensation of being at ground level, were added those of being taken captive and of being dragged in humiliation through the capital. Wills talked continuously and vehemently – but not to his passenger. As we jolted across the city an angry stream of vituperation was directed at the drivers who crossed our path.

At last we juddered to a halt.

'Well, Terry,' I groped for the handle, 'thanks for the lift . . . *and all the best.*'

Wills stared straight ahead, hands clenched on the wheel. When at last he responded, it was in a broken strangulated tone. '*What am I going to do without you?*' It was a cry of pure loss. What had tormented him all along was not anger but grief.

Here at last was what I thought I wanted – a full-blooded emotional love scene.

'You'll get somebody, Terry.'

'But you're so.... so ... so *perceptive*.' His hands left the wheel and flapped helplessly, the eloquent speech of the broken heart. 'Who'll deal with the technicians for me ... the technicians ... and *everything*.'

I got out, shut the door and leaned down to speak. But before I could say a word he started up and rocketed off, leaving me tottering and bereft.

Clare was sitting in the lounge watching Lucy toddle from chair to chair. (Despite my attempt to deny her this pleasure, she had been present for Lucy's first, and for most of her subsequent, steps.) Now she looked up from Lucy to study me carefully – not in overt annoyance but without joy. A spouse. 'What's the matter with you?'

Overwhelmed, I sat down. 'Nothing.'

Groping in my jacket pocket for a tissue, I came on the hateful pen case and flung it onto the sofa. Lucy assumed this was a game and eagerly set off in pursuit.

Clare observed the child for a moment and then turned back to me. 'Wasn't the present good enough for you?' Her tone was condescending and tart and cold; 'sarky' was how she had once described it when I spoke to her in a similar way. 'Did you expect a gold watch?'

'I don't give a damn about presents.' The turbulent seethe of emotions was threatening to overcome expression. As though to help the words out, I came forward on my seat. 'It's just ... I've been there a long time ... it's been a long time, *you know?*'

She considered this near-inarticulate appeal. 'But you told me you hated that school.'

'I know that ... I know that ...'

I raised my hands in a plea for mercy – but now Clare was the pitiless rationalist demanding consistency and logic. 'You told me you couldn't wait to get out of it. You said you'd go to Greenland for a lecturing job.'

Lucy had suceeded in opening the case and now flourished the ballpoint in a triumph which quickly turned to consternation.

For the tears had finally welled up – silent, bitter, copious, unstaunchable. Clare turned away, apparently in anger and disgust. No – her shoulders were heaving.

'I'm sorry, Martin. I shouldn't laugh. But you're just too ridiculous. I'll leave you now for a while. But can I just say one thing. We had another offer today. A thousand more than the one we agreed. I keep telling them the place is sold and they keep coming back anyway. And a *cash offer* this time. *Cash*, Martin. That would really put us in a great position to buy when we get home.'

Now that our youth was coming to an end neither of us had any desire to go naked in the icy penetrating wind. I wanted the protection of a prestigious job and Clare that of a prestigious home. She and I were meant for each other after all. It was the symbiotic union of status and money. We were worshippers of the oldest idols known to mankind – pomp and gold.


Terrified, Clare lags behind Martin and his mother as they advance across the hotel foyer to Eugene and Colette who greets the frightened girl not just as an old friend but as though resuming a conversation interrupted only a few moments before. Has Clare seen an eleven-year-old girl anywhere on her travels? Nuala has spent the night at a friend's and is to be delivered to the hotel *dressed by herself*, possibly wearing clothes *borrowed from the friend* and certainly looking like *nothing on God's earth*.

'And where's Fergus and Adrian?' Mrs Ward enquires.

'Adrian's at home studying and Fergus is at his granny's ... thanks be to God. That child has us *mortified*. We were in Devlin's the other day and says he to Mrs Devlin, we have to go on to Granny's *so we can't stay for drinks*.' Speechless for a moment at the memory, Colette lays a hand on her sister's arm. 'And you know Mrs Devlin – *a teetotaller these fifty years*.'

The implication is surely that Colette is partial to a finger of hooch – but when a waiter approaches the group she orders lemon and lime. Eugene, Mrs Ward and Clare have the same – but Martin defiantly opts for Guinness, cold and black as his heart ('I will not change. I will not reform. I have already snuffed out, amended, suppressed or gagged so much in myself that I am weary of the task' – Flaubert ).

The rest of the party arrives, Jean fussing to clear a path for Mairead who is pushing Greta in a wheelchair. Ward has not seen the bull aunt since her stroke and rejoices at the sight of a tyrant broken. Despite the busy solicitude of Jean and Mairead, it seems to him that they too are not entirely displeased. Mairead positions the wheelchair and cries triumphantly, *'Now!'* All regard the stricken empress who would once have revelled in the initiation of a new connection wife. Now she barely responds to their attention. Authority has drained out of her features, leaving a grey magma of bewilderment, fear and disgust.

'There's Clare now!' Mairead shouts, as though Greta is not only crippled but also retarded, blind and deaf. When there is still practically no response Mairead turns to Clare herself. 'Lord that's a beautiful coat.' For this momentous introduction Clare has borrowed the most expensive items in her sister Kathleen's wardrobe. 'You're like one of those ones in that American thing ... that thing on a Saturday night ... what-ye-may-call-it?' Mairead looks for assistance to Ward who indeed knows the soap opera's name but would never desecrate his lips with such filth ('Having attained a purity of feeling inaccessible to the profane, we should become liars in our own eyes if we adopted the consecrated names with which the vulgar herd is content' – Baudelaire).

'Do you watch it, Clare?' Jean cordially enquires.

'Ah ...' The girl utters a stricken cry. 'Ah ... no.'

'We always look at it. Just for the style, you know.' Jean chuckles indulgently. 'They're a terrible crowd.'

Perhaps sensing the youth's contempt, Eugene mentions a television play that he is sure Martin would have loved. Eugene loved it himself – but unfortunately can remember neither the title of the work nor the name of its author. He looks hopefully at the youth but receives no encouragement. ('His pure-featured physiognomy does not seem to belong to a man of our time and place but eerily recalls the hieratic and regal likenesses stamped on the most ancient coins of Medea' – Villiers). Eugene is obliged to turn to the company in order to tell the story of the play. It concerned an old minister, a gentle sort of man, who keeps bees in a garden at the back of a beautiful old rectory. Then one of his daughters, his *favourite* daughter, comes up from London with ... a fella ... a *sort of a fella*

293

. . .' Eugene glances about the company. 'Ye know?'

They know.

Now the table is ready and with considerable commotion the party makes its way to the dining room. Jean accompanies Ward and the girl. 'I was talking to Pascal on the phone, Martin, and he says he sends his regards to the *brainy* one of the connection.' In preparation for the helplessness to come she lays a hand on Ward's arm. 'Says I, *Is that me, Pascal? Is that me ye mean?*' And now she yields to a paroxysm of laughter which swiftly becomes smoker's cough. Undaunted, though still supporting herself on Ward, she turns to Clare to repeat the witticism. 'Says I to him, Clare, *Is that me ye mean, Pascal? That must be me ye mean.*'

As Mairead positions the wheelchair at one end of the table Clare and Ward move to the other.

'Come up here!' Jean cries. 'Clare! Martin! Come up this end!'

Ward turns with cool aplomb ('Calmness is strength' – d'Aurevilly). 'We're all right where we are.'

Clare leans her face into Ward's. 'Do what they say,' she hisses fiercely. '*Just do what they say.*' Moving up beside the wheelchair, the girl turns to the invalid. 'I hear you were over in Lourdes. Did you enjoy that? Did you enjoy Lourdes?'

Greta becomes agitated, shaking her head in an apparent attempt at speech. Mairead leans forward, eager to interpret – but the old lady manages the key word: 'Sweltering!'

Mairead immediately expands. 'We were *roasted!*' she cries, in apparent delight. '*Baked alive*, look see!'

Greta's head tosses wildly. 'Couldn't sleep.'

Clare nods in sincere sympathy and regret. 'The heat?'

'We went down to Knock a fortnight ago,' Jean comes in. 'And she enjoyed that a lot more. An easier journey . . . and a lot less hot.'

However, the memory of the Irish pilgrimage also seems to trouble Greta. With a good deal of help from Mairead and Jean she explains the outrage that has stung her into speech – a Hummel Blessed Virgin statuette which she bought in Scott's of the Diamond for thirty-five pounds. While in Lourdes she priced an identical figurine and it was fifty-two pounds. In Knock she priced the same item again and though you expected to be robbed in the Free State she was scarcely prepared for the extent of the shock. 'It was . . . it was . . . it was . . . it was . . .'

'Eighty-seven pounds,' shouts Mairead with every sign of satisfaction.

There is a brief silence, broken by Mairead who turns beseechingly to Clare. 'And the wedding's to be real quiet, Clare? None of us old ones?' Clare shrugs awkwardly. 'I know I'm not invited to the reception.' Mairead pauses for an odd chuckle in which the intended humility and acceptance are undermined by a note of scorn for the eccentricity of the arrangements. 'But could I just come to the chapel?'

Clare looks desperately at Ward who has agreed to marriage on condition of a brief austere ceremony in a remote country church with neither the connection nor Jack Barrett soiling its purity. But already Clare has been unable to resist Barrett's confident assumption of attendance. And now the connection is also wheedling and begging for an invitation.

'Even just to stand outside the chapel,' Mairead begs, desperate and abject, practically grovelling. 'Just to see your dress, Clare.'

As Clare is about to yield, there is help from an unexpected quarter. So demeaning is Mairead's behaviour that the broken autocrat regains her authority for a moment.

'You'll do no such thing,' Greta snaps at Mairead. 'You'll not push yourself in where you're not invited.'

There is an awkward silence. Jean turns to Clare. 'The heat was desperate in Lourdes. But we had the best crack in Dublin and on the way back. You see, when we were crossing the border we were searched by the British army and they couldn't get over all these bottles in the boot. *What is it?* they asked me and says I, *Holy Water.*' Already the cough is threatening – but she manages to keep it at bay. '*What*, they said, *twenty-eight bottles of water? You went all that way just to bring back WATER?*' And now, not only managing to continue, she actually throws in an impersonation of an incredulous cockney. '*Waw! twenny-eh bottles o' waw-ah!*' Coughing, she leans on the girl at her side. 'I suppose they thought we were madwomen, Clare. *Is your soup all right?*'

Clare regards the acrid emulsion of wizened packet vegetables. 'It's *lovely.*'

'Don't talk to me about the Troubles.' Eugene suddenly enters the conversation from the other end of the table. 'I had my windows blown in again this week. Third time in six months. Haven't even had the compensation for the first time yet. And burgled twice for good measure.'

Here is another challenge for Colette whose genius can create from the most lumpen ingredients the most exquisite of soufflés.

'The thing about the bombs,' she begins, immediately commanding the table's attention, 'is that every time there's a loud bang these days everyone thinks it's a bomb. Eugene's poor mother nearly had head staggers last week when the dining room ceiling collapsed on top of the table. Nothing to do with bombs – but it really put the heart across her. She was in the house on her own and she ran out into the garden screaming, *Jesus, Mary and Joseph where's Fergus and Nuala and Adrian?*'

'Destroyed the table completely.' Eugene turns significantly towards Colette, another attribute of the ideal connection husband being the ability to act as straight man for the wife. 'We haven't had much luck with tables. That's the second we've lost.'

'The first table was beautiful,' Colette sighs, expertly pacing the anecdote. 'But the centre section fell in.'

'Oh, Colette!'

It is obvious that the best is yet to come – but Colette compels them to wait, maintaining a perfectly deadpan expression. '*With all our Waterford glass sitting on it.*'

While the listeners wince and wail the actual victim of the catastrophe seems to become more composed.

'I don't know if you've ever heard a lot of Waterford glass breaking.' For the first time she permits herself a laugh, light and rapturous, as of one ravished by exquisite Mozartian grace. 'But I can tell you now that it makes ... *the most superbly musical sound.*'

'*Colette!*'

'Your Waterford glass!'

'No, Colette!'

Was there ever such gypsy abandon, such a bejewelled and scintillant insouciance? The connection looks at Clare to see if she is capable of appreciating genius. The girl laughs with a touch of bewilderment which is neither inappropriate nor unbecoming.

Still Colette has not finished. 'I wouldn't mind if the glass had been *dirty*,' she goes on, 'but I'd just put it back on the table after washing it. And you know how careful you have to be with Waterford. I'd just washed and dried the whole lot ... *ever so carefully.*' Using her glass and napkin, Colette mimes a cleansing operation of fanatical fastidiousness and caution.

Connection merriment is uninhibited and universal. Even Greta manages a laugh. Only Mairead is a little reluctant in her mirth (though who could blame the girl for envying brilliance she herself could never match). But no one participates more enthusiastically than Mrs Ward. Anxious and wary up to now, she has sensed that the connection is taking to Clare and is almost euphoric in her relief. For, just as the Lord rejoices most at the return of an inveterate sinner, so bourgeois joy is most intense at the redemption of a shop girl from Ardowen.

More heady than sparkling wine is this mood of compatibility that provides the perfect accompaniment to a main course of plaice with white sauce for the ladies and a sirloin for Eugene, though Ward as usual arouses comment by ordering pork kebab with rice ('There is something independent in us and about us that will always result in our being held in suspicion' – Huysmans).

After the sherry trifle Jean turns to Clare with an official confirmation of acceptance. 'We have a wee thing, Clare. Just a wee thing.' Here she pauses to glance significantly at Mairead who, as so often, is dilatory and obtuse. Only after an actual grunt from Jean does Mairead leap to her feet with a cry of recollection and apology. 'We have a wee thing – but we'd like to get you some sensible stuff as well. Things you'll be needing. You'll have to tell us what you need.'

'Oh I'll be getting them a few things too,' Mrs Ward wildly comes in. 'Can you come out with me after the meal, Clare, and we'll get a few things.'

Ward, the maestro of silence, is finally stung into speech. '*What things?*'

Euphoria is not easily discouraged. 'Don't heed him,' his mother cries, actually seizing the girl in her excitement. 'He'd have you sitting on orange boxes all your days, look see.'

'Pay no attention to that character, Clare.' Jean takes hold of the girl from the other side.

Colette leans forward in a quiet intimate confiding way. 'Martin's a bit of an oddity really. Always his nose in a book.'

Even Mairead, returning with a large cardboard box, makes an incoherent contribution. 'Oh Martin . . . uh huh huh . . . Martin and the ornaments . . . uh huh huh . . .'

Powerless to combat this rampant imperialism, Ward slumps back in his seat. ('Did I not once have an exquisite youth, heroic and fabulous enough to be set down on tablets of gold? By what error, what crime, was my weakness earned?' – Rimbaud).

Taking the box from Mairead and opening it, Jean turns to Ward. 'Now this is for Clare not you . . . *so don't you open your mouth.*' Then, withdrawing a large object wrapped in tissue paper, she turns to the girl. 'It's only a wee thing, Clare, but it'll get your collection started.' With a triumphant flourish she strips away the paper and, like an athlete bearing aloft the Olympic flame, raises on high a huge Waterford glass bowl which immediately gathers light and converts it to shimmering iridescence and sheaves of dazzling white rays. The connection regards it in silence – and then looks at Clare who keeps her wondering eyes fixed on the bowl.

'It's *absolutely gorgeous,*' she breathes.

'How is she?' Angela enquired as soon as she opened the door. 'She's come round a bit,' I said. 'She can talk but not move much.' My mother had suffered a stroke and we were just back from visiting her in hospital.

'Your children are in bed asleep,' Shotter said to Clare. 'No problems at all. Come into the living room for a drink.'

Angela lingered, reluctant. 'Can't we use the front room, Tony?'

'Fuck no.' Shotter grimaced. 'The living room's far more comfortable.'

As with most of its other problems, Ulster had failed to solve the conundrum of how to humanise front rooms. We passed a majestic chamber of heavy dark furniture and dark Persian carpet and made our way to a small parlour at the back of the house.

Shotter opened a sideboard and produced a bottle and glasses. 'I got a case of port as a present at Christmas and I've been saving it for a special occasion.'

Angela's laugh was slightly shrill. 'He's most of a bottle in him already.'

'You always claimed you'd never settle in Ireland,' Shotter said to me as he poured.

'*Agh!*' I paused to monitor the filling of the glass. The years had taught me to reverse my Magnificent Seven priorities and attend to ocial ladder, it could be that they had chosen me in order to move up a rung. The old human error of claiming a volition exercised elsewhere. And with that the familiar depressing sensation of being in the grip of mighty forces that can scarcely be understood much less controlled.

Angela was now addressing Clare as the only other sensible person in the room. 'Nobody in their right mind would buy in Mount Pleasant now.'

Who would have dreamed that the choice could come to this – no longer the Crag or the Cross but Mount Pleasant or out the coast road?

'What Jack Barrett was saying,' Clare immediately came in, 'is that we should buy a plot well outside Belfast and build our own house.'

This was enough to jolt me out of fatalistic torpor. '*What?*' I shouted in sudden anger – apparently I had some spirit left. '*Buy a plot? Build a house?*'

'You've accepted everything else.' Angela was clearly relishing her opportunity to attack. 'You're back in Ireland. You've taken a job in a Catholic college. You're working for nuns.'

'I have plenty of experience of that.'

'Not the way it is here,' Shotter grimly came in. 'I had an interview for a new teaching job recently and they asked me what I understood by *transubstantiation*. And these were all laymen. I told them I taught English not Religion.'

'So you can guess what happened to the job.' Angela coolly regarded her husband.

With a harsh laugh Shotter produced twenty cigarettes and tore the cellophane off the packet. Angela's displeasure changed to outrage.

'This is a special night,' he said, with a hint of his legendary snarl.

Watching him light up and inhale, Anglela chose her words with care and issued them one at a time. 'If . . . you . . . go . . . back . . . on . . . cigarettes . . . Tony . . . I . . . shall . . . be . . . *very . . . disappointed.*'

Lying back in an armchair, Shotter was the perfect Irish study – a cigarette in his left hand, a drink in his right, fatalism on his ravaged features and bitterness in his heart.

Was this another demonstration of the consequences of autonomy, nihilism and disdain? I had always been impressed

practical matters before indulging in abstraction. 'I also said I'
never marry, never have children, never own property and abo
all never teach.' A good moment to sample the port – full-bodi
and rich but not cloying. 'What I said I'd never do is the definiti
of what I've done.'

There could be no objection to Shotter's remark – but neit
was there any objection to a counter-attack. 'And how about yo
self? It's weird for a slag who hated snobs to end up in a place l
Mount Pleasant.'

'What's the house worth now?' Clare asked. 'We could proba
buy it.'

Clare was as exhilarated by estate agent's lists as I by the sylla
for third-level Physics. We had prospered as a result of the Lon
episode, whereas Homewrecker claimed he had been blighted
ever. This may not have been an exaggeration. Clare kept in to
with him over the years, occasionally meeting him on holida
London – and he never formed a lasting relationship or did n
with his life. After losing his post in the savage public sector cu
the following decade, he eked out a living as a part-time y
worker and drifted into a regime of drinking, increasingly c
lent, coarsened and embittered. Despite his appearance and r
views, Homewrecker was the only romantic idealist in our tri
– and its only real victim. The story was another illustration
melancholy law which states that it is always and only the
geoisie who are the beneficiaries of turbulence.

'I'm sure you could.' Just a touch of bitterness from Angela
see, it's not a good area any more. Since the Troubles
Protestants have moved out. You can hardly blame th
Ardowen's just up the road and getting rougher and
republican every day.'

'Make us an offer,' Shotter suggested.

'Ah!' Clare raised her glass in playful delight. 'What wou
make it for *cash?*'

'Mount Pleasant was Tony's idea.' Angela did not want t
facts obscured by facetiousness. 'I said we should buy someth
the coast road. That's the area that's just gone up and up and
nothing would do Tony only Mount Pleasant.'

Suddenly it occurred to me that, whereas I had alway
imagined I chose Shotter and Clare in order to move d

by Shotter's contemptuous non-involvement and cynical manoeuvrings but, if you do not subscribe to something, eventually the disgust will turn inward and consume your own soul.

Angela turned back to Clare and said in a lighter tone (though one from which indignation had not been entirely expunged), 'And what are you going to do with Mrs Ward? She may not be able to look after herself.'

'She was always very close to her sister Colette. And Colette has a big house.'

Though not for much longer. What had shocked me most in the hospital was not the enfeebled condition of my mother but the behaviour of Colette. Of course nothing was said – but the awkwardness and brevity of her visit spoke for themselves. Afterwards my mother admitted, angrily and grudgingly, that Colette was leaving Eugene and moving into a bungalow with the younger children. How to explain the terrible impact of an occurrence that was nowadays routine? It was not just that here the older marriages remained as unbreakable as the tablets of the law – but that this particular marriage had been so emblematic and central, a living example of the efficacy of an entire philosophy of life. For the connection, the marriage of Colette and Eugene was a flagship, a showcase, an inspiration, an ideal – and its breakdown was as devastating as the slaughter of a royal family to monarchists. On my mother, Colette's last surviving sister and now the senior relative, the blow fell hardest of all. And it was specially cruel coming after the stroke. Her entire world was being shattered along with her body.

Despite her disappointments and illness the question had to be put: 'But why are they breaking up?'

Her face took on a familiar grim set. 'Oh ... I suppose ... *Eugene* ...'

Again the belief that a name uttered with sufficient intensity was a full explanation.

'And you fell out with Colette about it? You disapproved of her leaving?'

Her face set into granite. Yet once again I had the feeling that she dearly wanted to talk. Given the way her sisters died – the first stroke followed in a few months by a fatal second – she must have known time was short. But not even the threat of death could

301

override a lifetime's repression. *Use it or lose it* – surely the truest and most terrible of our salutary maxims.

Perhaps it was enough to know that there was something passionate struggling for expression. Madame Rimbaud could not communicate with her son but when the contemptible Verlaine wrote to her threatening suicide, this virtually uneducated and apparently hard-hearted woman sent him a reply of astonishing sophistication and empathy. 'You complain of your unhappy life, poor child! But how can you know what tomorrow will bring? Have hope! You're too sensible to imagine that happiness can merely exist in the successful carrying-out of a plan, or in the gratification of some whim. Indeed nò! A man who would find all his desires fulfilled would not be happy, for as long as the heart has no aspirations no emotion is possible and hence no happiness. The heart has to be moved by the thought of goodness, of the good one does or hopes to do. I too have been desperately unhappy. I have suffered and wept but been able to turn my misfortunes to profit. God has granted me a strong heart, full of energy and courage. I've struggled against adversity and I've thought very deeply. I've looked around and become convinced, yes totally convinced, that each of us carries in the heart a wound more or less deep. My own wound seemed to me deeper than those of others and this was quite natural. I could feel my own wound but not those of others.'

My mother was incapable of intimacy but the volcano underneath was still active and every now and then erupted so violently that it blew a hole in the granite crust.

'You know I'm not ready to go,' she suddenly blurted out.

'Go where?' I asked stupidly, thinking she meant leaving hospital and realising too late that this was the old human cry of desolation at the end of rehearsals for a performance which will never take place.

Immediately the granite crust re-formed. There was nothing for it but await the next outburst. It was not long in coming.

'If I had my time again I would do it all differently.'

*Each of us carries in the heart a wound more or less deep.* Was she about to expose her secret wound? Examine her life and come to conclusions?

Not without the usual prodding. 'Different in what way?'

Immediately she was displeased. 'Many ways.' Her tone

curt and final.

'Mention one. Give me an example.'

Suddenly she pushed herself up off the pillows, angry passion blazing in her haggard features. 'I wouldn't put up with you hounding and lecturing me for a start.'

'I couldn't live with Martin's mother,' Clare was saying now to Angela. 'I know I couldn't do it. She makes me so uncomfortable. Sits and stares at me *all the time*. And, I mean, *really stares*. I feel like something in a zoo.'

'We'll sort something out,' I muttered wearily.

Our lack of piety infuriated Angela. 'I don't know what you've got against that little woman. I meet her all the time when I'm shopping and she always speaks to me and she's always the best of crack. I don't know how anyone can think of her as some kind of *enemy*.'

'It's nothing personal. It's just that whole respectablility thing.'

'*Respectability!*' Angela snorted in impatient contempt. 'That's dead and gone long ago. The only thing that matters now in this town is money.'

My mother's world was certainly dead or dying. I was fighting with skeletons, phantoms, dust. But if the enemy were so insubstantial why were they winning?

'It's not herself I'm against but her presence in me. The terror of intimacy. The hatred of marriage.'

Angela was no longer listening. 'Equality with Protestants,' she scowled. 'That's the only issue for Catholics. That's the only issue here now.'

'Marry your housekeeper,' Shotter cried jocosely, raising his glass as though to toast an actual union. 'That's my advice. Marry the housekeeper.'

I was blaming my limitations on the previous generation, just as my mother had done. But realising this did not prevent me from making yet another complaint. 'The enemy within is a kind of cowardice and meanness of spirit.'

Of course this kind of talk was too ponderous for a social occasion. Putting stones in a paper bag saturated with alcohol.

Sedated by his twin narcotics, Shotter was the first to speak, intoning with the calm strength and wisdom of Buddha, 'You judge people harshly.'

'No more harshly than I judge myself.'

'You're a zealot,' he said. 'A zealot in search of a God.' His serenity finally disturbed, he shuddered and took a restorative slug of port. 'And God help yourself and us all if you find one.'

This was even more solemn. The rolling bass had entirely drowned out the tinkling right hand.

Into the ensuing silence came the Shotters' eldest boy, Stephen, carrying the large format paperback I had noticed on the table during a previous visit. Intrigued by the title, *Structured Reasoning*, I had picked it up and opened it – and was immediately swept away on a tidal wave of involuntary memories. For *Structured Reasoning* was none other than the old 11-plus intelligence tests I had sweated over as a boy.

'Saturday is the first day of a certain month. There are 5 Mondays in this month. How many Fridays does the month have? What day is the 20th? Write the name of the last day of this month. How many Mondays will there be in the following month?'

Exactly the same! If only life had presented me with problems like these.

'Fred, Bob, Jill and Alice have a parcel each. Fred's parcel is lighter than Bob's but heavier than Alice's and Jill's. John arrives with another parcel which is heavier than Jill's but not as heavy as that of Alice. How many parcels are lighter than Fred's? Whose parcel is heavier than only two others?'

In the hospital, after the long silence following on my mother's violent accusation of harassment, I re-started the conversation on a lighter note by mentioning the *Structured Reasoning* book. 'To think of the 11-plus going on all these years . . . exactly the same as when I did it.'

'They tried to do away with it once,' she said. 'But there were ructions. There was murder. It was just after I got the Headship . . . wouldn't you know it? Instead of an exam, head teachers had to assess which children were of grammar school standard . . . which ones would have passed the 11-plus if they'd done it. The pushy parents just assumed their children would be chosen . . . and there was blue murder when it got out that some of them wouldn't be. The doctors and dentists were the worst of course. Oh you've no idea. They were up on their high horses. They were up to a million. What I had to put up with! What I had to listen to! The pressure to let some children through was just incredible. *Incredible*, look see.'

All at once there was the possibility of a strange unlikely late gift. If only we can be patient life will offer its bounty when we least expect it. 'And did you let any of them through?'

For an instant something fierce and implacable galvanised her ruined form. She sat up straight with wild blazing eyes. 'I never added one name to that list. Not one, look see. And the bad feeling afterwards was nothing ordinary. I've never known the like of it in my life. Many's a one in this town has never spoken to me since.'

'Did you finish those exercises?' Angela was saying to Stephen. Then she turned to us with a laugh. 'You know he's doing his 11-plus this year ... and his class have *the most easy-going teacher in the school!*' Taking a swift drink, she released an even more musical laugh, as though the irony was so exquisite that she had to pay it homage despite the terrible human cost. 'The most easy-going character you could meet.' Now she flapped her arms in a parody of irresponsible blitheness. 'Says he won't distort the curriculum for the sake of one exam. Of course I know the educational argument – and the kids *adore* him ... but *I mean ...*'

Stephen bade us goodnight and went off with *Structured Reasoning* under his arm. Perhaps he was already enslaved to the fetish of theory – and if he did well in examinations the enslavement could become permanent. When he was the only European in a settlement of mud huts in Africa, Rimbaud drove his mother wild by making her send him books on thatching, iron-forging, glass-blowing, candle-making and brick manufacture and also learned treatises on hydraulics, mechanics, astronomy, the construction of railways and subterranean tunnels.

Imagine the Kid, already grey-haired, gaunt and ill, squatting in a mud hut in Harar, ignoring the sounds and smells of the African night to study a volume on trigonometry by a guttering candle. Theories, religions, convention, revolt – our necessary attempts to master absurdity are merely further examples of it.

I took a long consoling drink of port. 'If I were a novelist, Stephen would be my ideal reader. The parallels are almost uncanny. Intelligent academic boy. Sheltered provincial bourgeois childhood. Catholic schoolteacher parents. Dominant, frustrated, ambitious mother ... weak father ...'

Shotter cast a sharp look at his wife. 'He's getting at us, darling.'

His concern was unnecessary. Angela laughed as musically as before. 'He's only *teasing*.'

*Teasing* – the perfect word for converting criticism to flattery. Apparently the punishing years had made no impression on Angela's impregnable self-esteem. All around her was a magical force field and everything that passed through turned to praise.

Imagine trying to inform Angela that her Stephen was not on the grammar school list! The charge of cowardice against my mother would have to be modified. She was no more a monster of bourgeois meanness than I was a hero of satanic revolt. *We are one people –* what a commonplace to be left with at the end. But of course the winding road leads not to the profound but the banal. The purpose of life is to invest the clichés with a terrible truth.

My father's plea for school milk and my mother's stand against her own – these hardly constituted a remarkable legacy. But then I was not a remarkable person. I set my empty glass on the coffee table in a manner which, without being downright impertinent, was sufficiently ostentatious to alert my host. Grave, sagacious, not at all offended, Shotter brought over the bottle at once.